OH GLITTERING PROMISE!

Oh Glittering Promise!

A Novel of the
California Gold Rush

By ANNE FISHER

THE BOBBS·MERRILL COMPANY·INC.

PUBLISHERS

INDIANAPOLIS • NEW YORK

First Edition

TO OTHETO WESTON, ARTIST AND PHOTOGRAPHER OF
THE MOTHER LODE, WHOSE COLLECTION OF UNPUB-
LISHED DIARIES, DOCUMENTS AND FIFTEEN YEARS OF
RESEARCH MADE THIS BOOK POSSIBLE.

OH GLITTERING PROMISE!

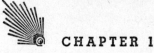

CHAPTER 1

1849

The twelve o'clock whistle blew at a Pennsylvania coal mine one sweltering June day in 1849.

Charles Morgan, the hard-bitten young Welshman, threw down his shovel and came out of the black pit to eat his nooning on the gray slag heap.

"Hear the news?" a fellow miner asked, as Charles poured cold tea from a bottle and made ready to bite into the bread and cheese Anne had tied up in brown paper. "Jim Teller's hit it rich out in California. Them pieces in the paper about gold is true. He says only fools stay here in the pits getting consumption and pulling out their guts, just to have a place to sleep and food for their children. Jim's picked up more gold in a few days than he could earn here in a year. Want to see what he wrote?" The fellow tossed a rumpled letter across the slag and it fell at Charles's feet. His grubby hands grasped the paper and smoothed it, and eyes bleared by coal dust and dark squinted at the penciled words.

Before he read the finger-blackened letter, Charles Morgan had been satisfied. These miners in Pennsylvania didn't know the horrors of Welsh coal miners who, for wages scarce enough to hold the bones together, constantly fought the fine dry dust and almost daily fires that broke out in the pits.

A dollar a day and the freedom of America seemed as close to heaven as a miner could hope for—but the heaven faded now as the blurred words of Jim Teller's letter sank into Morgan's brain.

"Men here are rooting gold out of the earth like hogs let loose in a forest after acorns. All they have is knives and the nuggets are right on top of the ground."

9

Charles was quiet. He looked over the heaps of loose gray slag at the dingy "company houses" clustered against the hill as if they were in constant fear that they would be covered by the work of their occupants. He saw coal-begrimed children playing in tiny flat places and gray washes on the lines in yards marked off by tumble-down picket fences.

"God, but I'd like to go!" Charles sighed. "Me with three boys to look out for! It might mean that they'd never have to go into the pits." He rubbed a black hand across his brow.

"Not for me," one burly chap roared, as he lighted his pipe and stretched his legs to rest. "Sounds fine here, when we got our bellies full of food, but by the time a man sails from Philadelphia to California all that there gold'll be picked up. Then what's he to do? Nobody ever heard of coal mines out in California, where a man can work for wages. I'll stick to my dollar a day."

"You got to take a chance," Charles argued, and then swigged the last of his strong black tea. "Jim Teller did."

"Him and fifty thousand others!" another chap called out, and sent a stream of tobacco juice onto the slag. "Jim ain't back yet with his gold."

All afternoon, as he heaved coal onto cars and sweated in the black tunnel, Charles thought of Jim Teller's letter. If he could only take the chance, his sons—Henry, Bill and Charley—would never have to bring their young bodies into the pit to sweat away youth and energy and life as he had done and his father and grand-father before him.

There were other things to consider. Anne, his wife, had plans to escape from the pits. She made cheese as they made it in Wales. This had caught the fancy of American miners and sold well. Right now Anne was scraping and saving out of his wages to get enough to build a little stone cheese factory, so they could all forget the coughing and aching bones and weariness, and stay above ground forever.

Charles shoved a loaded car along the track, straightened brawny shoulders and then began filling an empty as the foreman went by.

California was the answer—enough nuggets to build the cheese factory! Surely the God who had been good enough to guide them to this fine new country would give willing hands sufficient gold for a cheese factory. He was not yet thirty and Anne twenty-seven. They had a grand long life ahead! A few months in California, then the cheese factory and the black pits outwitted! He could hardly wait for quitting time to tell his news to Anne, to see her eyes brighten with hope.

Anne was such a good lass, and thrifty too. She could make a joint last longer and be more filling to a man's belly than any woman in the mines. She could turn old pants into small ones for the boys, and fashion a jacket fit to wear to chapel out of an old skirt. He groaned as he thought. It would take all her carefully hoarded savings to go to California. But if he got gold the lass would never have to skimp again!

That night as he climbed wearily over the hill and headed for the company house where Anne would be waiting supper, Charles planned how he would break the news to her.

A trip to the privy, then stripping to the waist and dousing head and body from the tin wash basin beside the back door. A quick wipe on the grimy towel, a comb through his yellow thatch, and he was ready for food and a rest for his tired bones—and the news.

With changed eyes he saw the little dark-green painted kitchen that sent out a warm comforting scent of stewing onions and meat when he opened the door. Six-year-old Bill sat near the lamp beside the table with the red-and-white checkered cloth, scowling over a picture book, and Charley, by the stove, fingered the ears of a dingy yellow cat. The little chap Henry, his wet didie seat blackened by coal dust, made a crablike scuttle across the floor toward his dad.

Anne stood before the stove in a clean brown and white calico, stirring the stew with a great spoon. What a picture she made for a homing man when she turned to greet him! Her bright brown eyes lighted up, and the feeble glow from the lamp couldn't cheat the shine out of her smooth hair that was parted in the middle and knotted at her neck. The very innards of him cried out in love for her as she put up her face for his kiss.

"You must be hungered." She smiled as he sat down. "Made it home faster than usual. Five minutes ahead of time." She held the spoon aloft, and glanced at the old wooden-turreted clock she had brought from Wales.

"Might be you and the young ones made me walk the faster," he managed as he unlaced his great boots and pulled them off to ease his feet. "A man doesn't *always* think of his belly." He swung little Henry to his knee and pushed back the tousled yellow hair.

What a bonny family they were! He could see them all now, away from the mines and running around the new stone cheese factory. It was all he could do to keep from blurting out the news right off but that would never do. The business must be managed, for it meant all Anne's savings must go for the trip.

Anne set the great dish of stew on the table and sent Charley and Bill out to wash up. "We must be quick with supper tonight," she said. "Tonight's prayer meeting, you know, and there's the new minister. The choir ought to be early out of respect. Your second best is laid out on the bed all ready for you."

But Charles's news wouldn't wait for chapel singing and prayers; it spurted out after the last cup of good black tea. Each detail of Jim's letter was so clear in his mind that he had no trouble remembering the blurred words.

"There's thousands of men in California," he finished. "Jim says the gold is right on top of the soil—nuggets."

Anne's eyes turned big as saucers. She stopped buttering bread for Bill and just sat, as if the word gold had addled her noggin. The very soul of Charles hurt as he watched her. The lass had lived through poverty all her life, and the miners' revolution in Wales; she had taken the bit in her teeth and made him come to the new country of America and the mines of Pennsylvania. Now this news was too much to be swallowed.

Finally she spoke. "If there's gold to be picked up like that, it's time the Morgans were moving, Charles. We'll get ready and be off."

The scrap of her, scarce weighing a hundred pounds, and three children wanting to go with him were something Charles hadn't figured. He got up, went over to where she sat and smoothed the satin brown hair with his cracked coal-roughened hand.

"You can't go, little love," he said gently, "not with the children. California is full of Mexicans with daggers, and Indians there scalp people."

She fingered the wide gold band of her wedding ring. "Charles," she said, "I've always gone with you, wherever you've gone. I'm your wife. You need me. We—we ought to be together." Her eyes were begging.

"But California's such a *long* way, and the trip is full of hardships," he managed. "Besides, it'll cost too much for us all to go."

That last weakened her a little. Anne could stand hardship and face danger, but she looked nine times at a bit of money before she spent it. The poor girl had seen so little money in her life.

"But, Charles, if gold is to be picked up atop the ground, what's the odds if it costs so much to get there?" she asked after a bit. "I can pick as good as anybody and so can Bill and Charley—once we get there."

There was a great din then, and Bill and Charley put in their oars and wanted to go.

"I won't hear to you taking little Henry," he said firmly and stroked the child's head. "Use reason, lass! Let me go alone, stay for a few months and bring back the gold for the cheese factory. Then we'll all be safe and happy."

Not until they came back through the warm night air from prayer meeting was Anne finally convinced that this time she must stay and let her man go it alone in the wilderness of California.

They had a cup of tea and some fresh-made scones. Anne ran her hand lovingly through his hair, sighed and then went to the little chest under the bed and brought out the savings—paper dollars and a few gold pieces.

They counted them carefully, but Charles knew this was only to put in time and so they could handle the money a bit before they parted from it. Surely Anne knew every hard-saved dollar that came from her grandmother's camphorwood chest.

"I'll keep a third for me and the boys," she told him. "Without a man around to be bothered with and cook for, I can make enough cheese to sell and keep us. Maybe I can get old Granny Davis to mind the young ones, and I can go out to work by the day. We'll get along, and it takes money to travel to foreign parts."

He kissed her, then grinned. "See here, you're shoving, aren't you? Let's wait a bit and think it over. Takes time to plan a trip, lass," he told her. "I've got to work out my week."

She turned impatient then. "Fiddlesticks!" she snorted. "If you're going after gold, get at it. No use working out the week just to wait for payday. Draw your wages in the morning and off with you."

That was Anne, he thought; no sooner said than done with her. No time for sorrowing or changing the mind once it was made up.

With a set face, she brought out the sea chest they had carried onto the boat at Liverpool six years before and began packing his big boots and woolen shirts and underdrawers. On top of all went his best black suit.

"I'll not be wanting *that*," he told her. "There'll be no need for good black in California. It's a place of miners and flannel shirts."

"But you'll be going to chapel if there be one," she insisted. "There's bound to be a Methodist chapel the world over. Chapel folks are strong; they've had to be to fight the Church of England and the Papists to survive."

Charles doubted. California was new and wild. He didn't think the church had caught up yet with the savages out west.

Then Anne told him what was really in her mind. "If anything happens," she said, "you'll have your good black for burying, Charles Morgan, and you'll meet your God respectable."

There was a tug at the heart of Charles as he pulled off the "britches of his second best" in the little bedroom that was crowded with sleeping children. He watched Anne carefully unbutton her black bombazine dress, draw it across her firm young breasts and over her head. Then she examined the white crochet bits at throat and sleeves.

"They'll do another time, before washing," she told him and smiled as if she would be telling him the same thing most any night to come.

He wanted to cry out to her with sadness; to tell her how much her courage meant to him, and that her brave way would bring him back the sooner into her arms. But one look at her eyes told him that, if he put into words what he thought, all she had labored to build would be destroyed.

As she stood a moment in her little white nightgown with ruffles at the wrists, he wanted to remember the picture—his last night with her for God knew how long! Then she leaned over to blow out the lamp and her dark braid slipped around to caress the breast of her.

"A little love for your man?" he asked gently when she was beside him.

"Of course—don't be silly." And her arm went around him.

The coal-roughened hands caressed her every curve, as if to hold the feel when she was far away.

"Charles . . ."

"Yes, love?"

"You're big and full-blooded and—" she sighed—"and good to look at with your blue eyes and thatch of golden hair. You have a way with women. You won't forget my arms?"

"No lass—never fear."

But Anne was different tonight as she took him to her. She talked about gold even as he caressed her!

"Someday," said she, as passion shot through him, "when you come back with gold, we can go together under fine blankets instead of pieced quilts and never have to worry that there might be another mouth to feed."

The words turned Charles heartsick. For this last time he wanted Anne to be free and abandoned with him, as she had been when Henry, the little nipper, was started. He dated time from that night when she had forgotten everything in the joy of giving.

As passion was spent, he knew suddenly why Henry was the favorite child!

The thought must have carried to her. "Charles," she breathed from within his arms, "if anything should happen that—that you didn't come back, we'll all work and see that Henry gets educated to be a minister and never goes into the pits. That would please you, wouldn't it?"

"Aye, lass, that would please me."

The next morning everybody was excited. Bill wanted a real Indian headdress sent from California, and Charley wanted a nugget. But little Henry sensed there would be loss, and small as he was sorrow came. He clung to his dad and could scarce be pried away long enough for Charles to go and collect his pay.

They had a bang-up good dinner that noon, a joint with roasted potatoes and stewed fruit as a treat.

"We'll be having this every day when I'm home again," Charles told them as he carved the rich brown meat.

Afterward he shouldered his sea chest, and, with only one turn back at the bottom of the big slag heap to wave at Anne and his boys, Charles started the walk from Pottsville to Philadelphia and the boat for California.

CHAPTER 2

1849

San Francisco!

Charles Morgan stood on the crowded deck of the old brigantine and strained his eyes for a look at the hills of California. Men shoved against him, and he jabbed with his elbows to push the hairy sweat-smelling bodies away.

Bone-chilling thick November fog dampened the spirit, and sharp wind made him pull his jacket closer over his chest. Four months of homesickness tugged at his heart.

What a nightmare of a trip! Scurvy had turned many a man into a bundle to be tossed into the sea. No prayers, no mourning. Some folks even rejoiced, for each one overboard made a bit more room.

Scanty rations and salt meat left a man's belly gnawing day in and day out.

The miserable trek across the Isthmus was still a hell to remember, with every devilish pest on wings or legs nipping and biting without a minute's peace, heathens ready to run a knife through the back and swamps reeking with chills and fever.

Worst of all were the weeks of waiting for a boat on the Pacific side, while savings melted away and the highest bidders got out first.

Then the damned ninety-seven days aboard the leaky old brigantine crowded with a cargo of sweating, cursing humanity, and costing more than half a man's purseful for room enough to lie on the deck at night.

The fog lifted a bit. The harbor was clogged with Chinese

junks, five-masters, sloops, all stripped of shore boats and humanity. They nosed at one another, silent and deserted.

"Left by the skippers and mates and crews that sailed them
here," said the ruddy-faced mate by his elbow. "Gone to the gold
fields. I'm doing the same thing myself this trip. What's the
odds? I'll pick up a few twinkling nuggets and to hell with the
skipper and hardtack and scurvy and saying, 'Aye, sir,' every time
the old bloke spits my way. On to the diggings, I say." He went
whistling off about his business.

Men scarce would wait for the plank to be let down. They
shoved and crowded and cursed any who got in the way of them
and their bundles.

Charles shouldered his sea chest and plodded with the mob
along the muddy road. At a wet place he sank near to his knees in
the mire. A poor little gray jackass heavily burdened and up to his
belly in mud had been left by his owner and brayed frantically.

This was no town of stone houses and shops, or even brick
places. The road was lined with flimsy flapping tents and frail
wooden shanties. Canvas-topped shops were open to the gusty
cutting wind with only a wooden frame to hold them together
and shelter their wares. Signs in all languages were tacked to the
frames.

Charles cast his eye toward the English signs as he walked.
Pickaxes ten dollars, blankets twenty dollars, red flannel underdrawers twenty and woolen shirts fifteen.

The prices made him shudder as he thought of the fast-dwin-
dling savings sewed to the inside of his jacket. One eating place
told the passer-by, "Eggs cooked any style seventy-five cents each."

"Them eggs is shipped all the way from France, pard, and about
ready to crow when they get here," a Yankee beside him said.
"One blew up in my face t'other day."

A head of cabbage cost two dollars in this bewildering California city by the Golden Gate! Wait until he wrote Anne that!
She'd be out with a trunkful of cabbage seeds and a shovel.

Horses sloshed by in the road and splashed him with mud.
Heavily burdened men with pale strained faces jostled one another

and ground through the mire. Chinese with long black braids carried baskets slung on a pole from their shoulders like huge animated scales.

Saloons, without benefit of swing doors, belched men of all nationalities and colors. Gaudily dressed dark-eyed hussies with painted faces ogled the men as they picked their way around mud puddles. One, cheekier than the rest, patted her breasts under the tight-fitting bodice.

"Very solid, señor," she called out. "Come with me and see for yourself."

There was a sidewalk but it soon failed. Between shops marked SIMMONS HUTCHINSON COMPANY and ADAMS EXPRESS OFFICE, cookstoves, sacks of flour and bags of coffee had been chucked into the swamp to make a place to walk.

On one side of the "Plaza" Charles saw a shanty labeled CITY HOTEL. He was past thinking of money now. Any place to find a bed, a bite of food and a rest from the everlasting jostle and racket.

The hotel was a rude affair with a loft over the ground floor.

He pushed past the loiterers at the door. Bearded men and one loudmouthed woman in a purple dress crowded around a long table at the far side of the room, where a moist-faced card dealer plied his trade and money jingled.

The yellow-headed fellow sitting at a counter under the sign OFFICE barely glanced up from a paper he was reading when Charles asked the price of a room.

"Bunk with another man—four dollars a night. Meals two dollars each, all in *advance*." His eyes went back to the sleazy bit of newspaper. "If you stay a week it's twenty-five dollars for the room and twenty for the board."

He didn't even bestir himself when Charles put down the money for a night; just motioned to the steep, narrow staircase.

"First door to your right."

The "room" was a small box, part of an unsealed loft, drafty and cold as a barn. Wind whistled dirges through cracks and knotholes. There were two chairs, a deal table and two built-in bunks hardly wider than a coffin. On one was a heap of brown blankets. A sweat-stained shirt lay on the chair beside it.

Charles banged down his sea chest and stomped angrily back down the stairs.

"There's no bedding, no pillow!" he roared at the bleary-eyed clerk. "I rented a room with my hard-earned savings—not a stable."

"Bed yourself down. We only aim to give you shelter from the elements. You can buy blankets across the way."

Welsh blood was up. This was an outrage!

"Where I come from they treat us like humans, not animals."

"Then go back where you came from, mister. There's plenty would gladly have your place. We didn't invite you." The clerk turned back to his reading.

Charles went out into the drizzle, into the damp chilly dusk of his first day in California. He was cold and empty and doubtful now, wondering if his brother coal miners were not wiser than he to stay in Pennsylvania with that sure dollar a day instead of spending their savings to wander like a lost sheep in this strange barbaric place.

He wanted a drink of whisky to buck him up. But whisky came high—a whole dollar a drink at the crowded plank bar.

He talked a bit to the man at his elbow, a sallow sour-visaged creature with dull eyes, and asked him if he had been to the mines.

There was a nod.

"Get any gold?" He couldn't keep the eagerness out of his voice.

"If I had I wouldn't be telling you, partner, but since I only got diarrhea, you're welcome to know I didn't." He told Charles that he'd been up near where Marshall first found gold, but grub was so high that his savings were gone before he even found one nugget.

"When my insides settle down, I'm going to work here. You can get eight dollars a day helping to put up shanties."

"I'm going to Stockton, and up somewhere to a place called Sonorian Camp. I have a friend picked up nuggets——" Charles didn't have a chance to finish. The man put a hand on his shoulder.

"You might as well know right off. There's three kinds of men out here: the hopeful, the discouraged and the gamblers. Gamblers is what gets the gold—all of it eventually. There's nine gambling tents to a block here, going night and day." He nodded to a place where lights glittered out into the mist.

"Over there at the El Dorado, men bet twenty thousand dollars on the turn of a single card! Gamblers and fancy women and saloons finally get every miner's poke. Bleed him they do until he won't bleed no more, then he either just dies or goes up some gulch and blows out his fool brains." He put down his whisky, wiped his mouth on the back of his hand and walked out.

Charles looked over the stock in several musty-smelling brush and canvas stores. Shopkeepers were indifferent.

"Take the stuff or leave it," one surly fellow belched out when Charles opened up a shoddy blanket. "Don't go unfolding it so's I have to fold it up again. I'm here to sell, not for feeling purposes. There's plenty will buy."

Charles would be damned if he'd buy then and stalked out of the place.

In a flapping tent that passed for a shop, he found a friendly face. The chap told Charles he had come from Philadelphia with the first ones over a year ago, tried his luck in the mines and finally settled in San Francisco as a shopkeeper.

When he learned that Charles had just come from Pennsylvania, he poured a drink and demanded news. He hadn't heard any in six months.

"Your boat brought in mail, but it'll be two days before the stuff is sorted and the office open. Then maybe no letter after hours of waiting in line."

In exchange for Philadelphia news and the purchase of two blankets at full price, the fellow opened up about this strange new country.

Over fifty thousand men had passed through Frisco on the way to the mines.

"God," the man said, "you should see how the soldiers deserted the damned barracks like rats when tales came back from the hills about nuggets big as hen's eggs! Lots of folks make it rich in a couple of months."

Then he told how good business was in San Francisco. Even the Chinese in Canton were getting rich from California's gold fields.

Charles asked how that was.

"Miners' washing. There ain't no women here willing to waste time washing when there's more ladylike ways of earning a living easy." The fellow winked.

"The Chinks send the dirty clothes to Canton, wash 'em for eight dollars a dozen and send 'em back. If a gent's got clothes enough to see him through all those weeks he's lucky. Otherwise, he wears 'em till they stink too much, then throws 'em away and buys more with the dust in his poke. The boat last week brought two hundred and fifty bundles and, Jesus, you should have seen the scramble."

All this talk of so much money fired Charles. He wanted to be about his own business of gold. He asked how to get to Sonorian Camp.

"You go by river boat up the San Joaquin to Stockton, where Webber's set up his trading post, then walk over the flats and up the mountains." The fellow grinned then. "Got to carry your own stuff unless you got enough purse jingle to afford a jackass."

A rush of customers came. Charles thanked the shopkeeper, took up his blankets and started out.

"Take the boat down at the wharf in the morning," the chap called out as he weighed sugar. "Fare's thirty-six dollars. Good luck!"

As Charles walked back along the crowded roadway in the biting wind, the damned words "purse jingle" ran through his mind like a steel-blue knife.

Purse jingle for a jackass. There would be none of that for Charles Morgan. He was a two-legged jackass himself for ever coming to a country where things cost so much. He wished he was back in the coal mine. There, he had his belly full, he was warm and he had a good bed. Soon he wouldn't have two coins to jingle one against the other.

The man from Philadelphia had wished him luck. Why not take a chance at gambling? With luck on his side just *once* he would have more of a stake to eat and walk on when he headed over the hills. He shoved past the loiterers once more and into the City Hotel.

"Make your bets, gents," the sallow dealer called out against the banging of tin cups and drunken singing that came from a side room.

The crowd was thicker now around the table, and the woman in the purple dress was near the dealer. Charles shoved close.

In the wind-blown flame of candles stuck into the mouths of whisky jugs, he saw shining coins fall on the rough table. Coins of all kinds; coins he had never seen before clattered onto the table in a metallic rain until they were piled high.

What would Anne, the good chapel woman, say if she could see this? he wondered.

"No more bets."

There was the *slap, slap* of cards being shuffled one against the other, and a breath-taking pause, while greedy eyes watched the bony fingers of the black-coated dealer.

The ace of hearts glistened.

Silently one man drew the huge pile of coins toward him while the losers grumbled a bit.

"Make your bets, gents."

The business looked so easy. Charles reached into his pocket and felt of the bit of money there. If only . . . But there was so little left, and if he lost? He thought of the sweat that had earned it. Sudden weariness and the stench of stale whisky got him. He turned away and headed upstairs.

There was a fresh swat in the little box of a room. The lock on his sea chest had been broken and his suit was gone!

His roommate, a red-faced burly Irishman, sat beside the deal table where a smoky lamp burned. He was studying a tattered map and looked up mildly interested when Charles cursed his luck and groaned over the theft of his suit.

"Well, at least you can't blame me!" He grinned. "Your britches is big enough to make a tent for me. The box was open when I came in. Locks is just no good around here."

Then he asked Charles if he wanted to go to a fancy house after supper. "There's four right around here. I've tried 'em all and I know the best one. Where I'll take you, the girls are really worth the money and the drinks don't come higher than any place else."

Charles shook his head. "I haven't been to the mines yet. My money's in blankets instead of women."

The other nodded understandingly, then opined that the grub would be ready downstairs and shuffled out.

No one at the hotel knew anything about the theft of Charles Morgan's suit and no one seemed in the least interested.

Supper was a silent affair. Men sat on benches at the long trestle table, giving their full attention to biscuits and the thick plates of stew before them, pausing only to wash down the bites with strong black coffee or tea. Each seemed suspicious of all others. No one smiled. This gold rush was a grim business and each kept his own secrets and hopes and fears.

The next morning, while the Irishman in the other bunk snored off his drunk, Charles emptied his sea chest and rolled the contents into his blankets. This was no country to be loaded down with the weight of wood, when a man must carry all his possessions on his back for miles over the mountains. He looked around the room to see if anything had been forgotten and thought once more of his missing black suit. Poor Anne, she would be fierce, and her eyes would snap with anger, if she knew his good black was gone and he could no longer face his Maker "respectable" if anything happened. But at least the pack would be lighter by the weight of a suit.

It was not easy to shut the door of the bleak little room behind him and leave the sea chest alone—deserted, with the black letters MORGAN—LIVERPOOL—NEW YORK across the top.

That wooden box spelled home, conjured up the faces of Anne

and his boys, the life he had lived in Wales, and what he had left behind in Pennsylvania.

He could see Anne as he left, waving good-by in front of the company house, until he strode out of sight with the sea chest on his shoulder.

Now here he was in San Francisco, the city named for a saint, with his decent black stolen and the sea chest empty and ready to be abandoned.

No doubt some cold night when kindling was scarce in this wild place by the Golden Gate, some stranger would burn up the chest, never guessing the hopes and fears and yearnings of its owner.

He got up from the bunk where he had been sitting. This was no time to live in the past. He must be off to the wharf for a schooner. On to the diggings and gold enough for the cheese factory!

Other eager ones had most likely left more than a sea chest behind them.

CHAPTER 3

1849

His fellow passengers on the river schooner were a strange lot; Swedes, Frenchmen, Germans, Irishmen, Australians and Englishmen all chattered in their native tongues.

Mexicans dozed in corners, their wide-brimmed straw hats over eyes for shade, and bright-colored blankets pulled close around them. There were a dozen pigtailed Chinese with scarce a whole rag on their yellow bodies, herded together by an overseer.

Beady-eyed Indians sullenly watched this welter of newcomers. There was something ominous about the bronze expressionless faces of the savages that sent a gush of terror through Charles. He was glad young Charley, who wanted a "headdress," was not here to see them.

Later, when he had a bit of talk with a man from the mines, Charles mentioned his feeling about the savages.

The other only laughed. "Quell your fears. Those are Webber's Indians. He takes the gold they bring in exchange for cheap blankets. They've discovered white men's nuts are better than acorns and fork over as much as sixteen dollars in gold for a pound of almonds. They bring the nuggets to Webber in baskets."

Just the thought of nuggets in baskets nearly crazed the brain of Charles to fever pitch. Hard on this news he overheard a Yankee drawling pleasantly to a Southern gentleman who had brought six of his slaves to work in the mines. The Yank said that only a week ago he had picked up a thirty-pound nugget at Jimtown, a diggings not far from Sonorian Camp.

Charles pricked up his ears at that. Sonorian was where he was going to find Jim Teller. He wanted to shove the boat along!

They had gone through the straits and entered the river, and now progress was slow. Everything nautical crowded the winding river. Crude barges overloaded with goods, imposing clippers, whalers, clumsy flatboats and hundreds of homemade cockleshell craft all touched sides. Shouting and cursing filled the air as men fought for place in the water.

As they went up the river, the rickety old schooner had to be worked by hand around the bends that were lined with rushes. On the flatland beyond were hundreds of great oak trees growing as close together as trees in an orchard, and to the east were green rolling hills.

Charles was startled when the boat finally tied up at the wharf piled high with cargo. Was this shambles of tents Stockton? Recent rains had turned cow paths called streets into boggy mires where men cursed and lashed at straining horses and mules that churned mud. The one main thoroughfare was lined with brush shelters and open tents where men drank or sat at unpainted trestle tables gambling, their packs beside them on the damp ground. The voices of dealers were raised above the curses of roaring teamsters passing by with heavy loads. Miners were lined up at provision tents buying what they called "grubstakes" at unheard-of prices.

As he elbowed into the crowd to see what to buy, Charles heard one merchant brag that he was making a hundred thousand dollars a month pushing stuff over the plank counter.

Charles felt of the dwindling savings inside his pocket. This bit wouldn't take him far. He was a mouse among lions.

Bravely he stepped up and picked out a tin wash basin like the one he used at home to slosh off the coal dust of nights. A basin he must have, not to wash a face but to wash gold.

"How much?" he asked.

"Fifty!"

Carefully he counted out fifty cents from his pocket and held it toward the man.

"What's that for?" the other demanded.

"The basin. You said fifty," Charles told him.

With that all hell broke loose.

"Will you look, gents?" the red-shirted storekeeper roared out among the crowd. "Fifty cents the man hands me. Fifty *cents* for a gold wash basin!" Then they all laughed.

"Turn them cents into dollars and the basin's yours."

Charles banged the light tin thing down and walked out of the place. He didn't have fifty dollars to his name!

Bewildered, he watched the miners milling around him, all with grim determined faces and eyes bright with greed. Not a woman in the place! How he longed for Anne's smile, the feel of her warm body next to him in the big bed at home! It had been a long time now——

He turned away from the gold-crazed hucksters shouting out their wares and strode along the muddy, dank-smelling road and out into the soggy swamp where men had built scattered shelters of brush on the bare ground.

That night, under the shelter he had fashioned for himself from boughs, Charles took stock and planned his future.

He had good boots, two pairs of them, woolen shirts too and three suits of red flannel underwear, but he had no food, no pickax, no pan for washing gold.

A pan was important; even a miner from Wales could see that by the way men shelled out their money for the shiny wash basins.

A suit of underwear sold for sixty dollars here. That and the extra shirt he had never worn would easily bring enough for a meager supply of gold to see him to the diggings and a pan and pickax too.

These thieves would find they couldn't outwit a Welshman and keep him from his share in Nature's bounty!

The next morning, stiff and cold from a night on the soggy ground, he trudged back into the flapping tent city with his pack, stood up to a trestle counter and drank hot coffee and ate flapjacks that were worth their weight in gold. Then he walked bravely into the first provision tent he saw.

The sallow crafty-eyed shopkeeper looked at the heavy woolen shirt Charles spread out before him and at the bright-red suit of underwear. For a long minute no word passed.

"Well," he said, "what you want for 'em? Be quick about it. My time's worth money."

"A pickax, a tin and enough food to take me to Sonorian Camp."

The man threw back his head and laughed.

"Got a great idea of the worth of these rags, ain't you? Not much sale for such as these." He tossed the things away from him in contempt.

"They're only good for a chunk of sowbelly and a pan to fry it in, ten pounds of beans and ten pounds of flour." He paused. "And because I'm a tenderhearted man myself, I'll chuck in a pound of coffee and some sugar to buck up your guts."

"But a pan! I'll be needing a pan for washing—and a pickax."

"Use a pocketknife or your fingernails." The other sniffed. "Better men than you have gouged the rocks with their fingers and filled their pokes. The fry pan is good enough for washing. I've told you what I'll give. Take it or leave it." He turned to another customer and began weighing out beans. Men crowded around three-deep.

"I'll take it," Charles said and pushed the garments back across the counter.

He was jostled aside. A grubby pair of hands reached for the underdrawers and held them up.

"How much?" A voice boomed.

The storekeeper glanced casually. "Hundred dollars."

Before the promised provisions were weighed out, Charles saw the red flannel underwear, with his name that Anne had sewed in the neck, go out of the flapping tent under the arm of their new owner.

Charles was furious. The shopkeeper was a cheat, a thief, traveling under the name of merchant! He wanted to mash in the insolent face as hot anger flared up.

But what was the use? The deed was done. He had made a bargain. A fight would only get him into trouble with this race of cutthroats and perhaps he'd land in jail. That would only hold him back from the gold that he needed so desperately. Angrily he grabbed up the pathetic store of provisions and strode out into the muddy street.

He inquired the road to Sonorian Camp from a big colored man who had the only kindly face he had seen.

The man smiled. "Ain't no *roads* out here, boss—only kinda trails made natural-like across the mountains." The voice was soft and full-toned. "Over there where you sees the crowd aheadin' out—that leads you to Sonorian Camp." A black finger pointed, and the man went on.

Charles Morgan shouldered his pack and joined the sweating, cursing parade that slogged through the mud.

The largest number traveled afoot like himself, bent low under the weight of their burdens; some cast envious eyes at their more fortunate neighbors who passed by on horse or muleback.

Everything that could move was pressed into use in this mad rush to the rich grounds. Ox-drawn wagons loaded with supplies, pack animals straining and white with lather, mud wagons and every sort of cart and wheelbarrow.

There were Chinese, the muscles taut in their bony yellow legs and arms, pulling clumsy homemade two-wheeled affairs. One man pushed a baby carriage. All were creaking and groaning and squeaking their way across the expanse of flatland toward the rolling hills and gold!

At first there was talk about the big nuggets that had been found, about new diggings. Then, as mile after mile of bare flatland was covered, feet were shoved along in silence. Strength was saved for walking, for shifting the heavy packs or wiping brows now that the sun beat down so relentlessly.

Some, with muscles unused to hard work and walking, dropped by the wayside. Listless eyes in blanched faces watched the men clump by.

A young blond stripling with a drake tail still on the back of his neck shook and chattered with ague on the wet ground not ten feet away from the rutty trail, but no one stopped.

Charles asked God to remember this young lad so far away from home and mother, but he didn't stop to help the Almighty. There was no time to lose with food so scarce in his pack. He was thankful for muscles trained to hard work and a stomach used to little food.

Endlessly the string of human ants made its way off the soggy flat and up over green rolling hills that reminded Charles of the moors of home.

At night the warm red glow from a continuous line of camp-fires cheered and lighted the way for those who still had enough strength left to push on in the cool.

On and on and on Charles went, counting fires as he passed them, three hundred, three hundred and one—now dying down to a red glow, with sleeping men beside them who forgot the struggle for a bit, or perhaps dreamed of golden nuggets waiting for them in the mountains beyond.

Finally his twitching muscles could stand no more punishment, and he lay down with his blankets around him and the precious pack under his head where it was safe from thieving hands.

The soul of Charles was rent the next day as he saw men with blue lips and glazed eyes stagger off the trail in the pouring rain to face their fate alone on the strange bare hillside or under a spreading oak tree. A dead Chinese not ten feet away, with a few oak branches thrown over him; a man coughing up his very lungs, an ague victim shivering in his blankets—all these were passed by. No time for tenderness or a word of comfort here on the California gold trail. The stakes were too high to bother about a brother traveler's body or even his soul.

For comfort, and to keep his mind off the continuous picture of misery, Charles said over the Shepherd's Psalm, taught him so long ago in the little Welsh chapel above the mine dump.

But the Twenty-third Psalm was soon crowded out by tales picked up along the trail. There was the place where the Yankee Colonel Frémont had diggings on ground given him by the Mexican Government. On Frémont's ranch a man could take out all the gold he needed in a twelve-foot square.

He must go on!

Drenching rains came, then out popped the sun to sweat the very juices out of a body.

Up through the hills Charles trekked, the pack lighter with each bolted meal, but heavier by pounds to the weary back that carried it. Then down into the wooded canyons where waters from the Mother Lode roared to lower levels. Oaks and pines gave a bit of shelter, and it was well too, for traffic thickened up so that folks jostled to keep their places in the line.

"What's ahead? . . . What's holding us up?" men demanded. "Let's get on."

"The ferry" came back down the line. "Knight's Ferry across the Stanislaus River. We got to wait our turn!"

Step by step the mob of stinking, sweaty prospectors with creaking packs jostled one another nearer to the water, where shouting ruffians herded stubborn beasts of burden and willing men onto flatboats.

The ferry was a crude affair and crossing slow and tedious. There was a stout pole on each bank, with ropes across the racing torrent. Hand over hand men pulled, until the crowded flatboat was safely across, and burdened once more with traffic coming from the opposite direction.

Man and beast were charged two bits each. "And have your money ready."

Charles asked a fellow traveler how much this was, for he had never heard of a "bit."

"Two bits—a quarter." The man looked at him astonished that he knew so little.

Pack animals were four bits. "And drive the damned critters on yerselves."

Wheeled vehicles were rated at a dollar a wheel.

Charges for crossing, compared to the importance of gaining the other side, were very moderate, Charles thought, but there was a lot of grumbling. Progress stopped when two Chinese tried to get across for a single fare by one carrying the other on his shoulders. The Chinese insisted that his friend was his "pack."

The bargeman disagreed. Harangue started in singsong Cantonese. A pack was a pack, and the fare included a man and his pack.

"Let the Chinese go over," Charles cried impatiently from the crowd waiting in the hot sun. "Stop the row. On to the diggings!"

CHAPTER 4

1 8 4 9

Travel was slow now. The hills were steep and long; loose outcroppings made a man slither back with each step. Muscles complained louder, and many feet were raw from sweat and rough rubbing shoes.

Charles saw great hulks of men sitting by the wayside nursing their hurts and cursing feet that made them lose precious time when the glitter of gold was so near.

Roistering, drunken men came down the trail on horseback and added to the impatience by shouting out that a new find had been made on Wood's Creek.

"The richest in the diggings! Nuggets big as peas all over the place and men thick as flies washing them out."

The words acted as a lash. Weary ones, barefooted and blistered and ravaged by hunger and scurvy, strained every bit of strength for the last spurt. Then they would suddenly be stricken with fever and chills and were no longer interested in the struggle.

Swelled, parched lips begged from the roadside for "Water—a little water. *Please*," but few heeded; if anything they stepped along more briskly past the pleading eyes.

Twice Charles stopped, feeling somehow if the dying were deserted in their hour of need, how could the living expect God to send them luck?

One lad from Nantucket was delirious and thought Charles was his mother. A doctor saw Charles with the boy's head cradled in his lap and left the trail. But the "pill roller" would waste no precious medicine.

34

"Too far gone" was all he said, and then went through the boy's pack. "I'm short of flour. This chap'll not be needing flour where he's going." The precious flour was extracted and the doctor moved on.

When the boy gasped his last, Charles pulled him into a ravine, rolled him in his blanket, and with bare hands covered him with soft woodsy-smelling leaf mold from the tree that would be the sole mark to tell that a boy from Nantucket had passed by this way.

Taking things from the dead was a regular practice here. When a man gasped his last, it was not many minutes before the food he had carried so far or his pickax was caught up and added to the pack of a total stranger.

At first Charles was sickened by this form of thievery, and then reason said, Why not? A dead man had no need for food or a pickax and both were scarce enough.

The trail was clogged with traffic as they neared Wood's Creek.

Some, impatient to be at the gold, left the trail to search along the waterway which was already lined with crouching men, but Charles pushed on. He hadn't enough provisions to waste. He knew about Sonorian Camp. Jim Teller was there and would put him onto the "sure thing" he had written about in the letter.

Bough and canvas shelters came in sight on the mountainside.

"Jamestown," someone called out.

"Jimtown," said another. "Richest diggings in the Lode—with four stabbings a night!"

Then suddenly around a bend in the grooved little gulch Charles saw hundreds of excited men feverishly scrambling for gold.

Weariness was forgotten along with Sonorian Camp. Charles shoved and pushed other men out of the way and rushed toward the creek bed.

He had the advantage now. A big man could plow through ordinary men who came up to his shoulders, just as a bull elephant could break a trail through the jungle.

Men up to their waists in the stream gouged up pans of pebbles and sand from the bottom, their packs still on their backs. Some used hats instead of pans, others just cupped red hands.

Charles had scarce scooped up a handful of gravel when a gun was poked into his ribs.

"This here's my claim," a brusque voice roared. "Five feet of this crick where you're standing right now. See the paper yonder on the bank?"

The speaker was a great rawboned chap with many weeks' black beard on his face. "Get the hell off!"

Charles waded out and shoved on up the gulch. Everywhere there were tickets marking claims, everywhere people loudly disputing.

Jimtown was a squalid place of tents and brush shelters, its single main street lined with drinking places and provision tents. Candles here were a dollar each and flour and pork five dollars per pound.

These people couldn't talk in less than dollars! Even a bit of saleratus to raise biscuits cost a dollar a pound.

His appetite for gold slaked some by the gun in his ribs, Charles decided to eat a meal in a tent where men were standing around waiting to be served.

"Grub!" a red-shirted man roared as he set down plates of sowbelly and beans. "Take your places, gents, and no bickering over the food." He licked off a grubby thumb that had gathered sauce from the beans as he carried them in. "Only three clunkers to a customer."

"What's a clunker?" Charles asked of his neighbor as they climbed over the bench and took their places at the crowded trestle table.

"Biscuits," the sandy-haired youth told him. "Ain't you never heard of biscuits?"

"Never heard them called clunkers."

"That's 'cause they're so heavy they clunk down and squash everything else in your belly." Then he asked Charles if he was another mick that had come over from Ireland because of the potato famine.

"We already got too many micks here! Three hundred up yonder on Paddy's Hill, and the fightin'est outfit in the hills, except maybe the Frenchies." He grinned and shoveled beans into his mouth.

Charles admitted to Pennsylvania.

"Want to be put onto a sure thing?" the fellow asked. "I got a claim can be bought cheap. Asthma! I got to get out of the mines."

Charles shook his head. "No money to buy a claim. I have to hunt my own."

From then on his neighbor was not interested in talk and turned surly when Charles asked how far Sonorian Camp was.

"Four miles further up. But you ain't going to have any luck up there. It's full of throat-cutting greasers."

"Oh, I don't know" came from across the table. "We got troubles here at Jimtown, when a man can't wash out his shirt and hang it onto a tree to dry without having it stole. It ain't Mexicans that does the stealin' either, but folks as claims they come from the States."

The youth beside Charles turned bright scarlet. In a flash his hand was out and a gun pointed at the man opposite.

"Take back them words. I didn't steal your damned shirt!"

But the other was quick too. A gun was pointed directly across the table, too dangerously near Charles for comfort.

"I ain't saying—" the man across the table spoke slowly, his eye fastened on Charles's neighbor—"but the shirt you're wearin' right now has the hole I burned in it one day when a spark from the campfire was outa place. I can see it from where I sit." With that guns went off, and the sandy-haired youth toppled backward from the bench.

Charles, used to the Saturday night brawls in miners' pubs, was horrified now.

"You've killed him!" he shouted out, and left his own food to lift up the youngster's head as blood began to stain the shirt red.

"Why not? He's a thief," the man opposite cried. "There's no place here for thieves—when we catch 'em." Long legs strode to the sandy-haired boy lying dead in the yellow dirt, and soon the murderer was busy stripping the disputed shirt off the inert body. "Guess his asthma's cured for sure now," he said, "but I've got to wash his God-damned blood off my shirt." And he threw the garment over his arm.

Charles turned away, sickened over the sight. Hungry as he was he couldn't finish his meal.

Miners affected by the affair jumped up and headed for the opening, but were barred by the man who had passed the food. "Not yet, gents! There's the little matter of mulligan to pay for. Stick out your pokes—or you don't get out."

The men stopped, shoved their pokes across the table toward the grubby man, who licked his finger, stuck it into the little leather or canvas bag and cleaned off the gold dust that clung to the spit. The process was repeated until all had paid. No one gave so much as a glance in the direction of the sandy-haired man lying in the yellow dirt.

Charles, minus poke and dust too, paid his ounce. Four dollars for three clunkers, a plate of beans flavored with sowbelly and a dish of dried-apple sauce. Then, disgusted, lonely and bone-weary, he struck out on the final four-mile stretch to Sonorian Camp.

As he trudged along, doubt crept into his mind. Why had he come to such a God-forsaken country where shopkeepers were thieves and men murdered other men because of a shirt, and no one cared? Why hadn't he been satisfied with a dollar a day in the mines and Anne's happy face waiting for him of nights? These were heart questions born of homesickness and weariness.

But Jim Teller had picked up more gold in a few days than a miner could sweat out in a year. Jim Teller was most likely rich by now, richer than ever a coal miner could hope to be. Everything would be all right once Jim Teller put him onto things. He'd get his pile of gold for the cheese factory and be out of the damned country. These were the glistening golden answers that whirled in his head while rough boots shoved on up the hill.

Sonorian Camp was larger than Jimtown. Lights twinkled all over the hillside. The main street was scarce thirty feet wide. Loud shouts and curses were going up as men tried to pull packed jackasses along in the mud or drive mules past knots of men congregated around the flimsy shelters.

The voices of faro dealers rang out into the night and there was the din of revelry coming from a place where a fiddle and guitar played. Twice, as Charles walked along, shots rang out.

But no one knew Jim Teller. No one had even heard his name. "Holy Mary, pard!" one man said. "How in hell do you think I'd know anybody here by name, with fifteen thousand men crawling like lice on the hillsides? You don't ask no questions as long as folks leave you alone and mind their own business. Try the saloons."

But Charles was too weary now. He needed a shelter, a place to sleep, and so he turned into a branch affair with a canvas top marked HOTEL.

The air was thick with smoke and the stench of whisky. Americans, Kanakas, Frenchmen and Mexicans crowded around a plank gambling table.

Over in the corner beside a whisky keg, Charles found the proprietor shoving drinks across another plank. He was a dark button-eyed little Frenchman whom the men called Baptiste. Baptiste was kind and talked a bit to Charles after the price of a "slug" was carefully counted out of the little hoard. But he didn't know Jim Teller.

During a lull when the men were all watching the card dealer, Charles told the Frenchman all about Anne and the cheeses and how he had hoped to get enough gold to go home and build a cheese factory. Then he showed Baptiste Anne's picture.

The Frenchman looked a while at the daguerreotype, but when he heard how long ago the letter had been sent from Teller, he shook his head.

"My son, that is a long time! So very long in this place. Men change so fast. Here today, gone and forgotten tomorrow if bigger nuggets turn up. The friend may be now in Jacksonville making dams along the Stanislaus, or at Hangtown to the north—or a dozen places by now. They jump like crickets, these miners, if someone else finds a new diggings."

Baptiste warned Charles about the Mexican settlement in Sonora, called the *Tigre*. It was a nest of thieves and cutthroats and harlots, because Mexicans were here first and they resented white men.

Then he offered a place on the floor to Charles, "for the bedding down with his own blankets," where he would be safe.

"And it don't cost you even a fraction of an ounce. Tomorrow you look around and if you don't see the friend, Baptiste grub- stakes you for a week or two. The rest will be the affair of the good God." He turned to sell a bottle of whisky and weighed gold carefully on a crude scale made from sardine tins slung to an upright pole.

For two days Charles searched in the milling crowd of men on the main street, but no Jim Teller. Wearily he went back past saloons and gambling places and confessed his failure to Baptiste.

"Have a brandy on the house, son," Baptiste told him and shoved a cup toward Charles. Then, when no one was near enough to hear, he told that a drunken miner had let drop about finding gold in a new place.

"Not crowded yet with diggers," Baptiste whispered. "Three miles straight south of Jimtown. The gold is on the surface. Men there call it 'Utter's'. You could maybe find the cheese factory there for your Anne. Baptiste finds out where the trail takes off by an oak tree, before the drunken one left here to lose his nuggets to Conceptión over at the *Tigre*."

He shoved a bit of rumpled paper into Charles's hand. On it was a crude map with a cross marked where the trail took off.

"Baptiste your friend tells you this. See that you are sharp enough to get there before the drunken one spreads his news! Be- fore Conceptión caresses him too well and then tells her lover and the rush starts." He pointed to flour, coffee, some candles and a bag of beans.

"The grubstake is there ready for you."

What could a man say of such kindness? No words would come. Charles promised to leave in the morning as soon as it was light enough to see the trail.

"And one day if I strike it rich, Baptiste, you shall have gold in return for the only friendship I've found since I left home," he finished gratefully.

"Hush, not so loud," Baptiste warned. "Even the branches that make a shelter have ears around Sonorian Camp. Baptiste maybe take his pay in cheese, yes?" He smiled and motioned to the corner where Charles had slept before. "Sleep now, so your legs will be rested to take you far and—and well, tomorrow."

But there was a letter to be written to Anne first. She must know he had arrived safe at Sonorian Camp, and that he had lost track of Jim Teller, but had found a good friend in the Frenchman and was on his way to gold.

Out of the pack came the little tablet she had put in along with a few envelopes. He sat with a stub of pencil and wrote on his lap.

He would not tell her of the hardship and death and misery, for that would worry her; instead he wrote about the old schooner crawling up the river through the rushes, and the long-legged gray birds that stood in the marsh like sentinels. He described the ferns by the trail and red berries heavy on bushes that looked like holly but didn't have prickly leaves. Aye, it was a fine letter, fit for a queen to read, he decided when the two pages were finished and he read them over.

As a P.S. he scrawled:

No chapel here, but they have a French priest, Father Arnault, who goes about by muleback to help poor sinners who are sick and dying, and complains that only Mexicans come to the little church he has built on the hill. And I've seen no women except two Mexican chippies. Write me all about the boys and send the letter to Sonorian Camp.

Baptiste told him where to find an express messenger to carry the letter down to the settlements and send it on its way.

Alas, the letter was not to go after all! The expressage of a letter cost four dollars and he had but two left in the pocket of his jacket. The lass would have to wait until he found gold at Utter's and came into town for provisions.

He shoved the envelope into his pocket, walked back to Baptiste's and rolled up for the night.

But a Welshman was not to sleep long. Just after midnight, there was a frightful uproar and the terrifying word "Fire!" rang through his dreams and into consciousness. "Fire!"

Charles pulled on his boots, rolled up the grubstake in his blanket and ran from the shelter.

The whole town seemed to be ablaze! Flames turned the sky crimson. Men clogged the narrow street, shoving and shouting.

When the wind blew embers that ignited their tents, shopkeepers couldn't get their stuff out because of the jam of men.

All hell let loose!

Someone began a bucket brigade, but it soon gave out in the fierce battle with the wind, and people scattered to save their own necks.

The fire had started in a gambling tent at the edge of town and was racing up the narrow gulch. One wooden shelter after another made its spectacular final show and collapsed. In less than two hours the whole of Sonorian Camp was gone.

Charles Bassett, a cook who had deserted ship and come to the mines, organized four ex-soldiers from Stevenson's regiment who were camped in the gulch below town to protect the smoldering ruins from those who would thieve.

Men standing at dawn in the rain before the blackened remains said forty thousand dollars had been lost in provisions. There was danger from famine now that rains bogged pack trains down in the mud. Other men searched in the ashes for melted gold where they had once kept the cash.

Charles Morgan was never to forget that morning of November 15, 1849, when he went back and saw little Baptiste standing in faded blue jeans beside the mass of smoldering wood and broken bottles that had been his hotel.

"I'll stay," he offered. "I'll help you. I can't go now, Baptiste, and leave you like this. You're my friend."

The Frenchman shrugged. "And what is there to help me about?" he asked. "Nothing left to carry, nothing left to sell. It is good that your grubstake was saved, for the sake of the cheese factory and the one who waits for you. Go on. Baptiste goes on too in *his* way."

"Then I'll be back," Charles promised. "I'll be back as soon as ever I can with some gold for you." He shouldered his pack and headed down the trail toward Jimtown.

CHAPTER 5

1849

THE sun broke momentarily through the clouds when Charles Morgan spied the oak tree marked on his bit of paper. But there were too many men on the main trail watching. Gold seekers used their eyes well. He pulled off, sat down by the tree until the line thinned, then shoved through the tangled bushes and along the thready pathway like a wild thing.

He had gone barely a mile when he saw the flat and two or three brush shelters nestled against a hill. Utter's!

Cautious, he left the path and commenced looking down in the red earth. It would be better not to let any here know that he had news of their find. Let them think he was just a prospector hunting a good claim.

He moved closer to the cluster of shelters, washing panful after panful of earth in a runnel that trickled through the flatland, just as he had seen miners do it in the stream at Sonorian Camp.

Then suddenly at the bottom of the pan there was a shiny gold nugget the size of his thumbnail!

Something stirred deep inside Charles when he looked at it. His first nugget! The Shepherd of the Psalm, who had guided a poor Welsh miner to this new country of America and to California, was surely not far away now.

He stood quite still in the drizzling rain with the fry pan in one hand and the nugget nestling in the other. It seemed that he was in chapel, so full of gratitude was his heart.

Off came the battered hat. His face tilted up to the threatening sky. "Thank you, God—for all blessings," he murmured. "And God bless Baptiste."

Out came the bit of crumpled paper and a stub of pencil from his pocket. He had learned well the rules of the gold seeker during his few days in the diggings.

A stick, split with his knife at the top and driven into the ground; this paper with his name and the date shoved into the slit.

He was so taken with staking the claim that the true meaning of the nugget hadn't penetrated his thick skull. As the paper fluttered, he suddenly realized it all.

His first nugget! He had a gold claim of his own! He was going to be rich. Anne would have the cheese factory and a lot besides. Tenderness ran through him as he thought of her. If only she could be here beside him now. All this was because of Anne. She had made him leave the misery in Wales and come to the new country, and her savings had brought him to California.

He looked at the bright nugget shining in his palm. Now, with the claim, his dear little Anne could have silk dresses like the ladies he had seen swishing along the streets of Philadelphia. Their boys would never know the black of coal pits. His brain whirled with the things gold could buy.

Crazed with his thoughts, he worked at cutting oak branches to make a shelter, come night.

When dusk was falling, he longed for a good cup of tea and Anne beside him to share in the excitement. He'd have to do without the lass, but she had put a little leaded packet of tea tied with a shoelace in his things. Now was the time to open and celebrate.

He was sitting over a smoky fire trying to make tea in the fry pan, when he heard the sound of boots approaching.

"Howdy, pard," a voice drawled. "I'm your neighbor up the line. Simmons is the name."

The man came into the fire's weak glow, a great chap in blue pants and red woolen shirt; blue eyes twinkled above a thick black beard. He glanced at the pan where Charles's brew bubbled.

"Ain't you got no pot?"

Charles shook his head. "I don't have anything much, except the strength of a coal miner and enough food to last a few days.

Sit down. Have some tea, if you can drink out of the pan," he offered.

The big fellow squatted beside the fire, but he would have no tea. Tea was weak stuff—a woman's drink.

Sharp eyes took in the few possessions Charles had put into the shelter.

"You ain't got much of an outfit, pard. Where's your shovel and your pickax?" he asked.

Charles explained that such things were luxuries he couldn't afford yet.

The other looked with astonishment and shrugged his shoulders. "A pick and shovel ain't luxuries, man, they're God-damned necessities!"

There was silence for a bit. A log burned through and sent out a spurt of golden sparks as it fell to pieces.

"I ain't aimin' to run your business, nor to give you no sugar-tit, but if you walk back to my place, I'll give you a couple of empty oyster tins so you'll have something to boil up a mess of beans in, and to use for that tea you swill."

Simmons had a good shelter with a canvas top and a bed of boughs up off the damp ground. He showed Charles how it was made.

"If you don't put plenty of boughs so's your body can't draw the damp you'll sure as hell get rheumatics," he warned.

When Charles left with the empty tin cans, there was a warm invitation to return and "sit a spell, when the coyotes howling and the rain make you wish you'd never seen the damned place."

For days Charles worked in the rain and picked up small nuggets. Nights were spent drying out his clothes and cooking beans over the smoky fire at the side of his drippy shelter while the wind whistled dirges through the branches.

Food in the grubstake dwindled so that it had to be rationed carefully.

He longed to send a letter to Anne and tell her his news, and he wanted to take some of his gold to Baptiste, who had helped him, but he was afraid to leave the claim. Other men might pick up his nuggets while he was away and steal his fry pan and blankets to boot.

A big nugget made him decide to stay with the job until starvation itself forced him to take the chance of a trip to town. He'd pick up his own big nuggets before any other man. A little more time would give Anne's letter a chance to come over the hills.

He was working late one afternoon not far from the shelter, when a low voice called out: "You all want to borrow my shovel, boss? I ain't got much use for it myself now. I'm sick."

Charles looked up and saw a friendly face, black as a coal miner's just up from the pits.

The colored man he had seen in Stockton! The kindly chap who had taken time to smile and point out the trail to Sonorian Camp.

The poor fellow was thinner now. His eyes were deeply sunken in dusky cheeks. He was wet to the skin and his clothes were dripping. As the darky stood, apparently waiting to see what his reception would be, a racking cough tore at his lungs and he crumpled weakly into a heap on the wet grass.

When the paroxysm was over, Charles helped him into the shelter and took off his pack. The pickax and shovel lay outside where the Negro had dropped them.

Charles stirred up the coals of his campfire and blew hard on the sodden wood until there was a blaze.

The Negro's eyes were bright with fever. His breathing was so labored that it frightened Charles. Each great heave seemed bound to be the poor fellow's last.

As soon as water was hot in the oyster tin, Charles took a pinch of Jamaica ginger from the white parcel Anne had put in with his things—bless the lass—and dropped it into the water. A quick stir with his tin spoon and he put it to the poor chap's mouth.

"Here, drink this," he ordered. "You're perished with wet and cold, but you'll buck up. This'll warm you. Then I'll give you beans and salt pork."

Grateful eyes followed him. The man took the tin in his own hands after a swallow or two and Charles cut up the last bit of sowbelly and put it in the fry pan.

When the darky had eaten, Charles greased the big black chest with hot bacon fat and spread his own extra flannel shirt over to warm and protect.

All night he fed the fire with what dry wood he had and watched the heavy breathing, wondering how long a body could stand such punishment.

At dawn the Negro fell asleep and Charles went out into the soggy gray morning to forage for more wood.

He would have to go in to Jimtown or Sonorian Camp now, for the darky had eaten the last beans he possessed, and pork grease for today's flapjacks was on the black chest.

The big lump of gold would be enough to help Baptiste and buy food. The sick man was safe enough to be left with the things. His legs wouldn't take him far even if he was a thief. Perhaps the black man had been sent to a Welsh miner by the Shepherd of the Psalm.

The Negro wakened while Charles was mending the fire and trying to brew a weak concoction that would have to pass for coffee.

Anyway, it was "wet 'n' warm" as his granny used to say in Wales when wages were scarce and only a pinch of tea left in the cannister.

"I'm better, boss, and thanks to you" came weakly. "But Artemus don't aim to be no drag on you. I'll push on today, sir, and always remember what you done."

Charles gave him a flapjack that had stuck to the pan and was burned from lack of grease and a tin of hot drink and took the same himself.

Warmed and rested, Artemus told how he had followed the trail toward Sonorian Camp for three days in the pouring rain, until he had been taken with a cough and shivers so bad he wasn't right in his head. He had a gold pan to wash, but everywhere along the line white men had run him away from the creek beds until all his food was gone. He didn't know how long he had wandered until he found Charles. Was this place Sonorian Camp?

Charles explained where Sonorian Camp was.

"Then I'll be goin' on there today," the man said between spells of coughing. "There's gold at Sonorian."

Charles looked at the pathetic dull-eyed man.

"You can't go. You'll die out in the wet with that cough. Stay here today and rest, Artemus."

The black man was too done-in to argue. He closed his eyes and turned limp.

Charles saw that there was wood within the sick man's reach and then headed toward Simmons' shelter to borrow coffee, a handful of flour and two fistfuls of beans to tide them over until he could leave the poor devil long enough to make a trip to town.

That night with a belly full of beans and flapjacks and plenty of hot coffee, and while Charles busied himself with the fire and a mess of beans for the morrow, Artemus told his story.

He was a slave from Virginia, come to the mines for nuggets enough to "buy hisself" and be "free as any man born on earth." That's what his master had told him. His master, Mr. Henry Bodine, was a good man and wanted only half of the gold Artemus found. The rest was for him to pay off on his freedom. Mr. Bodine had bought his ticket on the boat and his outfit too. Mr. Bodine was a good man.

Now that he was away, Artemus wasn't so sure he wanted to be free. The master "saw to his niggers good when they was sick, and there was always big plenty to eat on the plantation—yams and chickens and pork and corn pone." Maybe a nigger was better with a white master to look out for him, when the master was good like Mr. Bodine and "never beat no nigger, no matter how much of a black rascal he was."

"He gwine to write me reg'lar to Sonorian Camp," Artemus finished proudly. "Him and the mistress sure fine white folks. He got five ruffled shirts to his name. And he let a nigger Artemus come away and hunt gold for hisself."

"Know anyone at Sonorian Camp, Artemus?" Charles asked.

There was a shake of the kinky head. Mr. Bodine had read in the Norfolk paper about Sonorian Camp and the big nuggets found there and thought it would be a good place for Artemus to go. Mr. Bodine liked games of chance and he had a luck angel.

Charles told Artemus that Sonorian Camp was crowded with men hunting nuggets, even on city lots where places had burned down. There was little chance now for a newcomer.

"You'd better stay here in Utter's Camp. There's gold here. You can take the claim next to mine or maybe another," he suggested. "You can still go over to Sonorian Camp for Mr. Bodine's letters. He won't care where you find the gold as long as you get it."

The darky was astonished at the words, so astonished that he had a fit of coughing.

"You mean it? Near you?" he asked, his dull eyes watching Charles's face.

Morgan nodded.

"But, boss, you don't want to be livin' so close to no black nigger like me. It ain't decent," he objected when he had breath enough for talk. "White folks, they don't think nothin' of folks live near niggers unless they workin' in the house for 'em."

"God may have spilled His ink bottle on you, Artemus, but you must be honest or Mr. Bodine wouldn't have trusted you so far away when you could run away without paying for your free-dom——"

"Artemus not run away!" The darky put in. "Not when he can get nuggets to pay right and fair. Nigger men strong as Artemus cost good money to a master."

"I don't forget that you had time to stop in Stockton and show me the trail," Charles went on. "As long as you behave yourself around these diggings, you'll be as good a neighbor as any."

"Thanks, boss. Thank you, sir." The colored man's eyes were brighter now; new life seemed to come into the black face. "It's like havin' the master right here 'side me again—a white gentle-man lookin' out for things."

Charles promised to stake a claim for Artemus as soon as it was daylight. Then they rolled up in blankets near the fire to sleep.

Staking out the claim was a great affair. Artemus could neither read nor write, so Charles wrote out the paper that was to start the black man on his way to freedom.

"And now your other name?" he asked, after the date had been put down.

"Just Artemus, ain't never had no other name 'ceptin' Artemus Bodine," the darky said between gasps for breath as he watched the procedure with eager eyes. "Won't that legalate it?"

Charles reassured him. Artemus Bodine it was, and the paper fluttered in the pale sunshine.

Then Artemus told what was on his mind. Charles had saved his life. He was too weak to work yet. "But I still got me a mouth and a belly to feed—and I got me a pickax and a shovel too. Mr. Bodine he seen to that. He bought it in Norfolk before he put this nigger on the boat.

"Gwine to work for you, Mr. Morgan, same as I did for Master Henry Bodine," he went on. "Artemus give his free money into your hands, all the gold he gets and you takes half. Then when I gets enough to buy me, and enough for to take back to Master Henry I give you my claim. We gonna be partners, sir—if you all wants this nigger for a partner. Two pairs of hands workin' better 'n only one, sir, and sometimes this black head get a idea too."

Charles smiled. "We'll be partners, Artemus. We'll both work hard and split everything, because two of us *can* work better than one. But you keep your claim. After you're free you'll need to live. Mr. Bodine won't be paying for your keep."

Black hand met white in a clasp that bound the bargain. The partnership of Morgan and Artemus began its bumpy career in Utter's Diggings.

CHAPTER 6

1849

ARTEMUS was much better the next morning when Charles gathered together ropes and a blanket for carrying back provisions and then set out for Sonorian Camp.

But the trip was disappointing. New shelters were up on the ashes of their forerunners and the main street was thronged with men, but there was no letter at the express office from Anne and Baptiste hadn't been seen since the fire.

"And a good thing too," one chap said. "These damned Parleyvoos here getting the gold that ought to be in pokes of red-blooded Yankees. Too many foreigners here. String a few up, I say, and they'd make themselves scarce."

Anger flared up in Charles as he thought of his good friend Baptiste as a damned foreigner who ought to be strung up!

"Shut your jib," he snarled and turned away.

The man at Wells, Fargo tent weighed in his gold and gave Charles a hundred and twenty dollars.

That was a thrill to warm a man with no provisions and a sick partner to feed. His first gold weighed in! He was on his way now. The letter could go to Anne with a postscript about his find, even if it did cost four dollars!

He was disappointed in not hearing from Anne, for he had made reckoning on a letter, but letters took a long time in these parts. A man must be patient. He left his own letter in the hands of the carrier and headed for a grub place.

The great riches melted away in the newly fashioned provision tent. Everything had gone up more than half again, because pack trains couldn't get through the mud.

When Charles complained, the man turned furious. "What in Judas Priest do you expect," he roared, "with them jacks eatin' their fool heads off on oats at a dollar a handful and hay a dollar a handful?"

Charles looked at the pathetic little stock of groceries. There was only what he could carry on his back without being weighted down, but he didn't have enough gold to pay for what he had picked out.

He subtracted, pound by pound, until purse met the demands, then rolled what was left in his blanket and strode out into the driving rain for the house of boughs he called home.

It was dark when he arrived at Utter's Camp, and the heart of him was cheered by the warm glow that came from the fire by his own shelter.

The colored man had dragged himself out for more wood and now lay spent and gasping by the fire.

"I remembered the good Lord and the star that told the Wise Men where to go," he managed between coughing spells. "But all Artemus could do for you was wet wood, boss, and it don't make much shine out. The good Lord He know what you done for a sick nigger man and He light your way, I bet. Nobody come near this place whilst you was gone—or I'd gone after 'em with this yere knife." He pulled a ferocious-looking dirk from under his blanket.

They had scarce finished their supper when Simmons came over to get back his coffee and the other stuff Charles had borrowed. He didn't look kindly on the black man.

"I didn't know I was helping to feed a nigger when you came to borrow," he told Charles. "I don't like niggers."

Artemus slipped away from the fire and into the cold outside, to make himself scarce.

Charles Morgan, scrapper for the underdog in the saloons of Pottsville on Saturday nights, would have none of that! His temper came up with a bang.

"This is my claim," he snapped. "If you don't like what you see

here, get out and stay out. That black man came here sick. It was
my idea to have him stay, and anybody as can't swallow an honest
Negro tending to his own business can just stay away."

Simmons touched a grubby hand to his battered hat in salute,
whirled on his heel and stalked out.

Artemus came back into the shelter. He was upset and offered
to leave before dawn. "I don't want to make no trouble 'tween
white folks. They's plenty of mountains. Someplace else'll be
good for a nigger."

"We're partners," Charles snapped. "They can take us or leave
us alone. You're staying right here." Then he smiled. "Besides,
you have a good sharp ax——"

"Now, boss, don't you go runnin' after men with my ax—Mr.
Bodine he was allus agin that!"

"I'm going to need the ax for something else," Charles said.
"We're going to cut down trees and build us a decent cabin to live
in out of the wet."

Artemus was relieved. He knew all about building cabins.
Colored folks put up their own places on the plantation where he
lived.

They cut the first logs the next morning, then strained and
heaved to pull them into place not far from the shelter. It was
hard work and made the muscles ache, but there was satisfaction
in the effort as they saw one log after another fit into the notches.

Each day there was work on the cabin in the morning, and
panning for grub gold afternoons.

Twice a passing miner gave them a "heft" when the logs had to
be lifted high on the walls. Artemus always took a little gold from
his poke to pay, or offered a meal of cooked beans.

"It ain't good to take nothin' less you give. The master teach us
that in Virginia, and this nigger still goes by what he say to do."

It was while they shared beans with one of these passing prospectors who had helped boost logs that they learned what was
going on over the hills.

"States' men" at Sonorian Camp were for running out all
the foreigners. Frenchies and Sydney convicts and Swedes and

Germans and Chinks and Kanakas—they were against them all.

"That Sonorian Camp ain't no place for a nigger," Artemus put in. "I glad I got me a white man partner in a safe diggings."

Charles didn't remind him that right in their own camp a miner had been found only the day before with his head cracked in and his poke "vamoosed."

When the visitor had gone, Artemus put more wood on the fire. "That man, he ain't gonna get no place, boss. Ain't ever goin' to be rich. He don't stay no place long enough to even rest his feet, 'cause he's afraid he missin' somethin' someplace else."

Utter's Camp was changing fast now. News had leaked out about the diggings and every day more men came over the hills and settled on the bare places. The little valley was black with prospectors and campfires glowed all over the hills at night.

Two gamblers had set up tents not far from Utter's claim. These fancy-shirted chaps slept all day while miners worked in the rain and muck. But the card men brightened up at night all ready to spirit away the day's take from grubby hands.

Charles was worried about the turn of affairs in the little camp and spoke his mind one night when Utter dropped by to see how the cabin was coming on.

"I don't mind the Chinese. They're quiet and tend to their own business," he told Utter. "But the Mexicans are always shooting it out over those two fandango women they've brought in."

Gentle, blond little Utter rammed tobacco into his pipe. "Not being as big a man and a scrapper like you, Morgan, I'm not up to fighting the greasers or anybody else," he said quietly. "Besides, we can't keep 'em out even if we were here first. There's too many to fight, so we've got to put up with 'em."

By the light of the fire Artemus cut notches in logs for the cabin, and they all watched. Utter suggested that work and time would be saved on slabs for the door. There was a fellow now at Jimtown who had planks hauled up from a sawmill down the line. Charles could get him to cut some planks the right size for the door, fasten them together, and the thing would be done.

The day before Christmas the cabin was finished, a fine one-room affair with a loft above under the steep-pitched roof, and all chinked well with mud to keep out the raw December wind.

Artemus had carried four planks, cut to fit the door opening, all the way from Jimtown on his back. They had cost four dollars each. "These my Christmas to you, boss, and the money taken from my own poke," he told Charles.

The trip to Jimtown alone had been a great adventure for the darky. He had used his eyes well at the place where the planks were sold.

The miners were buying cradles to wash gold. Wooden boxes they were, with rockers. The dirt was shoveled in, water put on top and all rocked like a baby until the dirt washed out and the heavy gold was left. "We could go over a hundred shovels a day that way, boss, with one to shovel and the other to rock."

These new affairs were packed in from below all ready to use; they cost a hundred dollars, but were worth every cent. Even a black man could see that.

"If'n I had me a saw and some nails and some boards, this nigger could make us one, boss, quick as the flap of a rooster's wings when he after a old hen."

Charles was thoughtful as he cooked up three squirrels Artemus had trapped, along with two onions, for their Christmas dinner. This talk of cradles brought back the longing for home and Anne and the boys.

He thought of the little cradle he had made in the new country of Pennsylvania for Bill, his first-born, and of Anne rocking the boy with her foot while she knitted woolen socks. Pretty as a madonna she had been with her hair smooth over her ears and shiny as brown satin.

He thought of the times he had plodded over the hill after the letter that had never come. What in Satan's name had happened to Anne? She had promised to send a letter every week. Surely *one* should have come by now. Was she sick? Had she slipped on the slag heaps and hurt herself? Were the boys sick so she didn't have time to write?

Worry gnawed and loneliness for her poured through him like black ink that Christmas eve. He saw pale faces and deathbeds and Anne lying in the bottom of a gully—but there was nothing to do but wait. He tried to pull himself out by remembering what the chap from Philadelphia had said in San Francisco. No word for six months.

Wind whistled around the cabin, a doleful carol in memory of a Child born long ago in a manger. The fire puffed and smoked in the corner. A dark-skinned man sang softly to himself as he looked over nuggets by the red glow.

Anne would be singing real carols in her best black at chapel tonight. He hoped the little fellows would have a few sweets to remember the day, and not forget Father when they sat down and said Christmas grace before their dinner.

"Just got enough for one of them cradles, boss," Artemus said, as Charles laid down the spoon and put more wood on the fire.

"We'll get the damned cradle," he told Artemus, and ground his teeth. "We've got to have it if it washes a hundred shovelfuls a day, because I want gold and I want it fast! Then I'm high-tailing it out of here and home to my wife. God knows what's happening."

"Yes, sir!" The black mouth spread in a wide grin. "Me too. And maybe next year we all be home safe with our folks and eatin' good things instead of just tough old squirrels and clunkers."

"Let's hope we can forget this damned Christmas out here in the wind and rain and the cradle that doesn't rock a baby," Charles said as he kicked at the fire with the toe of his heavy boot.

Music, wild and furious, rang out from the Mexican fandango house down the line, and coarse drunken greetings were carried by the wind across Utter's Camp that Christmas Eve in 1849.

CHAPTER 7

1850

THE cradle was a wonderful affair, well worth the cost. Charles had carried it home alone from Sonorian Camp right after New Year's Day, when Artemus refused to budge out of their diggings.

Artemus was afraid. Too many tales had come over the hills about the knifings and robberies and killings at what was now called Sonora Town. "Good men" were threatening "foreigners."

"Them might think me is a foreigner," the darky told Charles, "and string up this nigger for doin' nothin' at all."

Charles knew Artemus was thinking about the story a passing miner had told them.

Just a week before, Procopio Murieta, a Mexican cattle raiser who sold fresh meat in Sonora, had been accused of stealing the horse he rode. Some "good men" fired with brandy and the idea of ridding the town of vice, hanged Procopio on an oak tree, to die before the very eyes of his brother Joaquin. When they took him down Joaquin found the bill of sale for the horse in the dead man's pocket.

Now there was real trouble. Joaquin had gathered other Mexicans and swore to get gringo blood a hundredfold to avenge the death of his brother. Almost nightly there were robberies and killings in Sonora and the near-by camps.

When the grub ran low, Charles trekked over the hill for provisions while Artemus worked alone at the rocker.

Each time as he neared the thronged narrow street of Sonora, his heart beat fast. Maybe a letter would be waiting from Anne! Each time he turned away from the office unrewarded. He wondered if the thrifty lass begrudged the money he told her a letter cost.

That squeezing of pennies brought up resentment. But for Anne he might be at home instead of grubbing for gold in this Godforsaken place of Utter's Camp, where already miners were grumbling.

The gold was running out. Only an ounce or two a day. At this rate, with grub so high it would take a hell of a long time to get anywhere.

Poverty Hill! That's what some thought of Utter's Diggings now that spring had come. A damned good name, Charles thought, for such a niggardly place. But where better could a man go?

He worked himself to the point of exhaustion, and the cradle was near banged off its rockers in an effort to grub out more of the yellow stuff.

One day the last of March, great excitement rocked the camp. "A new diggings! Richest yet! Just over the hills!" Doc Hildreth, a "pill roller" from Maine, had picked up nuggets, big nuggets that lay on top of the ground thick as fleas on a dog, just three miles northeast of Sonora.

Blankets were rolled and grub packed. Some men with little to carry raced toward the new place in the hope of beating others. Little gray jackasses struggled under loads of cradles and picks and shovels.

Lupines and buttercups were trampled under hoofs and boots as the horde left Poverty Hill and trudged toward Hildreth's Diggings.

Before the week was out the hills no longer glowed with camp-fires at night. Even the gamblers had folded their tents and gathered up their cards for bigger stakes beyond the hills. Coyotes yowled to take the place of fiddles and guitars at the fandango house.

"We going too, boss?" Artemus asked one night when lonely

dark closed in. "If they are gettin' them big nuggets maybe us should take our carcasses over them hills too."

Morgan sat down by the new mud fireplace they had just finished and thought the matter over.

They had no jackass to carry their possessions. They didn't know for *sure* about these new diggings. There was always the cry of "Gold! Gold! Gold!" Sometimes it was gone almost as soon as it was discovered. But the pull to get home nagged. He was too proud to crawl back home and face Anne and his pals without gold.

"Oh, hell, let's go," he said finally. "We have a cabin where things can be locked up. If we see Hildreth's is better we can stake out a claim and then come back and pull up here."

Artemus was delighted. "But we leave our cache of gold, my free money, here where it's safe, boss. Never can tell who's athieving along the road. We better be safe."

Charles agreed that the gold would be left.

The place was locked at sunup the next morning and the big Negro and his Welsh partner, with packs on their backs, struck off over the hills to Sonora and Hildreth's Diggings.

Sonora now was just a place to grub up and pass through. They headed for the post office first shot out of the box.

There was a letter from Anne! Artemus got one too from Mr. Bodine.

"Please read it?" Artemus asked and held out the worn envelope.

But Charles shoved the darky and his letter away. "You'll just wait until I read my own," he snapped, as he tore open the seal with shaking hands.

The boys were fine. She was making cheese for sale and getting along. She hoped he would be home soon with the gold, for there was a good piece of land she'd seen with a spring on it. A fine place for the cheese factory. There had been bad cave-ins and fires in the pits, and she was glad that she didn't have to go and stand with her shawl over her head and wait at the pit mouth with the rest of the women to see if her man came up dead or alive. There had been a reduction of wages.

Was there a chapel out in California where he was? She hoped so, for the horrible things she read in the papers about the murders and robberies and gambling made shivers go up and down her backbone when she thought of him. He was to be sure and not get tangled up with camp women, and to get down on his knees and say the Lord's Prayer every night before he went to bed.

She hoped he'd come soon with plenty of gold. Henry was running around now and it took lots for shoes and clothes for three boys. Charley helped out some by digging potatoes for a neighbor, but Bill was lazy and had to be nagged even to bring in coal and wood. Perhaps that was because he was growing so fast. She hoped this letter wouldn't cost much for carriage up to the mines, and was his loving wife, Anne.

Charles shoved the letter into his pocket. Disappointment and hurt pricked him. There was no word about Anne missing him; no bit of love or affection. All she seemed to think about was expenses and the cheese factory and gold. Homesickness clawed at his heart and the world seemed suddenly cold.

"You goin' to loosen all your teeth if you keeps on agrindin' 'em so hard, boss. You goin' to need them teeth for the tough meat," Artemus said, and put a gentle hand on Charles's shoulder. "Don't take it so hard. Bad luck always passes; got to spread herself out to bother other folks." Charles saw a tender look come into the darky's eyes. "You goin' to read mine now?" Again he held out the letter.

Charles tried to push hurt and homesickness from him and be decent to Artemus. After all there was no need to vent his disappointment on the darky. He took the sheets that Artemus had all ready for reading.

There in the crowded road, with men jostling them, Artemus had *his* news. The master and mistress sent their best to Artemus and hoped he was doing well and getting plenty of gold. Everybody on the plantation missed him. The tobacco crop had been good. The mistress wanted to be sure Artemus had enough clothes to keep him warm in the mountains. He was to have someone write how he was getting along.

Charles handed the letter back to Artemus without a word, but he was thinking a lot. Even the wife of a darky slave's master had more softness to her, more concern for a black man, than his own wife had shown.

"Come on," he snapped to the happy-faced Artemus. "Let's be on our way. No use standing here getting corns." He shouldered his pack and joined the rabble of men headed toward Hildreth's Diggings with no backward look to see if Artemus was following. He couldn't bear to see the happiness that his partner was unable to share.

But Artemus made tracks. Soon they were walking together along the road to the east that was a churn of manure and struggling jacks and mules.

Gamblers with white ruffled shirts and fancy black suits shouted out that they would set up the finest faro tents and monte banks at Hildreth's.

A Mexican drove cows ahead of him and sold milk at a dollar a pint whisky bottleful, and two hogs were bought as they trotted along in the mud.

Folks with shoes, tattered ones without shoes or packs and Indians as naked as the day they were born all headed toward the new find.

Fancy girls, knowing well the price of their charms, rode by on anything that would move, with bundles tied behind them, ogling men, shouting invitations, patting firm half-exposed breasts as a lure.

Men, starved for women, called out from the muddy road, "A poke for a night with you!"

Each bidder was soon walking beside his prize, lest she change her mind before they reached the diggings.

"Those trollops will soon be coming down in their prices," a fellow traveler muttered. "Look here." He shoved a worn newspaper into Charles's hand. It was the *Stockton Times,* a boxed notice.

IMPORTANT TO BACHELORS!

New York papers state that no less than one hundred tons of ladies were shipped from that port to California in the space of a week!

Charles shoved away the paper in disgust and thought of Anne's words that he must not get tangled up with any camp women. Who in hell wanted to get tangled up with these hussies? But he wished she had told him that her arms longed for him now, that she missed his caresses and his home-coming of nights. He wanted to feel that there was an empty place at home and in Anne's heart.

Then suddenly everything came clear as he walked along. He was a jackass. Anne was never one to express herself, to show her feelings on her sleeve. Anne let a man know of her love through her actions, by being brave and strong and full of courage. Hadn't she turned over her savings without a murmur? Hadn't she always worked by his side to *show* her love for him? Just the simple words that she loved him and needed him—and she was "his loving wife, Anne." What more did a man want? It was the damned country that had made him boil up in anger against his faithful lass in Pennsylvania. Suddenly all hurt and resentment drained from him and the world looked brighter.

CHAPTER 8

1850

W<small>HEN</small> they dropped down the last hill toward the new diggings, Charles saw a sight that near blew his hat off.

Hildreth's had been discovered only two weeks before. Now the ravine was black with men working, and the whole hillside was a babel of voices talking French, German, Spanish, Chinese; a milling crowd of greed on two legs.

At brush saloons miners waited their turn to dig into their pokes for whisky that was shoved across barrel tops in tin cups.

Monte and faro dealers were all over the place, crying for bets, slapping cards down on rough planks, cursing and abusing customers between deals for crowding them.

There was a whole row of tents where "fancy ladies" held forth for business. Men drunk with gold and rotgut were standing in line twenty-deep waiting for caresses.

One sapling shelter, larger, had a crudely painted sign across the front: A<small>N</small> E<small>STABLISHMENT FOR THE</small> Q<small>UENCHING OF</small> T<small>HIRST AND</small> P<small>ASSION</small>. Near the entrance two men were fighting to buy drinks for a Mexican tart in a red dress who had her legs exposed to the crotch while she picked gravel from between her toes.

That Mexican chippie stirred up the passion in Charles and made him think again of Anne's cold-knuckles letter. He wanted to fight!

The chance came in less than ten minutes, when they stopped to watch a sharp-eyed man shifting thimbles on an upturned box.

"Which one is the bead under?" the chap demanded, and shoved his hat back on his head. "Any gent with eyes sharp

enough to spot gold should be able to follow my fingers! Make
your bets, gents. Which one hides the bead?"

He held up a red bead between thumb and cigarette-yellowed
forefinger and then rolled it around under the two thimbles.

Time after time, miners bet half their pokes on the little red
bead and lost, but enough won to hold the crowd fascinated.

"What's the matter, *hombres?*" the red-faced one taunted. "Your
eyes need washing. Can't you see where the bead's gone? Step
up and try your luck."

Charles, head and shoulders above the others, shoved his brawny
arms out and plowed through the crowd.

He bet on first one thimble and then the other—and lost!

In a second his hammy fist mashed into the barker's face, and
then both thimbles were lifted. No bead at all!

"You dirty skunk," Charles cried. "You cheat!"

He gave the fellow another belt that knocked him across his
own box and tipped it so that thimbles and nuggets fell on the
ground. "Get up, your face needs washing."

"Good!" rang out through the air. "Bravo!"

With admiring eyes the crowd moved away, while Charles re-
trieved his nuggets from the ground, and the injured man wiped
his bloody nose.

"You was sure wonderful, boss," Artemus said as they moved
on. "Acatchin' of that polecat at his own game like you did."

The words were scarce out of his mouth when a shot rang out.

"Another long tom robbed," someone said casually. "When
will they learn it ain't healthy to take another man's gold?"

"Let's get out of here quick," Artemus urged. "You might be
next." His eyes were bulging with fear.

But Charles was feeling fine. There was nothing like a bit of a
fight to clear a man's spleen; besides, he had just caught sight of
Charley Bassett behind the counter of a provision tent across the
way. Good old Charley, the ship's cook, who had organized the
guard the night Sonora burned and Baptiste had been left with
nothing.

Charley was hearty in his greeting and treated them to a drink from a bottle he pulled out from behind a stack of red flannel underdrawers.

He was doing fine. He had this provision tent and a butcher shop too, and he'd made a deal with a Mexican who had cows. He sold milk at a dollar for a pint whisky bottleful.

"Miners here are crazy for milk," he told Charles. "They'll pay as much for a good swig of cow juice as they do for a snifter of whisky."

Charley had come to the diggings only three days after Doc Hildreth and his crowd found the gold. It was terrific! "Them fellows averaged eight ounces a day each!" Charley cried out. "Then in comes Captain Anent to locate a claim, and he knocks hell out of what the others found. Gets a pound and a half of pure gold the first day! Now he's taking out a pound a day or better, in spite of scarce water for washing."

Charles saw Artemus start. "Boss, we ought to skin our shirt-tails out into them hills quick and get us a claim right now."

Charley Bassett laughed over the black man's eagerness to be off. "That's what about eight thousand others thought ahead of you. We're lousy with miners in these diggings. They'd cut a throat over a rich claim and bury the loser under the dirt while they're looking for gold, and no questions asked."

A rush of business came. Charles and Artemus moved out of the crowded little tent into the dusk.

Candles and lanterns were flickering on in the tents all around. On a corner, with a pine torch for light, a miner stood on a whisky barrel. "Thieves and robbers should be tried and hanged," he roared out. "And them as helps them should be treated same way."

"Aye, aye!" came from the crowd.

"And anybody that steals clothes or tools or anything valued at less than a hundred dollars ought to have his head and eyebrows shaved off, be lashed and made to leave camp in twenty-four hours."

"Aye, aye!"

A wag opined that there would be a busy time for the shavers and a lot of colds in the head—and no one to run the diggings after a few days.

Charles pulled at Artemus' sleeve. They went off by themselves on a slope to make a fire to fry pork and warm up beans they had cooked at Poverty Hill.

"What do you think?" Charles asked. "Shall we scout around for a claim?"

Artemus shook his head. "I seen some mighty big nuggets handed around here today, boss, but the Devil, he sure in this yere diggings along with the gold. Didn't you hear most the men atalkin' about water runnin' out? Gold ain' no good unless you got water to wash it out. Them two men selling water at two dollars a gallon is makin' a lot of money too. Lots of folks can't even use cradles. We got us a claim with some water now and a cabin too. Better we rolls up in our blankets tonight and take the trail back to Poverty Hill come sunup."

There was something in what Artemus said. Buying water at two dollars a gallon would soon bust a man unless he made a rich find fast. But Charles left Artemus by the fire and went back to the lights alone. He wanted to hear more of the strikes.

He was weaving through the throng when he saw her, not a fancy painted-faced thing bold as brass like the others he had seen along the way, but a small woman with big brown eyes and dressed in a dark brown dress like the ones Anne wore. She stood next to the monte dealer in a tent where pine torches flared bright as comets. She made him think of his own little Anne. Her breasts rounded under the bodice like Anne's and her hair was smooth and plain.

He went up to the table near her, shoved close by the push of men behind him.

Was the monte dealer her husband? he wondered, as their eyes met. The look of her wrenched at his loneliness and made him want to talk to her for just a few minutes. It had been so long since he had even seen a decent woman.

"Are you playing?" he asked with a smile. "If you are, I hope luck is with you."

She smiled back, her teeth bright in the light. Then she shook her head. "I have no money for gambling."

"Then perhaps you're here to see that your man doesn't lose his poke?"

Again she shook her head. Her smile and the friendly eyes made him fair dizzy with happiness, and he grew really brave.

"I'd like to set you up to—to a drink, ma'am, if it wouldn't offend," he ventured. "A woman like you is a treat for a miner's eyes."

She nodded. "I'd like that, and we could maybe talk."

"Make your bets, gents," the voice of the dealer rang out as Charles made way for her through the crowd around the table.

Outside in the fresh-smelling air, she took a great breath, as if she would clear her lungs of the smoky stench in the gambling tent. "Drinks are better down a ways," she said softly, "and it's quieter too, for—for talking."

As they walked past the flare-lighted noisy tents, Charles was eager. "Are you American, from the States?" he asked.

She shook her head. "Chile—and that is a very long way from California. And you?" She sounded eager, friendly.

"Pennsylvania."

Then Charles, ever cautious for all of his loneliness, wanted to be safe. "I say, your old man won't be upset about you coming off with me?" he asked. "I wouldn't want to stop a bullet or have a knife dulled on my ribs."

She laughed, a gay girlish laugh. "Don't worry, señor, there's no husband to care what Maria does." She walked a bit closer to him then until they reached the stall, with two pine flares in front, where a man handed drinks across a barrel top.

"In my country men do not have golden hair and blue eyes," she murmured. "I suppose other women have told you—the clear blue eyes of you twinkle. You are very very handsome, señor."

He felt his face flush. "California's done that," he managed, pleased. "You wouldn't think I was so good to look at if you'd seen me blackened by coal dust in Pennsylvania.'"

As they drank and the liquor brought red to her cheeks, she told her story in broken English. "I came from Santiago on the boat with my brother to hunt for gold." She shrugged her shoulders, and the face turned sad. "He died of scurvy—here at Hildreth's. Now Maria is alone . . . no money—no way to get back home." There were tears in the beautiful brown eyes.

A woman crying and the liquor warm in his innards brought a quick spurt of sympathy. Charles put his arm around her and drew her from the glare and sharp eyes of the man pouring drinks. Then he reached into his pocket for the bandanna.

"Here," he said, "wipe your eyes, little love, and don't cry. There'll be some way. There's *got* to be a way. Just trust a Welshman."

She sniffed a bit, and her head pressed against his breast. With the feel of her soft body against him, the pent-up passion of months rushed over Charles Morgan. He caught her to him, covered the wet cheeks with kisses, then found her warm mouth.

"Oh—*señor*," she breathed as her heart beat hard against him.

God, how he wanted her! Everything in him wanted her—the very belly of him cried out with eagerness after that kiss. He promised her the gold in his poke, his friendship, anything, as hot passion shot through him! He must possess her, must feel the warmth of her. He needed a woman.

She snuggled closer to him. The very smell of her crazed him!

"Maria has a little brush shelter not far away, if the señor will come," she murmured.

On a bough bed he took her. Never had love-making with Anne or any other woman been like this! Maria knew tricks to send a man clean daft with rapture. She knew how to set him afire and then use her body well to quench the fire! She made rapture last and last!

Gamblers still called their bets, when Charles Morgan passed the lighted tents on his way back to Artemus. His heart was lighter than it had been for months—and he was lighter by his poke too. But what did that matter? He had taken a woman in a brush shelter. Maria had given him her soft body willingly and called him her friend. She would be glad to see him *often* before she went back to her home in Chile.

There was a bit of a prick when he thought of Anne and his boys, then quick resentment came up. To hell with Anne who was too stingy to send a letter to the man who sweated for her and her damned cheese factory! He pulled his hat jauntily to one side and strode past the last straggly shelter to where Artemus slept by the dying campfire.

But the next morning life was a different color. He had to face Artemus over the boiling coffee and admit he had no gold left. Artemus must buy the provisions to take back.

The darky shook his head and went on cutting fat strips of salt pork.

"I knowed last night the Devil hisself had you by the tail feathers, boss, and you wasn't pullin' too hard to get away, neither.

"Now this mornin' I knows it better. You got the look in your eyes of a nigger that's been wenching, that's what you got. We gonna get our grub quick and go back to Poverty Hill before that old Devil he pick you clean."

Charles tried to convince his partner that he had lost at gambling, but Artemus only sniffed as he wiped out the fry pan and tied it to the blanket roll.

There was no sign of Maria when they passed her little shelter on the way out of town.

"Make your bets, gents. Red or black? Win or lose?" came from a tent behind them.

"The Devil he sure works night and day too, in Hildreth's Diggin's," Artemus said dryly and glanced at Charles as they hit the trail to Sonora. "I gonna be glad to get you back safe to Poverty Hill, boss."

CHAPTER 9

1850

THERE was hard scrabble now on the claims at Poverty Hill. Early buttercups wilted down and sun-loving May brodiaeas starred the hillsides with blue. Water was scarcer with each sweltering day, for the spring was drying up. And what good was a rocker without water?

Charles and Artemus had to save every drop of Saturday night bath water for washing their clothes on Sundays.

One night Utter dropped in on his way home from Sonora. He was full of news.

"The California legislature's passed a foreign miners' tax of twenty dollars a month!" he told them excitedly. "It's to be enforced on the first of June, and the governor's appointed Besancon in Sonora as tax collector.

"All the damned foreign miners around are heading for Sonora to fight the Americans. Likely to be plenty of blood spilled too, before they're through. There was seven murders there last week."

Utter didn't seem to realize that Charles Morgan was one of these "damned foreigners" who would be taxed.

When he had gone, Artemus looked with solemn eyes at Charles. "Boss," he said sadly, "looks now like that there cheese factory of yours ain't going to come on very fast. Don't see how we can make enough to put none by with next to no water and grub high and you payin' our four ounces a month just for to be here."

Artemus was right. Dry! The hillsides turning brown by the hour now. No water. Grub high. What chance had he? He would have to pay twenty dollars for every month he stayed whether pay dirt came out of the hot hillsides or not. The tax was unjust—unfair!

Charles set his jaw. "You'll have to work alone," he told Artemus. "I'm going to Sonora tomorrow—to fight!"

The black man was terrified. He begged Charles to stay and work on until this Mr. Besancon came to collect. He offered to carry dirt on his back over to the water at Campo Seco and pay for washing privileges. They might find some big nuggets any day and then the tax money wouldn't matter.

"If you goes itchin' for a fight, you sure likely to get it, and if'n you killed they won't be no gold and it don't do you no good anyhow. Mr. Bodine, he say if'n you ain't in the way of a shotgun or a razor you sure stand a better chance of livin' to see them as has been nicked!"

But no amount of argument affected Charles. He had a right to fight against this unfair tax. All his money sweated out in coal mines, and Anne's savings too, had gone into this gamble on the California hillsides. Here was a Welshman who wouldn't give up without a fight!

Long before sunup he shouldered blankets and a bit of grub and struck off over the hills to Sonora.

When he reached town, thousands of men in an angry mob milled about in front of the tax collector's room in the wooden hotel. They demanded to know whether he intended to enforce the tax law.

With the assurance from Besancon that he did, Charles joined the sweating crowd that shook their fists at the collector and threatened to murder Americans and take the law into their own hands! To prove he meant business, Charles shot his gun up into the air.

"Halt!" The word rang out over the great crowd as a Frenchman stood on a box and waved his hands. "We must organize to fight Americans and take the town," he roared out. "To the flats, men!" He jumped down and, brandishing his pick, ran along the street.

"Kill the gringos. Take the town!" someone shouted, and a cheer went through the mob. Sticks and picks and clubs were raised.

Charles could feel his blood stir. These men unjustly treated would not be downed! They had fight in them. He, Charles Morgan, was glad he had spent some of his gold for the gun he carried.

Mexicans, *Chilenos*, French, raised their national flags and roared out their own battle songs.

Close to dusk, when they were ready to head for Sonora to get Besancon and string him to a tree, a man, red-faced and wet with sweat, fought his way through the crowd to the leader.

"Judge Tuttle, the *Americano*, sent riders!" he shouted as soon as he had enough breath. "Men are coming to fight us! Soldiers with guns are on the way here to shoot us! People from Sonora are with them. They all have guns."

"I have a gun," Charles roared. "How many have guns?" He raised his own high over his head with pride.

But there were only nine more beside his.

"Fight with sticks, with picks," Charles cried out. "We have our rights!"

Before they had time to move, the soldiers were upon them. Riding into them on lathered horses and slashing at both sides with gun butts.

"Break up! Go back to your diggings," they roared, and were followed by citizens from Sonora with guns.

Life seemed to ooze out of the miners. The Frenchman who had been so brave an hour ago shrugged his shoulders with a helpless gesture. They were without a leader.

But Charles would not go down. "Where are your guts, men?" he shouted. "Where's your courage? Don't let them shove you down."

He was clattered on the side of the head with the end of a gun and reeled against the man beside him.

"Get on to your diggings or we'll shoot. The law in California is the law. You pay your tax or you get out."

Horses plunged through the mob. A shot or two rang out as men scattered to keep from being trampled under hoofs.

What could men with only picks and clubs do against sharp-shooting well-armed soldiers? Perhaps each miner was thinking of his own hide.

Charles righted himself, rubbed his throbbing head. "Are we to be licked like dogs, without a fight?" he shouted, as a horseman shoved him aside.

"Get on to your diggings, or we'll throw coal oil and light up the lot of you."

Charles was furious. Because they had no leader, no one with guts, the angry miners began to hit the trail. What could one Welshman do? Charles picked up his pack and went with the rest toward Sonora.

"There are other ways, señor," a sharp-eyed Mexican told him. "Sometimes a brave one stands alone—to die alone. But there are other ways of getting the gringos. A knife in the back on a dark night, perhaps, or an accident of falling over a cliff or a gringo found dead in his bed. Joaquin Murieta knows the way, and there will be plenty to follow him."

There was a heavy guard around Sonora when they reached town. No foreigners could enter.

"Get on. Back to your diggings and have the tax money ready," the soldiers shouted, and prodded the tired backs of "foreigners" with their guns.

Charles resented the poke in his rump, but he mended his pace and struck off down the trail toward Jimtown and home.

Artemus had a fire glowing and was on the watch for Charles. He shook his head when he heard what had happened. "I knowed it was no use," he said, as he put on coffee and stirred up batter for flapjacks. "A nigger like me, boss, found out it just don't pay to fight. The others that's law above you just got more of everything to work with in a fight."

Then he offered to pay half the tax. " 'Cause I no good here without you, and you some better off with a nigger that's me. That's what Mr. Bodine he say. One nigger alone ain't no good at all, but let him have someone to talk to and hands works at least half as much as their mouths and *something* gets done!"

Artemus and Charles deafened their ears to the tales of bloodshed and hangings between foreigners and white men from the States and worked furiously in the few days left before the tax was to be collected, but there was little to be picked up without water to wash.

The first of June, 1850, dawned. Tales came back to Poverty Hill about Americans, in the name of the law, swooping down into the diggings everywhere to demand money from tattered miners who sweated on dry hillsides for enough to eat. These members of the law took properties and gold—and even life if there was the slightest objection and the claim was said to be a rich one.

Artemus was terrified, but Charles worked on.

Men started to come by on their way out. Some walked, some had jackasses, all fleeing in terror from the mines, making for the highlands or the lowland cattle country, anywhere, to be safe from the horrors they had gone through or seen. The hunt for gold was forgotten in an effort to save lives and what "color" they could hide inside jackets.

When the collector came to Poverty Hill, Charles handed over his poke for the gold to be weighed out. The man was generous in helping himself—four ounces and a half!

Charles gritted his teeth and offered grub for nooning.

"I don't eat nothin' from you lice. Like as not you'd poison me." And he rode off.

A terrified Frenchman, hungered and weary, came by. Charles recognized the leader of the revolt outside Sonora. Now all he asked for was water to wet swelled, sun-burned lips. He was going out of this inferno forever—to sell snails near the Seine in Paris. Let others fight and die for gold.

He ate some beans they offered and sold Artemus a small gray jackass that he claimed was too slow and held him back. He had little enough now to carry. The Americans had taken his pick and shovel and blankets.

Artemus was delighted with the purchase. "We'll call her Angie," he said proudly. "Angie, my mistress' pet name. Angie goin' to lug us our water from the spring and save us a lot of sweatin' and we can wash more gold."

Charles pointed out that Mrs. Bodine wouldn't be flattered if she knew a jackass had been named for her, but Artemus knew the mistress would be proud to know that he still thought of her. Besides, this little gray Angie was gentle and kind and had eyes like his mistress. "They is alike that way."

Charles was worried over Maria of the soft arms and warm caresses. She was a hated foreigner too, even though she worked no claim. How had she fared? She might even have been raped by Americans! Just the thought turned him frantic. He could hardly wait for the excuse of provisions running out—to get to her. Artemus was such a watchdog.

One day the black man came from the spring with their drinking water. His eyes were big and frightened. "Boss, they somethin' wrong down to Simmons' tent. He lyin' there agroanin' and he don't know nothin'. They blood around. I come straight back for you. He don't like niggers. You better go."

Charles dropped his shovel and ran over to the shelter. Simmons' hair was matted with blood, and his eyes were wild and staring. The little shelter had been ransacked. Charles cleaned Simmons up and poured coffee between the parched lips.

For days Charles and Artemus nursed the unconscious Simmons until he came back to his senses.

Simmons' story was short, and tragic too—when they looked under the bunk and found all his savings stolen. A year and a half of sweating and washing and digging.

"A New South Wales man came into my tent one night just after I'd blown out my candle and got into bed," he told Charles. "I knew he was from Australia because of his accent. 'Give up your poke or I'll kill you!' he says to me. Before I could reach my gun or the money either, he cracked me on the head. That's all I know." Simmons was furious over the loss and cussed the air black.

Charles waited until the man was spent. "If it hadn't been for Artemus, you'd have died, pard," he told the battered Simmons. "He saw something was wrong and fetched me. Artemus knew you didn't like black men, so he quit nursing you after the first two nights, in case you'd wake up and find him here. But he's been working your claim to hold it. He's working now."

Simmons was quiet for a while. The muscles around his mouth twitched. He reached out of the bunk and put a rough hand on Charles's shoulder. "Bring him in, Morgan. Bring that black fellow in."

Charles called Artemus from the muckle of dust he was making. The Negro blinked in the sudden darkness of the brush and canvas shelter and stood respectfully by the opening flap.

"Come in!" Simmons said. "Come over here to the bunk!"

Artemus shuffled across the bare dirt floor.

"Shake!" Simmons put out a hand. "You're whiter than I am. I wouldn't have done for you what you've done for me—and I thank you. Nigger, you've taught this Yankee a better lesson than Jesus Christ himself."

Artemus shook hands, then he put a black paw into the pocket of his frayed coat. "It's all I got out 'n your claim for a week, Mr. Simmons, sir. This yere dirt don't pay good in dry weather." He dropped three good-sized nuggets into the sick man's hand, then turned and went out.

That night, by flickering candlelight, Artemus dictated a letter to Mr. Bodine. "To tell the master what the white man said about me." He grinned. "That makes Mr. Bodine and the mistress feel good and know this nigger don't forget what they teach him, even if he don't get gold enough yet for to buy hisself free."

The next time they needed provisions Charles rode astride Angie, who would carry the grub back. He warned Artemus not to pay any more miners' tax, and to show the receipt if anyone demanded more, and then hurried off.

"And don't you get in no fight, boss," Artemus called out. "This time you got to look after my Angie, you know."

Charles quickened his pace as soon as he was out of sight. He had planned well. With the little jackass he could make better time. He would go to Sonora all right, and find out if there was a letter from Anne, then quick up the hill to Columbia to see his blessed Maria.

A great feeling of passionate tenderness came over him at the thought of the hours he had spent in the shelter with Maria. She was far more gifted in love-making than Anne. God, what caresses! He dug his heels into the belly of Angie to move the beast faster. Maria might have been abused—or even killed. He would tell her in the first minute how he had counted the days until provisions were low enough for the excuse to get away.

Sonora was like a dead town now, without water and without foreigners. The streets were nearly empty of men, and those left were talking of "pulling their freight" for the Tuolumne camps where there was water. Dozens of provision shelters were empty. Storekeepers who were left grumbled because trade was dull with so many foreigners gone.

"At least the lousy foreigners had to eat and bought with their dust," one man told Charles. "Now bacon and sowbelly melts on the shelves and I got to cancel orders for flour and beans."

There was scarce enough water to drink. Those left in camp got bellyache and diarrhea from drinking the stuff, and they didn't eat much.

"Business is shot to hell in Stockton too, because of the tax," the shopkeeper mourned. "Men are circulating a petition to repeal the damned tax law a hundred per cent."

There was a letter from Anne at the office. He opened it, and the sheet fluttered in the breeze.

She and the boys were well and getting along all right. She hadn't written because letters cost so much and money saved was money earned.

What was keeping him so long? Other men had made their gold and come back home already. She hoped he hadn't fallen prey to some woman out there! He must remember he had boys to think about—and the cheese factory.

She hoped his next letter would tell her he had started for home. She was his loving wife, Anne.

Charles shoved the letter into his pocket and went to the bar at the City Hotel for a slug of whisky.

Not a word about missing him! Just hoping he'd be home soon with money for the damned cheese factory!

After two more slugs paid for from his limp poke he clattered heels to Angie's gray belly and headed uphill for Columbia and Maria.

There was a warm, comforting lass for a man! And a smile she had too, as if she wanted to hear about you; plenty of cheer to Maria *Chilena*.

Be damned to the cheese factory—to the poke he hoarded! A man needed something else besides gold to keep him ticking.

CHAPTER 10

1850

THE road to Hildreth's Diggings, now called Columbia, was hot and dusty where a little while before the mud and manure had churned under so many boots and hoofs.

The red earth of June hillsides had nothing to offer but dried grasses and yellow-flowered weeds that gave off a pungent odor in the heat waves.

No men at work. No picks flashing in the sun. No bawdy calls from claim to claim on the flat.

A cow tethered to a tree bawled. Buzzards, black against the blue sky wheeled above the bloated carcass of a jackass.

Charles rode on. Soon he would spy the ravine and Maria's brush shelter.

Would Maria be pleased to see him again? After all she had seen him only at night and there was an old saying among miners in Wales after they had been on a jaunt to the hurdy-gurdy women: "In the dark all cats are gray."

His heart and passions stirred. Anne's letter crackled in his jacket pocket. What did she think he was? A stone image of a man in no need of affection and love?

Then came the shock as he crossed the dry creek—there was scarce a handful of men on the main street of Columbia. Crows cawed on the tops of deserted shelters, and ground squirrels scampered in and out of holes abandoned by men.

The roof of the shelter where he had laid up with Maria was caved in. The place was just a pile of brush and sticks.

Eight or ten men lounged in the hot narrow roadway. Charley Bassett's place was empty. There were no gambling tents and the fancy women had gone.

Charles drifted into the one provision tent open for business. The storekeeper was sour. The damned miners' tax and lack of water had fixed things up fine in Columbia. There wasn't enough business to keep a Chink alive. Before the miners left for river diggings they'd had a mass meeting to talk about forming a company to dig ditches and bring water in from the rivers but it was too late for that this year.

Not much here to talk about over a slug. No news except coyotes yelping on the hills of moonlight nights. There had been a murder though, when a Mexican found a chunk of gold that weighed five pounds and six ounces, and a man from the States knocked him on the head for it.

The news sickened Charles. He changed the subject to the one nearest his heart, the one that fired the very veins of him.

"Do you know Maria, the *Chilena* woman?"

"Sure. Women's noses ain't so plentiful that a man ain't likely to know all of 'em." The fellow grinned, a nasty lustful grin that ate into Charles. "If that's what you came here for, it's too bad. All the fancy women cleared out early, along with the gamblers and confidence men."

Charles drew up to full size and more. "Shut your jib," he roared. "Maria's a poor unfortunate and my friend. One more word about chippies and her in the same breath and I'll break your damned jaw and shut your mouth for good!"

A knowing look brushed over the brown-bearded face. "Put your feathers down, cock. All the fancy women around here are some man's bosom friend. They have to be to fill their pokes. I ain't meaning no personal stuff. We men always fall for that 'friendship,' don't we? And glad to get what goes with it."

Then he told Charles that Maria worked now down at Pine Log in blue denims and red shirt like the rest of the miners on a claim of her own. She sometimes came into his place for grub.

Charles felt life come back to him now.

"And some gent always puts it on his back or on his jenny and carries it home for her," the man went on.

Charles had to be sure. Maybe this was another Maria. He described her. "Smooth black hair drawn close over the ears, and very quiet, she was."

There was a nod. "Oh, yes. We're talking about the same one. She's your canary that's flew," he said dryly. "You might head you down to Pine Log with some salt to put on her tail and catch her." Then he added that Maria didn't have any trouble over foreign miners' tax. "And she don't dig into her poke neither."

What was the use of fighting? Control yourself, man. The store chap is useful. He can tell you the way to Pine Log if you keep your temper and his jaw intact.

Patience and a drink of redeye did it. The fellow told Charles how to strike the trail to Pine Log. "Up over the mountain and down so steep that it's like a chute straight into hell. The camp's at the bottom. As good place as any to drop your dust."

Charles started for Pine Log on the back of Angie. He had grub enough to last for three days, and if the woman was Maria she would be glad to see him. He wanted to think that. He *knew* she would be glad—no woman could give him what Maria had given a man and not be glad to see him again. He dug his heels in to make Angie move faster.

Maybe—if Maria was there, and water too—it would be better for him and Artemus to pull up stakes and move over to Pine Log until the rainy season began and they could wash again at Poverty Hill? With a cradle they could do well.

Golden dreams of nuggets and the yearning for Maria helped put in the time as Angie picked her sure-footed cautious way through scarlet poison oak and scrubby manzanita and the clinging branches of oaks.

The camp was wedged in the river bottom between steep mountains and, to reach the sandy bar where the tents were, Charles had to force Angie across the Stanislaus on a great fallen log.

Dusk was falling as he entered the diggings. Music rang out from a fandango house and a sharp-eyed painted woman watched him pass by. Maria wouldn't be in there—he knew that. But what if Maria had taken another man and would have none of him?

Faro tables were just getting under way for the night's business in tents where the air was filled with dust. Men plodded up from the river with pans and picks and shovels on their backs.

Charles led Angie to a stump and tethered her, then drifted into the single boardinghouse where the sign MEALS was printed in wobbly letters. Be damned to saving dust! He longed for company and a decent meal. Sowbelly had sickened on him.

The good-natured crowd cheered him up just to look at them when he wedged his knees under the plank table with the rest of them. Scotchmen, Irishmen, Americans they were, with a sprinkling of Swedes. They opened up their shirt necks for a bit of comfort while they drank brandy out of tin cups and jollied the man who passed the food. They treated Charles as one of them. No questions asked.

The grub was good: a fresh meat pie and greens they said came from a little garden watered by the river, with dried-apple pie to top it off.

They talked of things along the Sierra. Because of the scarcity of women at Georgetown, Thomas Springer, the magistrate, had granted a divorce to a wife one afternoon and married her to a new husband that evening. The whole town got drunk over the wedding and the bride slugged her new husband over the head with a whisky bottle to stop him from kissing her so much in public.

They all had a laugh over that.

Aye, it was good for a lone man to be with others for a bit and learn the news.

Sandy, a Scotchman, had a grudge because the Yankees were going to take away all firearms—"on account of the foreigners kicking up such a hell of a row over the tax."

With that Charles came up with a bang. "The tax isn't fair!" he roared out. "A man can't make it! You're foreigners. Do *you* think it's fair?"

"No, but it'll be settled," Sandy came back. "There's been a lot of rotten foreigners here killing and stealing. The innocent always has to suffer. If *we* stick to the law and behave, the Yankees will see it's a mistake. Business is shot into hell because of the tax. The peaceable way is always the best," Sandy finished as he lighted his pipe.

With that a roar of laughter went up. Sandy was poked good-naturedly in the ribs by an American. "What about you shooting up the town last Saturday night because Maria *Chilena* turned you away? It'll be safer for us all when that firing rod has to be handed over. You and your 'peaceful ways'!"

"Who calls me? Who says things about Maria *Chilena*?" came from the door. Maria walked in, tiny and big-eyed, dressed in blue jeans and red shirt.

The men chaffed her about being late, and she smiled at them. The boarding tent man chuntered about "them as want grub getting in for it before things is cold as a wife's kiss," and he banged stove lids around.

Then she saw Charles and her face was all alight. "Carlos!" she cried and ran to where he sat. Her grubby hand with broken fingernails was on his arm, and his heart was near to bursting with joy.

Charles could feel the red rush to his face as all eyes turned on him. But his heart was warmed too. Maria hadn't forgotten!

There was a shuffle of feet on the sandy floor. Fine dust floated into the air as men left the table. On the way out good-natured jabs drifted toward Charles as Maria stood close beside him looking into his face.

The cook banged a heaped-up plate onto the plank table and put a knife and fork down beside it.

"You two might know what you like—but get on with the grub, Maria. I want to deal monte."

Maria smiled at Charles. "I waited for you—but you didn't come back," she said softly.

Charles tried to explain about Artemus and how hard it was to get away. Her nearness took possession of him. It didn't matter that now the shirt hid the full bosom and miner's pants took away some of the womanliness of her. Here was Maria, soft-voiced and glad to see him. Charles thought of his flattened poke and wondered if Maria would be so pleased if she knew.

Might as well be frank with her. "I've had no luck, Maria," he began as she ate. "My diggings are dry—no water, no nuggets. My poke's near to flat!"

He watched her face. The warmth didn't fade. Instead there was a tenderness in the dark eyes. "Come—to my tent," she said when her meal was finished. "Maria does well on her claim. Big nuggets—plenty of them."

Together they walked along the sandy footpath, past monte tents where men who had eaten at the table had now forgotten everything but the spots on cards. They went past the fandango house where a gay song in Spanish was chanted to guitar music.

Maria took his hand and led him in the dark. The touch of her fingers stirred his body with impatience. "To keep you from falling over my big tom," she said.

There was the blue sputter of a match, a smell of sulphur and then the flicker of a candle.

The tent was quite comfortable and very neat. Two boxes to sit on, a plank table supported by two chunks of log and a bough bed.

He took her into his arms. She let him kiss her, but when he tried to pull her toward the bed she shook her head.

"Not yet," she said quietly, and pushed him onto a box. Then she dug under the boughs of her bed and produced a canvas poke which she emptied onto the table.

"See, from Maria's claim—because of you."

"Me?" Charles looked at the big nuggets that glittered on the rough plank and forgot for a moment his passion. There were not one or two nuggets, but several dozen!

"Yes, *amigo*. Didn't you give all your gold to Maria that night?"

Charles admitted that. "But you let me take you—I want you now. To hell with the nuggets!" His need came stronger than ever.

Maria didn't listen. "Now your luck's left you and come to Maria—and you follow it back to her," she told him. "We will be partners, Carlos, and use the long tom together—then you get nuggets too. The river is full of nuggets at Pine Log."

She was so eager, so bright-eyed, so much woman in spite of the pants and red shirt.

Charles was no longer interested in the glittering gold on the table. Any man could have gold if he worked hard and waited long enough, but a woman warm and passionate and tender like Maria——

"To hell with the nuggets, all I want is you!" he told her. "I came here for you." He pulled her to him and pressed his face against the red shirt into the softness of her breasts.

"And that too, Carlos. We're partners now," she said softly and blew out the candle.

CHAPTER 11

1850

CHARLES had forgotten all about Angie, but the little jackass had not forgotten her temporary master. Some prankster among the miners had tied her near Maria's tent during the night, and at dawn she brayed loud and long.

A prick of conscience ran through him as he went out to see after the little gray one's needs. Angie had been supperless. He had given nary a thought to bedding her down.

But the patient little burden bearer held no grudge—just fell to on the hay he bought at the camp provision tent.

When he came back, Maria had slapjacks with bacon instead of sowbelly, and plenty of good strong coffee. Like a regular wife she was! By sunup there was a kiss and a hug and they were at the long tom.

It was not until Charles was helping Maria wash gold and she talked continually about sharing the take with him that the great truth dawned on him.

Last night all he had thought about was her arms and the satisfaction she had given him. But now, as they washed together and the big nuggets glistened in the sun, their very rays sent a light to his brain.

This woman wasn't after his poke. She was different. She wanted to share with him and make a home for him. Maria wanted to *give* to Charles Morgan! A woman willing to give her gold as well as her body to a man must love him.

He stopped in the midst of pouring water into the long tom to hold her close and press his mouth against hers.

The kiss was returned in a way to turn him crazy with longing. It was all too much for a lone man at once. The big nuggets near numbed his brain with their glitter after so many hot days of sweating for nothing in the dry diggings of Poverty Hill—and he had love besides!

What would Artemus say when he saw the returns from just one afternoon's work? Nine ounces at least in a few hours!

For a week Charles spent the days with a shovel at the river, and nights with his loving partner Maria. Could anything be better? He whistled and sang old songs from Wales, freshened into being by gold luck and happiness at loving.

The other miners gave him sly or jealous looks, and one day at eventide "Lanky," a slab-sided thin miner from Missouri, stopped by the long tom and sang out a meaningful ditty, while he rolled his eyes toward Charles.

> "The dusky-eyed señoritas
>   Are very fond of me;
> You ought to see us throw ourselves
>   When we get on a spree."

Maria didn't mind. She only laughed and her eyes shared happy secrets with Charles about what went on after dark when gold was forgotten for the day.

But there was Artemus to think about, up at Poverty Hill where it was hot and the spring near dried-up. By now the darky would have few provisions and no Angie. Artemus would be wondering what had happened; perhaps thinking that Charles Morgan was lying dead up some gulch with blowflies at work on him.

Maria pleaded with him to stay, but return could be put off no longer. The cached poke at Poverty Hill might be empty by now if Artemus hadn't managed to glean some color.

Leave-taking was hard. Maria's warm lips clung to his and made the pull almost more than a man could stand. Charles promised to be back soon with a treat for her from Sonora and plenty of provisions and Artemus to help work; then, with his bulging poke close to his body, he headed up the steep hill for Poverty Hill.

In his frenzy of love-making and gold Charles had forgotten the date. Time had not existed when he was with Maria. But Americans left in Sonora hadn't forgotten it. The Stars and Stripes waved in the wind from the tall pine pole on the hill above town. Five-shooters were going off at a great rate and men were reeling with drink. This was a Yankee holiday—the day of freedom from old England! July 4, 1850. There might not be many miners left in Sonora on the narrow street but they made up for lack of numbers by making plenty of noise.

This was a great day! The first issue of Sonora's newspaper, the *Herald*, was just coming off the presses. No white newspaper this, but tinted brown as the skins of miners who held it in their grubby hands. Printed on wrapping paper it was, and the whole town fair going wild to buy the paper at fifty cents a copy.

Judge Marvin, the editor, was selling the papers.

He set everybody up to so many drinks that eyes were too bleary to see the mistakes in the first wrapping-paper issue of the *Herald*.

Charles dug into his poke with the rest and bought a copy. He read the sheet as he trudged over the hills toward home. One bit caught his eye and delighted his soul.

Americans now saw the foolishness of the huge tax on foreign miners. Provision men in all the diggings were donating to a fund for fighting the tax.

There was a fire in the cabin when Charles arrived at Poverty Hill.

Artemus was stewing a coyote he had caught in a trap. He left the fire and looked Angie over with critical eyes, then, satisfied with her, came back into the cabin.

"Boss, did you clean forget you had a partner?" he asked, shaking his head. "The sowbelly gone, saleratus gone, flour gone, beans gone, and still you don't come home. This nigger sure you got yourself killed." The great eyes rolled.

"You would have heard," Charles told him. "Bad luck always travels fast." He unlaced his boots and pulled them off, then stuck his feet out toward the fire. It was nice to have a hearth again.

Then Artemus turned accusing. "Been eight days now since you left. This nigger sees in your eyes you done forgot all about him and you been wenchin' again."

"Think so?" Charles pulled out the bulging poke from under his jacket and scattered nuggets on the table. "Half of this is yours. I've been working down on the Stanislaus where there's water."

The Negro's eyes fair left their sockets. He evidently couldn't believe what he saw. A black hand went out and fingers touched the gleaming yellow bits. Then Artemus shook his head. "I don't know—I don't know," he said slowly. "This nigger'd swear on a stack of Bibles, boss, that you all had been awenchin'! But this gold! You *couldn't* have been wenchin'." Then he looked slyly at Charles. "'Ceptin' I think that gray Angie of mine could explain them looks of yours if she had a tongue instead of just old brays."

Charles told the story then and proposed they leave Poverty Hill to wash at Pine Log until the rains came again.

"We can even get so much there in a little while that we'll have our pile and high-tail it out without ever coming back here," Charles said. "Look at the gold! You never saw that much in all your life before, Artemus."

Artemus looked at the gold then glanced around the snug little cabin and out toward the pile of earth he had shoveled ready for washing. Still he was doubtful.

"Time we gets back to where you been, the gold likely to be gone."

"It can't be. I've got a claim there," Charles insisted. "In three months you can have enough to buy yourself free and pay Bodine and still have a pile to live on without working."

"Mebby you right, boss. But it cost six hundred dollars to buy this nigger for hisself and six hundred for Mr. Bodine's share."

Charles turned impatient. "You fool nigger!" he roared. "You talk in hundreds. At Pine Log they talk in thousands! Tom

Baxter on the claim next to mine took out four hundred dollars in a single panful. There's near to two thousand dollars there on the table."

"Sound like them golden steps or somethin'." Artemus shook his head as if he were trying to wake up from a dream. "But Mr. Bodine he say, take it easy, Artemus. Don't go gettin' foam to come out of your mouth in excitement till you sure you can get you a drink of water to make you some more spit."

Then Charles felt sorry. Artemus had worried and struggled along without even enough food in these damned dry diggings and had been carrying drinking water all the way from Wood's Creek. The Negro just couldn't believe there was so much gold.

He explained there was plenty of gold and water to wash it on the Stanislaus River, and his friend Maria had a long tom they could use on shares. Maria was holding down their claim for them for the week demanded by law. They would have to get back and work it or everything would be lost.

At the mention of Maria, Artemus understood. He grinned. "I knowed there was some wenchin' in this somewhere, just the same as there's seeds in gooseberries! You sure you ain't goin' to get no knife in your ribs for this here gold when the Devil he catches up with you?"

They talked until midnight over the proposition. Charles pointed out the advantage of Maria as a partner. They would give her a third and work three claims and use her long tom. Long toms cost money, and here they had one all made and carried to the diggings. Only a fool would turn that down!

Finally Artemus shrugged. "When a man's legs wants to go somewhere else, ain't no talkin' goin' to change they direction," he told Charles. "A nigger like me can't stay alone in dry diggin's just alookin' at old Quartz Mountain and ahonin' for rain.

"But, boss, how you know this yere fine lady, Miss Maria, goin' to take to a nigger man like Artemus for a partner?" he finished. "Don't seem she would like it."

"She knows about you. I told her you were my partner too, and she was willing."

Artemus was still dubious about the combination. "If'n you

two don't go sashayin' off into the woods and leave Artemus by hisself to work them three claims, boss. You sure gets forgetful sometime about the minin'."

Before they went to bed Charles wrote to Anne and told her of his rich find and that he was moving to Pine Log. He told her about his new partner down there who had a long tom that made gold washing easier, but was careful not to mention the partner's name. If luck held, there would be money in no time for the cheese factory and he would shake the dust of California from his heels forever. He would be rich! Conscience pricked slightly. He told Anne that she was to drink an extra cup of tea and think of him, and to tell the boys to be good and do all chores their mother asked of them or he'd see to them when he came home.

Artemus wanted a letter written to Mr. Bodine about the change. There was big nuggets now, and before the hills around Virginia were pink with laurel blossoms they were likely to see Artemus again all fine, with money to buy hisself and plenty to boot. Maybe they'd let Artemus stay on the plantation and work a little in tobacco season when the days were not too hot, after he was free. Did the yellow yams still taste sweet as ever? No yams out here. Only beans and sowbelly and pancakes. Artemus was going to stuff hisself on beaten biscuit until his black skin was tight, when he got home. He was their loving slave Artemus.

The next day the cabin was abandoned and the black man and his partner headed for Pine Log, leading the heavily burdened Angie.

Charles couldn't bear to look back at the cabin, built on the first place where he had picked up gold. That seemed so far away now, such a long journey washed with rain and cold and sweat and hope.

Would someone else sit beside the fire now that the place was deserted? Would someone else fight drought and heat and be in possession when the rains came? He thought of the pile of earth all ready for washing. Would another miner write home about his big find because of a black man's patient work?

He heaved up his faded blue pantaloons. A miner in this country must never look back—but ahead. Forget the dreams of other nights and just remember what was at Pine Log. Maria and gold were waiting on the Stanislaus!

He was relieved when they were over the mountain and there was no temptation to turn and look back just once.

Charles didn't forget the promise of a treat for Maria. At the Chinese shop in Sonora he bought ginger in a green jug and coconut dried in sugar. The slant-eyed Chinaman seemed to understand the deal. He showed fancy silk shawls and slippers made from white fur. But Charles only shook his head. What would Maria do with such things? She was a miner now, even though mining was forgotten at nights.

Artemus watched the purchases with unchanged face, but he refused to have Angie burdened by the gifts.

"Angie, she ain't cottonin' up to no strange woman, boss. You got to tote your own presents to that Miss Maria—that's what."

Charles was a bit fretted as they made their way down to Pine Log. If Artemus was awkward and didn't like Maria there was bound to be trouble. He kept telling the Negro about the big nuggets they would get and how dependent they were on Maria and her long tom.

"She gonna come out all right, boss," Artemus said finally. "Don't you go to numbin' your head with how things goin' to work. That Miss Maria, she gettin' best of the deal with two men workin' for her because of that washer. She goin' to make a lot of money from Artemus' old black hands—just 'cause you can't stay no more from them there smiles of hers!"

CHAPTER 12

1850

CHARLES needn't have worried. Maria turned on all her charm. She greeted Artemus, who stood waiting respectfully at a distance. "I'm glad you came too," she told the black man. "Maria welcomes the partner of her partner, Carlos!" She shook his black hand.

"Yes, miss," Artemus said. "I gonna work good too." Then he smiled. "Maybe this nigger even works better than the boss here 'cause not so many things goin' around in his black head 'sides minin'!"

That evening while they made camp, Maria cooked a good meal in her tent. She was even willing to have Artemus sit at the table, but the black man shook his head and said it wasn't decent for a white lady to eat with colored folks and took his plate off to their own newly pitched tent. The crisis was over.

There were a few raised eyebrows and some glints of jealousy at first over the new tent pitched so near to Maria the *Chilena*, but most miners at Pine Log took the strange partnership in their stride. Every man was too intent on pay dirt and his own dreams, to give more than a passing thought to the Welshman and his Negro partner.

Tom Baxter, the big Scotchman on the next claim, often came of nights to sit around the fire and have a little "mouth wag," as he called it. When Maria invited him to have a bite with them, he always brought more than his share.

One night when he walked with Charles from the provision tent, Tom opened up. "You know, our friend Sandy MacGreggor's got his nose out of joint a bit over Maria shining up to you like she does," he said. "But I told him, 'Man, the lass has the right to choose her special friends.'

"And as for *me*," Tom went on. "Ye need have no fear about yer Maria. I don't take to dark women. Big Tom Baxter'll be waitin' till the golden-haired lasses, like he's used to, come along the trail."

The combination of Latin, Celt and Negro along with the faithful Angie was unbeatable.

Maria did her share and more as a partner. She cooked the meals and helped them at the long tom. She washed for Charles of Sundays while they kept the fire going for hot water, and other miners had to wash their own clothes.

Sandy MacGreggor, who was sweet on her, washed his clothes and plagued Maria no end by roaring out a ditty loud enough for the whole camp to hear:

> "I miss thee at the washing tub
>   Where my sore and blistered digits
> Have been compelled to weekly rub,
> Bringing blues, hysterics, fidgets.
>   'Tis then I miss thy timely aid
> Oh, do have pity, gentle maid."

Outside of old Sandy ogling and making a fool of himself in public over Maria, everything was going fine at Pine Log.

For weeks the three partners labored together, and Maria learned English from Charles, so that she rarely had to substitute words in her own language.

And she was a good lass too, as well as a loving one. Father Alaric, the Roman Catholic priest, had only to enter camp on his jackass, before she was out of the blue pants and into the brown dress, looking like a nun while she waited her turn to confess so she could kneel with the Mexicans under a tree on the hillside while the priest said Mass.

Father Alaric was a good papist and enjoyed eating Maria's cooking as well as the rest. He never asked a chapel man how he felt about God. Just ate and drank wine they fetched to celebrate and stretched out his legs for a brief rest while he told the news from the outside. The last two times it had been dreary news about the dry diggings and men who were bloated with scurvy and blotched by erysipelas while they hung on and waited for the rains to come.

He had seen big oak trees explode right before his eyes because of drought as he had come along the trails in the hot sun. There was so much territory for one priest to cover, and Mass had to be said under trees or in tents, when all the time men's minds were on gold. They even looked in the soil for gold when their heads were bowed at a graveside!

Artemus listened intently to the father's words from a discreet distance. At the end of each visit he went over and pressed gold from his poke into the father's hand.

"Ain't that I knowed much of what he say, for I is a Shoutin' Baptist myself," the darky admitted to Charles later. "But this nigger he just figure on being on the right side."

Charles decided to work out his salvation in a different way. Several Sundays while other miners were gambling and drinking, he and Artemus cut logs and built a little cabin on Maria's claim.

She was as pleased as punch. Carlos must share the lovely new cabin with her. He must try for himself the bunk built up off the floor with the soft mattress she had made from sacks filled with pine needles. It was only right that such luxury be shared. How could she, Maria, sleep in a cabin so fine when her partner Carlos was in a shelter with his bones on boughs?

After that Artemus saw his partner only by daylight.

One day they were all three working peacefully in the hot sun, and they could hear the clink of Tom Baxter's pick, when suddenly there was a great commotion on a near-by claim.

Charles looked up to see a wiry little man, red-faced and angry, talking in a foreign tongue to three other men who had torn down his claim notice and posted their own. In no time fists were going as the little chap tackled all three at once, his yellow wispy hair flying wildly.

"They're jumping the little Swede's claim!" Big Tom Baxter yelled across to Charles as he dropped his pick and ran toward the fight.

By the time Charles reached the spot, Tom had waded in and knocked out two of the attacking force. The third was mopping a bloody nose.

"Now what in hell is this about?" Baxter demanded.

In excited broken English the little man tried to explain. They had torn down his notice. They had tried to jump.

"Ain't no good anyways," the man with the bloody nose put in. "The notice ain't even in English. Who knows *what* it says?" He held the paper to Baxter. "We're Americans. He's a stinking Swede. If he can't write English he's no business here taking out *our* gold."

The little man stood by helplessly with pleading eyes, trying to understand.

Tom grabbed the ticket. "You know damned well what it *means*," he roared. "Never mind what it *says*. Now drag the carcasses of those two polecats off this ground and get off yourself." Then he turned to the little Swede.

"Go get you some paper and a pencil," he ordered. "Understand—*paper* and a pencil." He wrote wildly in the air.

A grin spread over the Swede's face. He nodded, picked up his hat from the dirt and clapped it onto the back of his head, then short legs cut across the gravel to his pack. He came back with a scrap of paper and a pencil. The tip of his hat scarce came to the hairy armpit of Big Tom.

A brawny knee went up, the pencil stub was well wetted between Tom's thick lips.

"Now. What's your damned name so's I can spell it?" he asked.

A long rigmarole of Swedish came out.

"Don't make sense," Tom said. "You're going to be Shorty from now on. Shorty—" he thought for a minute—"Shorty Palmer."

He wrote the words down with a flourish, put in the date and other essentials, then two eyes twinkled.

"Understand, pard?" he asked. "I've just given you a baptisin'. You're Shorty Palmer. S-h-o-r-t-y P-a-l-m-e-r."

"Ya?" The little chap nodded and grinned. A grubby hand hit his skinny chest. "Me—Shorty Palmer!"

The defeated men picked themselves up, banged the dirt from their denims and red shirts and went off glowering as Big Tom stuck the notice up and then stood back to survey his work.

"There you are, Shorty," he said. "Ain't anybody going to bang you down as long as old Tom's around."

The little man looked at the notice, then gratefully at Tom and put out his hand. "Shake, pard."

Tom's big dirty paw went out. "That's right—from now on, Shorty, we're pards. Let's go drink to us."

That night, Maria, bless her, cooked up a stew that she called by some Chilean name and they all celebrated the new partnership.

The only sadness at Pine Log came with the tax collector who never failed to arrive on his jackass to demand four ounces in the name of the law.

Charles always fumed over the deal, but Maria took it well. She would smile and remind Charles of what he had said about clearing out when he got his pile.

"This keeps you longer by four ounces, Carlos," she would say and look sadly into his eyes. "Just a little you pay and Maria pays to be here together and take out the gold and have happiness. You should be ashamed, *amigo*."

One day when Maria had knocked off early from the long tom to go and cook supper, Artemus took Charles to task.

"Miss Maria sure sweet on you, boss. Do she know about you having a wife and kin of your own makin'?"

Charles had to admit he had neglected to tell her. Maria had never asked.

The black man shook his head. "Ain't no good comin' of this, boss. Even a black man knows that you can't go on with two sets of arms alovin' you up. The Devil he got a pull on one set of arms for sure, and he goin' to take it out 'n your hide one of these days."

Charles tried to shrug the affair off. When they got their pile and left, Maria would soon forget him. There were too many men. But even as he said the words his heart was not convinced to forgetfulness.

Artemus wasn't convinced either. "I smells trouble. Ain't the womenfolks forgets. It's the men does, you know that, boss. Miss Maria ain't goin' to let you go away free like you come here."

There was no further time for argument or even a prick of conscience for guns went off. Men shouted and roared with joy like mad creatures, and miners rushed from shelters all along the river to see what was up.

Maria, Charles and Artemus joined the crowd around Mr. Radcliffe's provision tent.

Sandy MacGreggor, flushed and excited, waved a copy of the *Sonora Herald.* "Justice at last!" he roared.

Gamblers, fancy girls in bright-colored dresses, provision men and miners pressed close, eager to hear.

"It's come, lads! It's come!" the Scotchman shouted excitedly.

"Stop blathering, get to the point," Big Tom called out. "What's come? We don't want to hear you talk. If there's news in the paper, *read* the piece out to us."

Sandy accepted the challenge, cleared his throat, and by the light of Mr. Radcliffe's lantern read: "Americans! Greet kindly the stranger who asks your hospitality and protection. You may entertain angels unawares. The burden of the tax on foreign miners has been rendered less obnoxious. The following notice is being distributed throughout the country:

"NOTICE: The collector of taxes for governor to receive twenty dollars for the privilege of laboring in the mines until the last day of December next and to issue a license for that period. He is instructed to protect all who comply with this requisition and punish all others as violators of the law. The collector's office is at the head of Washington Street, Sonora.

"August 3, 1850   L. A. Besancon"

After the ruddy-faced, excited Scotchman finished, everyone near went wild with joy. Men chaffed one another and asked who were "angels entertained unawares."

They roared off to saloons and soon reeled in the narrow roadway. Noise was terrific in gambling tents and fandango houses. There would be a good take everywhere on this night of celebration. Men now had only to pay one ounce instead of four for thirty days.

Someone raked up a fiddle and a dance got under way. Charles grabbed Maria and away they went in a whirl of dust on the roadway.

"Promenade and treat your partner" rang out from the caller after a bit. "My whistle's dry."

Irishmen, Scots, Swedes, all reeled drunkenly toward the bars where drinks were rapidly running low.

Sandy MacGreggor, tipsy as a loon, put his arm around Maria—and she put her arm around him!

For a minute Charles saw red. Which was worse—the tax or seeing Sandy so close to Maria because the damned tax was off?

He pulled up his fist ready to knock the damned Scotchman down when a black hand caught his arm. "You ain't got no *real* claim to Miss Maria's arms, and this nigger goin' to keep your head from being busted in like a eggshell."

Charles suddenly felt a rush of guilt and shame. He turned away and headed home through the whooping, hollering, wild mob.

That night he stayed with Artemus and read one of the papers brought into camp—to punish Maria for her sins.

Jenny Lind was sailing from Liverpool to sing for the first time to the people of America. That made him homesick. He had heard Jenny Lind when she sang for a benefit of miners' widows. Jenny Lind, the Swedish nightingale. He had sat next to Anne that night—before Bill or Charley or little Henry was even thought of. Anne had squeezed his hand and they walked home through the crisp starlight of Wales, singing the tunes Jenny had sung. Anne's clear fine contralto and he himself booming out the alto. He was glad for a minute that he hadn't punched in Sandy MacGreggor's soft face. Anne would be shocked over her Charles, but here in the mines all was so different, so cruel. A man had to be hard to survive.

As Charles Morgan sat in his own tent away from Maria "to serve her right," he thought how far he had traveled from chapel singing. He had nigh forgotten the Sermon on the Mount that Anne read aloud of a Sunday afternoon.

But with all of it, Maria had no business clarting up to Sandy. If she really loved Charles as she said she did, it wasn't decent! He folded the paper, pulled off his shirt and pants and crawled into bed. She'd miss him tonight and jolly well good for her!

Sleep wouldn't come. Had Maria taken Sandy to the cabin? Without a candle he dressed again and went out into the night.

Stars twinkled above the deep groove made by steep mountain-sides, and twice August fall stars made a golden slit in the black. The dipper was clear as it shone in Pennsylvania of nights. By now Anne would be abed and thinking of no dipper.

Charles sat down on the rough stony hillside. What was a man to do? There was Anne who had given him three sons and always pulled by his side. She gave herself to him any time he asked— but that love was so different from Maria's soft eager body. Could he ever forget her? Hot anger went through him as he thought that right now Sandy MacGreggor was enjoying Maria's charms to the full.

He sat for a while, head in hands, trying to figure a way out. Then when no solution came he made for Maria's cabin.

A candle flickered. Charles banged on the door. He'd kill Sandy MacGreggor if he was inside. A hand went to the holster.

Maria was alone. She was expecting him. Why had he been so long?

He took her to task about Sandy. She had been common as a Mexican chippy standing with her arm around Sandy at the bar. He was ashamed of her!

But Maria only smiled as he cursed Sandy and all his ancestors. Her eyes twinkled bright as stars. Warm arms went around his neck and her kisses fair covered his face.

"Then you do love me, Carlos. Maria caressed Sandy to find

out!" She was delighted with the whole affair and turned so loving that anger was swept away in his need for her.

As he lay in her arms, Maria told him her dreams. Now that she understood about him loving her, everything would be easy. Next time Father Alaric came through the diggings they would be married.

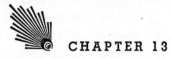

CHAPTER 13

1850

MARIA in cahoots with Alaric! Charles turned numb at the thought, while he worked at the long tom.

He recalled a thousand things he had said around the fire when Maria chinned with him of nights.

She had been so free about her life in Chile; how they had fiestas on the coffee plantation; the gay music natives played; the cold nights when mountain wind swept down.

She had prodded him too, to know of his boyhood, and he had told her about his folks in the coal mines of Wales. He'd had to watch his great tongue too. Twice it had nearly slipped and Anne's name come out.

Once Maria had asked him why a great fine chap like himself had not married. He'd put her off, saying there was nary a woman so perfect that he'd been willing to slave for.

She had smiled then. Didn't he want some fine strapping sons to carry on the Morgan name?

God, how conscience had stabbed then, and the sweat run down his legs!

He could see Anne, singing in chapel in her best black and he roaring out his lungs beside her.

What would the parson say to such doings as he was up to now? Charles Morgan living in sin with a papist. What a turmoil of a predicament he'd got himself into!

The great glistening nuggets in the long tom did their best to try and make a man forget his sins. There was relief too in knowing that lowered taxes would swell the poke. In spite of the blistering sun and the drought there was a chance now, if he could stay a little longer.

Lowered taxes had changed everything. Thousands now were rushing to all the diggings. At Sacramento and Stockton men with packs waited in line for stages bound for the mines. The paper told of twenty to thirty coaches all starting, one after the other with cursing drivers, to tear across the flat and up the grades groaning under their burden of men seeking fortunes.

Would Alaric discard his four-footed transportation and come over the hills in one of these fancy coaches and then suddenly drop down in Pine Log on foot, in answer to Maria's prayers?

The very idea made his blood run cold with fear. He worked like mad against time and prayed to God that the roads and coaches were too crowded for Father Alaric.

By the middle of September, which was hotter and drier than the month before, a shortage of food threatened the whole Sierra. Low water made it impossible for boats to travel the rivers now and people were coming too fast.

Sonora was running out of food and prices went up. There was scarce enough on hand to last a month. Men were robbing tents for food and even murdering in order to stay and sweat on the dry hillsides while they dug and waited for rain.

Father Alaric didn't come, and here was Maria excited and bright-eyed over the prospect. Most likely the father was too busy saving souls from the Chinese opium dens of Coulterville or the fandango houses of Hornitos where there was at least a murder a week.

Charles and Maria had to watch the sluices constantly now, because Pine Log had filled up with men, and it was no unusual occurrence to have long toms robbed while you ate mulligan or took a breather in the saloon around dusk.

Horse thieves were busy all over the place. On the Calaveras road a horse thief was caught in the act of stealing. A jury of camp men sentenced him to be hanged. A partner begged for his life, and the fellow received fifty lashes and was branded "Horse Thief" with a hot iron.

This news made Artemus more solicitous than ever of his precious Angie, who now was tethered to the tent stakes.

Maria grew restive. She decided to go to Sonora and buy clothes for a real wedding and see where the reverend father was. She had always planned on a pretty silk dress with a veil and slippers with buckles. Wouldn't Carlos like his bride to be that way? And a fiesta too for every old friend in the diggings, so no one would forget the day that Carlos put the ring on the finger of Maria. She had plenty of gold in her own poke to pay for everything.

Sweat ran down Charles's back as he helped her onto Angie for the shopping trip that he suspected was a scouting jaunt for the priest.

After she had gone, Artemus rolled his eyes. "The Devil he sure got you by the tail feathers now, boss. What you goin' to do? The Angel Gabriel don't let no man with two wives into the pearly gate." Then he finished with an opinion that a nigger with the love of a braying jackass was better off than a jackass with two legs that brayed after a woman he had no right to love.

As he worked Charles tried to think of a way out. Then his heart ached. Did he want a way out? Maria was beautiful. Maria was love itself. She worked beside him by day always cheerful and she made the night glorious with her love. But he was terrified at what might happen.

Last time he had gone to Sonora for new shirts and pants and a bit of a drunk, the chapel man, Reverend Long, had stood in a tent and ranted about men's sins catching up with them, and how God would punish when you least expected.

The Reverend Long wanted money to build a church. Charles had felt better for a bit when his poke was lighter by a few ounces transferred to the preacher's canvas bag. He knew Anne would be proud to know he had helped. Her letters pointed an accusing finger when she told of revivals where everybody had come out with "the Spirit" and singing was glorious, but they missed his voice. The boys always went to Sunday school come rain or snow. He should be proud of them.

The prick went deep. What did he, Charles Morgan, have to be proud about, living with another woman and trying to salve his conscience by giving a bit of gold to the parson?

The first morning after Maria left he wanted to bolt, and he confided to Artemus. "Ain't goin' to work," the black man said, and shook his head. "A man can't run away from hisself. The Devil in him runs faster." Artemus went on about sin. Wicked San Francisco had just burned down for the fourth time in a year, hadn't it? And folks no more crawled out of the ashes when cholera came on a boat from China and dead wagons busy. Scared folks had high-tailed it for Stockton and Sacramento—and were eating up miners' grub. "Just show what the good Lord can do to sinners."

Charles was terrified, desperate. What if Maria brought the priest back with her?

That night, by the light of two candles, he put all his gold together and looked at it.

Artemus sat for a long time in silence, watching. Finally he spoke. "Boss, has this nigger got enough to buy hisself now? And to divide with Mr. Bodine and still have yams and clothes and chicken sometimes without doin' nothin'?"

Charles nodded. "You're a rich man, Artemus. You'll never have to work again unless you want to."

The darky looked long at him, rolled the big eyes and nodded. He got up, pulled his blankets from the bunk and rolled up his gold and extra clothes in them. Then carefully he divided the few provisions kept in their own shelter now that Maria was away.

"What are you doing?" Charles asked, as he watched the busy black hands.

"This nigger gettin' right out of here back to Mr. Bodine before everythin' bust wide-open. I gonna give Miss Maria my Angie —'cause Miss Maria she goin' to need sompin' to love after a while, and she been powerful good to my Angie, feedin' her scraps and all. Artemus he just can't stand by and see sweet Miss Maria that been so good to him hurt and cryin'."

"You're not leaving for good?" Charles asked.

"Sure am—by this yere moonlight tonight, and no foolin'." The provisions were dumped in the pack. "Mr. Bodine he say smart rabbit he go home 'fore snow start fallin' and he leave no tracks."

A black hand met Charles's in a warm clasp, and there were tears in the eyes. "Been good to me, partner—I goin' to pray like hell for you while I walkin'."

"But Poverty Hill," Charles called out as the darky went out. "All the ground you shoveled ready for rain and washing. You can't go, man! It's not safe for you alone with all that gold on you."

There was no answer. Artemus had disappeared in the night. Charles ran through the dry crackling brush, calling the Negro's name. Only hoot owls answered. Heartsick, he returned to the cabin to tussle with his thoughts.

Artemus gone. Terror struck into Charles when he thought of the lone black man on the trails. The diggings were worse than ever now and bristling with crime and hatred. Indians plundered white camps and killed men for horses and provisions, and Mexicans killed for gold and because of hatred for those who had treated them cruelly and unjustly.

Memories of that first day when Artemus came crowded his mind. Artemus was his partner who couldn't read or write. A partner had obligations to the one who had helped him in the tough days. Charles wanted to button on the deerskin vest where his money was distributed and rush off.

But there was Maria, his other partner. She had rights too. He knew what would happen if he left the claims undefended. People were robbing all over the place. Jumpers descended on the claims the minute there was no one to protect them.

There was no sleep. Charles sweated in his own memories. If he hadn't been such a fool and had told Maria about Anne in the beginning this would never have happened. Now Artemus might be the sacrifice on the altar of the selfishness of Charles Morgan! Miseries came, such as he had never known before, and not even a steaming cup of coffee helped.

God, how he wished Maria would come back! For two days he worked at the long tom like a man pursued by the Devil, to try and run away from his thoughts—but they ran ever faster. How wise the ignorant darky had been when he said you couldn't run away from yourself because the Devil could run faster.

A way out came to his mind. He loved Maria—why not stay and marry her when she came back with the priest? Men buried in their blankets on California hillsides with no marker were never heard from again. Pottsville was far away. Charles Morgan could just disappear, and no one be the wiser. Anne's letters could go back unclaimed.

No! He brushed a hand across his eyes, to blot out Anne when she turned away from the company post office with one of her own letters returned. He loved her. She was his wife, the mother of his sons! If he did this terrible thing he would never again see his boys. Little Henry would grow up without a father.

But what was he to do if Maria came back with the priest? He loved Maria too, and he couldn't bear to see the hurt in her eyes when he told her—in front of the father too!

Oh, God, was ever there a sinner like Charles Morgan?

He could protect the claim for Maria, then hide in the brush until Father Alaric was weary of waiting and went away.

But there was no need to hide. On the second evening Maria returned alone. She was very excited. Father Alaric was coming in a week or two. He had given his word. There had been so many murders that the poor padre had been busy saying rosaries for the dead. But he was coming. He was glad Maria and Carlos would be bound in holy matrimony. She spread out finery on the bunk. Petticoats and a white dress made of silk from France with real lace on it and black slippers with shiny stones in the buckles.

The stuff had been ordered by Mexican girls in the *Tigre* to charm their men, but Maria had offered more and the shopkeeper decided the Mexicans could wait. She was like a child in her happiness.

She wanted to know if he'd missed her, and opened tins of delicacies, oysters and fruit. When the fiesta was eaten Maria was tired; besides, there was love-making to be done and plans to make.

After the candle was out and his arm around her Charles broke his news. Artemus had gone!

She couldn't believe it. Maybe Charles was a poor cook. Men were helpless things, just dipping biscuits in pork grease and cooking beans with no flavoring.

Charles suggested that perhaps the Negro was frightened of cholera. He had mentioned the scourge in San Francisco. Negroes were afraid of sicknesses. Didn't she remember how faithfully Artemus wore the holy medal she had given him?

While Maria was still thinking of that he went on and told her he was afraid for the darky alone. Now she was home to watch the sluice box and the claims, he was going to search for Artemus. Out here in the mines anything could happen to a black man loaded down with gold.

Maria understood that. Up in Sonora she had heard many tales of men killed in their tents or robbed on the road.

Her hands caressed him and she told him what a good man he was to be worried about Artemus. She was deeply touched and wept when Charles told her Angie was a parting gift from the black man. "You go fetch him back, Carlos, even if it takes weeks to find him," she cried. "He is our good partner. He must always stay near us after we are married. I will watch the claims and work while you are gone."

Maria was so tender and loving that she bothered him the next morning as he prepared to go. Her eyes grew big as she watched him fasten on the deerskin jacket under his shirt.

"You taking your gold with you?" she asked. "Why, Carlos?"

He looked right into her eyes then and lied as would befit no chapel man of Wales. "Too many robberies, lass, to leave everything here. I'm taking it to Wells, Fargo for banking. A Welshman *never* keeps all his eggs in one basket. It's safer that way, now we have so much." And he fastened the heavy damned strait jacket filled with gold around his middle.

If she was suspicious then, the suspicion was thrown off later when he took no pack, only blankets and extra suit. Once when she went out for a minute, he slipped in the picture of Anne that had been hidden for months.

He wanted the worst way to say good-by to good old Tom Baxter and little Shorty Palmer, who were always in on good times and bad ones too. But that would make the lass wonder. Tom and Shorty would have to take the will for the deed.

When time for leaving came, Maria was brave. She hugged him close and kissed him and wished him Godspeed, and was sure he would find Artemus before sundown. She stood waving as he struggled across the pine log with his unseen burden and threw a kiss when he started slowly up the hill.

CHAPTER 14

1850

CHARLES sweated and puffed and struggled up the steep mountain. The deerskin vest nearly sweated the life out of him and his legs complained about so many extra pounds. He began to wonder if he could make it to Sonora and the stage that would take him out of the diggings forever.

The heart of him was torn nigh unto killing him. Maria had looked so dear and good when she threw that last kiss. As he climbed the steep parched hillside alone, he couldn't help but thank God for the black man who had made the parting as easy as it was, and who had saved a Welshman the misery of seeing the lass suffer too.

He plodded on, weighed down by sad thoughts, and heavy of body from so much gold. One step, two steps, and a rest to let the heart stop its fearful pounding. Would he *ever* make it up the steep hillside and onto the flat?

Once at Columbia the way would be downhill to Sonora. Maybe Artemus was still in Sonora and they could go out of the diggings together.

It was dark when he finally arrived at Sonora with legs aching like a sore tooth from his extra burden, and heart wrenched for Maria, who waited alone on the Stanislaus with her wedding dress, and Artemus, poor black man wandering alone among cutthroats and thieves. All this because of a fool who had sung his lungs out at chapel prayer meetings and forgotten in a year the commandments of his Lord.

Things were popping in Sonora. Major Barry, the coroner, took a drink at the saloon in the City Hotel beside Charles.

"I ain't seen no black man but one lately. That nigger bought a horse for a hundred dollars and a saddle for two hundred and headed out." The judge went on to tell that the coroner's job now was no easy one in Sonora. There had been three murders to examine in a week, and no one caught to accuse.

Charles was weary and the tight jacket filled with gold made his body sore. They had some more slugs together to put in time until the stage was ready. He was careful to have the price weighed out of a flabby poke he carried in his pocket.

But the whisky went to his head. By the time the driver called out for Stockton, Charles couldn't manage his legs under burden of gold and drink.

The loquacious old Barry didn't desert his drinking companion. They reeled together to the coach and Barry shoved and cursed and struggled to help Charles into the vehicle, where four other men were already seated.

"You sure are solid and heavy," the coroner complained. "Must be all brawn."

Charles was not too addled to see the men exchange looks—significant looks—as they gave him a hand up.

"Sorry you had bad luck in the diggin's," Barry shouted out drunkenly as the driver got on his box. "But try and not forget old Sonora. Come back. Next time you may strike her rich."

The coach rumbled over the bumpy road toward the cow country. There were twists enough to break a snake's back, that made a man fair sick with their suddenness. The driver drove furious as the Devil himself, and the affair rattled like a dead wagon with a loose coffin bobbing about.

The men shouted out a bit of talk over the racket and cursing of the driver. They grumbled about the drought. There had been rain this time last year.

Charles was thoughtful. He remembered last year and the rain. Artemus had come to his shelter of boughs in December. The water had poured down for a month. Poverty Hill! Once he had wanted a last look at the cabin there, but now he was glad he had neither the energy to pull his load of gold over the scorched hills nor any desire to see the cabin. He tried to picture Anne and the boys when he returned so rich with gold.

The cheese factory Anne longed for was on him now, to blot out Poverty Hill and Pine Log and the murders and poor food and struggle. A year ago he would have been happy. Now he was weary and heartsick and sore in body because of the damned gold. Thank God he hadn't taken to gambling along with his other shortcomings, and could go home with his pile. Many didn't even live to get their hides out of this Godforsaken place, let alone their gold.

Where was Artemus, the black man who had stuck by him and helped him? He must forget Artemus now. The black man was part of the past—to be forgotten in happiness with Anne and his boys.

Maria was not so easy to forget. He broke out into a sweat every time he thought of her laying up with Sandy MacGreggor who was always hanging around like a buzzard. Maybe she'd even take to some damned *Chileno* now her Carlos was gone. Maria was really his. Hadn't she bought a wedding dress?

He tried to sleep as the stage rattled through the night, but the gold was lumpy and would give a man's sides no peace.

Each time they stopped for rest or food, the two dark men who hung together followed Charles like dogs. He had only to turn and they were on his trail. That made it necessary for him never to be alone. Damned old Barry and his talk about weight. Why couldn't the old fool mind his own business?

How quickly they got to Knight's Ferry, compared to the walk up a year ago! Stockton was different too. There were two-story frame shops and wooden shanties where the brush shelters had been. Stockton was a big town now, choked in dust and business.

But the biggest change was in San Francisco. It was newly built with frame shops and a wharf. The El Dorado gambling house on the Plaza had changed from a tent shelter to a three-story building.

Everybody in San Francisco was hopeful and full of business. Crowds thronged the dusty thoroughfares. Rain would come.

Didn't it feel damp now? Then they nigh choked on the dust
when a horse and wagon raced by. Gold was worth seven dollars
an ounce in San Francisco. Charles was tempted to change his
horde into flat money, but turned canny. If gold was worth that
much an ounce in San Francisco he could likely get still more for
it at the Philadelphia mint.

When he turned away from the office his companions of the
stage were near by and eager to treat him in farewell at the El
Dorado. Those two had dogged his steps through Stockton—
they had never let him out of their sight! Now, on the busy dusty
street of San Francisco, he shook his head and harked an ear to
the barkers from rival steamship companies.

All the agents called out their prices telling how swiftly the trip
back to the States could be made. "First-class three hundred sixty,
steerage one hundred and fifty. Plenty of room. Sailing at high
tide."

As Charles made ready to stride up the plank he turned and
thumbed his nose at his companions of the stagecoach who had
tried their best to get him into a saloon for a treat and probably
to drug and rob him. He'd show them a Welshman was no fool!

Cattle were driven on board, decorated with festoons of paper
on their horns. Fresh meat for the journey. Boxes and bundles
were loaded. All was busyness and cursing and shouting as people walked up the plank. Some came with quick step and vigor-
ous bodies and others, dirty and discouraged and tattered, dragged
themselves aboard. There were quite a few parsons, bespectacled
and pious and mostly looking down on ordinary folk, and two
or three women with strained faces and no sign of men with them.

Just after noon the vessel slipped away from the wharf and out
through the slate-colored water. The golden hillsides of California
were blotted out by time and distance, but Maria would not fade
from Charles's mind. He still saw her on the Stanislaus waving
good-by and Godspeed.

CHAPTER 15

1850-1851

CHARLES upset the whole applecart of the Philadelphia mint when he stalked in and told the pasty, black-broadcloth-coated man at the counter that he had come from the California gold rush and wanted to weigh in his gold and change it into money.

Then before they could catch their breaths, he slipped off his jacket, his shirt and undershirt, right there before them, and unfastened the deerskin jacket.

Eyes popped out, mouths gaped in startled surprise as they watched!

He knew. They had thought he was crazy when he came in, a poor tramp of a fellow in tattered blue pants and a dirty worn hat. But they found out!

For months he had dreamed of this. When he was heating up beans over a smoky fire in the rain, and when he was grubbing on the banks of the Stanislaus with the sun near beating the very life out of him, he had pictured this minute. It was worth the wretched seasick trip home and the misery of carrying the burden, to watch them change when they saw the bright pure gold he pulled from the pockets of the dirty deerskin.

They asked his name while he fastened his shirt and they looked at the gold. Soon it was "Mr. Morgan" this and "Mr. Morgan" that and "Yes, sir," when he talked to them, when before they saw the gold they were near to shoving him out of the place. He was somebody now—richer than any piddling clerk in black broadcloth. For the first time in his life, Charles Morgan of Wales knew the power gold could bring to a man.

Charles was near frantic with the joy and freedom of being shut of the damned jacket so filled with lumps, but he couldn't give all the gold up for mere money. He reached over and took one big nugget. That was to show Anne, and later to be beaten into a ring or a brooch for her, so she would never forget where the cheese-factory money had come from.

Several men weighed the gold and checked it and tested the stuff for purity. There was lots of excitement. Folks came to see the gold pile and have some talk with him while he waited. He was quite it. They didn't mind *now* that his boots were thick and had been polished over scuffs and his shirt was patched and the seat of his pants worn thin. He had gold! Some of the men knew about Sonora. Lots of people had gone there from Philadelphia. Did Charles know Dr. Lewis Gunn? He had gone last year to Sonora and written letters back that in June there had been twelve murders in the camp in a single week! California must be a horrible place.

Charles watched these yellow-livered ones shudder under their black coats while they gaped the more at his pile of gold.

"Aye," he told them, "it might be a horrible place, but the mines are lousy with them that wants California gold, and more coming by every boat."

"You know young James Coffroth, the writing chap?" one man asked.

"Never heard of him," Charles snapped. "You don't mix much in a place filled with Sydney prisoners they call 'clipped ears' or others who might put a bullet through your head if you ask questions."

They laughed then. "Folks out in California will hear about Jim Coffroth all right."

"Jim writes that he don't mind the murders out there in Sonora," one man told Charles, "but he don't like what they have to eat."

Charles told them what he had eaten for a year. California strawberries three times a day. Warmed up in the morning with grease, warmed up at noon and again at night and eaten with clunkers.

They wanted to know what California strawberries were.

"Beans!" Charles roared, and then, with a bored look, went over to watch the counting-out of greenbacks.

Across the table they came in piles neatly banded; not in hundreds but in thousands! Twelve thousand and seventy dollars!

The bills fair dazed him. He cashed a fifty back into gold pieces for gifts to Anne and the boys and slipped them into his pocket, then opened his pack on the mint floor showing red flannels and all, and chucked the packets of bills into it. All eyes were on him as he rolled the pack and slung it to his shoulder.

It was jolly to shock them. He liked being the center of attention, while officials of the mint weighed his gold.

With great deference a man opened the door, and they bade him good-by.

Charles didn't bother to speak, just saluted with a hand touching the battered hat and went out into the dingy smoky streets of Philadelphia feeling like the King of England.

New clothes to make an impression? Another thought: No, Anne wouldn't like that. She always had a look at the wool he bought and raveled a bit to be sure he was not being cheated. Besides, a fine dandy in a new suit carrying a blanket roll would attract too much attention. The lass would have to take him as he was, seeing he'd brought back her dream for her.

In the coach racketing over twisty roads to Pottsville, Charles looked out on the peaceful snow-crusted rolling hills of Pennsylvania. No gold or murder here—just plowed ground or pasture watered by snow and waiting for God's goodness and sunshine to bring green from the sleeping ground. He settled back. On such a hill as these there would stand the Morgan cheese factory, where he and Anne and their boys would prosper, and maybe their grandchildren after them, because a Welch miner had come home safe with California gold. He looked at his grubby cracked hands. His children would never know such labor. What a fine bonny country this was, where a man had freedom and money and peace!

At last Pottsville and the mine came into sight. Charles shoul-

dered his pack, swung off the coach and started along the last mile
to home!

What a dreary place to live with fine coal dust powdering everything black. More pickets out of the yard fences—probably used
of a cold morning when kindling was scarce. The great oak tree
he had watched so many springs and autumns was gone, covered
now by the growing slag heaps. There were new faces around
the stoops of company houses, men and women with pale thin
faces. Children he didn't know played on the flat places.

Before long the Pottsville slag heaps would be behind the Morgans forever. Charles had come marching home into the muck
and dirt with a treasure of gold to rescue his family from the pits!

Anne was haggling Bill from the doorway. His heart near
jumped out of him at sight of her. But she didn't see him. He
burst out in a bit of a song for her:

> "For he was a dandy man
>   With his pick and his pan
> And it took him quite a while
>   Before he made his pile."

Words stopped dead in Anne's throat, but her lips stayed parted
when she saw him. She caught up her skirts and ran into his arms.

Anne was just the same after near onto two years. Same brown
calico with the bit of white at throat and cuffs. (He'd see to that
quick. Only silks for his lass now!) Her hair smooth over her
ears. It seemed as if he had never gone away now with her arms
around his neck and sobbing out while she nuzzled his cheek.

But when he looked at the boys he knew time had passed. Bill
and Charley were a full head taller than when he left, and the
juicy Henry out of didies and standing like an owl in his blue
pants, watching the show.

When he was in the house and held Anne off at arm's length for
a good look at her, Charles tried to forget Maria. Anne was a
bonny lass, but in a much more calm, quiet way than Maria. He

missed the snap and fire of Maria's black eyes. She would have caressed him and been really excited.

Anne only looked at him and said, "Charles, you're thinner and too pale. You need good food." There were tears in her eyes and she turned away from him and rattled the stove. "First thing you need is a good cup of tea to buck you up."

The boys turned frantic then and climbed all over him. Bill told of the apples he had stolen for a pie from Farmer Grews, and Henry with a mucky ring of jam around his mouth shoved a picture book into his father's face. Charley roared to know about the Indians in California. Were they really naked and scalped folks like the papers said? Had Dad seen any scalped people? Did they bleed much with their hair off?

He tried to give each attention and told about the whales spouting in the Pacific as the boat went along, and how everybody ran to one side of the deck to watch when the call of "Whale!" went up. And how all the crew down to the cook rushed on deck at the opposite side for balance, and gave passengers a good helling for tipping the boat!

They were all interested in whales, and Bill wanted to know how far a whale could spit Jonah?

The kitchen was just the same, with the jiggle-legged table and the cracked lids on the well-polished stove.

"I've missed you, Charles," Anne said as she spread a clean tea cloth on the end of the table and set out the cups with yellow flowers on them that she had brought from Wales. "I began to wonder if you'd *ever* come home to us again." She reached over and kissed his cheek. "I prayed every night and morning that God would save you from sin and death."

He tried to close his ears to what she said. "It's like old times, lass, with the teakettle aboil and real bread to eat." Then he told her the eggs in San Francisco came from Lyons, France, and were old enough to crow for seventy-five cents each, and Frenchmen who baked got a dollar a loaf for their bread. "Flour was three dollars a pound at Pine Log."

The boys guzzled their toast and jam and slopped tea all over

the place in their excitement. Did gold really stick out of the
ground in California?

Anne spread more toast with jam and gave each lad a piece.
"Here, stuff your mouths full and be quiet," she said. "Your
father wants a bit of peace and rest. No more noise out of you or
you'll go to bed."

After they'd finished tea, Charles opened his pack, pushed the
tea-things aside and piled the packets of greenbacks on the table.
He tossed a golden coin to each big-eyed lad.

Such a grand feeling it was, to be tossing gold about like an
earl or a bloated rich lord at the very least.

"There she is, lass, the cheese factory and more for you," he
said as he enjoyed Anne's surprised face. "We can be done with
the slag heaps forever now."

He shoved piles of bills out of the way, took the plan of the
cheese factory that he had drawn on board ship and spread it out
on the table.

"See, here's the spring house, big enough to keep all the milk
and cream cool. Here're the vats. Here's the cellar where we'll
ripen the cheeses."

But Anne didn't seem to hear. She just sat staring at the piled-
up bills on the fresh white tea cloth.

"Are you listening, lass?" he asked and put an arm around her.
"Here's your dream on paper as we planned and the money to
pay for it."

She fingered the dog-eared plan with work-worn hands, not
tense and eager, but preoccupied.

For a long time there was silence; the only noise in the room
was the teakettle singing on the stove. He knew the whole thing
was too stupendous for Anne. She was dazed with so much money
all at once.

Finally she looked at him. There were tears in her eyes. "I—I
didn't know there *could* be so much money in the world," she
murmured. "And you got it in just a year!" The old eagerness
was in her face.

He got up then and held her soft little body close to him and

told her how much he loved her and how proud he was to bring
such riches back and that seeing her face was worth all the hardship and misery. In that moment he knew the true meaning of
love, of marriage. Two people with their dreams fused into one
great dream.

"The pit's outwitted at last! We'll be business people now," he
finished and covered her face with kisses.

From his arms Anne looked again at the money—and then
pulled away a bit. Her jaw was set, her eyes had a faraway look.

"Charles, we're not going to build that cheese factory," she told
him. "We're *all* going back to California. If you can get twelve
thousand dollars in a year out of the earth, we're going back to
where that gold is."

He could scarce believe his ears! The money on the table suddenly sickened him. He had sweated and struggled for the cheese
factory to please Anne. Now she didn't want it. They were rich!
Couldn't she see that?

He turned his head away and brushed his eyes with a grubby
hand. "No, Anne," he managed. "A cheese factory you wanted,
where we could all be together and work together. Something for
the boys to grow up to. I've brought it back. We'll build the
cheese factory and settle down to being prosperous."

She turned tense and pulled away from him. "Don't you see,
you great Welshman, that with a cheese factory we'd only be
tradespeople?" she cried. "Tradespeople grubbing along and worrying about prices and taking all the customers' grumblings. But
with just maybe a year or two in California we could be so rich
our boys would never have to turn their hands to work. They'd
be rich gentlemen, and Henry a minister of the Gospel!"

Something seemed to die inside Charles. He left Anne standing
beside the table, her hand fingering the greenbacks, and flung
himself into a rickety chair. "I can't go back," he groaned. "I
just can't go back and face the hardship and drought and murders,
not even for Henry's sake."

But Anne's jaw was set. "Fiddlesticks! You're tired now and in
need of my cooking and a woman. You'll be right as rain in a

month or two and as ready to start back as I am to go. With me along everything will be different."

"Don't be a looney," he cried out as he fought for his future, for his dreams. "If you and these little chaps had to eat what I've eaten in order to bring home gold you'd fair puke. The pork is the stinkin'ist salt manure ever brought around the Horn, and there's no bit of grease but that. Salt pork! I've fried it for breakfast and my supper, and boiled it with my beans for dinner and I've sopped it on my slapjacks—and the last I bought cost me eight dollars a pound."

'Twas only the money part that bothered Anne. No salt pork anywhere on earth was worth that much.

"I'll feed you up with fine stews and good joints until you sicken of rich food and get gout," she told him. "Then you'll be glad to go back to California and eat salt pork."

The boys soon forgot their mother's threat of bed and added their voices to the California din. They wanted to go and pick up gold for themselves and see Indians and bandits. Bill had read all about California. Everybody had a horse out there and they drove thousands of cattle and sold the hides when they weren't picking up gold and shooting Mexican bandits.

While the child talked, Charles had thoughts of his own. He knew the signs. That brightness in Anne's eyes was gold fever working in her blood, and the shine of greed. He had seen that same look in the eyes of men who sweated on hot red hillsides and had seen it again in gambling tents around the tables of monte dealers. Misery went through him just thinking of Anne out in California where Maria was, of the struggle and hardship and danger.

But there was no use arguing now. Anne was set on California and he was wearied to death. The homing hadn't been at all what he dreamed it would be.

He grabbed up the plans and muttered about getting some rest.

In the boxlike bedroom with crewelwork mottoes of Scripture on the walls, Charles flung himself fully dressed on the clean patchwork quilt that covered the bed and buried his head in a pillow. Maria would never have done this to him! She would have been glad of fine clothes and a house and peace and quiet. She would have understood a man's dreams and tried to help him with them. Why had he ever left her? He had been happy on the Stanislaus. Why had he come home? Was Maria, sad-eyed, still waiting for him, with her wedding dress? Then he fell asleep.

CHAPTER 16

1850-1851

THE next morning his money was in the chest and out of sight, thanks to God. Life suddenly seemed to drain out of Charles, in spite of Anne's good food and her fussing over him. He had managed to keep going while it was necessary, but with the sudden letup of the burden and responsibility he felt flattened out.

Old friends from the mine came in to hear about the gold rush, but Charles was too heartsick to talk much. He couldn't even get excited when one day a fellow miner came in with Stockton papers sent him by a friend out there who sold provisions. He wanted to know about the things he read.

Did Charles know where this place Shaw's Flat was, where miners had taken out two hundred and eighty-nine ounces of gold in two days?

Charles did. "It's between Columbia and Sonora where a man called Caldwell planted an orchard."

The news crazed Anne. She begged leave to borrow the paper for a while and read the grubby ink-smeared lines.

Charles cursed the damned *Stockton Times* that had followed him home and pushed reason clear out of his wife's head. Now she was more set than ever on her boys going to California to get riches greater than had ever been known!

He grabbed the sheet from her, scanned it for the murders and hangings he knew were sure to be there, then shoved it back into her fists.

"And what do you say to that?" he demanded hotly. "I suppose you'd like your boys to be in the midst of that too?"

James Savage, the scout, and the sheriff were trying to stop the uprising of hostile Indians. Three men had been murdered at Mariposa and one body had eleven arrows in it. They had found nine other men murdered by arrows.

When Anne looked up from reading about the horrors the thirst for gold was slaked for a bit. She didn't talk about California for three days, but instead busied herself with washing windows and curtains. Then suddenly the damned thing burst out all over again.

"You know," she said, "I've been thinking about those murders and troubles, but you don't get anything in the whole world without *some* risk." Her hands fumbled with the wet window rag. "Didn't we risk everything to come from the old country here to the new? And look what you have now? If we treat the Indians right and the Mexicans too they won't hurt us."

Charles drew a long breath and launched into the next round in the fight for his freedom. He told her of the hardships just coming home on the boat, when there was a storm, and they had nothing to eat except hard bread that was in boxes lashed to posts so they could grab a handful. Hard bread and salted meat and water for three days in the Gulf of Mexico. Everybody so seasick they wanted to die. The man from Texas moaning out, "I don't know whether I'm going to hell or heaven or Texas—but, oh, God, settle it for good!"

"You lived through it," she snapped. "It was only a few days. Surely you can stand a little hardship and suffering to give your wife and sons a chance to be rich!"

There was no stopping the lass. He told her of men dying in the diggings, with blankets for coffins, and not even a marker. Of the parson who was eager as anyone for gold and said there would be preaching on Sunday unless he discovered a *better* diggings. She didn't even mind that there were few women except Mexican tarts, who took men's pokes after a night with them.

"Then the mines need good women," she insisted. "I don't mind wet or drought or murder or salt pork as long as we *get* somewhere in life and find more gold. You're sick now, that's all. You'll soon be well enough from this trouble the doctor calls scurvy. Aren't we paying through our noses for bottle after bottle of lime juice that he ordered? The doctor *said* that would cure you. Are *you* afraid to go back because of a Mexican tart, Charles?" she asked in a cold voice.

Needles pricked at him. Had the lass turned suddenly fey? She had been born with no caul over her head! He drew up large and strong and faced her. "I swear to God, Anne, I've never been in a fandango house or slept with a Mexican. 'Tis just that I can't bear to think of you and the boys among Sydney convicts and rabble from all over the world. It's no place for boys and decent women."

She smiled with a knowing look. "Who patched your underdrawers? No man on God's green earth could put on a patch with fine stitches, nor so neat."

He tossed Maria off with an easy speech. Maria was a *Chilena* woman whose brother had died. Maria had a long tom and shared it with him and Artemus. She had washed their clothes and patched them too. Maria was no tart, but a good kind woman.

"Is Maria still in California?" Anne watched him narrowly. "Because if she is I want to know her. We could be friends since she's such a *good* woman."

But he was ready for that too. "Maria's most likely back in Chile with her California gold by now. She was only staying long enough to make her pile and return." He hoped his voice was more calm than he felt inside him at the sudden picture of Maria waiting—with her wedding dress.

Anne's voice cut through his thoughts like a knife. "That settles it! If this Maria was such a *good* woman and could be in California for gold, there's no reason why I can't do the same."

The row stopped short when young Bill came in with a letter, an answer to one Charles had sent to Mr. Bodine to inquire about Artemus.

There was sad news, an enclosure from Judge Barry, the coroner of Sonora:

A big colored man was found under a tree near the outskirts of this camp on December 18, 1850. His head was crushed in and he had evidently been robbed, for no gold was on his person. Letters found on him were addressed to Artemus Bodine and were signed Henry Bodine. As coroner, R. C. Barry was communicating with said Henry Bodine. Would the latter please send twenty dollars to pay for coroner's services and burial?

Mr. Bodine thanked Mr. Morgan for all he had done for his faithful slave. The whole plantation was mourning Artemus, who would now never have his fill of yellow yams. Mr. Bodine trusted that Mr. Morgan was well and was glad he could be back once more with his family.

The letter slipped from Charles's hand to his lap. He looked out across the slag heaps to the gentle rolling hills beyond. Artemus, the faithful black man who had labored beside him on the hot hillsides, was gone—forever. Artemus, who had worked so hard to buy "hisself free," knew a freedom now that was not purchased by gold. The hills blurred. Charles closed his eyes.

Anne came over. She took the letter from his lap and read it. For a minute her eyes saddened. She knew about Artemus, for Charles had written about the black partner and his quotations from Mr. Bodine.

"Too bad," she said. "He would have been so happy showing off his gold to the other black people."

"Artemus offered to give me his shovel when I hadn't one, and we shared the pick." Charles said, more to himself and those other days than to Anne. "Something fine and strong and good went out of the world with Artemus."

The letter about Artemus brought things to a head in the little house on the slag heaps.

Charles faced his wife. "I can't go back, I just can't go back. You'll have to be satisfied with what I brought you."

Anne's jaw set. "Then I'll go alone with the boys."

The sleeping winter hills of Pennsylvania had scarce turned warm enough for the planting of spring vegetable gardens when the Morgans left to begin their trek to California and gold!

CHAPTER 17

1851

THE last week in June 1851 Charles Morgan stood on the deck of the groaning old side-wheeler beside his wife and their three pale travel-weary boys. Men around them near shoved Anne through the railing in their push. Poor lass, she had put on the brown broadcloth cape and the hat with the ostrich feather, that he had bought for her in Philadelphia, to impress San Francisco. Now her cape was twisted and pulled and her hat askew from the shove and jostle of those whose eyes were only for gold.

"By Patrick's holy poker, keep yer shirts on," a tar roared at the restless mob. "There'll be plenty of time to lose them shirts once you get into the hills. We'll tie up the minute it's time—and no sooner!"

At last the plank went down and boots clattered against wood in a lively tattoo. Everybody in the Morgan family took up his burden. Anne carried the two carpetbags; Charley and Bill struggled under the weight of their own blankets, proud to be such big fellows. Charles shouldered his own great pack.

Henry got separated from them and bawled his lungs out for his mother as they were all pulled first one way and then the other in the rushing crowd.

Anne was shocked at the number of saloons to the block and the unshaved miners who had sopped up drinks until they reeled; she resented the men who ogled her as she passed them on the rough wooden sidewalks and was terrified when she heard San Francisco had burned several times.

Charles thought of his own poverty-stricken arrival in the city by the Golden Gate. He would give his family the best now! Proudly he led them into Delmonico's past the broadclothed proprietor.

Anne was careful of the boys; she seated them so they couldn't watch the bedizened, painted tarts who laughed and drank with a crowd of men at the bar, and told them to look at the beautiful crystal hanging lamp.

The prices on the food card near blew the feather out of her hat. An omelet two dollars and oysters three dollars! With such prices they must be out of San Francisco. She wouldn't hear of staying overnight, unless there was no river boat to take them out. They had come to get gold, not to spend it. The minute they finished eating, she pulled her cape close, took up the carpetbags and ordered the boys out of Delmonico's ahead of her.

They had to stand in line for hours with sweaty miners four deep, before there was a place for them on the Stockton boat. Bill and Charley got tired and began to belt each other on the head, and Henry whined.

Charles bought chunks of meat wrapped in *tortillas* from a Mexican vender. This shut the boys up while they guzzled, but the food was too hot and young Henry puked it up all over Anne's best cape. Then he began to bawl. Charles gave her his bandanna to wipe herself off and tried to shut Henry up.

There was no closing the young one's mouth until a grizzled miner took Henry into his arms and told him about the circus that had come to Stockton, and how beautiful Mrs. Foley looked in a short dress and long pink stockings as she rode a white horse bareback and jumped through paper-covered hoops.

At last they were on the boat. Anne sat on the deck with the sleeping Henry in her lap. The lass was wearied to death and her face looked pinched around the mouth. The heart of Charles went out to her.

Charley Bassett was aboard. He caught sight of Charles and moved through the crowd toward him. Charles was terrified. All his sins came up to face him. He tried to think if Charley had ever seen him with Maria. He hadn't been particularly careful not to be seen with her, for he never dreamed of Anne in the diggings. His hand was wet with sweat when Charley shook with him.

But if Charley knew he didn't bat an eye, just welcomed Anne to the mines and told her there was a "good" woman in Columbia now—a Mrs. De Moile. "She's French and runs a boardinghouse. God! What fine grub she serves—puddin' and everything."

Then he made them laugh as he told how old Long, the parson, had outwitted the miners one Sunday morning when his church was empty. They'd let him use the bell that was for calling people to a hanging. It was understood that he was not to ring it furiously and confuse the issues, but the old parson whooped her up that Sunday morning when everybody was getting over the night before. Men thought there was real excitement and ran to the place. Old Long grinned then and pointed out their sins to them right as they stood there in the street expecting to hang somebody.

Bassett told Anne to be sure and bring the boys to the Fourth of July celebration at Sonora. There were to be big doings with a bull and bear fight. Then he drifted away to talk to someone else.

Anne was worn out when they reached Stockton, which was a muckle of dust and roaring drunks and mule teams clogging the roads. She didn't want to look around. For her, just a cup of tea and a bit of bread and to bed with the lot of them.

In their room at the City Hotel, she took off her hat and shook out the feather and brushed a hand carefully over the broadcloth cape and vowed that tomorrow she'd take to calico. She wouldn't hear of spending money for a room for the boys; instead she laid out their blankets on the floor, and made herself ready for a night in the iron bed.

Charles was glad to be done with the lot of them and have a quiet walk by himself. But there was no peace to be had. In the saloon where he stopped for a beer, men told of Indians up the trail skinning a Mr. Johnson who had been caught out alone after dark!

He wiped the beer foam from his mouth and turned away. Oh, God, why had he let Anne talk him into coming back to California, where the saloons and even the streets were filled with tales of suffering and cruelty? He wondered what was going on in the woman's mind now she was here in the muck of it all? Her and her gold fever!

He thought of Maria. Where was she? It was jolly lucky he'd met Charley Bassett on the boat instead of Tom Baxter or any other miner from Pine Log. What if Maria had come to Sonora and they met on the street when Anne was along?

Sweat broke out on him. First shot, he must get away for a trip, head for Pine Log and explain things—if Maria was still there. Just the thought of her brought longing to his heart and kindled the passion in him. And then he remembered Anne in her fine cape, and Henry white and puking the Mexican food, and was ashamed. A Welshman with a family, a chapel singer at that, had no business with thoughts such as Charles Morgan was thinking about another woman!

He headed up to the room, undressed and crawled into bed beside the sleeping Anne.

The next morning Anne blamed Charles because Charley and Bill were constipated and meaner than Satan. If he hadn't given them red-hot food only good for savages they would have been all right. Served him jolly well if they died on the way! How long did they have to wait in this dusty place among men whose curses reached her even inside a room with the windows shut?

He groaned and wondered what Anne would be like after the nine-and-a-half-hour ride over the hills, with the driver using every known curse as he lashed the horses.

The stage tickets, five of them, cost twenty-five dollars each, but Anne figured the boys ought to go half-fare, and she created a swirl of dust with her brown calico as she marched over to the coachman and told him so.

The big red-faced chap would not be put down by her. "Your two older boys has backsides big as anybody else," he roared. "Why should they ride cheaper?" Then he told her if she wanted to hold the little one on her lap, that was up to her, but she'd find him a load and herself sweated out of the seat long before she got to Sonora.

There was not much peace in the coach. Everybody talked about people found robbed with their heads "stove in." It was no secret now that Joaquin Murieta, whose brother had been hanged, and himself flogged and his wife killed, had organized the band that was doing the deviltry.

Anne pulled young Henry close and rammed Charles against the side so hard that he could scarce breathe. She tried to look away from the bleary-eyed loquacious duffer opposite who kept ogling her as they strained through the dust and the driver let out red-hot curses to force the horseflesh.

Outside, the view was little better, with bleached carcasses lying all over the flat where mules had gone down into the winter mud and been left to rot.

To make matters worse, Bill and Charley insisted on counting the ones that still had hair on them.

As they wound around the hills hour after hour in the creaking stage, Charles had his worries. Meeting Charley Bassett made him wonder if it was wise to take Anne to Sonora. What if Maria was there or someone from Pine Log met them and shot off a mouth?

Poverty Hill was the place. Simmons was likely the only old-timer left in the diggings and he didn't know about Maria. He might be able to buy back his old cabin. Anne would like the comfort of a well-built cabin with a mud fireplace, and he had money enough now to buy.

By the time the horses began to sweat and strain to make the long Wood's Creek hill, he told Anne his plans, and how he wanted her to be comfortable. That cheered her, until she remembered that their tickets were bought to Sonora—and paid for.

He explained that Sonora was only four miles beyond.

A wail went up from Bill and Charley. They wanted to go to Sonora. Mr. Bassett had told them about the bull and bear fight and the Fourth of July was only three days away! They wanted to see the fight.

"Well," Charles roared impatiently as the stage pulled into Jimtown, "the lot of you can please yourselves. I'm getting off here." He jerked open the door, waited for the driver to give him his pack and strode along the dusty road. Anne and the boys grumbled along after him.

It was past midday and things were quiet in the diggings. Two red-faced drunken Irishmen stopped suddenly in their wobbling walk, grinned and bowed unsteadily with their battered hats clutched to chests, as Anne passed by.

Man, woman and children clattered into the fame boarding-house, ate beans from thick white plates, and two clunkers each, while the murky hotel man mourned. Things had gone to hell. Wood's Creek was dry and people had pulled freight for the rivers. He came close to Anne, put a foot on the bench where she sat and watched every mouthful she ate.

When he had gone away to attend bar, Charles told Anne that she had better stay here with the boys while he walked over to Poverty Hill and found them a place. But there was no use arguing with her. She was afraid! If he could walk she and the boys could too.

Charles looked at the peaked little Henry in his rumpled shirt and blue pants. They could never make it on foot after the long trip. He left them standing in the shade of a tree while he dickered with a teamster for the rent of a horse and wagon, then, boys, blankets and bags piled into the wagon, Charles helped Anne onto the seat. He climbed aboard, cracked the whip over the bony back of the horse and they headed off over Paddy's Hill for his old diggings.

CHAPTER 18

1851

POVERTY HILL looked sleepy as ever, and old Quartz Mountain shimmered through the heat waves. Simmons came to the door of his shack when Charles drew up. The New Englander nearly lost his teeth when he saw who it was.

"I didn't know you'd been away, now you turn up with a handsome wife and three fine boys!" he cried as a brown paw went out in greeting.

Simmons was delighted with the boys, and went into his cabin for a jug of molasses. He gave each one a big spoonful of the sweet as a treat. He wanted to know all the news from the States.

"Can't stop now to talk," Charles told him. "Got to settle my folks come night. Know a place?"

"Ain't no law against you holing in at your old camping grounds," Simmons drawled. "Nobody but varmints been in the cabin since you and Artemus pulled freight." He wiped his nose on a red bandanna while he looked Anne over. "Once I was going to go at that pile of dirt you two left. It would have been legal, because you was gone so long, but somehow I couldn't bring myself to dig into the stuff that poor nigger man sweated over, after him saving my life like he did. Thought he might come back sometime."

He was sad to learn that Artemus had had his head stove in and been robbed. Then he turned to Anne and said Poverty Hill was glad to welcome her and the little fellows and he hoped she would like it. Anything he could do just "holler."

The holler was not long in coming. The key to the padlock

on the cabin door had long been lost. Charles tried prying at the
hasp with a sharp rock, and had the Devil's own time keeping Bill
from busting his new pocketknife over the job. Then he sent
Charley over to borrow a pick from Simmons and in no time they
had the place open.

"Varmints" was right! A wood rat had gone down the deserted chimney and made a nest in the fireplace. There was rat
dirt like brown gravel all over tables and boxes and bunks, and
even in the cupboard. Mice had made nests in the first little gold
cradle that Charles had carried on his back over the hills. The
place smelled like a filthy menagerie.

Memories crowded as he took the cradle out and dumped the
mice nests by the door. Memories of Artemus so gentle and faithful, sitting by the fire while the beans cooked or bending over
the rocker as the sun set in a red glow. He saw the shiny black
face in the light from a flickering candle as they gloated over
their day's "color" on the table of a night.

Anne had cleared a place to put down the damned hat with
the feather on it, and now was like a general taking over for a
campaign. She bossed everybody at once.

Charles must clean out the rat's nest from the fireplace first so
she could make a fire for hot water and get the place cleaned up.
They could use the old ashes in the bottom for sweetening things.

This was a good cabin. She hadn't expected a fireplace and a
loft for the boys to sleep in.

The lass gave nobody's legs or hands a rest and worked herself
harder than the lot. Anne was a different person now. Eyes
bright, face flushed from work, mind racing like a colt as her
tongue wagged about plans. Dirty water ran down her arms to
elbows where the brown calico sleeves were rolled.

The boys were pleased with the loft and took great sport in
swinging up through the hole like monkeys.

They had a cup of tea off the freshly scrubbed table, to cheer
them on. Anne had seen to the bringing of tea, bless her!

"Charles, we'll be all right when we're settled," said she.
"There's the gold in that pile in front all ready to wash come

rain, and there might be nuggets in it. I can help you with the cradle as soon as we get water, and I'll have this place fixed up fine in no time. There's many a miner's family in Wales, with nine folks and the children living in one room, that have never seen such a good place as this. Our children won't have to go through that like we did!"

She got up and put her arms around him and kissed him as she used to before he had put the marriage band on her finger. "At first in San Francisco and Stockton I wasn't sure about this country, but we'll be happy here and rich too—you just see."

Off she went again with her plans. She had enough porridge for them tonight, but they must have provisions.

In five hours Anne had turned the deserted cabin into a sweet-smelling home for them, and the porridge for supper was boiling merrily over the fire in the mud fireplace Artemus had helped to build. But there were dark rings under her eyes as she spooned her supper. She was done-in. The boys must off to bed in the loft the minute the last bite was down them. They were fagged too from fetching so much spring water for cleaning. The rough bough bed would be like clouds of feathers to her own weary bones.

As Charles clattered along the flat through the growing dusk for provisions, the first star popped out, clear and twinkling, and brought to mind other stars he had watched along the Sierras. The night of the miners' tax celebration when he sat alone in Pine Log, angry and hurt because Maria had put her arms around Sandy MacGreggor. He had seen the August fall stars cut through the sky with their light above the deep canyon of the Stanislaus and never dreamed that he would be here on the flat below Poverty Hill with Anne in the cabin.

Maria! Was she seeing the stars at Pine Log tonight—or maybe too busy with Sandy to know there were stars shining? Maybe she was back in Chile? He wished to God he knew *where* she was.

Now, here in Poverty Flat, it was grand to march into the provision place and buy everything he needed without having to quibble about money, while the horse ate good fodder he had bought to fill its belly.

He had to near knock the door down to get in when he returned to the cabin. Over and over Anne asked him who it was. She jolly well made sure before she let him in.

The lass was like a ghost. "Oh, Charles," she sobbed. "Three men came to the door to ask the way to Jimtown. They had masks over their faces, but one man's handkerchief slipped down. They weren't Indians, they were white men!

"When they asked I said, 'If you found the way to this place you can find the way to Jimtown,' and I slammed the door and bolted it.

"'Open or we'll blow your bloomin' shack to hell,' one man roared, and I remembered how you told me about bandits firing cabins to drive people out—and I thought of my boys in the loft!

"'All right,' I yelled back. 'I'll see that you're shown the way. Henry! Bill! Charley!' I called out. 'Come quick, there's some men want to be shown the way to kingdom come. Bring your guns!'

"Then I heard a mad scramble, and they rode away."

She sobbed and shook with terror in his arms. The boys had been so sound asleep they didn't even hear her yell.

Charles near burst his buttons with pride over his lass with her quick wits, and he told her so.

When the candle was out and they lay together on the fresh sweet-smelling bough bunk, he took her into his arms and with her warm body close he comforted her. She was fine and brave and a hard worker, and she'd brought him three sons. Aye, a Welshman was lucky to have a wife like Anne. This thirtieth of June, 1851, was a new beginning. There was no end to what the Morgans, working together, could do in California. Riches, fine clothes, happiness——

They drifted off to sleep.

CHAPTER 19

1851

AT breakfast Anne was bloodthirsty. Charles must buy her a gun and teach her how to shoot. She was not going through another fright such as she'd had on her first night in the mines. She'd let any man have all the bullets any place they happened to hit.

They were having their second cup of tea when Simmons came. He said he was on his way to work a new claim, tunneling into the hill now; quartz mining they called it. You got the stuff out and smashed up with machines, all ready come rain for washing. They called the new machines Rhoades machines. "If I can just get me enough gold out to *buy* the danged machine."

Simmons smiled then at Anne and said how pretty her hair was; he'd always liked dark-haired women.

Anne flushed up like a schoolgirl.

Charles felt bile rise in him. Jesus, how a woman did change a man! Simmons had his gall coming almost before they were up!

Simmons gabbed over a piece he'd seen in the paper about some women coming to the mines wearing broadcloth pants and vests and top hats. "Now you know, Mrs. Morgan, what's fashionable," he finished as he pulled himself up from the door sill and knocked out his pipe. "And I'll be off to earn my Rhoades machine."

Charles was furious. This business of Simmons was transparent as glass! Woman-crazy that's what he was. It wasn't decent, a man suggesting wearing pants to another man's wife!

And then it suddenly occurred to him that Charles Morgan was a poor one to grumble about pants on a woman. Maria at Pine

Log wore blue denims and a shirt, and he had lived with her in sin and been happy.

Anne liked the fresh air and the gray mountain crags. She even thought the dry golden hills were pretty and she sang while she made them a treat of scones baked in a covered fry pan banked with ashes in the fireplace. Then she promised the boys that they could go to the Fourth of July celebration in Sonora.

Charles thought of his sins. "Sonora's no place for boys on the Fourth. Men from all the diggings come in to celebrate and get drunk," he told her.

She just sniffed and said Bill and Charley had seen plenty of drunks Saturday nights around Pottsville, and Henry was too little for it to bother him. If the boys were going to live among gold miners, the quicker they got used to new ways the better.

On the morning of the Fourth there was no urging needed to pull the youngsters out of bed. They were scrabbling around long before the sun, scrubbed ears and all, with clean shirts and slicked-back hair. They chattered like magpies about the bull and bear fight.

Anne made slapjacks and fried bacon to carry along and stay their stomachs in Sonora during nooning. Then they started out over the brown dry hillsides.

Charles carried young Henry on his shoulders and the boys clattered ahead over the loose stones.

When they reached Sonora, the hot midmorning sun was beating relentlessly on the narrow dusty main street, where thousands of men milled around.

Frenchmen pranced with the tricolor fastened to their hats. Cornishmen from Sullivan's Creek were drunk and roaring, "God Save the Queen" at the top of their lungs. A Scotchman in kilts sweated and puffed at a bagpipe that squealed out the "Bluebells of Scotland."

Tattered Indians peddled piñon nuts; one, naked except for a fine white ruffled shirt, darted in and out of the crowd gay as a child. Over all was a thin pall of red dust.

On a vacant space, Mexicans were clustered around a cock fight while the crowd shouted and bet on the fierce bright-feathered birds that capered and darted at each other. The boys wanted to watch, but Anne pulled them away.

Chinamen with baskets were doing a land-office business selling sugared ginger that they hauled out of pots with their long bony fingers. Charles bought the boys some of the Chinese sweets, and the slant-eyed Oriental smiled at the young ones, his yellow parchmentlike face a mass of wrinkles. He gave them three extra pieces. "Fourth July," he explained, and nodded his black-capped head.

They had just turned from the Chinaman when Father Alaric rounded a corner on his donkey. Would the priest recall out loud the days at Pine Log, when he had eaten at Maria's cabin?

The good father remembered a sinner all right! As he put out his hand to Anne during the introduction, the mind behind the bright eyes seemed to be computing years by the ages of the boys.

"I had no idea you were such a *family* man, Morgan," he said calmly and smiled at Anne and ruffled up the boys' hair. "Let's hope these young chaps will turn into fine men, and put some of their *elders* in the mining camps to shame." Then, quick as a darting swallow and while Charles felt heat rush to his face, Alaric said he must be on his way, for Jim Coffroth, the new writing chap from Philadelphia, was about to make the speech of the day.

A stir went through the crowd. Anne pushed back her calico sunbonnet and craned her neck to see, and Charles shoved Bill and Charley to the front.

A slender young chap mounted the steps of Holden's store, and a cheer went up. His voice rang out loud and clear as he talked about what this Independence Day represented in America, and urged men of all nations to get together and maintain law and order and create decent camps in the mines instead of dens of cutthroats and robbers. A gun was fired in salute and someone burst out singing, "My Country 'Tis of Thee."

A man came through banging a pan with a rock. "Two P. M.,

bear fight!" he roared. "A grizzly weighing eight hundred pounds, caught in Napa Valley and brought here at great expense in a heavy wooden cage, will fight the wildest bull obtainable. South end of town at two P. M." He went on, banging his pan and roaring, "First come get best places for their money. A dollar per person."

When Anne found they had to pay, she set up a fuss and thought the boys had seen enough for one day; money was too hard come by, with provisions costing so much, to be wasting it on bear fights.

With that a yowl went up from Bill and Charley, and even little Henry screeched. They didn't like old speeches. They wanted to see a bear fight a bull. Such a blubbering they made there in the street that even drunks stopped and stared.

"We'll go. We'll *go*," Charles cried. "It's not until after nooning."

Suddenly a big nugget dropped into Bill's hand, and a hairy man grinned.

"There, *garçon*. For you and the brother to see the bear fight a bull. 'Tis only that I wish I could see my boy in France this day." He stooped, kissed both lads on their cheeks, smiled at Anne and shoved on with the crowd.

They had their slapjacks and cold bacon sitting under a tree on the hillside, while they watched the crowd get drunker and drunker, and the sun sent shimmering heat waves over the dusty road. Henry got tired and went to sleep with his head in Anne's lap. Gamblers in the tent shelters below called for bets; a gay guitar tinkled from a tent farther down. Somewhere a shot rang out.

At last it was a quarter to two! Charles carried the sleeping Henry in his arms and they walked to the fenced enclosure where the bear and bull fight was to be held.

Hundreds of men were standing in the hot sun. Some swigged from whisky bottles while they waited. Anne pushed the boys ahead to where they could see.

The bear, a great black fellow, was in a heavy wooden cage on wheels, and not far away, tethered with an iron chain, was a big red bull pawing the earth and rolling bloodshot eyes.

A trap door was opened by the keeper who stood on top of the cage. Old Bruin ambled out with a chain fastened to his leg which was quickly attached to the chain that held the bull. Then the bull saw the bear, lowered his head and with a great snort roared at the grizzly.

The crowd cheered and men shouted bets at one another. "Bear! The bear will strangle him."

"The bull! Old *toro* will gore the grizzly."

A wild fight went on and the bear was gored by the horns of the bull. With blood running from his side old Bruin lammed the bull a belt that near knocked him off his feet. The bull backed off fiercely for a charge and the chain broke!

Everybody in the enclosure scattered for safety; there was a regular stampede of people terrified by the bear and bull loose among them. Charles grabbed Bill and Charley and hustled through the racing crowd, and Anne came after with Henry in her arms. They had to fight their way inch by inch. A man caught Henry from Anne's arms and ran with him.

Then behind them a shot rang out and the bull lay dead. The bear fight was over.

As soon as they were out of the crowd Henry started puking. "It's that heathen ginger coming up," Anne snapped, red-faced and all alather. "And my dress nearly torn off me, getting away from that pagan business. Let's go home before we get our heads shot off by these drunks."

They shoved and pushed past knots of men and took the road back to Jimtown. The boys dragged their feet in the dust, and Anne nagged about them wearing out their shoes. They were tired now and no bear and bull fight to egg them on. Charles was fair wearied with them and their grumbling and complaining all the way home to Poverty Hill that eventide of July 4, 1851.

In the next few weeks the money from Philadelphia just melted away. Charles tried his hand once more with the first little cradle he had carried over the hills, but it was no go. Only an ounce or two for days of work.

One day early in September he flung down his shovel. "There's nothing for it, lass, but to go down to Pine Log on the Stanislaus and see if I can get a claim," he told Anne as he pulled off his dusty boots. "We can't last many more weeks on the money we've brought, with five mouths to feed and grub so high. God knows when rain'll come."

Anne was delighted. "I'll be packed up in no time and we'll be on our way. This place is so dusty. Down at Pine Log there'll at least be enough water to wash our clothes."

Charles was bowled over. Good God! Anne with him at Pine Log!

"You and the boys can't go," he roared. "The trails are too rough, and provisions dearer by three times what they are here."

The fear of starvation convinced Anne. She'd stay with the boys, and if they needed a man, Mr. Simmons would be glad to help.

That was a thorn in the side of Charles. Simmons was a handsome duffer when he shaved, and his place not more than a stone's throw from the cabin. But there was nothing a man could do.

By candlelight Anne got his things together, and he tied up his pack, and at dawn she stood in the doorway and waved to him as he started through the gray light toward Pine Log—and perhaps Maria.

CHAPTER 20

1851

DISCOURAGEMENT dogged Charles with every step. All along the dry hillsides everybody he met had the same question as his own: "How long can men hold out against the drought?"

Columbia was more heartening to the soul for men there had hope. Capitalists had a ditch coming slowly over the hills to bring water.

But when Charles stopped in the saloon for a beer, a dreary low-spirited pair of miners had another tale. This fancy quartz-smashing machine that had promised so much was a curse! Companies of money men were forming to buy Rhoades machines.

"If a man has a good claim and has to leave to get grub, they watch like buzzards and jump the claim while he's gone!" one fellow roared. "He gets back and finds he ain't got no more claim than a Chink, and pretty soon there's a shooting scrape with some hired fellows belonging to the capitalists and he either gets killed or they have the law on him for protecting his rights. I tell you a poor man ain't got no chance against money unless we organize. Come on, join up!" He handed out a paper for Charles to sign.

Charles did a pile of thinking as he left the Long Tom and struck out for Pine Log. He hadn't signed the paper to organize for what was the use? He remembered too well the mob of foreign miners trying to stand up for their rights against the tax.

Now the gold he'd slaved for was going for nought. California was changing. So many people in the mines now; not just poor men, come to make their way as it was in forty-nine, but men with lots of money to begin with, buying stamping machines and tools for mining the earth that no poor man could compete with. And water! Other men with money were building ditches, so that only the rich could buy water for washing when the rivers ran dry in the spring. Those companies could charge anything they liked for what a man must have to survive.

Down the steep dusty trail toward Pine Log he trekked. If it hadn't been for Anne's greed he would be away from the hot hillsides where scarlet poison oak leered at him from both sides and threatened an itch that drove some men clear out of their minds.

As he neared the fallen log for crossing the river, a mad desire ran through him to turn tail and bolt from the lot. Disappear! Men were murdered, dozens of them a week. Then he thought of young Bill and Charley and little Henry all growing up into tall straight men. He had brought them into the world, and there was the need of a fat poke to feed them.

The sun had gone down behind the mountain and cool was coming into the deep groove of the Stanislaus. The riverbanks were black with long toms and cradles. Pots clattered in the miner's boardinghouse as Charles passed and headed toward the cabin he had built for Maria. His heart pounded hard enough to beat the shirt right off him.

How would she greet him after all these months? Perhaps she was married to that fathead Sandy MacGreggor and he'd be sent away at the point of a shotgun. Maybe she wasn't even there. He half hoped that was so, but again he was crazed to see the bonny, loving lass.

The cabin was locked. Charles rattled on the door that he and Artemus had nailed together.

"She's down to her claim," a man, naked to the waist, called out from a near-by shelter. "Don't come home till dark some nights."

Charles walked along the river to where he had washed beside the black man a year ago. There she was, in blue denims and red shirt that he had bought her, and bent over the long tom, just as if he'd never been away. The heart of him beat hard with a sudden burst of passion as he called her name.

Maria looked up. Her eyes widened. "Carlos! Carlos!" She raced to him and buried her head in his shirt front.

Then she began to sob. "Maria prayed, said novenas!" came up through the folds of wool. "I thought you were dead. Carlos . . . Carlos."

Her mouth found his. Her kisses were warm and eager with love. "And now you've come back to Maria." She ran work-worn hands over him as if she would not believe what her eyes were telling her.

"The good father said a Mass for you when he came to do the marrying of us. He was sure you were dead." Her arms held him tight. "But the soul of Maria knew you were not dead. Never again will we be parted! What happened?" she demanded and pulled out her shirttail to wipe away the tears.

The stomach near turned over in him with that question. "It's a long tale, lass, and a sad one," he managed. He couldn't tell her and take all the light of happiness from her eyes with his news. "Later, Maria. I'm wearied now and hungered too."

She was satisfied then, and chattered like a child as they picked up her tools and made ready for homing. "Carlos," she told him, "the wedding dress is put away all ready for when the priest comes. Every day I tidy up the cabin and think, This is the day my Carlos comes. And now here you are!" She stopped all operations to kiss him again.

As they walked along he asked about Sandy MacGreggor.

Sandy was gone. He'd made his pile and gone back to Scotland to see the bluebells blow once more on the moors he was always talking about.

"I suppose Big Tom Baxter and Shorty Palmer, the Swede, have gone, too?"

"No, just moved farther up the river to better claims." She sighed. "Maria doesn't see them much now."

Then she told him how she had held onto the claim Charles had left and Artemus' claim too, as long as she could, until a Swede had defied her and jumped. But she would share her gold with her dear Carlos. They would be happy together like they had been before. There was enough for two.

He told her the discouraging news from above then, and asked about claims along the river.

But things had changed in Pine Log too, she said. Miners now lined the river. They jumped a claim if a man was away from it a week. There were no more claims left where washing was good. But she had enough. He was not to worry.

Over plates of beans that she warmed up and fresh-baked biscuits, he told her about Artemus. Tears welled up in the big black eyes. She left her food to caress him.

Then she told him about poor little Angie. "Oh, Carlos, how the devoted gray one missed Artemus and mourned!" She sighed. "One night Angie broke her tether and wandered away—most likely to try and find the kind black man. We found her at the bottom of a gulch with a broken leg. Sandy MacGreggor shot the poor little beast."

But she wanted to know about her Carlos. Had he been laid up with sickness? A broken leg—like Angie? Where had he been?

In that minute all of him wanted her and the love she held out for him to take. He didn't want to think where he had been or that he was on the brink of a self-made hell. He begged her to wait until he was less weary. Now, he wanted to look at her, to be happy and loved.

But she shook her head slowly. "No, Carlos, it is not tired that keeps you from telling Maria," she said gently, and began tracing brown bean gravy with her two-tined fork across the heavy white plate in front of her. "Tired wouldn't keep you from telling."

She looked up suddenly, right into his very soul with her big round eyes. "Another woman keeps you from telling me, Carlos. Maria knows 'way down in here." She put a grubby hand on her heart. The color and brightness had suddenly faded from her face.

Charles couldn't stand that look! He got up, jerking the table and sending forks and spoons to the floor. That look of hers was killing him and he told her so. He tried to take her into his arms.

But Maria pushed him away. She seemed like another woman come into the body of his love. "Then Maria is right," she said in a strange shrunken voice without life to it.

"No . . . well, yes," he blurted, and grabbed both her hands. "But not the way you think."

There in the growing dusk he told her the whole story about his struggles in Pennsylvania, and Anne making the cheeses, and how he had come out to the California mines for a stake to build the cheese factory; and about Anne and the boys waiting up in Poverty Hill now, eating up what money he had left.

Fire died down in the stove, and cool blew in at the open door. When he finished there was no sound except the swish of water in the Stanislaus making its way past the door to the sea.

"But I love you, lass," he managed. "Can't you see I still love you? You made me happy." He tried again to caress her but she pushed him away.

"Yes, Carlos, I see," she murmured after a while. "We were happy—but Maria was only your *California* wife." She got up; her blue denims brushed against him as she passed.

His arms went around her waist and he tried to hold her to him, sitting as he was on the wooden box.

Gently she loosed his fingers and walked out of the cabin. There was something about her that stayed his impulse to follow. He was sick with the sorrow in his own heart, and the misery he had seen in her eyes when she first asked him about the other woman.

For a long time he just sat, then dropped his head on the table and cradled it in his arms. He asked God to forgive him for this terrible thing he had done.

Maria came back after a while, lighted the candle, picked up the scattered forks and spoons from the floor and sat down. She was very white and the sparkle was gone from her eyes. The old gay Maria had fled from the cabin and a new one come to take her place.

"Carlos," she said. "I have a claim here—a good diggings. To-morrow the claim is yours with love from Maria."

"No," he shouted. "I'll clear out tomorrow."

She shook her head. "You stay and work the claim. You need the gold it will bring you. I have plenty now to take care of me." Then she smiled wanly. "If you still love me—your California wife—let Maria's claim bring happiness to you and Anne and the little boys."

"No," he insisted. "I'll not take your claim on top of everything else!"

Maria brushed a hand across her eyes and looked at him wearily. "I'm tired, Carlos—too tired to fight," she told him. "I worked hard at the long tom today—my last day." Then she said there were beds at the new miner's boardinghouse at the end of the road.

Charles scrambled to his feet and shouldered his pack. "Maria, you don't understand. I love you. I'll always love you."

She didn't answer.

"I'll be over in the morning. We'll see everything different by daylight," he told her as he turned to go out of the door. "Try not to think the worst of your old Carlos."

By daylight everything *was* different! Charles banged on the cabin door. There was no answer. He lifted the latch and went in. The place was bare of Maria's things. Even the wedding dress was gone. The little black stove in the corner was cold.

When he reached the long tom there was a ticket flying white in the wind, to tell all concerned that the claim now was the property of Charles Morgan.

CHAPTER 21

1851

WITH a sorrowful heart, Charles unrolled his pack and put his store of provisions on the cabin shelf. There was no use going after a woman once she'd made up her mind. What had he to offer Maria if he found her? Besides, he needed gold for Anne and his boys. There was no time to be lost, with the poke flattening by the minute up on Poverty Hill. Into his work clothes and off to the long tom was the tune for a sinning Welshman now.

His mind worked as fast as his hands while the sun beat on his sweaty back. Maria was most likely headed for Chile with her gold. He hoped the poor disillusioned one would find more happiness there than she had among the rocks of California's Sierras. Dear merry-eyed little Maria who had sung the songs of her homeland beside this fire—was gone.

For weeks he slogged at the long tom, but Maria's rich claim seemed to have gone with her. He took only an ounce a day at best and many a day less than half an ounce turned up at the bottom of the tom.

Pine Log had changed too. The jolly crowd was replaced by surly "foreigners" who ripped wild in saloons and fandangos of Saturday nights and then went on their silent dour way for another week. A lone man worrying about his wife and children had a dull time. No Maria with her cheery ways, no love-making, just work, heating up food, and to bed with muscles aching from weariness.

The Stockton paper, brought in sometimes a week after it had been printed, was all he had to look forward to. Dry! Dry! That was the story all along the Lode, and yet thousands of prospectors were arriving by land and water. Fifteen thousand miners were in Columbia now, waiting for water in the promised ditch. Provision prices were out of sight with the drought and so many to feed.

The poke at Poverty Hill must be getting flabby as an old woman's chin. He thought of Bill and Charley shoveling away food with flour a hundred dollars a barrel and beans near as high, and was tormented.

Then, on the morning of December 22 rain spattered the dry hillsides for the first time and lifted everybody's spirits!

Men pulled off their battered hats along the Stanislaus to feel the moisture from the sky on their faces. They whistled at their work.

With discouragement pulling the hide off him, Charles left the long tom where it stood, took his few belongings from the cabin and closed the door for the last time.

At worst a man could be with his family for Christmas.

Life had been no dream at Poverty Hill. Anne was thin and worry lined her brow, but hope shone from her eyes at the sight of him. It was a shame to tell the lass he had little to bring back in his poke after four months of hard work. He put off the sorrow a bit.

With shoes around seventy-five dollars a pair, the boys went barefoot. Great fellows they were now, growing so fast that their wrists and half their arms stuck out below the calico shirts Anne made, and backsides so big they near burst the seams of their pants.

All three young ones talked at the same time, like crows, about robberies and hangings and shootings, and little Henry showed a bow and arrows that some miner had fashioned for him, and threatened to kill everybody.

Anne was pleased over the cabin that she had made into a cozy home and showed him the tick on the bed, made from one of her brown calico dresses and stuffed with pine needles. He must feel the soft pillows. She had gone with the boys on the hot flat to pick silk from milkweed pods to make them.

"I've made the money stretch and stretch," she told him. "For days now we've lived on porridge, while we thought of you com-

ing home with gold. The sides of the canvas bag are nearly together it's so lean. Twelve thousand dollars seemed such a lot
when we left Pottsville, and now it's nearly gone!"

After supper when the young ones were abed in the loft, Anne
caressed him. "Now let's see your poke," she begged. "I'm in real
need to see some gold once more to cheer my spirits, Charles."

He drew a great breath, reached under his shirt and threw the
flabby pouch on the table. "Bare wages I've made, Anne, and
nothing more. Luck has forgotten the Morgans."

All the light went out of Anne's face and tears came into her
eyes. "Oh, Charles—just this little bit when we need it so much."
Her head went down on the table in the cradle she made of her
arms, and her little body shook with sobs. "Folks everywhere
along the Lode are getting gold." The words were muffled by her
calico sleeves. "Mexicans, down at Frémont's trading post, just
made seventeen thousand dollars in eight days."

He put his arms around her to try and bring comfort. "I worked
as hard as I could, lass, and kept hoping from day to day that I'd
strike it rich." He covered her wet face with kisses. "I did my
best."

"I'm tired of living on hope," she sobbed, and then told him
there was so little water in the spring now that they had to mind
and not drink too much or there would be none left for tea. What
were they going to do? Dry up and die on the hillside while he
lived on "hope"?

Far into the night they talked ways and means. A few drops of
rain splattered on the roof. Perhaps that was the answer. With
a little more the spring might come up enough to wash.

He thought of his first days at Poverty Hill, when every mouthful had to be reckoned and the last grease had gone onto the black
chest of poor sick Artemus. Now after all the gold, he was right
back where he started.

Coals went down to a red glow and still the future was not
settled.

Christmas Eve was rainy. Anne would not let the boys see her
worry, and made a special treat for their supper. A dried-apple

pudding made from a handful she had put away in summer. Then she told them not to hang up stockings. Santa didn't know the way to the mines yet.

When they whimpered about no Christmas she gathered them around her knees by the hearth and told them about the little Lord Jesus who had no place but a stable to be born in, "Not even a bed and *He* got along." They must be big and brave and remember how great the little Boy born in a stable had become and what He meant to the whole world.

Bill asked to know exactly what the Lord had meant to the whole world?

Little Charley knew. "Jesus was born so we can sing Christmas carols."

That was it—Christmas carols! Charles boomed out bravely with "Hark! the Herald Angels Sing," and Anne added her clear voice to his, while she beat time for the little ones and their squeaky voices.

Then there were "Holy Night" and "It Came upon the Midnight Clear."

Anne turned suddenly to Charles. "It's Christ's birthday," she said. "We're supposed to give, Charles, and the Morgans from Wales still have something to give."

She looked at the boys. "On with your coats quick. We're going to sing carols in front of every cabin in Poverty Hill diggings and let the miners know that Christ is having a birthday."

Charles squeezed the lass's hand as she reached for the heavy brown Paisley shawl her grandmother had worn.

Out into the dark rainy night they went, singing and holding hands as they walked across the loose stones toward distant cabins.

Henry couldn't carry the tune very well and flatted the notes, but he made up by volume in the sweet reedy voice of extreme youth.

Anne sang out clear with all the strength of a Welsh choir singer:

> "Hark! the herald angels sing,
> 'Glory to the new-born King . . .'"

On they went splashing through the rain. Men came to doors and listened and called out, "Merry Christmas!"

Farther along the street they went. "Holy Night, Silent Night." Three little boys with their mother and father giving their Christmas to Poverty Hill.

A Mexican fandango girl crossed herself and stood listening by the door. Suddenly she bolted out, kissed young Henry and put a nugget into his hand.

Anne grabbed the golden gift from the child's hand. "He shan't have gold earned that way," she snapped, and was making off to return it when Charles caught her shawl and stayed her.

"My lass, take the gift as it was meant, in the name of Christ," he told her. "This is His birthday, and He didn't judge harlots."

The nugget dropped for the second time into Henry's grubby little hand.

"Hark! the herald angels sing . . ."

A guitar tuned up and men's voices joined the song.

" 'Glory to the new-born King . . .' "

Christmas 1851 had come to Poverty Hill.

CHAPTER 22

1852

By the fifteenth of January so much rain had fallen that miners along swollen rivers abandoned their claims and poured into Poverty Hill by the hundreds. Mule trains bogged in the mud, so that provisions couldn't move more than a snail's pace along the lowlands, and what little got through to the diggings was sky-high.

Anne resented the miners who stood around waiting for the whisky that poor straining mules carted up the hills, when folks needed food so badly.

"No use lamenting, lass," Charles told her. "Miners'll have their jackass brandy, come food or none."

Everybody in the Morgan family worked at washing gold. Bill and Charley rocked the cradle and carried dirt, while Charles and Anne shoveled, and young Henry kept the bag ready. But the take was small in spite of young arms and old, working from early morning until dusk. Anne grew paler and thinner. The lass was wearied with work all day and then coming in wet and tired to cook grub to fill five hungry bellies.

Finally she could stand it no longer. "We'd better leave this cabin and hunt something else," she told him with fear looking out of her eyes. "The food's so low we won't have much to carry, and I'm afraid, Charles. The thought of the boys going hungry scares me." She was sure now, with water, the rich flats around Columbia would give up their gold.

The next day she cooked the last beans and made slapjacks to carry along, while Charles divided their few possessions into four

packs with a little one to be carried by the proud young Henry.
Then they started through the drizzle for Columbia and riches.

Columbia was jammed with people because of the promised
ditch come real dry weather, but there was sadness too. Smallpox
had broken out and frightened some folks out of their wits and
the diggings. It had evidently come with the great horde of poor
half-starved Chinese coolies who had settled in the north end of
town in miserable hovels.

Charles dragged his family first to Sewell Knapp's store to ask
about a place, then to Jackson's, but nobody knew of an empty
shanty.

Anne bought some food and quarreled about the high prices.
Jackson got red in the face over her words, but he was at a dis-
advantage for a minute. He had to go to the door and let fly a
mouthful of tobacco juice before he could answer.

"You just listen here, Missis," he told her. "Jesus Christ Himself
couldn't sell any cheaper than I do, with it costing thirty cents a
pound to haul the damned stuff up in mule teams."

Henry sat on a keg and began to bawl that his feet hurt, and
Bill and Charley were fiendish, nagging for everything in the
place.

Charles was at wits' end with them all when a miner, bloated
with whisky and a breath to fair knock a man down, plucked at
his sleeve. "I'm headed out, pard, and you've brung in a little hell
of your own, I can see that. I don't aim to get smallpox and I'm
fed up. You can have my shack for your regiment and welcome."

He swung the bawling Henry to his shoulders. "Come on—it's
on the edge of town." With that he blasted his way along the
crowded street with the Morgans trailing after him like the tail
to a comet.

The place was a frail shanty of boards and boughs with a "linen"
top. There was a bunk, a table and several boxes to sit on. In the
corner was a tiny black iron stove with a crazily tilted stovepipe.
Anne offered to pay for the stove but the miner said he'd fry in
hell before he'd let her.

By dusk their wet clothes were drying at the back of the stove and Anne was heating beans and stirring up a batch of biscuits in the new home, while Henry whimpered and felt of his bruised foot, and Bill and Charley grumbled because they would have to sleep on the floor. They never had to do *that* in Pennsylvania.

Charles saw Anne shut their mouths with one look at them. He put his arm around her. "Don't mind, Anne, we'll make it somehow," he told her. "The boys are soured with the cold slapjacks they gobbled at noon."

For three months Charles worked and scrabbled on the hillside to feed five hungry mouths, as the water everywhere dried up.

Men found nuggets, plenty of them and dust too, right in the claims next to him, but the golden goddess presented niggardly gifts to a Welshman for plenty of hard work with pick and shovel.

Anne did her part at the cradle as well as stretching the food. At news of each rich strike the flame of gold fever burned in her eyes. She was sure they'd hit it rich maybe the next day. She figured that if you did the Lord's work when you were in want yourself you'd be prospered, so she helped the Presbyterian parson get funds for a real wooden church, since there was no Methodist chapel to help.

The miners liked Anne. They were willing. "Give 'em a place to pray in," they would say at the Long Tom Saloon when she went to beg. "Give 'em a sulphur refinery." And they dug into their pockets.

But when May Day dawned, Anne had no time to beg for the church. The wondrous day had arrived at last, when the new flume was to open and water flow into the flats around Columbia.

Irish were out early, and drunk by the time the parade was ready to begin. Anne and Charles took their places near Knapp's store where the boys could see well. Charles was proud of Anne as she stood in her hat with the feather and a freshly starched calico. Poor woman, she'd had to borrow Mrs. De Moile's sad iron to smooth that calico. His were not the only eyes that brightened when they looked at her. One grubby chap, who introduced himself as High Water Bill, couldn't take his eyes off her, and set the boys up to sweets as the parade marched by.

First came the bankers in fine black suits and beaver hats, smiling at everybody from the coach. Then came miners from every diggings, walking under homemade banners that told of their camps.

Indians with waterfalls painted on their naked bodies, shook their headdresses to thrill Bill and Charley as they passed by, and Mexicans strummed guitars and looked self-conscious in their best serapes, as gamblers in frilled shirts and fandango girls with gold hoops in their ears closed in after the procession.

There were speeches by the officials and Jim Coffroth, and cheers for the capitalists who had made possible this wonderful flood of water—and then the flume opened.

Everybody sang "My Country" as if their throats would burst from gratitude, as the first stream of water came into Columbia that May Day 1852.

Anne's new friend, High Water Bill, walked back to town with them. He said he lived in Squabbletown, a Mexican settlement on the flats, and not long ago had been robbed. "But I got back twicet as much within the hour."

Young Charley and Bill pricked up their ears and gave all attention to the bedraggled man.

"I was robbed of all the gold I'd taken out in six months, and no sooner do I start with my cradle again than a Mexican comes up behind me and shouts, 'Hand it over pronto!'

"You could'a shook a sack of meal out of me with that." Bill shot a stream of tobacco juice into the dusty road. "I puts up my hands and says to that bandit that if he could get anything out of me after the cleaning I'd just had he was welcome.

"That Mexican, he just listened a second and asked me which way the robbers went.

"I points, then he says, 'I am Joaquin. Come with me and I'll give the gringos a lesson in robbing.'

"We went up on the hill and spotted the men in camp below.

He told me to guard his back and went down to face them. In a few minutes a shot rang out and the Mexican came back.

" 'Go to your diggings,' he tells me. 'Here's half the steal. They'll never bother you again.' And he shoves a bagful of gold into my hands—almost twicet as much as was took in the first place!"

When they reached the fork in the road, High Water Bill said he was pleased to meet a real lady in calico, and turned to the right.

Charley called after him, "Why do they call you High Water Bill?"

" 'Cause I ain't never been known to wash." Bill grinned and shuffled away in the dust.

Water in the little ditch brought twenty-five thousand men to Columbia. Who cared that the damned capitalists charged twelve dollars a day for a four-inch-tom stream to wash? There was plenty of gold in the flats.

Almost overnight up went a new main street with tall-fronted wooden buildings. Gaily painted banners hanging from porch canopies told the location of the Long Tom, Finnegan's Place, Pay Ore Saloon, Lady Joe's Fancy House and Hog Annie's "also fancy" and dozens of other places of enjoyment and business.

"Ladies of joy" soon owned most of the saloons and "dango" halls and were doing a bang-up good business. There were houses for all kinds and classes. Frisco Martha's was a rowdy place; she limited her time with each man and the frizzy-headed brassy one bragged that she made three thousand dollars in a month!

Maria Querida's "Sporting House" had girls with "the best-shaped legs in the Lode," but beautiful Marquita had a luxurious "Blue and Gold Saloon" where only miners who were properly washed up and dressed in their best were welcome. Here the political barons congregated. No money passed across the fine inlaid bar. Glittering gold was tossed into gay Marquita's own jeweled hands for drinks and "favors." The vivacious little Mexican, only sixteen years old, was soon toasted a dozen times a night in champagne, "Queen of Columbia! . . . Columbia's darling!"

Anne was frantic over the prostitutes every time she went into town, and always took it out on Charles of a night while she rattled pans cooking supper. All men thought about was these harlots. All they talked about was fancy women.

"There's no use fretting," Charles told her. "With twenty-five thousand single men on hillsides you can't expect anything else. Men are always interested in women."

But she wouldn't let him talk. "Don't I know it!" she snapped. "Those two-legged creatures are even nosy about the washings a body puts out on the line, but I fool them. I hang my drawers inside my petticoats to dry!"

Charles was fed up with her grumbling. "Well, you *would* come to California for gold!" he snapped, and went out to stand under the stars and be away from her awhile.

CHAPTER 23

1852

WATER or not, the luck of the Morgans didn't change. Charles went farther and farther afield with his rocker and slept out under the stars to make the golden goddess smile on him while Anne waited with the boys in the flimsy shack.

Times were hard for even those who had dust, for gold coin was scarce because of the state law that no coin would be honored by banks except the hexagonal slugs issued by John Moffatt from his private mint at Mt. Ophir near Frémont's place at Bear Valley. John Moffatt had the whole Lode in the palm of his hand now. President Taylor had appointed him last year as United States Assayer of California, and he controlled the money.

The government promised a mint in San Francisco but nothing happened. The Philadelphia mint in the States was against it, so John Moffatt went right on.

Thought of the Philadelphia mint brought Charles up short as his mind went back to the day he had swaggered into the damned place with his load of gold.

How far away those days were now, with Charles Morgan back, poor as a crow and grubbing; Artemus rotting in an unmarked grave, and God alone knowing where good, loving Maria had gone.

The lid was off in Columbia on the Fourth of July! Charles and Anne forgot their meager larder of beans and salt pork that hot Sunday morning and took the boys uptown to see the doings.

The main street was thronged with thousands of people from recently burned-out Sonora and the neighboring camps.

The little chaps were delighted to see two or three other children—girls in calico pinafores and pantalettes, and red-faced boys in tight pants and straw hats—waiting for the parade to start. They talked of the last Fourth at Sonora.

Mexicans sold "dulcies," native sweets tied in cornhusks so they looked like great chains of beads.

It was hard for Charles to refuse his boys this treat when every other child's mouth was ringed with stickiness; there was a pinch in his heart too, as Anne looked at the scattering of other women who lined the street. Mrs. Dr. Gunn from Sonora stood not far away in a fine-figured blue silk dress, and a dozen women beyond were fixed up fancy, while his poor wife must be satisfied with her calico all patched under the arms.

And then of a sudden Charles stopped feeling sorry for Anne. If she'd stayed back in Pennsylvania where she belonged she could have been wearing a silk dress, his children wouldn't be longing for sweets and there would be no worry about the price of food!

Anne was no longer his sweet warm love when he took her into his arms of a night. A love-up now to her was just something that went with a home and family—another wifely chore. The greed for gold and the struggle had done that to the Morgans. He thought of Maria and the nights of love with her down on the Stanislaus.

The procession went by with the Hibernians carrying the green flag and the band all blowing and puffing off key in the muckle of dust that their boots kicked up. Folks cheered and turned in behind.

At the amphitheater in the hills on the edge of town they all stopped. The crowd stood in the hot sun waiting for the ceremony of the day.

A skinny little chap, with buck teeth and his blond hair split down the middle and slicked with grease, read the Declaration of Independence in a reedy voice, then Jim Coffroth orated while folks mopped sweaty faces; finally the Catholic priest gave a brief benediction and the doings were over.

The crowd broke up. Dinner was to be served to the ladies at the church, organized that way most likely, Charles thought, so that a man could head for a saloon and a beer or two to slake his thirst after so much ranting. Anne shook her head when Charles asked if she was going to the church. "My shoes are terrible, and my clothes not fit to be among the others," she sighed. "I don't want any of them looking down on me. Besides, I didn't donate any of the food—just put the wild flowers on the tables. That's not enough to entitle me to eat expensive vittles others brought."

When dark came there was a treat that delighted the boys— Colonel Cavaneau shot off fireworks. That was no sooner over than the Masons tuned up their band and there was a grand ball at the new Loring House, with all thirty of the fine ladies of "first respectability" invited.

The Morgans watched through the door as men and the few women took hands for the first square dance. Three gallant men invited Anne in to dance, but she shook her head and said she'd only be a drab sparrow among peacocks.

In that moment the heart of Charles was near bursting with hurt as he thought of the days when he too had a bulging poke, and now his wife couldn't take her place amongst the rest.

He'd been too quick to condemn Anne. The woman had worked like a horse beside him; she'd saved and scrimped and hoped and worried, and tried to get her man into better things the very best way *she* knew. He thought of Maria's finery at Pine Log; of the buckles on the shoes and the dress. Maria at least had the joy of a beautiful possession—all her own.

Anne turned from looking at the dancers and said it was long past eleven and that was too late for the boys. They must home and to bed. A loud howl went up. Henry bawled like a calf, and Charley and Bill pulled away from their mother with sour faces.

High Water Bill turned up just then. He shoved a string of Mexican dulcies into their hands and, already tipsy himself, invited the lot for a drink or two in honor of Columbus or whoever had created Independence Day.

Anne shook her head and strode out with the boys, but Charles hung back. "I'll take a drink and follow," he called after her.

In the saloon, with the glow of two drinks running through his veins, he blurted out to Bill all the sorrow in him: the hard luck and skimping, and how bad it was for a man to see other men's wives all decked out fine and his own lass in calico with patches under the arms.

Bill ordered more drinks, then Charles didn't feel so bad. Maybe tomorrow the luck would change. Lots of prospectors worked to their last beans and then hit a nugget or two that fixed them up for life.

Suddenly Bill clapped Charles on the back. "I got a good idea, Morgan," he cried. "May I remind you, my good kind friend, that extra gold came into these paws of mine because I was robbed a while ago?" He paused, lifted his beer to the thick lips and waited.

" 'Sright," Charles managed.

"Blood money—that's what it was," High Water went on. "Not a God-damned pinch of it earned by sweat. We're goin' to spend the filthy stuff right now—tonight!" Together they reeled along the street to Knapp's store on the corner that was doing a land-office business with miners in from all the camps around. Bill roared for "Sew" Knapp, the proprietor himself. No one but the proprietor would do.

Finally, when Sewell got around to them, Bill demanded to see "The best doggone silk in the house. The silk that costs the most."

Knapp took down a bolt of purple watered silk and waited while Charles and Bill ran their grubby hands over the folds.

"How many yards for a dress?" Bill demanded.

"Round seven," Knapp told them.

"Then give me eight!" Bill roared. "What you waiting for? The second coming of Christ?"

With a knowing look, Knapp began to measure the stuff. "Listen, High Water, you can make just as good impression on a chippie with less expensive stuff. You better think this over," he said quietly.

"Ain't no chippie I want to bother with and I got nothing in my head to think with. Cut her off, will you? And to hell with the advice." Bill tossed his poke toward the shopkeeper and leaned against the counter for support as Knapp weighed out the gold.

The poke was plenty low when it was handed back. Charles objected a little through the fog in his brain, but Bill brushed aside all objections. He shoved the bundle under his arm and they walked out with great dignity and a little trouble with their feet, and across the street to the Long Tom to finish up what was left in the poke.

Charles didn't remember how he got home that night of July 4, 1852.

Anne was furious at him the next morning, all crumpled up on the floor asleep as she found him. But her eyes lighted up when he opened the bundle and she saw the beautiful purple watered silk that High Water Bill had sent her. Silk purchased by the labor of unknown hands.

At first the lass would have none of it. She'd walk all the way over to that Mexican Squabbletown and plump it right back into Bill's hands.

"You know you hate waste," Charles told her. "Bill's got no woman, and he doesn't want one. If you take it back, the rats and mice in his cabin will just chavel at the stuff and ruin it."

The thrifty lass relented then, and two Sundays later swished into the new Methodist church and sang like a bird for the Reverend Gibbons. After services the pastor congratulated Anne on having been "renewed in the spirit of the Lord."

CHAPTER 24

1852

CHARLES had his own renewal in the "spirit of the Lord" twelve days later when he was slugging at the claim and a man passing by told him Mrs. Williams had been "took with pains."

The heart of him near beat out with excitement when he heard for sure at the Long Tom that the doctor had gone up the hill to Mrs. Williams' house and women were there tuning up the stove for hot water.

Everybody in town was concerned over Mrs. Williams' "interesting condition" and had been for days. Miners who had never even caught sight of the lady had put money on her.

Down at Pine Log, the miners had a big stake up and kept abreast of the news of the lady's state of health through Wilson, the butcher, who took meat down to them.

Dan O'Connell from Springfield had gone on a three days' drunk after the Fourth of July because he'd had half a poke up that the celebration would bring the "little feller" out to see the doings, and Joel Levy, the German who had opened up a new shop on Main Street, had promised free saleratus for everybody's biscuits if the youngster came on the seventh and he won the pot. But July seventh had come and gone without results, so folks bought their own saleratus.

Williams, the lady's husband, was a decent *hombre*. He had given everybody a fair chance to bet. "How in thunder do I know when things can happen?" he cried. "Can be any time at all—but it's *got* to be July—that's all I know."

Anne was the crafty one. She had looked at Mrs. Williams as the lady, muffled in a long cape, was purchasing calico. Anne

166

shook her head and sniffed over anything sooner than the fifteenth. What do men know about such things anyway?

Charles had listened to his lass very carefully that night and then sashayed down to the Stage Driver's Retreat and bet two pinches that the baby would be born on the seventeenth day of July 1852. He'd not tell Anne, for she'd scold, but the pot was too big not to take a chance.

Now, here it was the night of the sixteenth and the doctor already at the Williams place! Charles was so filled with fidgets he couldn't stay in the shack. If only Mrs. Williams wouldn't cough or sneeze or do any other fool woman thing, he had a good chance to take the winnings.

Out in the cool of the night, he looked up to the light that squared from the cabin window and told the little twister to stay put "just a little time—just a few hours to please me," then in pay a Welshman would sing outside the cabin "until his throat busts."

Down on the Main Street everybody was atwitter. Horny sunbrowned miners exchanged sage views about birthings over foaming beers.

Tim Riley, who had money up for the twentieth, bet that nothing was happening. "Might be the woman's 'et beans and got a stomach-ache. Didn't every miner get bellyache from sour beans, and no baby to show for it either?"

Pat Doyle, who had his money up for the eighteenth, exhorted God and told the Virgin Mary to "hold up proceedings for the sake of America, the Irish and Tim Doyle in particular," then he took a double whisky to steady his nerves and help him wait until the eighteenth.

Midnight came—and still no glad news from the little lighted cabin. Charles went home and crawled in beside Anne. Could it be that fool women sometimes spent days at the job and the seventeenth would come and go and leave a Welshman in the cold and Doyle to win?

At ten the next morning news came: The doc was in to wet his whistle after a hard night's work. Mrs. Williams had given birth on the seventeenth of July!

Charles Morgan, who had wooed old Mother Nature with no avail on hot hillsides, was rewarded by the old girl now. Proudly and tipsily he sauntered home bearing ten pounds of gold in the poke he had won.

Anne looked up from ironing when he came in and asked him if he was sick, coming back so early in the morning. Then she smelled his breath. "You've been drinking again," she scolded. "Drinking up what should go into your children's mouths for food."

Then he gave her the poke and her eyes near bugged out of her head.

"I bet on the baby—only two pinches!" he cried. "Mrs. Williams gave birth on *my* date—the seventeenth of July and the first baby born in Columbia!"

What a day of rejoicing!

Anne put on her hat and went right to Wilson's butcher shop and bought a turkey for twelve whole dollars and potatoes and onions and dried fruit that they hadn't tasted in months. The lass even forgot her piety enough to drink a toast to the new, red, wiggling little soul that had brought them luck.

Anne made everybody scrub up, and she laid out clean clothes. With such a dinner—after days of beans with nothing but dripping for their bread and sometimes not even that—they would let the Lord see how grateful they were for blessings.

Then suddenly her eyes grew big and she turned on Charles like a she-wolf. "You got it gambling!" she yelled out. "Gambling's wicked. You might not have won and then where would we be?"

Charles could contain himself no longer. There was no satisfying the woman. He put his arm around her. "Anne, we've been gambling for a year now with Nature, but you don't call that gambling. You'd best take what the good Lord has sent us and stop quibbling about the way He sends it."

When the turkey was ready, and brown gravy thickened with flour, and steaming boiled onions to boot, they stood around the rough table covered with clean tea cloths. Big and little said the simple grace. "May the good Lord make us truly grateful for

what we are about to receive." Henry was on his box all ready
for business before the Amen had faded into the air, and Bill and
Charley not far behind.

After dinner, Charles told Anne about the secret promise he
had made all alone under the stars last night. A promise to sing
as only Welsh singers could sing—if Mrs. Williams would only
hold off her baby until one minute after midnight.

"We'll *all* go," Anne said. "We'll go after dusk when everything up on the hillside is quiet, and we'll sing her and the little
one to sleep."

"Henry can't carry a tune," Charley rowed. "Henry can't go.
He'll spoil everything."

"I can too!" Henry roared. "I can sing louder and better than
you." He lammed out and shot a fist into Charley's eye right
where he sat on the doorstep.

The eye was already black when the little troop went up the
hill in the starlight to sing. Anne carried a plate, with white turkey meat and dressing for the new mother. Henry was allowed to
knock on the door and hand it in, while the others sang softly
the tender lullabies that had come across the sea from Wales to the
first babe born in the gold diggings of Columbia.

CHAPTER 25

1852

CHARLES was discouraged. D. O. Mills's Tuolumne Water Works had opened up new opportunity, but there was only water enough for three hundred long-tom streams. The price of twelve dollars a day took all the dust he dug. His recent windfall meant six hundred dollars, but with flour a dollar a pound and the same for sugar, beans and coffee, the little pile had melted.

Even his boys were gold-greedy now. When he entered the shack one night after a bad day, Bill held out at least an ounce of dust—with the fever from it glistening in his eyes.

"Me and Charley's got us good diggings," he cried. "The keep at the Long Tom lets us have the sawdust from the floor for sweeping out the saloon mornings, and look what we get after we burn it. It's the gold they drop when they pay." Charley showed his share then, with a gold coin among the dust.

Charles glanced at the boy's face. "Where did you get the black eye?"

"Fighting the Chink," Charley said hotly. "He jumped our claim and was going to take the sawdust away from us—and everything. The dirty skunk!"

Charles winced. The boys had near as much as he for their work. What would his old granny in Wales say if she knew her great-grandsons in America were fighting Chinamen for a bit of sawdust from the floor of a pub?

"Does your mother know?" he asked, and thought of Anne's fine speech that day on the Pottsville slag heaps. "A few months in California and we'll be rich. Our boys will be gentlemen and will never have to turn their hands to work."

"Sure Mom knows," Charley put in. "She's proud of us. She thinks we're hustlers and bound to be rich someday."

Oh, God! Charles thought. What has gold done, to make Anne, the chapel woman, willing to have her boys sweep out a saloon to glean the glistening California curse?

"Well, you're *not* to go over that damned sawdust any more," he ordered. "We'll manage some way without that. Let the poor Chinaman have your claim. I'll lash you if I ever catch you at it again!" he finished, as Anne came in with the provisions.

The lass was full of excitement as she rattled pans to make supper. "Collins and Company over at Grass Valley are averaging a thousand dollars a day, Charles, from the ten stamps they run!" she cried.

The pull came after supper. Anne wanted to go to Grass Valley. It irked her to know that others were getting rich while the Morgans had to scrimp along.

"But we've no money for stamp mills!" Charles snapped. "Are you daft? At the rate the gold is coming out up there at Grass Valley, most likely it'll soon play out like Sullivan's Diggings and a dozen other places left barren and deserted."

She turned fair shrew then. "What's the matter with you? Other miners right in the gulches here are taking out twenty dollars a day! Men are standing in line at Wells, Fargo and Adams until eleven o'clock at night weighing in dust. But no Morgan's there!"

It was Saturday night when, usually, the tub was brought up to the fire and each boy "bottomed" ready for chapel services on Sunday. But tonight Anne whirled on her heels, took out her best brown broadcloth cape and clapped the fine feathered hat onto her head. "I'm going down at least to watch them turn in their gold. I suppose that's all I'll ever see," she said and left the shack.

The woman was crazed by gold! Charles was afraid for her. Drunken micks were always in a brawl of Saturday nights. With a heavy heart he followed her. He longed for love, for affection, for a real mating, instead of this constant thought of gold, gold, gold. He felt alone, helpless, unloved.

Anne was standing in her finery at D. O. Mills's, watching with eager eyes the wondrous scales that could weigh out forty thousand dollars' worth of gold at once. Her face was a study as she feasted her eyes on other men's riches, while the miners around her shoved and jostled and talked politics.

Then a fight broke out, because one man said that the country would go to hell if Pierce was elected. Anne's feathered hat was knocked off when a miner missed aim, and she was caught in the tangling mass.

Charles was going to wade through the sweating men and rescue her—then resentment interfered. Let her get out of it the best she could! He went outside and waited until she came out, then followed her home.

Once inside the shack, Anne didn't mention the fracas; just busied her hands trying to pull the battered hat back into shape.

As they walked through the bright sunlight to chapel in the morning, Anne was evidently sorry for her outburst. There was tenderness in her eyes when she spoke to him. "You're right, Charles," she said finally. "We might land at Grass Valley with no place to live, and not strike it. After all, here we have a shelter to live in and a stove too, when stoves are scarce and high priced. And there's chapel. God knows what goes on up in Grass Valley."

She slid her hand into his and squeezed it. "Forgive me, Charles, for what I said last night," she begged. "It just seems that when I think of all that gold you brought home to Pottsville and what I expected to get once we came out here, I turn sort of crazy when I hear about the gold other people find."

Then she said that surely in a town with forty-three faro banks and so many gamblers, God would help decent people. Their turn would come.

But by the time frost turned the leaves yellow and the first rain splattered, a panic had broken loose in the States and everything tightened up along the line because of an election year. Fillmore had tied up the money. Then the water came down so fast that the roads were almost impassable and lined with bodies of dead mules sacrificed in an effort to get food to the mines.

Rain bashed against the flimsy little shack with the fury of seven devils. It took all the efforts of Charles and the boys to keep enough wood gathered to feed the little black stove. But they were thankful they had a stove! Stoves were hard to get and many miners in shelters had to build fires on the floor. The Morgans had a door to their place too; many folks had nothing but a bullock hide over the opening.

Thousands of miners headed for San Francisco on foot or horseback, and word came that people were starving on the streets there.

No mule-team bells rang on the road. Money in the poke was gone now, but gold was not much good. Even the lucky miner who had picked up a twenty-nine-pound nugget in Experimental Gulch found little to spend it on. Major Solomon at the general store trusted Anne, along with a lot of others, for weeks; then one day Leary the constable auctioned off the fixtures and counter for debt and Solomon's was no more. There was little left on Knapp's shelves or Jackson's either, except hinges and bolts that folks couldn't eat.

One by one the restaurants and boardinghouses of Columbia closed, and the bakery ran out of the small loaves of barley bread that they had sold for a dollar each. It too shut up shop.

Few gay tunes tinkled out from the fandango houses. Vigil lights burned instead, and Mexicans fingered rosaries, for death seemed to stalk the streets where such a short time ago men had swaggered with pride. So many cases of smallpox broke out that the doctors were going night and day, and boxes containing the dead went up Boot Hill at the rate of two or three a week.

Liquor gave out in the saloons, so there were no more roistering Irishmen.

Everybody turned to his own form of comfort and pleadings. Chinese lighted punk before their idols in the dank-smelling rickety joss house at the north end of town, and burned up sheets of yellow prayers in a petition for food. The Methodist Reverend Gibbons called his flock to the tiny frame chapel and held forth for hours with prayers and exhortations for the wicked to repent of their sins. Twenty grizzled miners who never came into a church if the saloons were open joined forces with Christ.

Still the rain came down and no jingle from bells on mule teams.

Father Alaric came on his donkey from Sonora in the pouring rain to hear confessions and say a special Mass, and Big Anne, the town's most notorious prostitute walked in her bedraggled finery to confession.

Father Alaric was a wise one. He used his time well among Irishmen who could no longer buy liquor or spend their money on riotous living, and pointed out that Columbia needed a decent Catholic Church, instead of the makeshift affair that must be used now. Nuggets dropped into his hands from those who would placate the Lord.

Charles stood in the musty-smelling provision shop and watched Father Alaric at work; all the priest's visits long ago crowded into his mind to torture. Slowly he edged closer to the good father, then, in a lull when no one was around, he took a great breath and faced Alaric. "Father, you may have forgotten me. . . ." he managed.

The priest shook his head. "No, I've not forgotten you," he said sadly. "Maria's asked for too many prayers for you—the poor child."

The words cut into Charles and shame made his face hot. "Where is she?" he asked, without looking at the father.

"Do you think you have the right to know?"

"No! God knows I *don't.*" Charles groaned. "But that doesn't keep my heart from asking, does it?"

"I suppose not," the priest spoke softly with gentleness and understanding.

"You say she asks you to pray for me—then she didn't go back to Chile! " Charles looked into Alaric's face.

"No, she didn't go back to Chile."

Charles thought his heart would burst with the news. "She's—she's not in want?" he got out. "She has food?"

"She has food. The good God has seen to that."

There was a moment of silence as the men looked at each other, then Charles sighed. "When you see her, tell her Carlos thinks of her—" he paused—"and sends his love." He tried to plead with his eyes.

There was compassion in the priest's face. "No, Morgan," he said; "I'll tell her instead that you want her to know that you are trying to be a good husband and father." And he turned away.

Misery tortured Charles as he walked toward home in the driving rain. Damned old Alaric! Why couldn't he have told where Maria was? Maria loved her Carlos or she wouldn't be paying for prayers. He wanted Maria. There had been no luck, no real loving, since those happy days on the Stanislaus. He was disgusted, disheartened, lonely. He wanted to leave greedy Anne and her greedy boys to fight it out for their damned gold. There were other things in life besides the glittering stuff. But alas, he didn't have gold enough to go searching for his love—and what did he have to offer if he found her, but arms that the law said belonged to Anne?

Charles was frantic. For nearly six weeks they'd lived on barley porridge flavored with salt. One morning he took his six-shooter and Bill and Charley. They would come home with something to eat—or they wouldn't come home!

For Christmas there was tough stringy stewed coyote with juice thickened by barley, and the Morgans were thankful, so thankful that Anne made them all get down on their knees to thank God and bless His Holy Son. She reminded them that there were many with pokes full of gold who had nothing but barley porridge and some without anything at all. Then she sent Charley through the driving rain to Mrs. Williams and Mrs. De Moile with legs of the creature for a Christmas treat, and planned carefully how long her own family could live on what was left.

January 1853 and still no provisions worth mentioning had come in. Food was exhausted at Sonora; livery stables were selling barley that should feed animals! The last flour had sold at a dollar and a quarter a pound. Mokelumne Hill folks were starving until fifty poor persecuted Chinese coolies had gone over the mountains on roads that only a human could travel, braved rushing rivers where ferries couldn't operate, and come back from Stockton, each carrying a hundred pounds of supplies on his back! What they had brought was now being rationed and the camp saved.

Charles laid down his paper and thought about these poor ones. He remembered how many times he had read in copies of this same Stockton paper about the killing and burning out and hanging of "heathen Chinese." And now, without bribing, without extortion, the "heathens" had done this great act of sacrifice to save the lives of their persecutors. How long would folks remember their good deeds? he wondered. Perhaps until the next time a Chinaman found a sizable nugget?

That night the Morgans went back on their diet of barley porridge and not much of that—until the bells of the first mule team clanged into Columbia on January 26, 1853. When Anne heard the jangle, the lass who had been so brave, so full of courage and cheer through the dark days, broke down and sobbed like a child with joy.

CHAPTER 26

1853

As soon as the roads dried up enough to get provisions, miners came back to Columbia in droves, and Joaquin Murieta went on the rampage.

Gangs of his band darted like flies from one camp to another, killing men wholesale and robbing like fiends. Sometimes there would be as many as twenty whites killed at one camp in a night, then a jump and two or three camps attacked and robbed the next night, with the dead left all over the place! Posses of miners formed, but Joaquin was too clever for them. The whole Lode was terrified and men were fleeing in fear.

Governor Bigler, near crazed by the number of dead, offered a reward of one thousand dollars for the capture of Joaquin Murieta dead or alive. Notices went up on the trees in all the camps, and a description of the bandit came out in the papers, but the murder and robbing went right on.

The flats around Columbia didn't escape Joaquin and his men. Caleb Dorsey, the Harvard-educated sawmill man, had the spit frightened out of him, so High Water Bill said. Caleb had been over near Squabbletown sizing up some timber when some friendly Mexicans came up and talked to him. They asked Dorsey what was being done about the robber bands. Surely the Americans weren't going to let things ride as they were.

Dorsey had explained that everybody was after the leader and they'd get him.

One handsome chap shook his head then and said he didn't think they'd ever get Joaquin alive.

"Then we'll get him dead!" Dorsey had promised.

The next day the Harvard accent was knocked out of Dorsey. Joaquin vowed to put Dorsey on his list!

Hot on this, word had come underground to McCrae, Dorsey's partner who ran the store and was banker for the miners, that Joaquin intended to attack on a certain night. McCrae sent a rider to Columbia for reinforcements with plenty of ammunition, so they would be ready for the robbers.

"You should'a seen them," High Water told Charles. "They cleaned their revolvers and rifles and loaded 'em and decorated their hats with patriotic feathers. They dragged the little brass cannon with 'em too, and shot her off every hundred yards until they got to McCrae's. The Columbia Guard will be ready for Murieta and they'll take him dead or alive!"

They had a few drinks at McCrae's while they waited, then a few more drinks and some eatables, until they cleaned out Mc-Crae's liquor and vittles—but Joaquin didn't come. McCrae said he didn't know but what he'd rather take his chances with the robber band than be eaten out of the place by a lot of roistering drunks for nothing but moral support.

Worry over Joaquin Murieta dampened a little the ardor of Columbia Hook and Ladder Company Number One, but they went on with plans for the grand Inaugural Ball in honor of President Pierce. Only Americans who could vote, and their wives, were invited to the ball. Printed invitations went out to all the "American ladies and gentlemen of prominence" in camps around, and the great day neared.

Champagne by the case came up the mud-rutted roads along with special delicacies that the Frenchmen around Columbia called by the name of "horses d'oovre." Not a bite to the things, but they would impress the ladies. There were good sound ham sandwiches for them that "liked to sink their teeth into solid vittles."

Everybody was excited. Doc Hildreth lent his picture of George Washington to hang in the ballroom. James Coffroth brought in his American flag. Some others fetched the French tricolor and the Union Jack in grubby hands and couldn't understand why their loans were refused. The room was a riot of color with streamers of red cotton and blue that night, when Tibby's Band struck up the Grand March.

Charles and Anne and the boys looked through the open doorway and the front windows, along with other "foreigners," as nearly fifty gaily dressed ladies danced the polka with their partners.

Anne turned to Charles. "I wish I was American." She sighed. "The tunes are gay—and I have my purple silk this time." Then her head went up. "Bill and Henry and Charley are Americans. Maybe someday *they* can dance at a President's ball."

But while the ball was going on and the horses d'oovre were shoved down gullets along with champagne at Columbia, Joaquin was killing faster than ever. During the next few days people were terrified. The State Legislature passed an act for the purpose of capturing Joaquin and his men, and also offered a reward for breaking up the number of horse thieves that were infesting the country. The matter was for soldiers; ordinary men were powerless. Captain Love and his Texas Rangers had volunteered, and were already after Joaquin.

Folks breathed more easily now that something real was being done. But let the papers come out and there was a line waiting to hear the news.

Anne only sniffed at that. "I think they want the papers so they can read all about the wild actress woman, Lola Montez, that's just come to San Francisco from Paris and New York. She's been mistress to half the men in Europe and brags about it —the brazen creature."

The hussy had let it get out even in San Francisco papers right after she landed, that five hundred men in Paris had offered her one hundred francs each, making ten thousand francs for one evening's entertainment. But she didn't tell what the entertainment was!

As he left the saloon late one afternoon in June, Charles Morgan's feet dragged. He thought of Lola Montez making money hand over fist—pretty clothes, everything she wanted—all because she could stir men's passions with her spider dances. There was his own lass old at thirty-one from hardship and worry. All he had been able to give her was a new iron washtub that she had begged for. Anne was still a bonny lass with plenty of spirit to her, but the soft girlish ways were gone. Sometimes she turned fair shrew because luck had not come to her man.

But he was no young fellow himself now. He realized his thirty-three years only too well when he remembered how many rockers he used to wash in a day. Now he could only do half as many and tired was his name. There was young Bill at ten and there was Charley too, no longer in school more than half the time because they had to do chores and run errands for others to help out with their keep. Should he be proud because Bill at ten could chop up a neighbor's woodpile in a day? California and the greed for gold had done this for the Morgans in the last five years.

He looked down at his faded blue denim pants with patch sewn upon patch. He was a lone man with only hands and pick and shovel against quartz-mining companies and their stamp machines grinding out gold at a great rate. What did he have to look forward to? Would to God Anne had been satisfied!

That night as Charles read the paper, the editor of the *Gazette* rubbed salt into his wounds.

Every miner who came to this country in '49 or '50 can now look back and see hundreds of instances where he could have made a fortune had he contented himself to remain where he was instead of going in search of Golden Lakes or Golden Cliffs.

Quick pictures went through his mind as he laid the paper down. Maria? The claim at Pine Log? Money on him going out—but no cheese factory. Poverty Hill? Artemus?

When Fourth of July rolled around, Charles was too discouraged to go to the supper at the Loring House. He didn't want to see the parade either and stand in the sun while everybody around bragged about how much they weighed in on Saturday night. He didn't want to listen to Jim Coffroth rattle his windpipes in any fine speech. To hell with California's hot dry hillsides, and to America too! It would have been better in Wales where hills were at least green in summer. Now he didn't even have the price to get back to the coal mines of Pennsylvania.

Anne had an idea. Why didn't they leave the boys in Columbia for the day, to see the celebration? They would go by stage to Jimtown, then walk over the hills to Poverty Hill and see what was doing in their old home. The change would do him good. There had been quite a find there, and Simmons would be able to tell them all about it.

CHAPTER 27

1853

CHARLES was pleased to see Anne merry-eyed as she had been in the old days, while she tied up their nooning in a paper bundle and gave the boys instructions about what they could do and what they must not do unless they wanted their bottoms warmed when she got home. Then she slipped into a clean calico, put on her sunbonnet, and they were off.

The new-style Concord coach was comfortable as a cradle, swinging gently from side to side over the bumps. There were cool smooth seats and a good smell of leather.

Anne moved closer to Charles. "I feel like a grand princess on holiday! I'm glad everybody else is celebrating the Fourth and we have a carriage all to ourselves."

When Jim Johnston let them off at Jimtown and they struck over the hills afoot, Charles talked out what had been bothering him. "I'm tired of coyoting around in the red dirt, Anne, and getting so little," he told her. "We've got to think of Bill and Charley and young Henry, almost seven years old now."

He thought perhaps it would be better for him to go to San Francisco and look for work. The place was picking up some, and there were bound to be jobs he could do. He had seen by the papers that laborers in San Francisco were striking for higher wages.

Anne listened to his arguments and with a wicked twinkle in her eyes she chided him. "Are you sure you don't want to get down there to see Lola Montez do her spider dance?" They laughed together like youngsters over her great joke as they plowed along the dusty road.

Then she turned serious. They had better stick together. She'd like to get out of Columbia and its wickedness for the boys' sake, but San Francisco was no place for folks with a family. She had talked to some men from Placerville. Philip Armour, the butcher there, had made lots of money and was planning on going into the packing business for himself, and John Studebaker, the blacksmith at Placerville, was hauling in a fortune, building miners' wheelbarrows.

"Folks don't have to *dig* for gold," she told him. "They can get it other ways, if they know what miners want."

Charles, discouraged as he was, had a mad desire to remind her of the cheese factory, but that would only spoil the lass's holiday.

Poverty Hill startled them. It had grown into a large camp, with stamps of quartz mills banging out their salute to the Fourth of July, and bunkers piled high with crushed rock waiting to be washed out when the rains came. Simmons was jogging along as usual. He hadn't made enough yet for a Rhoades machine.

A stout ruddy-faced woman stood in the doorway of the old Morgan cabin, with two children clinging to her skirts. She told Charles her husband worked for a quartz outfit, and asked them in for a cup of coffee when she found he had built the cabin.

Afterward they walked down the main road and stopped in at a provision tent, open on the chance of business when miners came back from celebrating in Sonora or Jimtown.

Dutchman Joe told them trade was brisk. He'd done well enough in his tent shop. "But hard luck's dogged me," he sighed. "I married a Mexican girl and she ran off with a monte dealer. I got money, sure, but I'm lonesome without no woman, and I get homesick for my folks in Germany."

Anne seemed to like the chap. She chattered about the shop and provisions he sold; nosed right into his affairs and embarrassed Charles when she asked so many questions. Joe was good-natured and evidently flattered by the attentions of a pretty woman.

Then the lass shot her bolt. "You want to sell your store?"

The yellow head nodded slowly.

"How much do you want—in gold?" Anne asked.

Charles felt his blood come up in anger. Why did the woman want to plague a man, to give him hope only to dash that hope in the next minute? Here was his own woman talking about the price of a provision shop, when the Morgans had to count every pinch of gold for the food they put into their mouths.

He tugged impatiently at her sleeve. "Come, don't make the man daft with homesickness by your bait," he scolded.

But Anne pulled away and listened to Dutchman Joe's broken English. For two hundred ounces any man in the State of California could have the shop, lock, stock and barrel, and be damned to it!

When they left the place, Anne said she was tired and wanted to sit down in the shade to rest; evidently Germans didn't ask women to sit down.

They found an oak with branches so gnarled that it had escaped the ax. Sitting in the shade was good. Anne took off her calico sunbonnet and mopped her brow. "Joe sure charges all the traffic will bear for his old beans and sowbelly and matches." She sighed. "But quartz miners seem glad to pay and save the time it takes to go to Sonora or Jimtown."

"What's it to us?"

"We're going to buy his place," Anne said. "That's what it is to us."

"You're sun-struck!" he shouted. "Where in heaven or hell do you think the poverty-stricken Morgans could rake up two hundred ounces of gold to pay for any damned store?" The woman was talking like a whisky bloat in his cups.

"It's not a *damned* store!" she snapped. "What would the Reverend Gibbons say to you blaspheming like this?"

She stood up, shook herself a bit then pulled up all her petticoats higher than a kite, right there under the tree in broad daylight, and unfastened a tape from around her waist. Three heavy canvas bags made a dull thud on the carpet of oak leaves. After she had righted her skirts, Anne put the pokes into his hands.

The weight of gold took the wind out of him. "Wherever did you get it?" he demanded.

"It's mine, Charles," she said softly. "Earned from months of washing the fancy, frilled white shirts of gamblers at five dollars each. Take it and buy the Dutchman's store, so we can live happy and not be afraid any more."

No words would come in his throat. Charles looked at the gold and then up at Anne and a great wave of love and pride and gratitude raced through him. Suddenly he grabbed her red work-worn hands and smoothed them. "God bless you," he managed. "What else can a man say?"

She pulled her hands away; ruffled up his hair a bit. "There's nought needed to be said," she told him. "Let's off and give the stuff to Dutchman Joe."

By sundown the deal was complete, and they started back to Jimtown for the stagecoach. Anne was happy as a lark. Didn't he, the silly lout, even suspect why she wanted the new tub? A woman was a good miner when she had a washtub and plenty of men around wearing fancy frilled shirts, while her man was off on his claim.

Then she told him how the whole thing was managed. She couldn't trust Charley and Henry to keep their mouths shut. But young Bill was in on the secret. He went to the gamblers and fetched the shirts and took them home too. Bill was proud to be such a fine businessman and bring back the money.

Charles squeezed her hand. "Running in competition to the Chinaman, aren't you?" he chided.

"But the gamblers like *my* shirts best," Anne told him with pride. She saw no joke, the serious one. "I put in plenty of starch and they stay clean longer." Then she laughed and said probably the buying of Dutchman Joe's was the best use ever put to gambler's money in California.

Charles and Anne were well established in Dutchman Joe's store at Poverty Hill on the sixth of August, when two miners brought the paper over from Jimtown and there was bedlam.

Captain Love and his Rangers had finally caught up with Joaquin Murieta! They had met the robber chief and his gang and after a desperate battle Joaquin and one of his henchmen were

killed. Murieta was past trickery now! His head had been cut
off, along with the hand of Three-Fingered Jack, and put in
whisky. Captain Love was on his way to Sacramento with the
trophies to claim the reward.

In a small space on an unimportant page of the paper there was
a note that Lola Montez had a fight with her new husband after
her appearance in Marysville, and the citizens had voted to boy-
cott her. She was now rusticating in Grass Valley. Joaquin Murieta's head had stolen the show from Lola and her spider dance.

The lid was off! Every miner in Poverty Hill diggings got
drunk to celebrate the beheading of Joaquin Murieta. Tipsy,
they came in to buy every delicacy on the Morgan shelves. Business was so brisk that Bill and Charley had to help wait on trade,
and young Henry was set to mind the food cooking on the stove
in the back room where they lived.

When things had quieted down and Charles had his shoes off to
rest his feet after supper, he chaffed Anne. "First and last the
Morgans have done well on Murieta. You have your purple watered silk because of him and see what business his head has
brought us today."

CHAPTER 28

1853-1854

OCTOBER came, and still Joaquin Murieta and Lola Montez were racing for attention from gentlemen of the press. Joaquin's head was exhibited at a dollar a look now, along with the hand of Three-Fingered Jack.

"Can't exactly call it a neck-to-neck race," Simmons told Charles when the papers came in and they scanned the headlines. "Lola has the edge on Joaquin with them legs of hers and the spider dance and him with only a dead head to offer."

Lola *had* streaked to a lead. She had fought with her husband in Grass Valley and thrown him downstairs. A minister had denounced her sexy spider dance from the pulpit. Then Lola, with her tame bear on a leash, had hunted out the parson and danced for him. In no time flat she had converted the sky pilot. After seeing her, he thought Lola "a study of beauty and grace" and said so publicly.

Anne was annoyed as the two men read the piece and laughed over the weakness of men, be they of the flannel shirt or the cloth.

She ripped into them for deriding ministers. "Where would folks be without spiritual advisers?" she demanded fiercely.

"To hell with the damned parsons and them knowing *everything* spiritually!" Simmons came back. Then he told about a Chinese woman working the tailings of a claim next to his, when the tax collector came. She had refused to pay, saying she was no man. The collector said how did he know? She was wearing pants. She told him to go ask the parson. "He knows for sure that I'm a woman."

"You and your spiritual parsons!" he finished, and slatted out of the shop.

Charles sighed and went to weighing sugar. Anne was a great crusader for the church and there was no use arguing. To her there was no gray in a man—just black in sin or white in the church. God! If only she knew what her own man had done at Pine Log when he had been happiest in all his life!

And yet even now as he was condemning her, if it hadn't been for Anne's willing hands at the washtub, he, Charles Morgan would not be weighing sugar in a store. They would have no old nag to bring provisions from Sonora—or to take her to church on Sundays.

Only last Sunday she had come back all aglow. The Good Lord was slowly winning the fight against sin! Gamblers at Columbia had now to pay a tax of fifty cents for every game they dealt, and the Temperance movement was coming on fine. Fifty of Columbia's best citizens had signed the pledge. God was in the Mother Lode fighting the Devil tooth and nail.

Charles thought the little Temperance band had its work cut out to change the taste of twenty thousand miners around Columbia from Bixel's beer or whisky to water, but he let the woman have her happiness.

By January there were forty thousand miners on the flats and in the gulches around Columbia for the pious ones like Anne to work on.

Marquita now had "Marquita's Big White House" up on the hill away from the "Blue and Gold Saloon." At seventeen she had created a sensation by importing the first "real blonde" girls for the miners' delight. There was a golden-haired Danish girl, and a Swede and a blue-eyed German doll. The camp went wild over them. When Charles hit town for supplies, that was all he heard about.

High Water Bill came over to visit and he told them that on Saturday nights after miners had weighed in their gold, they stood in line a block long waiting to be charmed by the blondes at Marquita's, but church folks were doing their best at Saturday night choir practice.

"They sure whoop and holler out the hallelujahs so's the men waiting to get into Marquita's place can't help but hear them. 'Most drowned out the fandango music too, with them 'Cling to the Lord' songs."

Then he told how waiting miners plagued the choristers as they walked home from practice; leathery throats, used to cussing and roaring all week on the hillsides, tuned up for sure on Saturday night with the "Hangtown Gals."

> "To church they seldom venture,
> Hoops so large they cannot enter.
> Go it, lass! You're young and tender;
> Show the pick and shovel gender."

Anne turned on Bill like a hornet then and asked him if he had a Bible.

"Sure I have." He chuckled and watched her face. "The leather binding is good for sharpening razors."

Anne's face was livid at his teasing. "You should *read* it, you sinner!" she stormed. "It's men like you keep the Devil busy."

High Water told her that she was prettier than ever when she got mad, and that the Bible was "too danged personal" for him to read.

Charles sighed and thought of High Water's way of doing the Lord's work. Hadn't the parson himself congratulated Anne on being "renewed in the spirit of the Lord" that first Sunday she had worn the purple dress to chapel? There was some great and good power at work in the rough miner who never read his Bible and went on a toot every Saturday night of his life.

Early one morning in July, nearly a year after they had arrived in Poverty Hill, Anne had her innings with sin. Hot wind brought a pall of black smoke over the ridge so thick that it obscured the sun. Miners raced for their horses, and the few women stood with their arms wrapped in their aprons and watched the great clouds rolling from the north.

At noon word reached them. Columbia had gone up in smoke! Columbia, the proud wild town, was no more because of carelessness in a bakery. Hook-and-ladder boys had done their best, and been glad for the willing hands of despised "foreigners," but there was too much wind.

Anne went on her knees, there in the store, and pulled Charles down beside her. She thanked God that the Morgans had not been burned out and were safe.

When she was on her feet again there were tears in her eyes. "You see? It's a visitation of the Lord!" she told Charles. "God takes care of his own. We might have been burned out along with the gamblers and fancy women and saloons."

"Then how do you Temperance folks account for Bixel's Brewery being saved?" Charles asked. For answer she went out and slammed the door.

That night Anne cooked extra beans and loaded provisions ready in the wagon, for the sufferers at Columbia. There were blue denim pants and calico for dresses they would need, pots and pans and flour, and canvas for a shelter over burned-out ones. Before dawn she was off with the wagon and Bill and Charley to help where they were needed.

There were great tales when the tired ones came back late that night. Bill and Charley wanted their father to see through their eyes everything they had seen. There was no stopping up the young ones' mouths, not even with fresh meat just brought in by the butcher.

When they arrived in Columbia, shacks were already up on the ashes. Wells, Fargo and Company and Mills's were open for business.

On every smouldering lot men were busy with saws and hammers on boards rushed over from the sawmills around Springfield, but they vowed that everything put up permanently after this would be brick—and fireproof.

Chinamen had squealed and chattered excitedly as they poked

among the ruins of their hovels, and Bill told of petting a yellow
dog that had been tied with a rope to a hitching post and sat on
his haunches howling. Charley had picked up some little terra-
cotta thimbles that Chinks used for shipping opium, but he had
given them to a Chinaman.

"You should have seen our mom," Charley put in. "We lugged
in our beans, and Mom, she rolled up her sleeves and went to work
along with the rest. And she gave Marquita a plateful too, and
Marquita thanked her and was grateful."

Then Bill told how Mom had said the boys were to go out
and help anyone that needed a hand, but they mustn't take any
pay for it because it was the Lord's work and she'd warm their
bottoms good if she caught them taking even a pinch of gold from
any poor sufferer with no home to his name.

Charley began to wiggle then and eyed his father.

Anne washed up the dishes, and Bill wiped. Charles cut a chew
from his plug and settled back.

But there was no settling back. Charley came up and insisted
that his father must put on his shoes and take a turn around camp.
No talk of being tired satisfied the lad, and Charles sensed something wrong.

When they were out alone under the stars, the murder came
out. Charley had been helping a woman fix a shelter for her sick
husband and children, when a pretty dark lady in a black silk
dress had come up. The lady had watched him for a long time,
and then, when he went to fetch some more nails that people from
Sonora had brought, she stopped him.

"I've been watching you," she said. "You are a good boy. You
look like the son of Carlos Morgan should look."

"Then I said I *was* Charley Morgan, and she said, 'Yes, so Mr.
Knapp, the storekeeper, told me.' With that, Father, she put her
hand into the pocket of her skirt and pulled out a nugget and put
it into my hand—a big nugget!

"I told her we weren't burned out, that we lived at Poverty
Hill and had just come to help," the excited boy told Charles.
"But she didn't pay any attention. She wouldn't take it back!"

The heart of Charles near burst through his shirt. He was glad of the covering darkness; glad his son couldn't see the excitement in him.

"And—and then what?" he managed to say.

"She said for me just to keep it and give it to my father sometime when he was discouraged in his mind and needed a treat. She said you'd understand, and then she hurried away like anything."

Charley put the nugget, a big heavy fellow, in Charles's hand. "But I was afraid to tell Mom. She said she'd lick us if we took anything when we were doing the Lord's work. The lady was pretty and she looked at me such a long time. Who was she, Dad?"

Who was she? The very blood of him warmed with quick passion at the thought of Maria's quivering ivory softness in the bough bed with him at Pine Log.

His fingers tightened around the nugget. "Charley," he said softly, "there are so many things in the world we don't understand, and women is among 'em. Maybe the lady just wished she had a fine son like you and wanted me to know, and that's the reason she sent the nugget. I'll always keep it as a pocket piece to remind me that a good son is better than any nugget a man can ever find."

They walked back through the soft night air in silence. Before he opened the door Charles turned to his son. "I think we'd best not tell your mother, Charley. She wouldn't understand."

CHAPTER 29

1854

JULY and August were the hottest Charles had ever known on the scorching hillsides. Men working their claims were fair fagged out by noon.

Bixel's schooners were more in demand than ever and as the miners downed beer, they grumbled with dissatisfaction. There was only enough water to supply a fraction of the men who wanted to work, and the capitalists were getting rich on what they sold.

Another thing bothered men "grubbing up" at Morgan's. A new method of mining had developed up north where there was more water. Hydraulic mining, they called it. "They have a big gush of water from a hose and wash away whole banks!" a miner told Anne and Charles. "Companies are forming to buy the hoses and wash mountains away. Where's the little pick-and-shovel miner coming out now?" He shoved back his hat and waited for an answer.

Charles shook his head.

The miner was a dreary fellow. What was the use of building the fine fireproof, brick buildings in Columbia like Sewell Knapp and Jackson were putting up? Knapp and them sold to the little miners; but when these big companies with money came in, they hired miners at day's wages and had their own company stores where they sold cheaper. Where was the merchant who had to sell for more to make his living?

Charles saw Anne's eyes grow big at the news, and he knew she was thinking of their own fine little business in Poverty Hill and the money she was laying away nights after the place was closed.

"Oh, I don't think we have to worry over hydraulics yet a while," Charles answered. "After all they've got to have water first. The hydraulics are up north where the finds aren't so rich anyway."

"That's it, hide your head under a barrel of flour!" the miner roared. Then he told them the curse was right over the hill at Sonora, and had been used to wash out Chinks, "cribs," shacks and all, and folks had panned the gold. The Chinks had gone! "Squealing like hell."

"Good!" Anne put in. "Now our men won't be tempted any more with the horrible sin those Chinese girls have brought in." She went into a long harangue about Chinese bad women spreading disease all over California.

Charles was astounded at Anne's cruelty. So kind she was, and faithful to her church, yet over it all greedy for gold as the greediest miner in the diggings; there was no give to her when it came to sin. His heart went out to the poor little Chinese concubines; half-starved wandering souls in a wilderness of cruelty.

He felt of the nugget in his pocket and thought of his own sins. He had traveled a long way from his Lord now, but he couldn't let such cruelty go unchallenged. He laid his hand on the lass's shoulder as she stood beside him at the counter.

"Don't put it into words, Anne," he begged. "The good Lord created them too, poor things, with souls and yearnings and hopes the same as he made you. The Chinese girls are no worse than the others, perhaps not as bad. Maybe it's the men who own them get the gains from their bodies."

With that she flared up, and accused him of going to the Chinese girls, "or Marquita's—only you wouldn't be dressed fine enough for *her!*" she ranted. "It always takes you a powerful long time to fetch things when you go to town."

"That ought to hold you, pard," the miner chided. Then he advised Charles to dress up and try Marquita's. Her girls were "hummers." "'Twould be an education to a man with a wife that trounces him so hard."

Anne banged down the dozen candles she had been counting out. "You red-headed Irishman, take your candles and get out," she ordered. "No one here is seeking your advice."

The miner winked at Charles, took up his candles and hummed the funeral march as he went out. But the door had scarce closed on his blue behind before he was back.

"The whole place is afire!" he shouted. "She's coming this way, and things dry as hell! Get what you can." Without stopping, he shouldered a sack of flour and tore out.

"The money!" Anne screamed to Charles as a roar and terrifying crackle hit their ears. "Charley! Bill! Henry!"

Smoke poured into the place and near choked them. Charles ran from the flimsy frame shelter with their hoard in the box and passed the boys lugging chunks of sowbelly to safety out on the flat. "You stay here, Henry!" he ordered as he set the box down and raced back. "Looters! Don't leave it."

Anne passed him, stumbling through the biting smoke, with her apron full.

Shack after shack was catching fire! Embers were floating everywhere in the wind. Charles heard men shout above the crackle and the crash of tumbling wood, as he ran back into the shop and groped blindly in the smoke for canvas.

Charley was coughing behind him. "Here, give me a heave," he yelled, as a wave of heat came and the canvas back of the place flared up like a great candle.

Anne was dragging blankets out. "Get the clothes!" she shrieked to Bill.

There was a crackle above, a board gave way and crashed. The roof was aflame! There was no more going back into the place now.

Thin tongues of yellow were racing in the dry grass toward the stuff they had saved. Henry was beating them back with his shirt. Anne darted toward him.

"Be careful of your calico dress," Charles yelled through the smoke. "It'll catch sure as hell!" But she paid no attention.

All of them fought then, in a circle with backs to the things they had saved, as the flames rushed toward them. Charles shoveled dirt with a shovel he had caught up as he ran out of the place. Bill and Charley swatted the grass with their shirts and Anne had a blanket. When things were safe and they looked up, the wicked red was licking grass on the hillside beyond, leaving its trail of desolate black. They stood panting, with blackened sweat running from their faces, and watched the two-by-fours collapse and fall into what had once been Dutchman Joe's store. Every shack and cabin in Poverty Hill was gone.

Charles saw Anne wave her blistered black hands to cool the burning. He reached down and cut off a chunk of sowbelly with his pocket knife.

"Here, rub it on. The grease will keep out the air," he said helplessly.

The poor lass did as she was told, then brushed back her straggling sweat-wetted hair and looked at the pathetic heap at her feet: canvas, beans, some flour, a fry pan and blankets. She reached under the pile and pulled out the purple silk dress and brown broadcloth cape he had bought for her in Philadelphia. The metal fastener jangled when she pulled, as if the fine jeweled bit would mock a woman on the blackened hillsides of California.

"Well," she said, as she shook the cape, "we're better off than a lot of folks. We have our money and enough canvas to shelter us and some food."

Charles closed his knife. When he dropped it into his pocket there was a clink as it hit the nugget Charley had brought home from "the pretty lady" who knew he would "understand."

He wondered how Anne felt about "visitations of the Lord" on the wicked now?

That night when cold crept across the flat, Anne cooked beans over a campfire for some of the burned-out ones. Simmons brought the coffee he had saved, and a dozen other rough men handed over what they had.

As they sat eating in the acrid-smelling dusk, each thought aloud and planned. Five or six would "pull their freight" to another diggings. Poverty Hill was no damned good anyway. Simmons vowed he'd stay on and build him another shack, and someday by God he'd take out enough for a stamp machine.

Anne talked about the poor Italian who had only the week before begged for a grubstake from their store, and the next day found a lump of pure gold that weighed twenty-seven pounds. It brought him four thousand, two hundred and twenty dollars! She thought now was the time for the Morgans to pull up stakes and really go after gold.

But Charles shook his head—Morgans were just not lucky on claims. Their way lay not in chance but in day-by-day labor. They still had the horse and wagon and canvas enough for a new roof, and money to start up shop again. They'd best stick to what they had. The miners staying on then gave the Morgans three cheers and promised business, and they all rolled up in blankets under the stars.

As Charles was drifting off to sleep, he heard the mournful wail of a coyote far up in the hills and thought of the old days here in the brush shelter with Artemus.

At dawn he and the boys measured for lumber to hold together the new tent, while Anne cooked flapjacks and sowbelly, and by midmorning, Charles was in the wagon on his way to Jamestown for lumber and provisions for Morgan's new shop.

The next day as Anne held the canvas while he nailed it to the pitchy-smelling new yellow-pine frame, the lass was very quiet. When Bill and Charley and young Henry had gone on some errand of their own, she spoke.

"Charles, I'm—I'm very sorry for what I said about things yesterday. And I'm sorry I accused you of going in to see the Chinese fancy girls," she told him. "You've been a good husband to me and patient too. You were right. The good Lord made us all, good and bad. Maybe it took a fire for me to remember——" She handed him up some more nails in bleeding grubby fingers. "And Charles . . ." she hesitated.

"Yes, lass?"

"I'm sorry we didn't stay in Pottsville and have the cheese factory like you wanted. We'd have been better off and never would have known about Chinese girls and the gamblers and everything out here. The boys would have had green hills in summer to play on instead of burned-out blackened hillsides. They wouldn't have known about the little earthen thimbles that opium comes in."

"Perhaps not," he comforted, "but if it's the wickedness you're thinking of saving them, just remember there's sin, as you call it, the world over."

"I wish we had enough to go back." She sighed. "The slag heaps would look good to me now."

"If wishes were horses, then beggars would ride," he told her, and thought how often his old granny in Wales had said the words to him when he was a young lad ayearning. "Now we've got to make the best of a bad job and have such a good shop that all the miners will trade at Morgan's place."

Morgan's place prospered. The miners kept their word and stuck by the Welshman, and the box under the bed was just beginning to fill up some when a muckle of rich finds made the gold fever flare up again in Anne.

When news was shouted out in the Stockton paper that Mr. Noyes, the agent of Adams and Company in Stockton, was showing a nugget of one hundred and sixty-one *pounds*, she was fair crazed.

"*One hundred and sixty-one pounds!*" she bawled at Charles. "That's twenty-five thousand and seventy-six ounces. It'll bring over twenty-eight thousand dollars! One nugget like that and we could be out of here forever."

She put down the paper and stood up before him, her hands on the faded calico hips. Her mouth was set, her eyes glittered. "Mr. Morgan, *you* may like to tend store, but I don't," she railed. "I'm sick of it. There's women working for themselves in the mines. I read about them in the paper. The water company up near Auburn even lets one woman there have free water. I'm going back to Columbia where there's gold. I'll get some too— before the hydraulics come in and wash everything out! You can go or you can stay here with your old store."

By the end of November the Morgans had moved into a shack at French Gulch just outside Columbia, where a discouraged Frenchman had given up his claim.

CHAPTER 30

1854–1855

ANNE was delighted to live on the edge of a metropolis. Her eyes were always bright when she came home from shopping and talked to Charles about what was going on, while he worked at the long tom and grumbled over paying twelve dollars a day for water.

Columbia was looking up, not just a gambling hell and a place for hussies to clean out pockets. There were ninety families, and a school. Law and order were being established so fast that there was no longer the need for a bell to summon miners from the hills for a hanging. The town had sold the bell to the church. Bells now meant "Come to church" when they rang.

For himself, Charles liked the new saloons with mahogany bars and fancy trimmings. It was wonderful to join his cronies on a Saturday night and look at the French paintings of nude women and the statues too, and see the gleaming glasses.

What a long way Columbia had come from the first day when the saloons had been whisky barrels and the drinks shoved over the barrelhead in tin mugs! Miners then didn't need nudes to whet their thirst. Now, the Pay Ore Saloon on the corner was a hummer to catch any miner's schooner or slug money, and it was doing a business fit to blow off a man's hat—in spite of the Sons of Temperance!

D. O. Mills's, the bankers, now had marble steps to welcome miners who came to leave their gold in safekeeping, and Wells, Fargo built a new red brick with a fine iron balcony brought all the way from Troy, New York.

Anne saw the sense of banks now. There had been so many robberies and so much gold stolen from cabins and miners' shacks in gulches that she was afraid for the money in their own box, nearly full now of their earnings and the money from selling the store. She was all for taking it over the marble steps to go into Mills's safe.

But High Water Bill was against Mills's. Weren't they the ones who had put money into the ditch, and now the damned bankers just turned a deaf ear and said they couldn't reduce the high-water rates?

"Adams is the place," he cried. "Adams is a fine man—all the miners trust Adams, and he ain't connected with no water deal."

Charles was against *any* bank. They didn't have enough to worry about, and most likely they'd have to dig into it anyway until the claim at French Gulch paid.

Anne set her jaw. They'd make the claim pay without touching the nest egg! She had earned the money for the store in the first place and it was *hers* to manage. Never again would the Morgans be stranded down to their last dollar.

One crisp December day, they walked together into Adams and Company and deposited their money, the first real bank account they had ever had in their lives. When they were out on the street again, Anne took Charles by the arm and smiled into his eyes. "Charles," she said, "with that as a backlog all safe, we'll go full steam ahead. The Morgans will never know want again. I feel it in my bones."

But Charles couldn't share Anne's hope and eagerness. The boys were out of school more than in, because their hands were needed to put more dirt through the rocker and make enough for grub and water rates.

Anne sang chapel songs while she papered the shack with old copies of the *Columbia Clipper,* or as she poured out elderberry syrup she made for their slapjacks. When Charles complained of the water rates, she told him that they would forget the price when they struck it rich and had fine things and could swish into the Oyster Parlor with the best folks—or when they were served dinner at the American Hotel like royalty.

One sunny spring morning, six months later, when Charles and Bill and Charley were slugging away at the long tom, for enough from the day's take to buy grub, bedlam broke loose on French Gulch. The Frenchies started talking fast and shouting in their own language. Then they threw down their picks and shovels and started running toward town.

"What you suppose is up?" Charley asked as he threw a shovelful of dirt into the tom. "The Parley-voos is sure excited."

Charles shrugged and went on with his pick work. A Frenchman had probably stabbed another over water or a claim. They were always getting excited about something.

Then he saw Anne running toward them over the loose gravel. Her face was white and pinched. "Charles, Bill, Charley," she panted as she stopped beside them. "A rider just came by. He says the bankers are closing—with attachments on the doors!" Then she started to cry. "Charles—our savings—our store money!"

"Oh, God!" he groaned, then, without stopping to put on his coat, he set off on a run toward town with Anne at his heels.

A man galloped past them on horseback. "Get your money out before all the damned banks bust!" he yelled. "They're still payin' in Columbia."

The trails were full of excited miners who had heard the news and dropped their picks and shovels. There was a stampede in Columbia. Hundreds of men milled around on Main Street. Wells, Fargo was still open and paying depositors and men jostled one another for place in line at Mills's.

But hundreds of sweaty, angry, red-shirted men stood cursing in the sun and battering at the closed doors of Adams and Company. "Give us our money!" they roared. "Give us our savings." But there was no response. The fireproof iron doors didn't move an inch.

Anne stood beside Charles in her faded blue calico. The sweat was running down her face, and life had gone out of her eyes. She picked at her fingernails.

"Damn you, give us our money," a great Irishman demanded of the door and kicked wildly at the iron. "If you don't we'll come in and *get* it!"

"Won't do no good to go in," a lantern-jawed Missourian drawled in a discouraged voice. "Brown, the Adams agent, just skipped out the back way with what was left and put it into the Tuolumne Water Company's safe."

Some of the frantic ones made a dash for the water office and the Morgans ran with them. They demanded that Robinson, of the Water Company, open the safe and give them their money.

Robinson shook his head. "I'm not authorized to pay anything out."

High Water Bill came up. He was crazy. All his years of work and sweat had gone. "Receiver!" he roared and banged his fist on the white paper posted on the Adams door. "Receiver of the money I grubbed for!" Then he turned away and headed back for Squabbletown.

Charles walked down Main Street with Anne beside him. Wells, Fargo was still meeting all demands. Someone said Daegner, the agent, had sent riders to San Francisco for money.

There was no use staying around. Silently discouraged men turned away from the place and started slowly back to their diggings. Charles and Anne joined the heavy-footed procession and cut across the hillside through fresh green grass that told of spring. Neither of them spoke. There was nothing to say. The money was gone and the hard scrabble must proceed if the Morgans were to eat and pay for water for the thirsty tom.

Just before they reached the shack, Anne sat down on a rock and cried. Her thin shoulders shook and the sobs cut into the heart of Charles. He could think of nothing for comfort. To cover up the hurt inside him, he whistled a bit, very low, an old tune his Granny had taught him in Wales.

Anne's head came up with a jerk; her eyes were fiery. "Have you no decency to you?" she cried. "This is no time for whistling! Besides, you flatted your G." She was up and off down the road, leaving him to take her dust.

CHAPTER 31

1855

MINERS without their savings to fall back upon turned rebellious against the damned capitalist bankers of the Tuolumne Water Company. Twelve dollars a day was too much to gamble when a man faced starvation! Twice, letters had been sent demanding reduction, but the Tuolumne stood pat. The amount received for water now only paid two per cent per month on the great cost of the ditch.

That two per cent stirred up the ire of men who sweated on the hillsides. "Two per cent a month—that's *twenty-four* per cent a year!" they shouted one to another.

"Miners—strike! Four dollars a day for water is enough!" The call went all along the streets of Columbia, over hills and into gulleys. "Strike, and put the damned water company where it belongs—in hell!"

Anne fair shoved Charles that night to Major Farnsworth's saloon where a meeting was to be held. "You've got to go or we'll likely starve," she told him.

As Charles dragged wearily over the hill, he wondered what a few miners could do against a great corporation? Too many times on the hillsides of California he had seen the weak fail in their fight against the strong.

But the threat of an empty belly made the men strong. No man was to work his claim unless water was reduced. All miners could register their unworked claims to protect them from jumpers.

"And put signs on claims—tombstones. 'Claim buried for the

season. Four dollars for water. No more!'" one chap shouted. There would be a black book kept with the name of any miner who broke faith with his fellow men.

The next morning church bells clanged. The cannon boomed.

Charles threw down his pick and headed into town. Every gulch and hillside spewed miners. The streets were a mass of angry determined men.

Senator Jim Coffroth, red faced and excited, made a proposition for his Stanislaus Water Company. Men out of employment and not able to work because of the water strike could leave their protected claims and work on the new ditch for four dollars a day in stock of the company, and they'd soon have cheap water. "If two hundred men will find provisions and tools for themselves we will begin work on Monday."

Charles signed up along with hundreds of eager men. The water war was on!

Beer flowed freely. Irishmen, Americans, Scotchmen, *Chilenos* and Frenchmen lifted glasses to the new ditch. "To cheap water! ... to bigger nuggets ... to more beer and stronger whisky"— anything to celebrate.

Miners, tipsy and feeling their power, thumbed noses and jeered as they passed the offices of the Tuolumne Water Company, or when they saw Mr. Robinson, the secretary, on the street.

Two nights later in the Long Tom Saloon Charles heard the news. "The capitalists have had a meeting. They're frightened for their damned investment now when we suckers ain't using the water and have set to work on our own ditch. Not a drop of monopoly water's leaked out into the flats through their sluices." Everybody had a beer then and lifted mugs to the future; the committee had a time of it quieting down the mob so the letter could be read. The Tuolumne Water Company made a proposition. If miners would work on *their* ditch to enlarge it, the company would issue script for the work and give the miners four-dollars-a-day water! The enlargement was only twelve and a half miles and wouldn't take long.

The proposition was accepted. Only twelve and a half miles

of work against three times that much for Coffroth's company. That would mean cheap water quicker.

A loud cheer went up for the capitalists. The strike was over and hundreds went to work on the Tuolumne ditch to make short work of that twelve-and-a-half-mile chore, and then get back to gold.

When the weary but satisfied ditchdiggers hit Columbia a few days later, bells began to ring and the cannon went off. The streets were lined to greet them. Charles saw Anne and his boys waving from the jammed sidewalk. Nearly the whole length of Washington Street had tables set and loaded with food donated by provision men and the bakers and butchers of Columbia.

When Charles climbed over the bench to sit down and eat, there sitting next was Tom Baxter, the big Scotchman, who had saved the claim of the little Swede down at Pine Log, near Maria's claim.

"Hello, pard!" Tom roared out in greeting and clapped his great hand so hard on Charles's back that it nearly knocked him off the seat. "Ain't seen you since the little black-eyed one left you cold down at Pine Log! Thought you was feedin' the maggots by this time."

Anne was passing coffee down the line, but the lass had the ears of a fox.

"Yes—it was a long time ago," Charles put in quickly while the sweat formed. "Where are you now?" he asked Tom.

"Oh, same old place. We turned the river and done pretty good down to Pine Log on what the other fellows left. Say, how in hell is that little black-eyed Maria of yours anyhow? Did you ever catch up with her again?"

Under the table Charles ground his heel onto the boot of the damned fool. "You mean Angie," he said in a clear steady voice. "She was as good a little jackass as ever tripped the trails."

Anne poured their cups full of brown liquid. Tom frowned and looked bewildered at the words, but at least he kept his big mouth shut until Anne was beyond hearing.

"Are you loco?" he asked Charles after a bit. "I'm not talking about no jack. I'm talking about a woman with two legs and—"

he scratched his head under the wide-brimmed hat—"and a long tom you used to have."

"I'd like to bash your fool face in," Charles said in a low voice. "I don't know where in hell Maria is, and that was my wife pouring the coffee when you took to running off your mouth."

With that Tom threw back his head and gave a belly laugh. "I get you, pard," he said and winked. "The black-eyed one was only the silent partner in the deal. I get you."

Then he stuck out his neck as long as a giraffe's and looked along the table at Anne. "You must have something," he opined. "This here one's comely too, but I'll wager she makes you step lively to *her* tunes." He shook his head. "I'll stick to what I get at Marquita's on Saturday nights and dance to my own music. It's easier that way. Only trouble is you ain't got no children to leave your money to."

Tom pulled his freight then to head for a saloon. "You don't have to be afraid of me no more, Morgan. After this I'll remember the name of your jackass that got killed. And when I get homesick to see a decent woman I'll be in to visit you and your present incumbent."

That night in the little cabin, Anne, weary from helping to cook and serve food to so many celebrating miners, slipped into the bunk beside Charles. All was well now. They would have water, plenty of it, at four dollars a day instead of twelve dollars. The Morgans could be thankful. She was proud that her man had done his part to help the whole; to make Columbia a fine town.

"But perhaps the miners today only signed their own death warrants, Charles," she finished.

"What do you mean, lass?" he asked. "It's just the beginning of prosperity for us—liquid prosperity!"

"Maybe." She sighed. "But didn't you think of something when Coffroth was talking about his company and even more water being needed to wash the treasure of Midas from Columbia's flats? The hydraulics, Charles."

CHAPTER 32

1855

WITH cheaper water came more gold and bawdy-house trouble aplenty. Shootings and knifings over fancy women burst like stars from a Fourth of July rocket all over the pages of newspapers.

The Methodist parson flapped his black coattails and roared against sin at the top of his lungs, but still men fought and died for favors from the "Sisters of Satan." The new Catholic priest, Father Slattery, quaffed with the "boys" in saloons and fought sin a different way. He told them they should be ashamed of the rickety wooden church, when good brick was ready to hand. If St. Peter knew that Catholics on the rich flats were weighing in gold enough to make the gates of Heaven itself, the Saint would be ashamed of them.

Charles Morgan saw Irish pride come up with a bang then. Norton Kane and his partners offered their claims on Kennebec Hill as ground for a church, and nuggets and dust were shoved into the priest's white handkerchief.

The jolly, kindly Father Slattery near bust his hind-side collar! The church would be called St. Anne's, for the patron saint of miners the world over, and stand with its cross shining out white and high on Kennebec Hill. Why, the church was well on its way this very minute.

But in spite of Protestant and Catholic, crimes of passion still swept on. The Legislature passed a bill to suppress the houses of ill fame and rid the country of these places of riot and bloodshed. The governor signed it and there was a law.

Anne was elated. "There, you see?" she said proudly as if she had done the thing singlehanded. "You and your 'men will be men.' You didn't think anything could be done, did you?"

"There's lots of laws but nobody pays any attention," Charles came back. "The chippies haven't gone yet."

With that, young Bill, the know-it-all, put in his oar. "The prices have gone up at Maria Querida's and Frisco Martha's too."

Anne whirled on her heel and faced him. "How do *you* know?"

"Heard the miners talking outside the American House the other day," Bill said and shrugged. "I couldn't help having ears, could I? You gave 'em to me."

Charles looked at the loose, rangy young one so cocky, and wondered if Bill at twelve was depending solely on his ears for wisdom about such things.

Bill's ears soon heard aplenty. The fine speech-making Senator Jim Coffroth was tangled up with a woman and challenging a man named Dobie to a duel for what Dobie had said about him. Dobie refused to duel. He was opposed to the barbarous practice, but he would retract nothing he had said, and held himself responsible in any manner provided by the law of the state.

Tongues clacked in excitement all along the streets of Columbia and in saloons and fandango houses too. "Good women" in decent calico made excuses to go uptown with baskets on their arms, and they gathered in little knots. Who was the woman? There were near as many guesses as there were tongues awagging.

What would happen now? At the Stage Driver's Retreat and the Long Tom and even the Oyster Parlor bets were up among the miners that Coffroth would plug Dobie some dark night. Others put their money on Dobie. Everybody forgot the dozen other shooting scrapes over women, for this fine big fish, and watched every movement of Dobie and Coffroth.

High Water Bill sniffed when he treated Charles to one of Bixel's schooners in the Stage Driver's Retreat. "Just a lot of words," he said. "Coffroth goes to the bawdy houses same as everybody else and everybody knows it, 'ceptin' because of politics and votes he wants to keep in with the sky pilots and their flocks. That's why he's aposing as a lily. Politicians got to be good setter-uppers of drinks and still be whiter than Jesus' lamb to get the votes of sinners as well as the white-feathered angels we got around here. Plenty of drinks at the right time and lots of talk about law and order on the side, and any man can get hisself elected in California!"

Everybody was waiting to find out what Coffroth and Dobie would do about their woman affair. Then the *Sonora Union Democrat* came out. Eager grubby hands thumbed through the fragile sheet. Aye, there it was! The cocks were at it again.

Dobie said that he had called on a certain lady who reported to him remarks derogatory to his character that Coffroth had made. Then he told her freely and candidly the general course of Coffroth's conduct in Columbia as a frequenter of houses of ill fame. "And I told her, too, remarks made relative to herself by a certain prostitute in Coffroth's keeping, and that I could give the proof. I now submit to the world this statement of facts for investigation, well knowing that my character will be found unblemished while his will prove rotten to the core."

"You see," Anne said when Charles put down the paper. "Dobie's talking to prostitutes too, or he wouldn't be carrying tales from one to the other and yet he's 'unblemished.' They're all tarred with the same brush!" She banged up a pillow to fluff it, as if she would like to bang his head. Then she went on with her ranting, sure that the prostitute must be that Frisco Martha, married now and calling herself "Mrs. Barclay," and still running a saloon and bad house.

Some folks who had their money up on Coffroth said he would never take what Dobie had said. Coffroth was a lawyer. He'd sue, that's what he'd do. But they lost the pot. Coffroth, the Honorable Senator, had business in the lowlands of Sacramento, urgent business that kept him out of Columbia.

High Water Bill went on a bust with the money he won on Dobie, and treated Charles to seven of Bixel's schooners at the Long Tom. Then Charles treated back a couple of times, because he had hit good digging on his claim and all was well at French Gulch.

Four days later, when the poplar trees in front of the City Hotel had been touched with the first fingers of frost and were yellow as gold itself, Columbia had troubles.

The day started peaceful and greedy as any other. Men were grubbing around, and some panned dirt from atop a new-made grave by the roadside as Charles and Anne walked into town in the early afternoon to do some marketing.

The Chinese "Bone man" was sorting out the bones of his dead countrymen ready to be shipped back to China.

"Come on!" Anne said and tugged at Charles's arm. "It makes me creep to think that one day I'll be nothing but bones."

He looked at her, with bonnet shoved back, and saw for the first time that there were silver hairs among the brown at her temples.

"Well," he said as they walked along under the yellow trees, "I'm glad the poor Chinese will be at peace and rest in their own country. That's more than we can expect, lass. I'm afraid it's the red clay of California for us."

"Nonsense," she snapped, "we'll get out our gold one of these days, and go back to Wales and watch the eyes of the Powells and the Morgans when they see how rich we are."

At four o'clock men rushed into Knapp's place where Charles and Anne were buying new flannel underwear for the winter and blurted out the news. A man named Smith had been drunk and quarreled with Frisco Martha over a pitcher he had broken, and Martha's new husband up and shot him! The marshal had arrested Barclay and taken him to the town lockup.

People poured from stores and saloons, music stopped in the fandango houses and the fancy girls came out in their gaudy dresses.

"You'd better get home," Charles told Anne as a mob formed outside the jail. "There's going to be trouble and this is no place for you."

But there was no reason to her. She wouldn't go home. Instead, she jammed her bonnet down on her forehead, gathered up her full calico skirts and wedged into the crowd.

Jim Coffroth got up on a chair in his fine broadcloth suit, his face determined. "Men," he said in a loud voice to the jostling men in red shirts below him. "Ordinarily I am in favor of sustaining the laws, but this occurrence is of such a character as to demand the speediest vengeance, to warrant the people's taking the execution of the law into their own hands, and to mete out justice on the spot!"

"Hear, hear!" came from below and faces turned eager.

"I held the deceased as a very near and dear friend," Coffroth went on. "He was a good man only a little the worse for drink. We all make mistakes. I hope the people will move and promptly. I have been elected to make laws, but upon this occasion laws should be put aside. Get Barclay, men! Try him under Judge Lynch!" he roared.

Scarce before the last word was out of Coffroth's mouth miners rushed the jail and Barclay was seized and half carried, half dragged toward the Tuolumne Water Company's flume.

Anne ran with the rabble and Charles took after her.

The trial was brief. Angry, bloodthirsty men would not let Martha testify in behalf of her husband. "No! Get a jackass to testify!"

"String Barclay up!" came from the crowd.

Barclay was quickly hoisted up on a rope thrown over the flume above his head. They had forgotten to pinion his hands! The wretched, frightened man went up with a savage yell of terror and clutched desperately at the rope above his head to stop the noose from tightening.

"Break his hold! Jerk the rope!"

Those with hands on the rope jerked it up and down wildly so that Barclay jiggled like a puppet on a string. "Let go, you damned fool! Let go!" one of the executioners roared out as he leaned over the flume.

Finally Barclay's strength gave out, the hands fell to his sides. Drawing up his legs, he gave a final convulsive movement and then hung straight. All was over.

It was a hideous affair to Charles, jammed in the crowd so tight he could scarce breathe. A great bonfire had been lighted and the flames cast a crimson glow on the heads of the men who stood below the suspended man. It lighted up their faces with fierce passion and the thirst for blood, and was like a scene from Hell itself, with the light flickering on the dead man as he hung forty feet above.

The throng below began shouting and yelling and jumping as they lighted torches from the fire. "To Martha's!" they yelled. "To Martha's, let's rip the house down!" Away they raced with their flares. When Charles and Anne arrived back in town, all the windows in Martha's house were smashed.

By midnight the streets were empty. Music sounded from the fandango houses, and gamblers called out for bets. Frisco Martha's husband kept his lone vigil dangling from the flume.

The next day Charles happened to be in town after tenpenny nails, when he saw poor hatchet-faced Martha and three of the girls from her house, following the men who carried Barclay up Boot Hill in the pine box.

The editor of the *Gazette* made a plea against hangings and trusted in heaven that this would be the last time he would have to print such terrible news. He congratulated all who had taken no part in the "lamentable occasion."

"It *was* horrible," Anne admitted to Charles and High Water Bill, as she folded up the paper and put it ready for lighting the fire. "But just the same I'm glad the decent folks are waking up at last to what fancy women and gamblers are doing to men in the mines. Maybe the hanging will help to get them out faster."

"Ever think who it was started the hangin' in the first place?" Bill asked as he cut a chew of tobacco from his plug. "It was Jim Coffroth with his silver tongue did it. And why was he so agitated about what went on at Martha's? Gettin' back at Martha, I'll wager, for all that prostitute stuff in the papers about him, and maybe helping himself along in politics at the same time."

"I wasn't thinking of that," Charles said after a minute. "Who knows—perhaps that mob may speak for itself when men read about it a hundred years from now—or a thousand. I was thinking that things last Wednesday must have been about like when the mob took Jesus Christ. Only difference was they yelled, 'Crucify Him!'"

CHAPTER 33

1855-1856

But not everybody was bloodthirsty. Father Slattery's new church on Kennebec Hill came on apace, while all the town watched and chipped in for more bricks.

Charles was surprised at Anne's interest in the church that would eventually bear the same name as hers. In Wales and even in Pennsylvania, she had been so rabid against the papists.

"Any church is good in this wicked place where folks are so full of robbing and shooting and gambling," she told him. "And if ever there was a saint among men it's that Father Slattery. It's not the church, I'm beginning to think, but the folks who live the life."

Then she told him that perhaps the bad luck of the Morgans was because God had given the gift of song to a Welshman and yet he never lifted his voice in a church choir of Sundays to sing the praises of his Maker.

Charles was not so sure about that. God had been good and supplied him with the wherewithal from the mountains of California to build a cheese factory, then the greed of that Welshman's wife had brought him back to grub in the red soil for a bare living. But if that was the way Anne felt, what were the odds?

After that, Charles put on his best black suit of a Sunday morning and sang out anthems louder than anybody else in the little church. Anne would never again be able to clap blame for the lack of luck onto his shoulders.

But not even anthems helped. Some days two ounces which was good, some but half an ounce.

At sunset one April evening, when Charles had to go to Columbia to the blacksmith for the sharpening of tools, he met High
Water Bill. Over schooners Bill told disconcerting news from
Squabbletown. Now that there was a new flume with plenty of
water, a hydraulic company had formed and was taking over
worked-out claims at a great rate.

"Hell, you should just see, Morgan!" he cried excitedly and
nearly tipped over his beer. "They're washing the hill away below
Slattery's new church!"

Charles tried to be calm against the wet moving finger of fate.
"Are they getting much out?" he asked, and ordered another
schooner to buck him up.

"Getting much out?" Bill roared. "Gold dust shipped from
here in the last three weeks amounted to three million dollars!
All the shopkeepers in town are roaring about the boom, but I say
it's the crack of doom for us little fellows."

As he walked home to French Gulch, Charles decided not to
tell Anne about the hydraulics. She would find out in time for
herself, and right now she was worried enough with the boys.

Only last night Charley had told how he and another lad had
gone to Chinatown and peeked through the cracks to see the
Chinks and some white miners too, smoking opium and dozing on
dirty bunks.

Bill, near fourteen now, was threatening every day to leave off
working for his father to go and work for wages at the quartz-
stamping outfit. And young Henry at eight was a fine-looking
Lord Byron and knew it too. He was entirely too interested in
what went on around the fandango houses that he had to pass on
the way home from school and bragged that two girls had called
out to him and said he was a "handsome boy."

Anne had news of her own when he went into the cabin, news
that blotted out hydraulics and the problem of the boys. She was
excited as a schoolgirl. John Leary was going to have an auction
that night—a real auction, not just job lots of wide-brimmed Palo
Alto hats or elkskin leggings and miners' candlesticks.

Then she went on to tell that she had gone uptown with Henry and they had seen the beautiful things all set out at Clarke's Hotel for folks to look at. Henry had his eye on a grand little music box from Switzerland, no bigger than a loaf of bread, and it played six tunes!

There were painted fans and silver bouquet holders with real gems twinkling in them and beautiful mirrors from Florence, Italy and china from Dresden.

Charles looked around the little cabin papered with *Gazettes* and said they certainly needed silver flower holders and Florence mirrors!

He saw the excitement fade from her eyes. "It won't do any harm to go and have a look," she begged.

She came over to him then with the skillet in her hand. "You've said yourself that John Leary auctioning things off was as good as any of those players that come to Cardinell's Hall. I do love just to *look* at pretty things, Charles."

Charles felt a bit sick inside at her words. Too many times he had seen the longing in her eyes when she looked at the new fine white-painted houses all fixed up with fancy-cut board trimming that looked like a wedding cake.

"We'll go," he told her. "After supper you just deck out in your purple silk. We'll swish into Clarke's with the ones that's pulled out big nuggets and make out we're rich too and building a fine house and need a mirror from Florence to put in the front hall-way."

Bill and Charley had no interest in the fancy stuff, but Henry wanted to go and bid for himself on the music box. Charles put on his good clothes, slipped a bit of dust into the canvas bag, and waited while Anne fiddled a long time to get her hair just right, then they started out with the lantern.

"Don't get your hopes set on that music box, Henry," Anne warned as Charles took her arm and they picked their way along the road left rutted and muddy from recent rains.

"But it's mine!" Henry came back. "I've got all my money from running errands right here, and it's a lot—almost five dollars." He smacked proudly on his pocket.

Everybody who was somebody, and a lot of nobodies too, in their gaudy dresses and frilled gamblers' shirts, moved across the Brussels carpets of Clarke's Hotel.

Marquita, young and merry-eyed, was there with one of her lovers. Charles watched her slender white hands draw a long, fringed wool shawl to her breast with eagerness and joy. She was a beautiful young thing in demure black silk, with her shiny black hair smooth as a madonna's. A man could scarce believe as he looked at her that she made a handsome living from the caresses of her blonde girls up at the "Big White House."

Anne was taken up with the Dresden shepherdesses until she saw the Staffordshire dogs, then she grabbed Charles by the arm. "Look!" she said. "Just like the one your old granny had on the clock shelf in Wales, Charles." When she lifted her eyes to his there were tears. "Don't you think we—well, we could manage a Staffordshire dog?" she begged. "Surely *they* won't cost so much, and it would be like home."

"We'll see," he promised.

Henry took his stand by the music box and paid no attention to the folks that bumped and jostled him in their eagerness to see and feel the lovely things that were spread out so temptingly.

The fiddler tuned up to catch attention of the crowd. Then he dropped his fiddle and announced that for the benefit and entertainment of all present and to warm up for the bidding he would do an imitation of the famous Lola Montez spider dance.

With that the skinny little red-bearded man capered all over the place with a shawl around him and nearly wiggled his behind off his spine. That brought down shouts of laughter and put folks in a wonderful humor for the business at hand.

John Leary got up and called for order. First he gave a long harangue about the costly wares from all the capitals of the world, brought at great expense by boat and mule team to grace the luxurious homes of Columbia. "And now, ladies and gents, the auction is on. *Don't,* I beg of you, let this *one,* this *only,* great opportunity slip away without buying something beautiful to nurture your souls, to bring you joy for the rest of your natural or unnatural lives."

He held up a fine mother-of-pearl inlaid writing case for all to see. "What am I bid for this beautiful treasure? Can be used by a gent to hold his love letters from home."

The fine box was knocked down for two hundred dollars to a horny-fisted sun-parched miner, who promptly handed it over to the girl beside him—and the show went on.

Jeweled, silver flower holders, paper cutters, luster jugs, all brought terrific prices, and Leary's assistant was busy with his scales weighing out dust.

Marquita, standing with her man behind Charles and Anne, got the Cashmere shawl and lost no time in putting it around her shoulders.

Then Leary put his great red paw on a Staffordshire dog! Anne's hold tightened on Charles. He glanced at her and saw the muscles in her neck grow tense. She scarce breathed as her eyes looked toward Leary and the dog he held.

"What am I bid for Fido?" he roared. "Don't cost nothin' to feed him. Don't wet on the floor. Don't even bark or chew up a shoe. Nice little Fido came all the way from beef-eating England to set on his behind and grin at folks on Columbia's hillsides. What am I bid?"

"Five dollars," Charles called out bravely.

Leary clapped his hands to his ears. "Gent, I'm deaf!" he roared. "I'm deaf to such piddling bids."

"Twenty!" Conlon roared out.

"Now we're talking," Leary said. "Little Fido all the way from England ought to be worth twenty-five of anybody's gold. Think how seasick he got! Think of the jiggling all the way up the rutted roads, and not even a chip off his shoulder!"

There was a laugh through the crowd.

"Twenty-five," Charles called.

Anne poked at him. "Oh, Charles," she whispered. "We can't. You know we can't—for just a—a toy. And there's little Henry and the music box."

"Thirty!" Conlon called.

Thirty went three times. Fido was passed down to the assistant and Conlon pushed through the crowd for his dog.

Leary had the second dog up now.

Charles felt in his pocket. His hand touched the nugget pocket piece he had kept ever since Maria had sent it to him two years before. Anne wanted a dog. Poor woman had so little now, and perhaps even less to look forward to. He bid thirty—the bid went three times and the dog was knocked down to him, while Anne tugged at his sleeve and tried to shake her head at Leary.

As he pushed through the crowd to pay his gold and take the prize, he gave a final squeeze of his fingers to the nugget, warm from two years next to his body. "It's more blessed to give than to receive" went through his mind.

Charles watched anxiously as Leary's man dumped his dust onto the scales. He held the precious nugget ready if it was needed.

"A little shy of making her," the man said in a matter-of-fact voice, "but we'll let it go." He handed over the bit of pottery. "Folks at auctions beats me. Thirty dollars for a fool dog that you can't even eat, come bad times."

Then came the music box.

Henry jumped up and down with excitement and trod on the foot of a miner next to him. "Jesus!" the man let out. "You got worms or something?"

When Leary asked for bids, Henry's birdlike voice chirped out, "Two dollars and fifty cents." But the words were lost in the fifty-dollar bid that came hard on them.

Henry wilted. Anne put her arm about his shoulders and pulled him to her. The boy sobbed into her skirts while Leary wound the infernal machine up and "The Bluebells of Scotland" tinkled out between bids.

Henry covered his ears then. Anne clutched her pottery dog, and Charles saw her blinking back the tears. She made a move to get out, but the crowd was too thick, too eager, in its pressing.

Up went the price as the tinkling tune ended. The box was knocked down to Marquita for two hundred dollars. Her lover shoved past young Henry to get it, and Leary reached for a jeweled dressing case.

"Come on, I can't stand any more," Anne murmured, as she led Henry to the door.

When they were outside in the cool misty night, a hand touched the sobbing boy.

"Here, little love," someone murmured softly. "Here's the music box. I bought it for you." Marquita pulled the lever and the little box began to sing as she handed it to the child.

For half a second there was silence. Then Anne grabbed the box from Henry while it still played and handed it back to the girl. "It's very good of you," she said in a stiff hard voice. "But if he has to get it this way, he's better off without it."

She grabbed Henry's hand and strode out into the night without even looking in the direction of Charles.

A great surge of real pain went through him as he stood in the dim light from the doorway and saw the hurt look on Marquita's beautiful face that had been so shining with the giving but a moment before.

He put a hand on her shoulder. "Thank you and God bless you," he managed to say, then turned and followed Anne.

Henry had set up a wail. He couldn't see why he couldn't have the box when Marquita had bought it for him and said so.

"We don't get things that way," Anne scolded. "I'm sorry you couldn't have the music box and sick about your disappointment, now hush your blathering."

"But you got your old dog," Henry blubbered as they stumbled along rough muddy road. "A damned old dog that can't even bark, let alone play a nice tune. She *wanted* to give it to me. I had it in my hands!" He began to sob as though his heart would break.

Anne stooped down and circled the little boy with her arms. "My little Henry, my son," she said tenderly, "I love you more than anything in the world. That's why I couldn't let you take the toy. There'll be other music boxes. One day you shall have the finest music box that was ever made." She kissed him and wiped away his tears with her handkerchief. "Now just think about that instead of what you've lost." She took his hand then, and the three of them walked home to the rhythm of dancing light shafts from the lantern.

Anne was like a child over the Staffordshire dog. She tried it out a dozen places in the cabin, until at last it shone on the shelf by the stove that she had decorated with cut-paper work.

When the boys were abed in the lean-to, she came over and put her arms around Charles. "That dog is a symbol," she said. "I'm grateful to you for buying it, Charles. It's a symbol of the old and the new. The old is Granny's clock shelf in Wales with the dogs smiling down——"

"And the new?" he asked, holding her close.

"That I discovered I'm going to have another young one, Charles."

CHAPTER 34

1856

In the months that followed, Charles chided Anne to keep up her spirits and to give his own a buck up too. She'd picked a fine year, a presidential year, to have another son. Would they call the boy Buchanan Morgan or Frémont Morgan when he put in his appearance in October?

Anne said he needn't bother his head about such names, because she had set her mind on a girl this time. The boys needed a little sister to tame them down.

Charles told her he'd never noticed the mind had much to do with the sex of babies. She laughed then, and went about dipping a sack of bluing into water and dabbing it on the newspaper-covered walls to make a pretty pattern and brighten up the place for the newcomer.

"If it *is* a little lass, let's call her Maria," Charles suggested.

Anne wanted to know why Maria? There was no Maria in the family. "I suppose it's for that Chile woman that mended your clothes. It's time you forgot her."

While he squirmed, she told him that since most of the business of having a baby was hers, she had prime right in the naming and the girl would be Sarah Ann.

"You and Slattery," he grumbled, "naming your babies after the patroness of miners. Let's be hoped this miner will have some luck along with the names."

Things boomed in Columbia! With the hydraulics, more gold than ever was taken out of the hillsides and flats, and scarce a week went by without the express riders being robbed on the road when they carried the gold down to the lowlands.

Politics were hot too; men got into arguments over Buchanan and Frémont in every saloon and gambling house, and more than one paid with his life for his political convictions.

Columbia boys were all for Frémont. The States needed a man from the West for a President. What white-livered Easterner knew anything of the needs of men who dug out gold in California and kept the whole damned country going with their labors?

Then Jim Coffroth hit town to make speeches. Republican boys of Columbia had helped elect Jim to the State Senate. Brows furrowed some when he talked. The cuss had changed his politics! He allowed that every rugged, well-informed miner in the "diggings" would do the same as he had done—for a man like Buchanan. They were to vote Democratic if they wanted real prosperity!

That was quite a blow. A few teetered when they thought of Moffatt and the private mints—maybe Jim was right.

After the speech, nearly every man from the hills got drunk and whooped and hollered for his particular candidate for President. The odds were about even when dusk came that night of the first parade. Two men had been killed in saloons defending Buchanan, and two killed for Frémont's sake, with a third stabbed in the ribs and not likely to live.

On October eighth, when the political fight was growing hotter by the minute downtown, Charles and the boys kept a worried vigil in the lean-to off the shack on French Gulch. Doc Oxley had come around seven, and a neighbor woman was clattering kettles and pans. They could hear Anne moaning.

Just before midnight, Doc stuck his tousled head in the door and said. "Come on, you gents, and look at your new little girl!"

Little Sarah Ann, whimpering a bit, lay rolled up in a blanket in Anne's arms. What excitement! The boys took one look and went out to whoop and holler on their own, and to plan years ahead about what they'd do for the little sister.

After they were abed, Charles hit off for the Stage Driver's

Retreat to tell his news. He hoped Doc hadn't shot off his mouth first. He, Charles Morgan, was the father—a baby couldn't be born without a father, could it? And he wanted to be the one to tell, not some pill roller brought in nine months after the important work was done!

But everybody knew when he burst into the place. Schooners were lifted, cigars went around and the boys near clapped the back off him for the fine job he had done to help out the woman situation in Columbia.

Jim Doyle opened his shirt, tore the holy medal from his hairy chest and gave it to Charles for the little colleen, and Mike Donovan shoved a bottle of champagne into Charles's hands "to take home to the little mother." Nuggets from Pine Log boys were dropped into his hands for "a few girl fixin's when she needed 'em," and Tom Baxter, the Scotchman, promised to bring the picture of his mother up for Anne to look at as a treat.

"I've not seen a little baby for so long I wouldn't know how to act," Tom said. "Man, these many months since we found you again, and never once did you ask us to come and see your woman and the bairns. If ye be afraid that me and little Shorty here will tell on your sins down at Pine Log, ye needn't be afeared. This Scotchman's not one to make any trouble between a man and his wedded wife—and Shorty can keep his mouth shut."

Charles promised they would meet Anne and see the new baby.

The next day High Water Bill came all the way up to the cabin. He looked a long time at the baby in the basket. "Them funny, helpless little maggots sure gets under a man's skin," he told Anne. "She ain't much to look at, but God-damned if I don't love the little squirt already, wiggling her fingers like she does."

Then he reached into his pocket and pulled out something wrapped in a scrap of paper. "I bought this for her, but I misjudged the size some." With horny fingers he presented a great heart-shaped gold locket big enough for a breastplate.

"See," he said delightedly, as he pressed a spring and the heart opened. "It's for pictures. I had mine took at the 'Dag' studio,

so's she'd know old Bill gave it to her." Then he looked again at
the baby and shook his head. "I guess *someday* she'll grow up to
it."

After the visit Charles took High Water out behind the lean-to
and reached under the floor for the bottle of champagne that Donovan had presented to the teetotaling Anne. "We'd best drink it
up," he said. "Anne wouldn't, and it'll only waste."

They finished off the bottle and High Water went weaving
home.

Little Sarah Ann was just four days shy of being a month old
when Father Slattery decided to have his great show. Bishop
Alemany himself was coming all the way from San Francisco to
dedicate St. Anne's!

True, the steeple and bell tower weren't on yet, but the church
itself was finished and who wanted to wait for the trimmings?

Anne dressed the wee lass up fine in a long white dress and a
bonnet with pink ribbons fit to kill, and gave her to Charles to
hold while she dressed herself up in the purple silk and ostrich-
feather hat to go to the dedication.

All along the way people in their Sunday best were headed toward Kennebec Hill. Women in full, silk hoop skirts and gorgeous bonnets loaded with flowers and feathers clung to the arms
of their men. Little girls with wreaths and white veils on their
heads, all ready to take their first communion, walked self-con-
sciously arm in arm under the warm sun, and boys in squeaky
shoes and their best store suits darted in and out among their
elders.

Even the little, wild, pink roadside roses seemed to know that
this was a great day, for they spread brightness and fragrance all
along the way—to honor the good Father Slattery and his new
church.

Some miners on the hillside, greedy for gain, had no time for
the affair, and the sound of metal picks against the stones clanged
out into the warm clear air.

As they reached Kennebec Hill the crowd thickened and progress was slow. Mr. Benoit, who was giving them a lift, had to
walk his chestnut horse and watch out for the excited children
who didn't look before they ran across the road. The great coach
bulging with folks from Sonora eased in ahead.

Out on Brown's Flat below, the hydraulics were washing and
men shouted above the roar of water.

There was a great cliff just to the south of St. Anne's, where
once flowers had bloomed on the gentle slope of a hill. Charles
saw Anne turn her eyes quickly away from that and look at the
crowd ahead.

Bill and Henry and Charley were off to find a place for themselves, and Charles helped Anne with the baby. They moved as
close to the doorway as possible to try to see and hear. Bishop
Alemany was splendid in his robes as he blessed the little young-
lings in white veils, and the boys too, as they knelt before him at
the altar rail.

After the Mass, Father Slattery, so tall and dignified in his gown
and white lace surplice, gave the dedicatory sermon.

The beauty of the words and the father's deep-toned voice
affected everybody. Handkerchiefs fluttered white in the breeze;
noses were blown violently when he finished.

Slattery seemed to make folks believe that it was worth-while
to fight for the good, true and the beautiful on the red-clay
hillsides of California.

When all was over the crowd began to move away. Little knots
stopped to have a bit of talk together. Charles was seeing to Anne
and the baby, when suddenly a woman in front of him turned
around. He looked up into the eyes of Maria.

"Carlos!" The word was tinged with joy, with eagerness and
love.

"Maria!" Her name came out before he had time to think.

There was silence for a split second, then he turned to Anne.
"This is my good friend Maria, Anne. She looked after me and
Artemus long ago at Pine Log. You remember? She mended my
clothes for me." He tried to keep his voice steady.

Anne shifted the baby to her other arm and took Maria's out-stretched hand. "I've always wanted to meet you," she said and smiled. "Any woman who takes care of a poor forlorn man in the mountains has her work cut out for her."

Charles saw that Maria seemed more at ease then. She smiled her beautiful smile and looked down at the baby. "Carlos told me about the boys," she said, "but now you have a *new* one!"

That just suited Anne. "A little girl. We're very proud of her too."

"Where are you now?" Charles asked, uneasy lest the conversation turn awkward.

Maria pulled her black shawl close. "You'll never guess, Carlos. I have a school to teach the children at Murphy's old diggings, Melones. It's small, only a dozen or so, but I love little children and I'm happy there."

"You're a long way from home?" he managed to say.

She smiled into his eyes then, and the heart of him near jumped out with its guilt. "It isn't every day that such a fine church as this is dedicated—and I love Father Slattery."

Anne fingered the pink ribbons on little Sarah Ann's bonnet for a moment, then she did a great thing, a glorious thing, for which Charles was grateful to the marrow of his wicked bones.

"When the little one was coming," Anne told Maria, "Charles wanted her Maria. If I'd known you then I would have named her after you." And she smiled like a madonna in a picture.

Tears came into Maria's eyes. With a quick movement she kissed Anne on the cheek. "May God and the Blessed Virgin light the way of you and the babe always, Señora Morgan." She turned suddenly and darted out of sight in the crowd.

"She must be a good woman," Anne said as they walked down the hill to where Mr. Benoit's wagon was hitched beside the coach from Sonora. "You can see it when you just look at her."

"Aye, she *is* a good woman," Charles agreed. "You'll never know how good, lass." God! How he wished he could have had just a minute to speak to Maria; to tell her how he cherished the nugget she had sent, and that never a day went by that he didn't think of her. Perhaps he could make it one day to Murphy's old diggings.

"She didn't wear a wedding ring," Anne chattered. "Does she have a husband?"

Charles took a great breath. "She *did* have one at Pine Log," he said, "a worthless good-for-nothing he was too—deceitful as the Devil himself."

Then Anne wanted to know what happened to Maria's husband.

"Went off into the hills one day and never came back to her," Charles replied, and kicked at rocks in the red dirt as he walked.

"Murdered, I suppose, like hundreds of others." Anne sighed. "It's too bad. She likes children and would have made a good mother. Did you see the longing in her eyes when she looked at our little Sarah Ann?" Then she hugged the wee one to her breast, fancy bows and all.

Charles fingered the nugget in his pocket and tried to forget that good-for-nothing husband of Maria's.

CHAPTER 35

1856

THE day after the dedication and the day before election, feeling ran so high in Columbia about Buchanan and Frémont that men were frantic in their zeal.

Big Annie, the prostitute, was washed out, shack and all by the fire boys with their new hose because she had spoken up for Buchanan in a store right in front of "decent" women.

"You should'a seen the mess," High Water told Charles. "Old Annie's shack just busted to pieces like an eggshell when the hose hit it, and the sticks slewed and whirled in the water—and old Annie herself sliding around on her backside struggling in the mud. Jesus, it was a show!"

Voting day came fine and sunny. Excitement was pacing the street in woolen shirts and thumping with every pair of boots. The Buchanan men were out combing the hillsides for miners with a vote. Both sides treated well in the saloons and then just hoped that the liquor they paid for was buying the right votes.

Charles and the boys knocked off work and went into town with Anne and the baby, to see the goings on. They were just coming out of Knapp's store when a rabble of miners came in sight, marching military fashion with brooms over their shoulders like guns.

On they came, sweating and yelling and cursing Frémont and stopping at each shack to grab up every broom in sight.

"Here we come!" they roared. "The Broom Rangers from Pine Log! Down with Frémont!"

Among the rabble were big Tom Baxter and the little Swede

Palmer. "You two can't vote!" Charles yelled out to them as they passed. "You're foreigners like the rest of us."

"Mebby I can't vote," Tom shouted back, "but I can make a bigger racket than them as can! Down with Frémont!" And he marched on with Shorty's little legs beside him, hard put to keep up.

Suddenly a shot rang out from the six-shooter of a Columbia Frémont man. The bullet was neatly guided to go between the pantaloon seat and bottom of a Broom Ranger and took with it a piece of blue denim as clean as a dressmaker could snip it.

"Some shot!" a bystander roared out. "Bully for Frémont."

Five minutes later there was a free-for-all in front of the Stage Driver's Retreat, with blue legs and red flannel arms whirling in all directions and raising a terrible dust.

"What on earth will happen at the polls?" Anne asked Charles as she stood beside him watching the rowdies. "They're so crazy with drink they won't be able to see any of the names on the ballots."

When the sweaty Pine Loggers lined up at the poles to cast their votes, Shorty Palmer and Tom Baxter came to where Charles stood with Anne and the children. The two of them were shy and awkward, with their hats in their hands, while Charles introduced them to his family.

Big bulbous-nosed Tom, with his thick red eyebrows bushed out over the twinkling blue eyes, reached up and gingerly pulled the neck of his shirt together and buttoned it over the red hairy chest. "Pleased to meet you, Mrs. Anne," he said in a deep burry voice. "We knew your husband when——"

"Artemus had a little jackass called Angie," Charles put in quickly.

Big Tom's eyes twinkled mightily then and Shorty Palmer laughed right out. Shorty nodded to Anne. He seemed like a midget standing beside the six-foot-four Scotty.

Tom chucked little Sarah Ann under the chin with his great horny fingers, and the brown-eyed baby cooed and laughed at him towering above her.

"Such a to-do you're making here, and can't even vote," Charles said. "You and Shorty must be daft."

"Aw, it gives us an excuse for a bit of a lark," Tom confessed. "We don't even know what it's all about, but me and Shorty gets fed up with our own company down there on the claim."

Then he turned to Anne. "I promised to bring this for you to see, but Morgan never gave me the chance." He reached into his pocket and pulled out a picture of a black-haired woman. "She's my mother, and she always goes everywhere with her Tom—even to election doings." He handed the little tintype to Anne. "One day I'm taking my pile back to Scotland and let her spend it for me."

Anne said she wished Tom's mother was in California. She would like to know her; she handed the smiling-faced picture back.

"If she was here, she'd probably be marching beside her Tom in the Broom Rangers," Tom said.

"Not a woman!" Anne cried. "Women can't vote—even in America."

"Neither can I." Tom grinned then and shook his finger at Anne. "Mark my words, Mrs. Anne, one day the women will be voting—and marching in political parades too—if I know my women."

Some of the Broom Rangers came from the polls and stretched out in the shade to "sleep it off."

"We'll be going," Tom said. "We've blathered here long enough. But you've not seen the last of us, Mrs. Anne." Then he asked her if he and Shorty could come to supper of a Saturday night if they brought grub.

"Better come tonight," Anne said. "You'll be wanting to stay until the votes are counted, to see if your man won."

There were merry doings at eventide in the cabin on French Gulch. Tom and Shorty brought fancy things from the bakery and from Knapp's as well.

While supper was cooked, little Sarah Ann sat on Tom's lap and played and gurgled, then afterward Charles walked back to town with Shorty and Tom, to stand with the rest and wait while the votes were counted.

The Broom Rangers from Pine Log had done it. Columbia was swept clean of Frémont—Buchanan carried the diggings! Major Solomon, who had gone into bankruptcy trying to feed the hungry from his store, would likely be United States Marshal!

Columbia settled down after the election excitement, but High Water Bill was stirred up.

Charles was in Riley's store one night, talking to Riley's new clerk, Matt Brady, when Bill came in looking black as a thunder cloud.

"I want to talk to you private, Morgan," he said without ceremony.

As they walked together for a schooner at the Pioneer, High Water opened up. "What's them two polecats from Pine Log hanging around your place for, Morgan?" he demanded. "Tom Baxter bragged how much little Sarah Ann likes him. Next it'll be your wife!"

Charles had a prick of conscience. He thought how many times he had tried to get down to Melones to see Maria.

There was the time he had appealed to Anne's greed for gold by suggesting he go down and see what was up at Murphy's. Anne had stopped that idea on the spot. Maybe she suspected what pulled at Murphy's old diggings.

"You needn't worry about Anne," he comforted. "Most likely she's only interested in saving the souls of Tom and Shorty. She'll be having them at church first thing you know."

"Just the same, you can't trust *no* man in a place where good women is so scarce." Bill's voice sounded frantic.

"How about me trusting you?"

"Oh, me. I'm different." Bill had to laugh at the trap.

It took three schooners before High Water was mellowed enough to admit that Shorty and Tom were not such bad fellows after all.

CHAPTER 36

1857

How good-natured little Sarah Ann did queen it over the men-folks in the months that followed! Everybody bowed to her whims. High Water Bill brought her a fancy embroidered-satin coat from the Chinaman's, and Shorty Palmer made her a little pair of rabbit-fur shoes.

After the horrible fire in August 1857 that gutted nearly all the fine brick buildings in Columbia, nothing would do but Anne must dress up the baby all fine so that big Tom Baxter could carry her down to see the grand new fire engine that "the boys" had bought in Frisco. He wouldn't take no for an answer, and only put up with Anne along, so she could "do the didie business" if necessary.

Everybody was in town to celebrate, and drinks were shoved across makeshift bars.

"Papeete," the spidery little fire engine, was a bobby-dazzler with leather buckets and ladders and her sides decorated with naked women! Anne was shocked and turned her face away in shame after one look at the painted hussies. "Wherever did they get the thing?" she demanded. "It's disgusting."

Then it came out that Kamehameha, King of the Sandwich Islands, had ordered Papeete made special in Boston. The little beauty had come around the Horn and there was no ship to take her to the Islands. The Boston people wanted their money. The King had tried everything, including diplomatic notes, but nothing happened. Then the Columbia fire boys hit San Francisco, put the money on the barrelhead and brought Papeete home!

"If King Kamehameha wants her now he'll have to come to Columbia to get her!" a drunken miner roared.

Big Tom held Sarah Ann close so her little dimpled hand could pat the glistening "pretty ladies" on Papeete's sides.

"Now the engine's christened right," he told Anne as he hugged the child to him and they turned away. "Can't help but have luck, now Sarah Ann has touched her."

Columbia forgot all about Papeete and King Kamehameha when John Cardinell, the dancing master's brother, made his rich find at deserted old Tuttletown early in October.

"Ain't that a devil of a note?" Leary asked Charles. "John Cardinell gets himself into a hell of a mess over a woman and sifts out of Columbia to fall on his nose in a pile of gold at Tuttle-town."

Cardinell and his partner had tried to keep the news of their find quiet, but it leaked out through Sleepers', the bankers who had bought up the gold. There was five thousand dollars' worth of gold in a twenty-nine-pound chunk of ore!

After they had read all about it in the paper, nothing would do for Anne but they must go into town and find out more about Cardinell's strike.

Little Sarah Ann seemed to know something different was in the wind, for she grinned and gurgled and dawdled over her food until Anne was frantic before the little one was finally abed. Charley and Bill wanted to go to town, but young Henry was quite content to stay and look after the little sister who was the light of his life.

Columbia had turned crazy with the news! The main street was crowded with miners who had abandoned their claims and deserted their cabins to shoulder packs and picks and shovels and be on their way to Tuttletown.

Jackasses and mules burdened until they could scarce waddle were nose to rump in a steady stream headed out of town. Merchants were loading mule teams with provisions destined for Tuttletown. Several gambling places were dark, their owners eager as any for the rich pickings over the hill.

Anne was frantic when she saw the stir. "There! You see?" she cried. "Those men are smart. They hear of a strike and they're off. The Welsh are too slow to pick up gold!"

"Let's us go too, Dad," Bill begged. "Maybe Tuttletown's the place."

"I'm sure it is," Anne said.

Charles was half a mind to try it, until he thought of several objections. "There's the tunnel we've worked on all summer," he said more to himself than the others. "It might be just ready to come into some good dirt about now."

"Tunnel nothing!" Anne snapped. "They don't even have to tunnel at Tuttletown."

"But we have water from the flume to wash," Charles argued. "This is a dry year and there's no water at Tuttletown."

"I suppose Cardinell thought of all that when he went over there, and he hit it rich!" Anne fair screamed the words out. "You're like the tail of a jackass, Charles Morgan—last after everybody else had found the best claims! If I didn't have Sarah Ann I'd go myself. You and Bill and Charley all working on a claim at Tuttletown could make us rich in no time—and you moan about your old tunnel."

Right in the middle of town at Knapp's Corner, she turned angrily. "I've seen plenty. I'm going home!" she shouted. "When the jackass has seen enough he can follow." She was off, digging her heels into the hard-packed earth.

"We could go," Charley said as they walked home. "Henry will be home with her and Sarah Ann. They'd be safe enough. Indians don't bother much now and thieves will go where there is real gold."

"Boys—" Charles sighed—"we've sweated and worked the flesh off us up in French Gulch on that tunnel. A man is only allowed one claim. If we leave our workings *anybody* can jump it while we're gone—you know that. Then someone else will get the benefit of all our sweating. I've seen it done dozens of times. I know."

"Let 'em," Bill said. "There's nothing but a dribble in the damned tunnel anyway. I'm sick of it."

"I am too," Charley put in. "If we don't take a chance once in a while we'll grub along all our lives."

They walked in silence as the first stars twinkled out in the black above. Charles fingered Maria's nugget in his pocket. With the boys feeling as they did about the tunnel and eager for Tuttletown, they would most likely bolt anyway to work for wages.

"All right," he said as their boots clattered over the rocks. "We'll put packs on our backs tomorrow and head for Tuttletown, and hope to God that with Anne in the cabin no one will dare to jump the claim."

Anne was pleased as punch and worked half the night mending blue denims and heavy socks and packing things ready. When Charles told her of his fears about claim jumpers, the lass was a smart one.

"I'm of age," she said happily. "I have a right to a claim too. Look at the women who come out to work for themselves. Turn this claim over to me! Henry and I will work it a little, to hold it while you are gone. Won't we, Henry?"

Henry was delighted with the idea, and pleased to be the man of the family with Mom and the baby left in his charge.

"We'll hold the claim all right," Anne said. "But you are sure to strike it in Tuttletown where everybody's getting so rich, and we won't even need this old place."

The next morning at dawn, Charles, Bill and Charley were off with their packs and tools. Anne stood in the cabin door with Henry beside her and Sarah Ann in her arms. The wee one in her blue dress smiled and gurgled and waved a tiny hand and then threw a kiss at her brothers and daddy when they took a last look before they disappeared over the hill.

"Only thing I'll miss is Sarah Ann. Don't seem possible we've had her near a year, does it?" Charley said as they went along, and Charles saw him blink fast. "If we strike it rich, she shall go to the finest finishing school and learn French and everything. Our Sarah Ann's got to be a lady, Dad," the boy finished.

"I'd like to buy her a silk dress as swell as any Marquita ever put on," Bill said. "Maybe she could do her curls with a red ribbon when she grows up. I like red ribbons on girls."

"Come on, let's strike out," Charles urged. "The quicker we get there the sooner the riches instead of dreams. Tuttletown's only six miles. We ought to make it in an hour."

CHAPTER 37

1857

THE land for miles around Tuttletown was staked off in claims. White papers on sticks fluttered everywhere. The place was black with hundreds of prospectors and their picks glinted in the sun. Jackasses were hobbled. There were brush shelters and sometimes piles of provisions just dumped on the ground. The main road of camp was lined with fresh-smelling, new pine shanties and gambling places that were deserted now in the early morning sun.

For three days Charles and the boys scrabbled over the hillsides keeping a sharp lookout for possibilities, for a bit of land that had not been claimed. In their blankets out under the stars of nights, they could hear the din from gambling houses and the strum of guitars that betold the fandangos were going full tilt.

Finally, next to two Mexicans, they found a place unclaimed. The Mexicans were crushing quartz that showed no gold at all on the surface; yet when it was ground in the arrastra they had, the stuff ran better than twenty dollars to a ton.

"Here's where we stay," Charles told the boys. "You set up camp while I stake out the claim."

Before dark that night they had a brush shelter up with the tent roof all snug over them. The white slip of claim ownership fluttered once more; Charles thought of the time he had written out a similar slip for poor black Artemus—who had no other last name except the name of his white master—and the slip that Maria had left fluttering at Pine Log.

The Mexicans were good fellows and they liked the boys. From the very beginning the smaller of the two, José, would call out a cheery *"Buenos días"* of a morning. After a night or two, they came over and sat around the campfire for a bit of talk, and Charles passed out some of Anne's sweet cakes as a neighborly offering.

Antonio was the serious one, but José was out for a little fun and excitement. He knew when there was a new fandango girl in camp, even if he never went off the hillside, and told in great detail about the fine cockfights men had down in Hornitos where his girl Anita lived.

"You know what?" Bill said one night after the Mexicans had gone back to their own camp. "I bet we could make a deal with them. They know me and Charley can't have claims because we're not old enough. But they know we can work as well as any man. Charley and me could run their darned old arrastra stone good as they do, and leave them time to mine out more rock. Then after we crushed theirs, they could let us use the stones to grind our rock, and we'd all be better off."

"You're your mother's own canny son, Bill," Charles said and promised to tackle the Mexicans about the arrangement.

"Only thing, I wish they didn't have to wear those long knives," Charley said. "I don't like knives so handy."

Antonio and José listened carefully while Charles explained the proposition the next night after dark, but they wanted to think about it. In a couple of hours they came back and told *their* plan.

"Your claim and our two," Antonio said, and held up three fingers. Then up went five fingers on the other hand. "Five people to work. Everybody work like hell. The *jovens* grind everybody's rock, then you get one third everybody's work. We furnish our arrastra and work too and we get two thirds everybody's work." Then he shrugged. "When rain comes everybody wash."

Charles thought a bit. After all there was no money yet for a stamping machine and the rock must be crushed. A poor man had to get along as best he could. The Mexicans already had the stones, but grinding was hard work for a couple of lads. Most folks used a jackass to go around and around and crush the rock between the two great flat stones.

"What do you say, boys?" he asked. "You'll be doing the grinding."

"Make the deal," Bill said. "We've a lot to gain if the dirt pays and we can always stop if it's too hard."

"José, Antonio," Charles said. "What if we take out plenty for a stamping machine on shares? Would that agreement of two thirds to one third still stick?"

"Sure," José said. "The stamping machine goes faster."

José, Antonio, Morgan and Company fared fine the first week with nearly thirty ounces of gold to split three ways when they walked over the hills at sunset on Saturday afternoon to weigh in at Wells, Fargo in Columbia. What a thrill Charles had going over the marble step with the crowd!

After the weighin nothing would do but they go to Riley's store for grub, for fresh tomatoes, raised by Chinese gardeners on the lowland near Stockton, and canned oysters and fancy crackers.

Jolly young Matt Brady was as pleased over their strike as if it had been his own. He passed out drinks in celebration.

Anne was delighted when they all trooped into the cabin for supper, and didn't even wink an eye when the new partners produced a bottle of wine along with the fresh meat and other things they had bought. Such excitement! It was a party.

Henry chattered like a chipmunk. There was no stopping him. His chest was big as a pouter pigeon's when he told that he had dug a whole foot of dirt in his mother's tunnel.

Sarah Ann was charmed by Tony, and insisted on sitting on his lap and bashing him in the face with a chunk of bread. Tony didn't even mind when her small fingers fastened themselves in his long black hair. He just threw back his head and said that was a way women had with men, and vowed he would wait until the niña grew up and then marry her.

Charles nearly fell out of his chair at supper when Anne, the Sister of Temperance, took a sip of wine to drink the health of the new partnership. "To riches!"

The claim paid well. Sometimes there was as much as forty ounces when the three partners weighed in at Wells, Fargo and then trudged up to French Gulch for supper.

After that every Saturday night was celebration night in the little cabin. Tom Baxter and Shorty Palmer always headed up from Pine Log for the jollity and brought grub, and High Water Bill came in from Squabbletown with his contribution.

At first High Water's nose was out of joint. He didn't like other men, no matter who they were, to share Anne's attention. Charles was sure High Water came to the celebrations only because he would be miserable if he stayed away, for he had asked Charles why Anne "had to have every God-damned man in the diggings hanging around the cabin of a Saturday night and stinking the place up with their pipes and Mexican cigarettes?" He resented jolly little José, and was going to bust in the Mexican's face because José mentioned the good-looking legs of some fandango girl! It wasn't decent even to speak of such things in front of Anne.

Bill didn't like Tom Baxter getting his face so near little Sarah Ann when he played peekaboo with her.

"Tom's breath smells of chewing tobacco," he grumbled. "A little girl shouldn't be bothered with smelling chewing tobacco until after she's married and can't do nothing about it anyway."

"How do *you* know so much about Baxter's breath?" Charles chided. "You been *kissing* old Tom?"

As the weeks went by, Bill's jealousy worked itself out, and he was good-natured once more. The other men, slicked-up and shaved, and clustered around Anne, worked a miracle on him. Bill took to washing up and using hair oil to meet the competition on Saturday nights.

Anne made fine rice pudding with raisins in it and they had roast beef too. Always there was a bottle of wine "to warm the heart," as Tony said.

Sometimes José didn't come to the celebrations. There was a *señorita* at Hornitos who had more pull than the cabin at French Gulch. Tony would be disgusted then, and refuse to talk to reckless José for perhaps a whole day—until his anger died down.

The Mexicans took everybody to see the Bachus Minstrels—the finest seats in the house—and High Water Bill, not to be outdone, treated to the Siamese Twins and to the Oyster Parlor afterward.

This was the real thing. Money helped a lot. They were all different, new people now, with happiness instead of just hope to live on. The flats around Columbia were recognizing the Morgans at last and giving them a share of the riches! With rain, folks would see what happened. Tuttletown men might have to wait for rain—but they had gold.

But on the way back from a week end, they learned that the folks at Murphy's were making a great to-do over their new eighteen-hundred-foot flume. Murphy's was showing the rain what it could do.

Murphy's! The name quickened the blood of Charles as he walked along. Maria wasn't far from Murphy's at Melones. He thought of the times he had tried to get over to see Maria, but the excuse was never enough to justify him in Anne's eyes. At Tuttletown he was away from Anne! There was nothing to keep him away from Maria.

"Think I'll take a trip over to Murphy's and have a look at the flume," he told the boys and José that night around the campfire. "It might pay us to see what folks there are doing."

There was no objection, no comment.

The next morning he started off bravely on the stage. Maria wouldn't care that he wore his old mining clothes. He was like a lad let out of school for a holiday, and excited about seeing his girl. But as the wheels ground through the thick dust he wasn't so sure. What did he have to offer Maria but heartache? What could he say now? Just telling her that he cherished the nugget was silly for a grown man.

The stage creaked on. That fine pink glow he had started with took on a daft tinge as he passed the great flume at Murphy's and rode on to Melones.

At a saloon he had a schooner and asked about schools.

The keep was a family man with kindly blue eyes. "There's two," he said. "One, public as hell, and the other run by a woman from Chile that tries to teach my young ones some manners." He swabbed off the bar. "Thinking of sending a youngster to school?"

"Yes." Charles didn't look into the man's eyes.

"Well, better go on over and see the *Chilena*. She's your woman. She's out with the little ones now." He pointed across the dry grass to a small board shanty where children played in the yard.

With lagging steps and an ache in the pit of his stomach and yet eagerness that was near to burning him up, Charles made his way across the open space. The heart of him jumped as he saw Maria sitting on the porch, her face calm and placid and gray hairs at her temples. Her head was bent over a book and she was reading aloud to a cluster of children at her knee.

He couldn't go on. She looked so peaceful, so content. How could a sniveling man spoil it all and open up the old sore just because his heart called out to her?

Charles slipped behind the trunk of a locust tree and watched. Maria's soft voice came across the dry grass on the breeze. "And the prince took his princess away and they lived happily ever after."

"There's a *man* hiding behind that tree!" a youngster's voice rang out. "I'm afraid of men that hide!" And he pointed to the locust.

Charles came out. There was nothing else to do, but his heart was in his boots.

"Carlos!" Maria's eyes brightened, her face shining as he walked toward her.

"*Amigo*," she said softly and clasped his hand, while all the children stood about her wide-eyed.

"I had to come," he managed. "I've wanted to tell you—to thank you for—for the nugget. I carry it with me always."

There was a moment of silence. They didn't need to talk. Each heart screamed out with its love.

Maria clapped her hands. "All you children into the school," she ordered. "Everybody write the multiplying tables as far as he knows them before I come in."

Through the racket and scramble of rough boots on boards Charles spoke. "I'll always love you, Maria. You're in my mind day in and day out. The heart of me mourns you." He tried to put everything in him into words, but they failed so pitifully.

"You have the wife—and the dear little *niña* that *might* have been *ours,* Carlos," she said tenderly. "You should be most thankful."

The dam burst then. "I was young!" he cried. "I didn't know love when I married her. Oh, God, what's a man to do?" he finished desperately.

Maria's eyes turned sad. "Would it help the pain, Carlos, if you knew that there's been no other man after Pine Log?" she asked gently. "And that Maria stays here instead of going home to Chile because she wants to be near you in case you ever need—" there was a pause—"your California wife."

All hell broke loose inside the school then, and she turned toward the door. "But you mustn't come again, Carlos. It only makes the hurt worse." With a last look that made the soul of him wince, she disappeared inside.

Heavy-hearted, Charles walked all the way back to Murphy's, took a look at the flume and headed for Tuttletown.

"The flume's all right," he told his partners, "but we have nothing to complain about here, with a good vein and five pairs of hands to work it. *We* don't need a flume. Rain'll come."

Rain did come, with a vengeance, in November. All hands of José, Antonio, Morgan and Company turned to the washing. God had sent rain and man must work with his Maker to harvest the gold while runnels flowed.

They didn't stop now of a Saturday night and head for Columbia, but worked right through the Lord's Day.

Antonio would cross himself and say the good God sent the rain, so surely He didn't expect a man to leave his gold for any other man to pick up. Every miner on hill and flat was doing the same thing.

Anne understood. She sent Henry over on a horse, borrowed or hired, with bread and cooked food for them.

Along with the provisions came a bit of news. Henry, all by himself, had taken out three more feet of earth from the tunnel on French Gulch. Mom had fastened Sarah Ann in a chair to watch, and helped Henry wash it in the cradle. They had two whole ounces of gold!

But now Mom couldn't work. Sarah Ann was getting teeth and was a crosspatch if ever there was one, so the washing of gold must wait.

Tony knew what to do for teething. In Mexico the little *niñas* gummed something hard and cold to bring teeth through. What could be better than a fine gold nugget worn smooth by a river long ago? He sent a nugget back to his "future wife" by Henry.

They were all sitting over the campfire one night at dusk two weeks later, when suddenly Henry appeared on horseback.

The little chap looked pinched and miserable, and slid off the horse to sob in his father's arms.

"What's up, son?" Charles asked as he held the bony shoulders close to him. "Tell us, lad. Out with it."

"Sarah Ann's dead," he sobbed. "She don't breathe any more. She's all limp and white on the bed."

"Oh, God!" Charles gasped. "Not my little girl! What happened, boy?"

"Doc was there all night. He said it was teething and she got cold on her chest, but the medicine didn't do no good." Henry went off in another burst of sobbing.

With that Charley buried his face in the blankets and started sobbing, and Bill walked out of the tent into the dark. Tony just sat like a man frozen, with tears rolling down his cheeks.

Through his awful grief, Charles could hear José murmuring prayers.

When the first terrible shock was over, and Henry and Charley quieted a bit, Charles tried to think. Bill had come in again and sat silent and red-eyed by the fire.

"We must get back to your mother," Charles decided. "She's alone. She needs us."

"We all better go to put the poor little angel to bed for the last time," Antonio said gently.

"I *can't*," Charley cried. "I can't go and see her—like that! She was so merry and I loved her so much. Her little hands waving—I can't, I tell you. I'll stay here and watch the claim."

In an hour the little group were off, Henry riding the horse, and all but Charley plodding sadly through the cold December night toward French Gulch and all that was left of little Sarah Ann.

CHAPTER 38

1858

THE shock of seeing Sarah Ann carried up Boot Hill in the little pine box nearly finished off Anne. She could talk of nothing else, no matter what Charles, the boys and Antonio and José did to try to cheer her. She wasn't even interested in the new gas works that would burn wood and give folks light for fifteen cents a burner for a night; just sat staring into space or sometimes looking at Sarah Ann's clothes.

With leaden heart Charles sent his partners and Bill back to Tuttletown and Charley. Anne needed him now by her side as she had never needed him before. The fact that their lovely little girl was gone forever seemed to be a bond that bound them together as nothing had done in years.

One afternoon nearly a week after the funeral, Charles was making a cup of tea for Anne, to buck her up a bit, when there was a gentle tap on the door. He was used to such taps, for High Water Bill was always dropping in with a treat for Anne or a paper for her to read.

"Come in," he called, and went on pouring boiling water into the brown earthen pot.

The door opened—and there on the stoop stood Maria, a pink-flowered bonnet on her head and a long black cape wrapped around her.

"Maria!" Charles banged down the teakettle and went toward her. Anne too came to the door.

"I—I just heard about the little angel," she said softly. "My heart went out to you. . . . I came as soon as I could." Her eyes met Charles's for a second in understanding, and then she took both Anne's hands in hers and drew the lass to her. "Poor dear," she murmured tenderly. "Poor dear——"

For the first time since Sarah Ann had died, sobs racked Anne as Maria held her close. Over Anne's shoulder, Maria sent a look of love and pity and sympathy to Charles, who stood watching— helpless. All his soul understood that look. She had come to let him know her sorrow—and to comfort Anne too. A great surge of love went from him to her, and he knew that she knew.

"She was so pretty." Anne's words were muffled in Maria's cape. "You saw her that day, all smiling."

"Yes, *querida*," Maria comforted. "I don't forget." Her eyes were bright with tears. Gently she led Anne to the bunk and they sat there side by side. It startled Charles a bit to see courageous Anne cling to Maria's hand like a sorrowful child. He pulled himself together. "Have some tea, Maria?" he said. "You must be tired from the trip. We're forgetting about you."

"Yes, and after you were so good as to come, too." Anne wiped her eyes on the bottom of her checked apron. "Take off your cape and your bonnet—Maria. The tea must be poison strong, brewing so long." She got up, laid a clean tea cloth on the table and brought the plate of sugar cakes Mrs. De Moile had sent over.

Maria took off her cape and put the bonnet beside it on the bunk just as young Henry banged in from school.

"You've never seen our boys, Maria," Anne said, as she poured tea. "This is Henry, the youngest."

Then she turned to Henry. "This is—is Maria, an old friend of your father's," she explained. "Shake hands with her. She's come by coach all the way from Melones to see us."

Charles was in a daze and worried too. A man with two wives in the same room! Maria was as much his wife as Anne who introduced his boy. He pulled up the two chairs to the table and a box for himself. Pricks of fear came through his happiness at seeing Maria. A hundred things might happen. What if Tom Baxter and Shorty came? Those big mouths would be sure to let something out about Pine Log days. And High Water Bill? He'd be smitten with Maria the minute he clapped eyes on her. Bill was no husband for Maria—besides, Maria loved her Carlos. Anne was clever and had a way of worming things out of folks. Maria was no match for her. In no time at all Anne would guess the truth! Sweat ran down his legs and the room turned suddenly hot as he sat close to Maria at the table. Oh, God! Were a sinner's sins really about to catch up with him?

Maria was smiling at Henry, asking about the new school just started and telling him she was a teacher herself.

"Henry's to be the minister of the family, if Charles here ever gets enough gold out of the ground to send him to school," Anne said.

Henry's face turned dark and savage. He swallowed a bite of cake. "But I don't want to be a minister. I want to have a fine saloon like Marquita's so I'll be rich enough to buy everything I want."

Anne looked pitifully at Maria and shrugged her shoulders. "You see what this place does to them. I wish we'd never come! We might have had our little Sarah Ann yet if we'd stayed in Pottsville or even Wales." And her eyes filled once more. "That Marquita doesn't care whose husband she pulls into her place where the girls are." She sighed and passed the cakes. "But I suppose you have plenty of *her* kind down at Melones too."

Maria stirred the sugar in her tea. "Yes," she said without looking up, "they seem to be everywhere, but some of them try to be very kind."

Charles thought he would die, when Maria spoke so gently and didn't look up. Was she thinking of the same thing that pricked at him? "That's what I tell Anne," he put in. "Marquita is generous and kind——"

"Well, she can just take her kindness and generosity somewhere else," Anne interrupted. "Her and all the others. I've seen enough of what they do to the men."

"Here, here, this is a tea party, not a Temperance meeting!" Charles tried to sound gay, undisturbed. "Maria doesn't want to hear a tirade when she's come so far to see us."

After that they talked of safe comfortable things, like the price of provisions and the new gold strikes. By the time young Henry had finished off his tea and gone out to play, the two women were chatting like old friends, about the new styles in dresses and how much starch to put into petticoats.

Charles grew restless. High Water might be dropping in any time now. He often came for supper.

Maria stood with a tea towel, wiping the thick white cups that Anne washed.

"You know, I was so surprised to see you that day at St. Anne's. Charles was sure you had gone back to Chile," Anne said as she wrung out the dishrag. "He said you had taken out enough gold to go back rich."

Charles could feel his pulse race. It was hard to swallow. The spit in his mouth dried up. Maria sent him a quick look, then spoke as she folded the tea cloth.

"There was nobody to go back to—in Chile. And the chance came to have a school."

"But your claim!" Anne cried. "Charles said you had a good claim and a long tom at Pine Log. What happened to that?"

There was a second's pause. Charles wanted to go through the floor. Why did Anne have to probe so damned much into the business of other people? She would catch Maria as sure as God made mackerel.

"I sold it," Maria said slowly. "I sold it at—at a very high price, *la doña Anita*—then left Pine Log." She brushed a smooth white hand across her eyes, as if she would blot away the thought.

As Charles watched her he remembered the night he had told Maria about Anne. She had done the same thing then, but her hand had been roughened by hard work and tanned in the sun. Oh, God! Was ever a man so miserable, having to sit helpless and hear his ring-and-prayer-book wife put the woman he loved through such a cruel questioning?

Maria's answer seemed to brighten Anne up. "Well, I'm glad *some* woman has taken riches from these wretched mountains besides the bad women," she said as she rolled down her brown calico sleeves. "The Morgans have struggled for years living on hope, and nothing much to show for their work."

"But gold isn't everything," Maria came back. "You have your husband and your boys. I have only memories."

That cut into the very heart of Charles.

But Anne wouldn't be salved. "Just the same, you need gold—to feed boys."

"Maria worked hard for what she got at Pine Log," Charles cried. "She worked from dawn to dusk at her long tom, and then cooked for the lot of us. On Sundays she washed and mended our clothes. She's earned everything she got."

Then he added a bit for himself—to let Maria know. "I was down at Pine Log after you left, Maria. You took your luck with you from that claim. The fellow after you didn't make wages—after the high price he paid."

There was talk of supper then, and that gave Charles his cue. "I'll be off down to get some oysters, Maria. You always liked tinned oysters we used to have as a treat, remember?" He smiled at her.

The answer came back. "I'm afraid I'm too old now, Carlos, to go back to the times passed away. Anything will do for eating tonight. I didn't come to bother, and I must catch the stage at seven."

Anne set up a protest. Maria must stay at least a day or two. There were so many things to talk about. They must have a good visit.

Maria shook her head. There was school. She must get back.

"But you don't need the money. You can take a day or two," Anne begged.

The head shook again. "The children love me and I love them. They'll be expecting me."

Charles begrudged the time away from Maria while he went to fetch the oysters. He wanted to be there and know what the women said, and yet the whole business made him heartsick and tongue-tied. He could think of nothing to say. Besides, he had to steer High Water away from the shack.

Tom Baxter and Shorty Palmer were safe enough down at Pine Log. Maria would not be staying until Saturday. He fingered the nugget as he strode along. There would be a bit of a chance to talk to Maria when he took her down to the stagecoach. He would tell her how much her visit meant and make excuses for Anne's probing. He would tell her again how much he loved her and that the nugget was his talisman to keep close, come hell or high water. A dozen things to tell her floated through his mind.

But after supper, when Maria put on her cape and bonnet, Anne had brightened up. She thought a walk through the fresh evening air would do her good. And damned if Maria didn't back her up!

They walked along the road by the light of the lantern. The stage waited in front of the Stage Driver's Retreat, and Jim Johnston was about to climb up onto his seat.

Anne kissed Maria and clung to her a moment. "I'm so glad you came. You've done me a world of good. Do come again!"

Maria smiled tenderly as one would smile at a child. Her teeth shone white in the gleam from the coach lights, and made Charles think of the night he first lay up with her in Columbia.

"I will say prayers that the good God will take away the hurt—from you and Carlos," Maria said. "Good-by my *pobrecitos.*" Then there was the quick clasp of Charles's hand with a squeeze of love to it, and she darted into the coach. Jim slammed the door shut, climbed the box and with a cluck to the horses they were off.

Charles had sad thoughts of his own as he and Anne started back over the hill. What a mess he had made of his own life—and Maria's too!

"Wasn't she good to come all the way up here?" Anne's words came through the misery. "You know at Pottsville, I got the idea that she was—well—common, working with men as she did——"

He let that pass. What was the use of talking now?

"Do you suppose, Charles, that she's just staying around here because of that good-for-nothing husband who left her?" Anne wanted to know.

"Might be." Charles hit a rock with the toe of his boot and cursed under his breath.

"Did you see her dress?" Anne persisted. "It was the heaviest corded silk I've ever seen, Charles. And that bonnet must have cost a fortune."

"I didn't notice," he got out, and they walked in silence for a time, their shoes clattering over the loose gravel.

"You know, I've been thinking something," Anne broke the quiet.

"Yes?"

"Maria's alone, with nobody to care about her——"

"That's true. There's no man now to look after her—or give her a hand when she needs one," Charles said softly. "And after all she's done for others too. But perhaps there's people down at Melones. Maria always made friends——"

Then Anne shot the bolt that hit him midriff like a bullet. "Charles, Maria's rich. She admits it. If we were to be friends, really good friends—you being her partner long ago and everything—if anything should happen to her, why maybe she'd leave her money to us. You heard me tell her how we wanted to send Henry to be a minister. Her without folks to leave her money——"

Hot anger boiled up. "No! I'll be damned if I'll be like a buzzard, waiting for Maria to die so I'll get her money!" Charles clutched hard at the nugget in his pocket and wanted to cry out with the pain. "You should be ashamed, Anne Morgan! Henry can rot on the hillsides before I'll stoop that low." The words rang out and echoed in the night air. "Maria's shared far too much with me already."

"Then maybe you can find some way of your own to make us rich like other people," Anne snapped. "I've done everything *I* can. Even Maria, a woman, has done better than you have. I'd like a corded silk dress too, and a bonnet that's from a store and not made over."

There was no more talk between them that night after they reached the cabin, and the next morning Charles left Anne with Henry and struck off for Tuttletown.

CHAPTER 39

1858

CHARLES persuaded the Tuttletown outfit into knocking off early the following Saturday. He wanted to be on hand when Shorty and Tom Baxter arrived at the shack in Columbia, heads fuzzy with whisky that might loosen their tongues. Anne was bound to pop off about Maria, and a sinner had to look sharp.

Sure enough, Anne was full of Maria's visit while she made the gravy and they all sat around waiting for grub. She told all about how Maria looked, the beautiful corded-silk dress, and how kind and sympathetic she had been over little Sarah Ann.

With the description Anne gave of Maria, Charles saw young Charley's eyes open wide. The boy stopped fingering the paper he'd bought and gave his father a startled look as if he was putting two and two together to make a damned five!

God! Charles thought, as a rush of uneasiness shot through him. I clean forgot Charley! She gave Charley the nugget for me and I told him not to tell his mother.

Charley started to contribute something to the talk, then evidently thought better of it and his mouth closed again. His eyes went back to the paper.

"Maria seemed right glad to see Charles and me," Anne was saying as she sifted flour into the brown meat juice. "She's rich too; she admitted she had taken out lots of gold at Pine Log and sold her claim for a high price. Maria's put the lot of you to shame. I'm proud of my sex."

Shorty Palmer didn't look up, but Tom Baxter did and his blue eyes twinkled.

"Remember that two-legged—I mean that four-legged little jackass you and Maria and *Artemus* had, Morgan? Right smart little black-eyed devil she was."

Charles could feel the heat rush to his face. His flannel undershirt stuck to his back in a sudden sweat. "Yes, and I remember too, the good things Maria cooked for *you* and Shorty and me of a Sunday." He glanced past the gathers of Anne's skirt at Tom sitting by the door.

Anne, with her back to them, talked on while she stirred. "Charles says she had a good-for-nothing husband at Pine Log but he left her. I can't see how *any* man would want to leave a good woman like Maria."

There was silence for a second then Anne rattled on. "Charles says he never saw Maria's husband. Tom, did you and Shorty ever see him?" she asked. "What did he look like?"

Shorty Palmer's big Adam's apple bobbed up and down inside his thin little neck and he busied himself by spitting tobacco juice out the door.

Tom Baxter grinned at Charles, crossed his great legs and cleared his throat. "Well, yes—I did, Mrs. Anne—several times. . . ." he began slowly.

All the while young Charley sat there taking notes, his eyes like saucers.

Charles was terrified. Baxter had taken several nips. How far would the fool go?

"He was a great big chap—handsome too," Baxter went on. "That is, if you fancy dark men——"

"From Chile, I suppose, like Maria." Anne took the meat out of the oven and brought it to the table. "You can't trust Latins. Come on, pull up your boxes and chairs."

"Can't trust nobody," High Water put in as he rolled down his shirt sleeves. "Not Latins or Irishmen either. A damned mick went off with my pick today when I had my back turned."

Tom Baxter let out a loud guffaw then, and there was an end of talk about Maria—in favor of food.

Later, when the boys and Antonio and José were off about their own affairs, and High Water Bill was helping Anne with the dishes, Charles went out into the cool dark to smoke with Tom and Shorty.

"Kinda got a little beyond your depth with Maria and Anne together, didn't ye, laddie?" Tom laughed. "The Devil must be grinning a bit to himself."

"Along with you?" Charles snapped. "I don't think it's funny."

Tom drew on his pipe to light it and threw the match away as pungent tobacco smoke filled the air. "Strikes me yer name's spelled wrong," he said and clapped Charles on the back. "Ought to strike out the *G* and put in an *M* and join up with that Brigham Young chap over at Salt Lake. I hear tell they let men have *six* wives all legal over there."

Then, as Charles ground his teeth and cussed him, Baxter seemed to feel compassion. "Don't worry, Morgan, we'll keep your secret. We'll watch our tongues with Mrs. Anne—for her sake. 'Course you can't never tell what might slip out, though."

"It's an *O*," Shorty said suddenly.

"What in hell's an *O*?" Baxter asked.

"Mormon—it's spelled with an *O*." Shorty was dead-serious.

They had a good laugh then, and Charles felt a great flood of relief go through him.

"So it is," Tom cried. "Go up in the class—yer improvin'. That *O* lets Morgan out."

From that minute, no matter what happened, Charles knew there was nothing to fear from his pals—unless they were tipsy.

Maria's visit had given Anne a great buck-up. For weeks, on Saturday nights and Sundays, she talked of Maria and her kindness and longed to see her again, until Charles was crazed by the chatter and trying to keep from showing his feelings before Charley and Tom and Shorty. Maria was good, said Anne, Maria was beautiful. It didn't matter that Maria was a papist. Maria, Maria, Maria!

At last one Saturday night the middle of April the damned Maria ratchet was lifted in Anne's mind. She could scarce wait to

tell them all that a man in Sonora had predicted the end of the
world on March 4, 1861. He had a long piece in the paper warn-
ing folks. He had read Revelations!

Antonio crossed himself quickly and decided to stay over at
the cabin and bunk with the boys so he could go to Mass at St.
Anne's next morning.

José said there was plenty of time. This was only 1858, nearly
three whole years to repent in and get ready for God. He was
going to have a good time first, down in Hornitos.

"Well, we'll all go down together, the good along with the bad,"
Charles said as he cut off seconds from the roast. "You never miss
a go at church, Anne. I'll hang onto the skirt of your calico when
the time comes—you ought to get me through."

They all laughed then, even the boys, and it annoyed Anne no
end. She thought they ought to be prepared in case the man was
right. She wanted them to go to the meeting and hear what this
Mr. Leiber had to say.

"One in the family's enough worrying about it," Charles told
her. "If the millennium only holds off long enough for us to get
that damned stamp machine over to the claim and going, I'll be
satisfied."

Leiber scared Anne stiff with the terrible things to come before
the end of the world. Famine was coming; earthquakes too, and
meteors would fall burning from the sky and kill folks right and
left. The whole thing was in Revelations. There was no time to
be lost. Men must confess their sins and get right with God, so
they could be saved and meet him at the golden throne.

Two weeks later, when May Day dawned, there were other
things to think about besides the end of the world.

"Rich gold strike on Fraser River in Canada!"

San Andreas heard the news first off, and the echo rang over
every hill and dale in the Sierras near as fast as a forest fire!

Men in Tuttletown, over schooners at nightfall, were full of talk
about the strikes at Fraser. Already hundreds had pulled freight,
and the big companies had bought up their quartz claims.

Anne had an idea about what Fraser could do for the Morgans, when Charles hit Columbia one Saturday with Antonio, José and the boys. "We can buy up a good claim cheap from someone who is crazy to go and *we'll* get rich," she told them.

But Charles would have none of that. He wasn't going on any more wild-goose chases and buy up somebody else's claim. The good ones would cost all the money they had put by for the stamp mill, and then they couldn't be sure. Men were salting mines like hell to sell and get out.

José and Antonio backed Charles up. They had a good claim now. Mrs. Anne would be a rich lady someday if she would only keep her ears deaf to the calls of other claims and let the men manage things.

But on the Fourth of July, when Morgan and Company reached Columbia to collect Anne and Henry and make a day of celebration there wasn't even a band of music! In two days two thousand miners had left. Some even skipped out without settling up their liquor bills.

The only talk along the streets was Fraser River. Water in the new ditch had failed completely, and there was only a dribble in the old Tuolumne Water Company's ditch.

Jim Coffroth and his Stanislaus Water Company were wild. One million dollars had gone into the new ditch that would bring water sixty miles over the mountains from the north fork of the Stanislaus!

Jim raced from group to group on the streets, his black broad-cloth coattails flying. "Just be patient, gents," he begged. "The Stanislaus Company knows your needs. We'll give you water for two dollars a day! Don't desert us."

Some men jeered at him then, as they stood in line near Jim Johnston's stagecoach waiting for seats to Stockton.

A sign was up on a lamppost that there would be no more gas light furnished. The mains were clogged with pitch.

"So we're going to be like Moses—in the dark," Leary said to Charles and Anne as they read the notice together outside Riley's store. "What with crazy miners stealing horses to race for the

boats at Stockton, and folks salting mines and robbing one another
—all because of this Fraser business, it might be that fellow over in
Sonora is right. Maybe the world *is* coming to an end."

Only jolly Matt Brady at Riley's store seemed to be getting any
fun out of life. He told them all his joke.

Captain John, the Digger Indian Chief, had come into the shop
to find out why palefaces were going away, and one of the "boys"
had made to read out of the paper that folks around Columbia had
decided to turn the country back to the redskins. All Indians
had to do was pick out the house they wanted to live in.

Anne was full of news next time they came home. Indians
were *demanding* their houses, and burning down cabins and robbing folks who refused to get out. Two miners had been killed
and Jim Coffroth had called a meeting for volunteers to go out
and quell the outrage.

"Coffroth better stick to his water works," Charles opined.

"They went out, but they didn't get the poor things," Anne
told him.

Charles sighed. "Indians will most likely have to go back to living on acorns, and be just where they started before the white
men came to educate them about almonds and rotgut—only now
they have no land to call their own."

But he had news of his own to tell her. The stamp mill was in
and crushing rocks at a great rate on the near-deserted hillside at
Tuttletown. The piles were all ready to wash, come rain again.

José ambled in with two bottles of wine then and chickens that
he insisted on cooking Mexican-fashion on a wire over the open
fire. There was a great celebration in the cabin on French Gulch
that night, and toasts went up to the new stamp machine.

"We have *something* from the Fraser River to be thankful for,"
Anne said as they ate supper. "The fandangos have most of them
caved in, and church folks don't have to listen to as much wild
music of nights."

Young Bill sniffed. "Marquita's is still going and Maria Querida's too, and there's gambling." Then he told that Mr. Strain, the
gambler, was doing all right for himself, dealing monte nights

and panning in the creek bottom daytimes after he got out of bed. Strain had just found a nugget worth seven thousand, four hundred and thirty-eight dollars!

"And here we sweat all day and dig out less than six inches of hard stuff and don't get much gold! Beats hell how some folks have all the luck," he finished.

"Wait until we wash big," Antonio cried. "We'll show them all."

"I'm waiting," Bill said, "and so is Charley. We're getting fed up. What in hell *is* ahead anyhow?" He shoved away his plate, left the table and strode out of the cabin.

The heart of Charles went out to the boy near man. How many times had he thought the same thing himself? What's ahead?

He got up from the table and followed the boy outside.

Bill was sitting on the chopping block, head resting on his hands.

Charles went over to him. "Buck up, Bill," he said. "It isn't all downgrade, you know. There's always the hills a man must climb. We'll get the breaks ourselves someday." He opened his purse. "Here's a bit of extra jingle, lad. Go have some fun."

But Bill shoved the gift away with his elbow. "I don't want pap," he said, "dribblings from your purse. I'm nearly sixteen now—a man, and I'm sick of the whole business."

"What do you want to do, son?" Charles asked after a minute, and tried to put himself into the boy's boots.

Bill lifted a hard angry face. "I want to clear out! I want to go on my own and work for decent wages at the quartz mines. I never want to see damned old Columbia again."

"Some girl?" Charles ventured.

"Yes, damn it, if you have to know!" the boy roared out. "Sophie, up at Marquita's place, has been my girl on Saturday nights for a year now, but Strain and his God-damned nugget have changed everything! She's gone on him. Won't even talk to me. I'd like to plug his old guts with lead for his pains!" Bill's eyes shone fierce with anger in the fading light.

"That won't help," Charles told him. "There'll always be another Strain or a Kelly or a Finnegan—you know that. Those girls are out after the money."

"I thought Sophie was different," Bill groaned. "I thought she really liked me."

There was silence for a bit.

"Maybe you're right," Charles said finally. "Maybe you'd better clear out for the quartz mines on your own. But leave Strain alone, Bill. Leary or the sheriff will only get you and you'll go to jail or perhaps be hanged for your pains. No girl like Sophie is worth that."

Bill got off the chopping block. "If I go to the quartz outfit, Charley wants to go with me. We've talked about it," he told Charles. "Charley's fed up with grubbing too. We want to make our own way."

"Charley's pretty young."

"Hell, he's stronger than I am," Bill cried out. "He has a right to his life too. You worked in the coal mines when you were his age!"

Charles sighed and put a hand on the angry lad's shoulder. "All right," he said. "If you two are set on going, you can leave from Tuttletown when we go back to work on Monday. I'll break the news to your mother when I come home next Saturday night. It'll save a rumpus with her that way."

Rebellion wiped itself from Bill's face. Charles saw the young eyes brighten. A rough hand squeezed his own horny one. "You're a good dad," Bill said. "You're a *wonderful* dad."

"I *hope* so. I hope God thinks I'm a good father for what I've done this night." Charles sighed, and turned away. Then suddenly he whirled on his heel. "Bill, *don't* go after Strain, will you? It'll only bring shame and trouble on us all if you do."

"No, Dad," Bill's answer came through the growing dusk. "I'll be a sissy as usual and let the damned stinker live."

Anne took the news well. If the boys wanted to be off on their own, they might make out better. Good wages were to be had at the quartz outfits, and they'd not forget to send some home.

"They aren't starting any sooner than hundreds of boys do in the old country—or sooner than you did," she told Charles. "I'd hoped things would be better for *our* sons. But at least they'll never die choking from coal dust or burn to death in a mine fire."

She pinned her hopes on Henry, still at home. Maybe for Henry things would be better. He was younger. By the time he had become a man, things were *bound* to be better.

CHAPTER 40

1858-1860

THE Mexicans missed Bill and Charley, but they were willing to work on the same shares with Charles, for after all without the boys there could have been no stamp machine. Each day the three men grubbed away, and the ten hammers crushed rock ready for the rain.

But the dry made bad times. The hydraulics had stopped with the water on Brown's Flat, leaving great cliffs and cleaned-away places as a monument that they had come, taken the lion's share and gone. With no water to use on claims the few miners left were laying in winter supplies to wait for rain.

Coffroth kept on promising water. The ditch would soon come in, he told them all. Nearly all the flumes had been calked. Sixty miles was a long way to bring water. They must be patient.

Every day more and more disillusioned miners back from the Fraser came through Tuttletown, and found that the big quartz companies had gobbled up their deserted claims. They resented Chinese who worked and took out even an ounce. Someone was always being stabbed or shot.

Charles took Henry to help at Tuttletown. It would give the boy some pocket money, Anne said, and get him away from so much hatred and misery. But after a few months they didn't need so much grub at the claim in Tuttletown. José had gone one week end to Hornitos as usual and didn't come back.

Finally, when five days passed and still no José, Antonio could wait no longer. He changed from work clothes into his best, and rode out of camp with the express rider along with the gold.

262

Two days later, at dusk, he walked into the cabin just as Henry and Charles were tuning up the cookstove to heat the beans. "We got no more José," he said and threw his wide-brimmed Palo Alto on the bunk. "He's had his last excitement at Hornitos."

"Run off with a girl?" Charles asked, as he stirred the pan.

"No, ripped in the guts and dead over that damned fool Anita down there. Got drunk and had a fight in a 'dango house. The other *hombre's* dead too. They're planted together on the hillside outside town."

Work on the claims went slower after that. Charles began to feel his age. Digging was harder for a man of thirty-nine than it had been at twenty-nine when he had first grubbed the hill with Artemus.

When Bill and Charley came home from Bear Valley one Saturday in August, they were excited as chipmunks. Horace Greeley had been staying at General Frémont's! He was such a grand gentleman in a frock coat and the finest set of whiskers as graced a face. He talked to everybody that worked in the quartz outfit, in language good as any parson used on Sunday for a sermon.

Anne told them then about Greeley having a piece in the paper —about women. Greeley had said California needed over one hundred thousand more women.

"Women! What in hell does Greeley know about women?" Bill demanded. "He's a writer. I wouldn't give a pickax for anything in petticoats!"

"*Madre de Dios!*" Antonio cried. "Not one hundred thousand more of the troublemakers! Where in hell will men go then?"

Charles knew the poor Mexican was thinking about his pard José, "planted" with the other *hombre* on the hill outside Hornitos because of a woman.

"Men's what need the protection. Women is what makes the trouble for them. Not even this Greeley fools *me* none," Tony finished.

Tom Baxter unwrapped the steak he had brought and opined that with the duel affairs of honor going around like they were, there would soon be no one left to fight over the silly wenches.

Anne shook the soup ladle at him, and said if he kept on spending his money at Marquita's on Saturday night, no decent woman would ever marry him.

Tom chucked her under the chin and grinned. "Aw, Mrs. Anne, you wouldna take a lad's fun away, would you? The bad lassies have their place whilst we wait for the good ones to come along," he told her. "We're all here clingin' to the skirts of the only angel we know to get through the Golden Gates, come the end of the world that Leiber chap told about. Only a little over a year now."

They all roared with laughter then, as Anne cracked Tom over the head with the soup ladle. Who could be sorrowful with the jolly Scotty and his Swede pard around?

But Charles had misgivings as he saw Henry laugh; he hoped the young one was only copying his elders and playing at being a man. Henry seemed to know considerable of what went on at Marquita's, and the business of the music box still rankled in Henry's craw.

"I can give ye a bit of bigger news than any ye have here," Tom burred as he planted his six feet four well out of Anne's way in the corner and took out his plug. "I got a letter from an old pard that's up in Grass Valley." Then he told that a prospector named Henry Comstock and another man, Judge Walsh, had been rambling over the hills into Washoe Territory and found wonderful ore there. "Black stuff that runs three thousand dollars to the ton in silver."

"Three thousand dollars to a *ton*!" Anne dropped a pan lid. She looked quickly to Charles. "Charles! Three thousand to a ton!"

"Holy Jesus, keep your skirts on!" Tony shouted out. "It'll only be like Fraser—nothing but clay—and they'll all be high-tailing back in a couple of months to find Chinks on the claims they left."

But Comstock and his "black stuff" could not be ignored, not even for the hectic, bitter political rows between the Blue-Bellied Black Republicans and the Hypocritical Democratical Sessionists, over what was to be done about black folks in the South.

A new disease, silver fever, had broken out in diggings everywhere. When Charles came into town all the talk was about "Comstock's lode at Washoe." Fabulous money was to be made there. Almost pure silver it was, and gold along with it for good measure!

"To the Washoe, charge!" was the cry in Matt Brady's store and on the street. Not even the water in Coffroth's new ditch stopped their jaws. There was work at good wages for miners in Virginia City. Strong backs and arms were needed!

In spite of rumblings of Civil War between the North and South in the States, men all along the Sierras kept their eyes on the Washoe and its dazzling silver. Saturday night suppers at French Gulch now had talk about Comstock's lode as relish for the meat.

"Not for me," Tom said. "There's enough for a Scotchman and his Swede pard down at Pine Log and there we stay, eh Shorty?"

August came and when they heard John Mackay had gone from Downieville and even Jim Fair had left Angel's Camp for Washoe, Bill and Charley were determined to go too. What was Frémont's forty-five dollars a month when a miner could make twelve dollars a day? They didn't mind that the water was like lye and food scarce and houses were blown down by the wind. Washoe was the place.

Charles watched Anne patch up the boys' clothes and get them ready for the trip over the mountains. He wondered that she wasn't eager to go herself. She didn't even urge him to head for Washoe. Was the lass finally growing as tired of the everlasting cry of "better diggings" as he was himself?

Not until they had gone to see Bill and Charley off on the stagecoach, and Henry went about his own affairs, did Charles find out the real reason why Anne had no desire to go to Washoe.

The lass looked pinched and white when they came home to the cabin at French Gulch. He told her to lie down on the bunk for a bit while he made a good cup of tea to cheer them.

266 OH GLITTERING PROMISE!

"We old folks must buck up and remember that the young ones have to fly for their own fortunes," he told her. "You've still Henry, and he's a fine lad for his twelve years."

"Oh they'll be all right," Anne told him. "They're used to roughing it. Bill and Charley will land on their feet and make their way. It's not them I'm worrying about." She got off her bunk, went to the shelf behind the stove and took down her beloved Staffordshire dog.

Charles watched her while he waited for the kettle to boil. The work-worn fingers caressed the shiny bit of pot, then slowly she opened the drawer where she kept her things and carefully laid the treasure away.

Charles set out the cups and saucers and put more sugar in the bowl and Anne took her place. When the tea was poured from the old brown earthenware pot, he put his hand over hers. "Why did you put it away?" he asked gently. "That dog is the only bit of beauty about the place."

She shook her head and the eyes of her looked into his. "Makes me think too much of the past, and Sarah Ann and what might have been." Then she took a great breath. "Charles, I'm going to have another young one come next March."

By the time the Blue-Bellied Black Republicans and the Hypocritical Democratical Sessionists had battled to the bitter end on November 6, 1860, and Abraham Lincoln carried the state, Columbia was beginning to show the effects of silver fever. She was slowly but surely wasting away. Some miners stayed gophering on her hillsides, a few gamblers remained to pick up what other men grubbed for, and several fancy houses including Marquita's kept proud heads and gay faces. But the main procession was toward Washoe.

Charles had his trouble. The vein at Tuttletown had given out. It didn't even pay now to run the stamp mill.

Something had to be done. He longed to tell Anne, but she was big with child and had enough to carry without sharing his burdens.

He sat with Antonio on the hillside at Tuttletown one day, fingered Maria's nugget in his pocket and tried to think of a way to plot the future.

Copper had been discovered thirty miles south of Stockton, and an English company had just brought in Cornish miners to work the mines.

Tony thought that might be a way out. "Washoe ain't for us," he told Charles. "Those letters from Bill and Charley about the churches blowing down all the time, and men having to live underground to keep from freezing, just don't sound good to this *hombre*. I guess it's Copperopolis, Don Carlos and day's wages."

"I can't leave Anne the way she is, and I can't take her with me without being sure of a place to live," Charles said. "She's held onto the claim at French Gulch. I'll work that until I can do better. I'll let her think I want to be with her now with the baby coming and her near thirty-eight, and tell her about the vein failing afterwards."

One bleak windy December morning they packed up the most important things ready for the teamster from Columbia to pick up the next time he was in Tuttletown, and then looked a long time at the hard-earned little stamp mill by the mine shaft.

"Guess no one would buy her from us," Antonio mumbled. "Nobody but big companies left and they wouldn't look at her."

"Guess not," Charles said. "Seems too bad to go away and let her rust here all alone, don't it?"

After a while they closed the cabin door for the last time and stood in the wind.

Charles wanted to say things to Antonio: to let him know what a good pard he had been, and to wish him well. But no words would come.

Antonio must have felt the same way, for he just pulled his faded tan jacket closer against the wind, and put out a brown paw.

Horny hands met. Antonio touched the brim of his battered

Palo Alto in salute, then without a word shouldered his pack and turned toward Copperopolis.

Charles took one look at the cabin and sloshed through the wet young grass to Columbia.

Green, he thought, as he crossed the hills. The green of resurrection, of spring, of new life coming on! Then the old and tired in him broke through, as he remembered that these fresh young pricks of green would turn lush and then tawny brown, and be a menace to men on the hillsides in August.

CHAPTER 41

1861

IN January the boys wrote exciting news from Washoe. Sun Mountain was gobbling up hundreds of tons of salt to process her silver. All day and half the night mule skinners lashed at their animals and cursed them, too, while they hauled salt, and still there was not enough. Now they had camels, ten of them, and each one carried two hundred pounds on its back. The poor defenseless things were pitiful when they arrived. They would whimper and groan and kneel to have the salt lifted from their bloody sore backs, and then pad quickly up the hill and look off sadly toward the flats, without anyone so much as washing off their hurts.

Twice Charley had fights with the men for abusing camels, but it did no good.

Henry was sick to his stomach when Anne read about the poor dumb camels. He had wanted to go to Washoe to earn money of his own, but now he said he'd stay and do odd jobs around Columbia and work over abandoned claims, rather than see so much suffering. That made things hard for Charles, because Anne wanted to know why Henry couldn't go to Tuttletown and work with Antonio.

He had to put her off about the claim. She thought the reason Antonio came no more on Saturday nights for supper was because he was shy and embarrassed to be around her now she was so big with the baby.

Once, when her mind was set on knowing how much gold came out of the quartz at Tuttletown, Charles used the death of

Lola Montez to switch her off the track. That had worked per-
fecly when he read it from the paper.

The "hussy" Lola Montez, dying poor and obscure and deserted in a shabby New York rooming house under the name of
Fanny Gibbons, fair cheered Anne as God's justice working
against wickedness.

Came March 1861 with warmer nights and greater trouble
about Civil War in the States. March, when Lieber said the end
of the world would come, and Anne was to give birth!

Charles still kept his dreary secret about the worked-out claim,
and was glad of the money put by during the flush days.

Shorty Palmer left Tom Baxter to work alone at Pine Log, and
stayed with Matt Brady in the store of nights, "to wait around in
case of need," he told Charles.

High Water Bill drifted over from Squabbletown every single
night after the first of March. "To be first to clap your damned
old back when the youngster shoots out."

They waited each night at Doc Parsons' Pay Ore Saloon for
word that "Anne had been took and come through the blizzard
right side up."

Little Aaron Morgan was born March 8, just four days after
Lieber had said the world was coming to an end. Charles was so
relieved that the affair was over and the little red twister all he
should be, so far as his works went, that he left Anne with the
church women fussing over her, and headed for the Pay Ore and
a roaring tearing drunk.

Shorty was so tickled that he poured a pony of liquor into his
own hat and clapped it onto his head to baptize the little devil.
Of course, it would have been even better if this sprig on the Morgan tree had been a girl—but no one could complain.

High Water said no other girl could take the place of Sarah
Ann, then clouted Shorty on the jaw and told him to shut up about
girls.

Matt Brady came in. They drank to Charles. To Anne. To

Aaron. To Bill and Charley at Washoe. To the camels at Washoe. To Abraham Lincoln, the new President of the United States, and lifted their glasses several times to America.

Anne wanted Maria to see the new baby. "She loved little Sarah Ann so much she'd be sure to like Aaron," she told Charles one night just after she was up and around. "I'm going to send a letter and invite her up."

Charles winced as he stacked wood behind the stove. He thought of Maria's eyes and what she had told him at Melones—that Sarah Ann might have been their child.

He straightened up. "No, lass," he said, "don't put her through that. Maria's always wanted a young one of her own. No use opening the sore."

"That's just it," Anne insisted. "She has none of her own. We can give her the joy of ours—and don't forget she has money. She might do something for little Aaron if we invite her."

"Money! Money! That's all you think about," he scolded.

But there was no use arguing, once Anne had her mind made up. He went out into the night and prayed to God that Maria would be saved this new hurt.

Anne sent the letter in spite of everything, and Charles lived in misery for days. Finally, a box came from Melones. There was a beautiful white crocheted blanket for little Aaron, with all Maria's love and best wishes. She was sorry that school kept her from coming to see the babe and his mother.

Anne held up the blanket and sniffed. "The wool in this didn't cost more than a dollar or two. I should think she'd have sent Aaron at least a silver mug." She tossed the white square onto the table and stamped out.

Charles went over and touched the soft wool. He thought of Maria's gentle fingers and the love she had put into the stitches. This little white blanket was her message to him. She was there at Melones, thinking of Carlos, but she wouldn't come again, to make things hard for them both.

He dropped the coverlet and quickly moved away when he

heard Anne's steps. Someday he would tell his son Aaron about the good Maria who had made a baby blanket for him.

Well before little Aaron was three months old, war had come and Abraham Lincoln sent out a call across the hills and dales for volunteers to come and fight for the rights of black men in the South.

Henry, at thirteen, wanted to go to war. He was an American and he fancied himself in a uniform.

"You'd only puke at the blood and seeing folks with cannon balls in their guts," High Water told the lad. "You're too young."

"I could be a drummer boy," Henry argued. "They need drummer boys."

"Your father needs a drummer boy more with your brothers gone and a new baby to take care of, and your Ma knowing that Tuttletown claim ain't worth a damn no more. She's sore as hell over that stamp mill going to waste," Bill snapped. "Besides, most likely there won't be no uniform. Only generals wear uniforms. They want folks to *fight,* not to dress up."

In Columbia and Sonora and all along the diggings thousands of miles away from the Civil War battlefields, folks began to fight private battles. Men were stabbed and shot because of what they thought should be done about the black men in the South.

There were fights up at Washoe too, so Bill and Charley wrote, but the fights were over silver. There were now twenty-five thousand men in the diggings. Nearly every mine had law suits over disputed ground. People *really* fought when a single share in a mine cost twenty thousand dollars or more, and some owners were taking out as much as ten thousand dollars a month!

By November, Anne could stand the strain of hearing about such riches no longer. She opened up on Charles one night at supper after they had read a letter from the boys.

"Here we are, grubbing along as usual, and you only getting out around two ounces a week on our claim, and having to help other miners put timber in their tunnels, for wages. Why don't you leave Henry and me and little Aaron, and go to Washoe after those *big* wages like the boys are making? We'll never get anywhere as it is."

"I can't go, lass," Charles told her. "I'm forty-one now, and forty-one is old in the mines. I couldn't keep up with the rest mining now. They won't pay a man twelve dollars a day unless he's worth it." Hard words they were to utter and they tore at his heart. For the first time in his life Charles Morgan, the Welshman, admitted defeat.

To make up for the disappointment he told her that he had been talking to a chap working an abandoned mine in Experimental Gulch close by. There had been quite a bit of dust and some good-sized nuggets too, and the fellow wanted him to go in as partner.

"Well, I expect you can try it—" Anne sighed—"but it makes you no better than the poor Chinamen gleaning from the tailings of what other men have left."

The needling about his gleaning from the tailings of others hurt Charles. "Anne," he groaned, "the mistakes of the Morgans hark back to the day I landed in Pottsville loaded down with gold that the good Lord had given us. We didn't take what we had and use it for the purpose it was given—the cheese factory." With that final shot he left her and went out to chop wood and work off his sorrow.

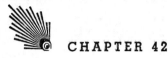

CHAPTER 42

1864–1865

BITTERNESS about the Civil War was everywhere. Henry came home one night with horrible news. During recess a fight had taken place. The Union boys decided to hang a Secessionist boy to the locust tree by the flume that carried water to sprinkle the streets. But the schoolmaster happened to look out of his window and rushed out just in time to save the lad.

"What a place!" Anne cried. "Young ones here get murderous before they're out of didies. It makes me sick—and all of us slaving to give calico balls and benefits to raise funds to care for the sick and wounded soldiers! What kind of a world are we living in, anyway?"

Then they suddenly *knew* what kind of a world it was! Grant took Richmond. Bells clanged out in Columbia, cannons fired, and bands tuned up that sunny April day in 1865 when word of Lee's surrender reached town.

Men poured into town in every direction, and drunks roared along the streets shooting off pistols and guns and the place turned into bedlam over the victory.

Charles and Anne saw Tom Baxter drunk as a lord, weaving along the road, with faithful little Shorty beside him, nearly as tipsy as Baxter.

Anne was disgusted. "I do wish men—good men like Shorty and Tom—didn't have to go the whole hog and try to empty every whisky keg in town whenever something happens," she snapped. "They work too hard for their money to spend it so."

" 'Tis their own to spend, lass," Charles said. "Whenever will you learn that men will be men, no matter how much talk and crusading comes their way? We've all our weaknesses. Yours just don't happen to be drink, that's all."

There was a different story the next day when sad-eyed Shorty Palmer came puffing up to the cabin on French Gulch with his dreary news. He and Tom had gone home to Pine Log as usual after the celebration. But when they came to the log crossing over the river to the diggings, Tom told Shorty he didn't think he could make it.

Shorty blew his nose then and wiped his eyes. "Just in the middle of the log, where the water was rushing, he must have turned dizzy, 'cause he toppled off the log into the stream."

Shorty had plunged in after Tom and rescued him.

"But when I finally got him on dry land, it was too late, Morgan," Shorty finished sadly. "His neck was broke and he was dead. The boys helped me hist his body to the back of a jackass this morning and I—" Shorty looked out of the door—"I led him up the hill into town. Tom's laid out on the floor of the Engine Company, while Old Coffin Pope measures him for—for his wooden overcoat."

There was little to say. Poor Shorty was desolate. He didn't see how he could go on without his big Tom pard. He asked them to go up Boot Hill with him that afternoon.

But things were not so simple as that. When they arrived at the engine house, little boys and curious folks stood looking at poor defenseless Big Tom and Old Coffin Pope was having his troubles. The day was hot and Tom had swelled while the coffin was being made!

Three times Pope had to enlarge the box to fit Baxter for his last trip up Boot Hill.

When Pope was ready to nail the coffin top on, Shorty dived into his pocket, pulled out the picture Tom cherished of his merry-eyed mother, and tucked in under Tom's arm.

"He'll be wanting her with him for company up there on that lonely hillside," Shorty said, then looked out into the bright sunlit street while Pope hammered at the last nails.

Not long after that, Shorty Palmer came up to the cabin and brought steak for supper and a bottle of wine.

Charles and Anne scarcely knew him, all dressed up as he was in a new store suit with a boiled shirt.

"You're not—not going to get *married,* are you, Shorty?" Anne asked. "There's only one thing takes a man out of blue jeans and a flannel shirt around here—and that's love. Who is she?"

Shorty shook his head. "Ain't no *love* would hold me to these hillsides without Tom." He sighed. "I've sold out my claim, Mrs. Anne, and I'm heading across the water to Sweden, for my old age. Pine Log just don't seem the same without old Tom. I can't stand them big tall mountains or bear to hear the water rushing under that log over the Stanislaus, without thinking all the time about Tom. Jim Johnston's taking me out on the stage tomorrow."

They had scarce put Shorty Palmer on the stage when muffled bells tolled mournfully. President Abraham Lincoln had been assassinated.

Word came that Father Bouchard would give a eulogy from the courthouse steps at Sonora, in honor of the martyred President. Anne was determined they must all have a clean-up and go to honor the memory of the fine man who had done so much to bring right and good and decency to this New World—America.

"It's all we can do, to honor him—listen to the good father," she told them as they jogged toward Sonora with High Water Bill. "Perhaps years from now, when we are dead and gone, and bitterness and horrors of the war are forgotten, men will see and understand what Abraham Lincoln has done for America."

"Jesus, but you're a good woman," Bill told her.

Charles thought of Artemus, who had worked so hard by his side, "to buy hisself free as any man born" and still never knew the coveted freedom. Because of the dead President, men like Artemus would never again be born into slavery to other men.

The father was eloquent and his words so beautiful that they touched the very soul of a man. Somehow, as they rode home through the growing dusk, Charles felt uplifted and filled once more with hope and the goodness of mankind, and faith that better things were ahead.

There was a light in the cabin when they trudged up the last hill to French Gulch. Charley and Bill had arrived from Washoe.

Henry was excited, and little Aaron turned shy in the presence of those big men he had never seen, who called themselves his brothers.

Anne rolled up her sleeves and went to work on a meal for everybody. High Water Bill tailed it to Matt Brady's after tinned oysters for a stew, and came back loaded with eatables of all kinds as a welcoming treat.

"Well, the hurricane's hit poor old Matt Brady for sure," High Water told them, as he banged things down on the table. "The man's gone clean crazy with love. Can't even draw a gallon of whisky or weigh out a pound of sugar, but he's got to look across the road at Fallon's Hotel, for fear he'll miss seein' that new girl Margaret Banahan, that Fallon's got working for him."

"I've seen her," Charles put in. "She's less than half the age of Matt. But she's a merry-eyed lass."

"No fool like an old one," High Water said. "Maybe Matt's going into his second childhood there in his store among the whisky kegs and sowbelly."

"Stop such talk," Anne snapped. "Matt'll make a good husband. Age doesn't matter if they really love each other and are suited."

After supper Bill and Charley told their news. The bottom had dropped out of Virginia City and the mines around. Comstock's lode was through. The cream of surface stuff was gone and all the tunnels full of water. Miners couldn't get work for even four dollars a day now.

"Maybe someday they'll find a way to drain her," Charley said.

"But a man can't stay up in those hot, hellish red hillsides and starve while he waits. Anyway, me and Bill ain't going to waste our lives away on a played-out hillside."

Henry, feeling big for his seventeen years, offered them a go at the place up the gulch where he made four dollars a day panning.

Charles stirred his tea and watched the older boys shake their heads. That was poor pickings for them after Washoe. They'd go back to Mariposa and Frémont's place. By now he would have plenty of stamp machines going. At Frémont's they were known and could get work.

CHAPTER 43

1868

For three years Charles plodded along at the claim just making wages. On days when she had time, Anne helped him. She heaved shovels full of dirt, her calico dress pinned up to keep it out of the muck. "Henry's likely to strike it rich before you do, unless I shovel too." She sniffed.

Charles always knew the handsome dandy was Anne's favorite son. She had a different look to her eyes as she watched him, and let Henry be off his feed and she turned all afuss like an old hen with one chick.

Charles had no fault to find with Henry. He was a good lad; worked away at panning where he could and never failed to put his share into the pot to keep the grub coming in.

Henry did a bit of gambling on the side, and twice, when Charles had been uptown of a night having a schooner or two with High Water, he had seen Henry come out of Marquita's place. But after all what was a father to do about such things? Henry was a grown man now, nearly twenty years old.

One night after the seven-year-old Aaron was abed in the lean-to and Henry had fixed himself up fit to kill and gone out, Anne sat by the fire with Charles.

"I'm worried about Henry," she told him. "He used to be so open and frank with me, and now he's taken to fixing up this way in a boiled shirt and going out without a word about where he's going. Henry's got a girl, I'm sure of that, but I can't get anything out of him." She sighed. "Do you know anything about who she is, Charles?"

Charles tried to comfort her. "Likely the handsome young devil's got half a dozen. I used to be a bit of a beau myself at his age. Remember, when I singled you out of the lot to take you to hear the Swedish Nightingale?"

Anne wouldn't be thrown off the track by romantic memories of her own past.

"If he'd only *talk* about girls," she complained. "It's natural for a boy of his age to brag about his girls."

Charles thought of young Bill that night sitting on the chopping block, and was thankful that Anne had never found out the lad's affair with Sophie at Marquita's big white house. That would have been enough to put Anne under the sod with worry and shame, because of her feeling about what she called sin.

Henry's affairs were not so easily settled as poor Bill's had been.

One evening, coming back from Experimental Gulch, Charles met Henry on the road home and decided that was the time to do a little prospecting along the vein of Henry's mind. "Let's sit down a bit," he said. "I want to talk to you away from where your mother can hear."

Henry seemed willing enough, but Charles saw the muscles around the lad's mouth tighten as he dropped his pan and shovel and sprawled out on the dry grass near the rock where Charles settled.

"Your mother's worried about you, Henry," he began. "She's sure you've got a girl because you've taken to fixing up of nights and going out."

"Well, suppose I have?" Henry wanted to know.

"I didn't tell her I'd seen you hanging around Marquita's. You know how she feels about the girls in houses?"

"So you've been snooping!" Henry's face turned hard and ugly. "Well, it won't do you any good, because I'm going to keep right on going to Marquita. I love Marquita and she loves me. I've loved her ever since she bought me that music box Mom wouldn't let me have." He kicked worn shoe toes into the red earth.

Charles could scarce believe his ears. "Marquita! Are you clean daft, boy?" he demanded after a minute. "That woman's twice your age! She was taking lovers when you were wearing britches made out of your mother's old skirts."

"What in hell do I care about that?" Henry demanded with a set jaw. "Old folks are always bringing up what's past. I tell you I love her and Marquita loves me. Maybe she does make her living in the saloon and with her girls, but the damned girls want to work for her. They're well treated."

Charles groaned. "Oh, son, why don't you find a girl your own age, a decent girl, and marry her? Marquita's near old enough to be your mother."

Henry just looked bored then and more determined. He sneered and repeated what his mother had said about old Matt Brady marrying a young girl half his own age, and how she said age didn't matter if people were really in love and suited to each other.

Charles tried to point out that this was different, very different, but he knew his words fell on deaf ears. There was no use arguing more now. He picked up his tools and started for home with Henry following a few paces behind.

After that talk, Henry and Marquita defied everybody in Columbia. They went about openly together on the streets.

Word of the doings came to Anne's ears by way of the church women; she was furious and blasted Henry about the company he kept, and turned the boy resentful.

He reminded his mother that she hadn't been above taking a big donation from Marquita and her girls during the war when she'd been collecting money for the sick and wounded soldiers, and then he went out of the cabin and near slammed the door off the hinges.

Marquita took to coming up the hill to French Gulch to see Henry, and calling softly for him near the cabin of evenings. Anne would pull the curtains close, bar the door, and slap the pans for a fare-the-well to drown out Marquita's voice in the hopes that Henry wouldn't hear.

Charles thought that if any other son except the beloved Henry had such an entanglement he would have been sent packing. But the tie was too strong: Anne's love was too great to banish Henry from the cabin.

One day when he came home from work earlier than usual and Anne was away, Charles had a shock. There was little Aaron, big as life, playing with Marquita. The youngster was racing about the place like a true pacer, with Marquita's long coin chain as a harness. Marquita, in a gay full-skirted red dress and jangling bracelets, danced after him as driver! They were both children together, shouting with happiness—a sight that made the heart in Charles ache.

Rather than disturb the play, he went over to the mine and let them have their bit of fun without grownups to bother.

But when he came home for the second time that day, all was changed. Aaron was red-faced and screaming with anger, and Charles caught sight of a full red skirt disappearing down the road.

Aaron ran to Charles. "Mom took it away from me!" he roared. "Marquita told me all about her long chain of dimes and how the miners gave her the dimes to make it. They're *seated* liberty dimes and three hundred of them! We counted them. She gave it to me for horse reins and we were playing. Then Mom came home and took it away from me and threw it down the privy." Aaron howled out the words and beat at Charles's chest with angry fists.

"That I did," Anne snapped. "And I sent her packing too, the trollop! Coming here and making over our Aaron. It's disgusting. What will the town folks say?"

"Marquita came to see Henry," Aaron sobbed, "but he wasn't here so she played with me instead. She's pretty and I like her. She told me about her chain."

"Such stuff," Anne snorted. "She'd better stay down where she belongs—with her tales." She took off her best town dress and slipped a calico over her shoulders.

"I like her!" Aaron pursed up his mouth in rebellion. "I like her to tell me stories. I don't like *you*! You put my beautiful dime chain down the privy." He went off again in a fit of wailing, and got his bottom warmed for defying his mother.

Henry was furious when he came home that night and learned what had happened to Marquita's neck chain. "Just like the music box!" he cried, and glared at his mother. "Well, it didn't work with me. You can see it didn't."

"I suppose that Marquita is having her way with you, poor weak thing that you are, to spite me for not letting you have the music box," Anne scolded. "Oh, Henry, can't you see, son, she's just making a fool out of you?"

"If that's what she's doing, I like it." Henry grabbed up his clean shirt and went into the lean-to. He wouldn't even come and eat his supper. Later they heard the outside door slam.

Anne was frantic. "Can't you go and see Marquita and talk to her?" she demanded of Charles. "Maybe you could stir up a little decency in the creature and make her let our Henry alone."

CHAPTER 44

1 8 6 8

CHARLES decided to tackle Marquita around dusk one day when he knew Henry would be home late. He washed, dressed in his best and sashayed into town to Marquita's Blue and Gold Bar, next to the Pioneer.

The place was like fairyland after the harsh, bare, red hillsides. Mirrors reflected the lights, and the inlaid bar was a gorgeous affair. The tinkle of glasses and gay laughter cheered a man's heart. Marquita, gayest of the gay, in a bright blue silk dress and hung with jewelry, was pocketing the due change from drinks with a smile and a bit of chatter that made men happy at their loss. The little Mexican was well along in her thirties now, but she looked young and blooming and merry-eyed as a lass in her teens.

Charles saw Marquita's dark eyes grow big with surprise when she caught sight of him. She pushed through the crowd and came up. "Don Carlos himself!" she cried in welcome. Her little white teeth flashed in a smile. "What will you drink? The Irish whisky? Or maybe the Scotch!"

Charles told her his choice, and Marquita turned to the handsome Mexican behind the bar. "The best Irish in the house for Henry's father," she cried, "and on the house."

Marquita went to the bar herself then for the drink, brought it and sat down at a small table.

"You don't come often, Don Carlos. Not for a *very* long time—

and you are always welcome at Marquita's," she told him when he was seated opposite her.

Charles smiled. After all he had no fight with Marquita. You took these women as you found them. "A man with poor pickings on the hillside like I have can't afford all this." He lifted his glass and made a wide sweep of the room. "This place is only for the tony ones who hit it rich, Marquita."

She lifted her small glass of cordial then. "To better luck for Don Carlos Morgan." She asked how little Aaron was. "Does he jingle all over the place with the fine new reins?"

Charles wondered if this was a trap. Had Henry told her what Anne had done? "No," he said. "The lad is in hot water, Marquita. His mother threw the chain down the privy."

Her face turned sad for a flash, the slender shoulders shrugged. "Poor boys who gave me the chain," she sighed. "They must never know their fine gift landed in the privy." Then she took a breath. "Aye, Don Carlos, why is it that pious women can *never* see any good in women not so pious?"

"That's a question a poor Welshman can't answer, Marquita— and the reason why I'm here now."

"Because of Henry?"

Charles nodded. "He's so young. Why do you plague him, Marquita?" he begged. "The lad doesn't understand the wiles of women and he's bound to be burned."

He noticed that all the fingers were gone on one of her hands, and remembered the rumpus long ago when John Leary, the constable, had come to question Marquita about a shooting and she had pulled a dirk from her stocking. But John Leary had been too quick and caught her hand in such a way that her own fingers were cut off.

Now, as Charles talked to her about his son, she was very calm. The big black eyes looked right into his own with almost the same expression Maria's had had long ago.

"You are a man, Don Carlos," she said in a low voice against the clinking of glasses and laughter around the bar. "You know that in the mines love and real passion between men and women do not always take the path pointed out by ministers and those never tempted. I love your Henry. He is the passion of my life! And Henry loves his Marquita."

She motioned to the man behind the bar and ordered him to bring Charles another drink.

"But what's to come of this love?" Charles demanded. "He's only a boy. You're a mature woman, Marquita, a woman of many affairs, many lovers. But you are Henry's first love, his only love—so far."

"*Si,* that's right!" she said and lifted the glass to her reddened lips. "Henry brings freshness into my life—and he is my only love now. You shall see, Don Carlos. Marquita gives up all this glitter. We will be married; go away perhaps to my home in Mexico, and be happy always. I forsake all this for young Henry, my lover."

The barman ambled over and gave Charles a hard look as he set down the fresh drink. Then he turned to Marquita. "They're asking for you at the bar. They want Marquita."

"Then let them keep on asking," she snapped. "Give them a drink on Marquita. I'll be over after a while."

Charles argued with her. There was the matter of money. Marquita was used to money, to jewels, to luxury. Henry could give her none of these things. The boy made only a bare living from his panning.

But she had an answer for that too. What did the father of Henry think she had been doing through the years when Columbia boomed and gold flowed across her bar in a steady stream? She had saved it. There would be more than enough for her and Henry as long as they lived. She shook her head. "It will take a bigger, a greater power than you, Don Carlos, to separate Henry and Marquita."

As Charles walked home through the twilight, dozens of thoughts whirled through his mind of other days—of Maria who had told him almost the same words as Marquita. "I have enough for us both."

It seemed to him that nearly every action in life had its effect and made other actions necessary. Cause and effect, cause and effect. Like a stream they were that flowed through living. Sometimes the causes and effects brought success and riches; sometimes just more mistakes and poverty. Cause and effect. Because of Anne's greed they had no cheese factory; they were back on the hillsides of California. Now they were reaping the effect of that action in Henry's entanglement with Marquita.

He felt of Maria's nugget in his pocket, and thought of the gay bright-eyed lass. Who was he, to judge the actions of another generation of Morgans on the hillsides of Columbia?

The greedy hordes of gold seekers had gone now. Their hopes, like shifting clouds, had blown away before the winds of circumstance. There were only a few left gophering about in the hope of luck.

Those who had come with their greed and lusts and passions left behind them the effects of that greed. They had left the bare, scraped hillsides, deserted flumes and sluices and closed shops with barred, iron doors, to tell of what had once been glory and glitter and riches. Some men left sons.

Men didn't change. Greed went on. Perhaps generations of gold seekers to come, with better methods and more education, would again claim the hillsides and take even more gold from the earth. And there would be the women too; the good and the not so good, wanting their share of the spoils.

"How did you come out?" Anne wanted to know first thing when he arrived home. "I hope you made Marquita see what a terrible thing she is doing to our Henry."

"I didn't," Charles told her. "She vows she loves him, and that it will take a higher, stronger power than me to separate them."

"What fools men are!" Anne scolded. "I should have gone myself to see her. A woman can always wrap a man like you around her little finger and make him think the moon's green cheese. I'll go myself to talk to her tomorrow."

Anne's talk with Marquita never came. Another power had moved.

About ten o'clock that night Matt Brady thumped on the cabin door. "There's been a shooting scrape at Marquita's, Morgan," he said in a low voice.

"Not Henry?" Charles managed. He heard Anne gasp, behind him, but he had no strength to look her way.

"Yes." Brady's voice came through the silence. "It seems her Mexican barkeep was jealous. He heard Marquita tell you that she loved Henry and was going to quit the place and clear out. After you left he went into a rage and took it out on Marquita. Henry came in and plugged him."

"Oh, dear God!" Anne cried. "Henry's a murderer!" She threw herself on the bunk and began to sob.

"The boy cut and ran," Brady went on. "But they've sent for the sheriff. I thought I ought to come and tell you, but you'd better stay up here out of the mess. There's nothing you can do now."

After Brady had gone, Charles tried to stop Anne's sobbing, but there was nothing to say in comfort.

Cause and effect, cause and effect—the words ran through his mind like a stream. If he hadn't gone down to talk to Marquita, maybe this wouldn't have happened—cause and effect.

Finally he could stand the din of the words and the hot cabin no longer. He put on his coat and walked alone under the stars, wondering where young Henry was now, wondering if the sheriff had caught him. When his legs grew so tired the bones in them ached, he went back into the cabin.

Anne sat, dry-eyed and peaked, by the stove. No words came from either of them.

For a week, Henry was never mentioned between Charles and Anne. Each day Charles went into Matt's for word, but there was nothing. Marquita had cleared out and left one of the girls in charge of her affairs. There was no trace of young Henry Morgan.

Nearly a month later, the sheriff knocked on the cabin door at French Gulch, to tell Anne and Charles the last chapter of Henry's life.

The brother of Marquita's dead Mexican barkeep and some of

his friends had tracked Henry down in an isolated camp where
Mexicans and Indians were working. They had shot Henry and
escaped. What did Charles want to do about Henry's body?

"Bury him where he lies!" Anne cried out. "He doesn't belong
to the Morgans any more. I never want to hear his name again!"
She strode past them out of the cabin, and Charles saw her calico
dress blow in the wind against her thin body as she went striding
over the hill.

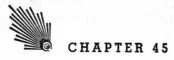

CHAPTER 45

1869

ANNE turned suddenly fierce and sting-minded as a hornet after Henry's death. She wouldn't talk with the parson when he came to see her, and she refused to go to church. She said she'd tried that for years. God had forgotten all the things she had done in His name, and God could jolly well look elsewhere for hands to work in the church.

Charles sighed, and thought with hurt in his heart how far they had traveled along the wrong road since that first Christmas in Poverty Hill, when they walked through the rain singing carols.

Now he must be the one to keep faith; he must guide little Aaron, his last-born, along the ways of his forefathers to something stronger and finer than the greed for gold. He wished Aaron could be with Maria.

Of Sundays he sent the little chap off to Sunday school with a bit of church money wrapped in paper and the Bible text firm in his mind. Then he asked the Shepherd of the Psalms to guide the young feet into better ways than his father had trod.

As the weeks went by, more and more Anne blamed Charles for the hard luck upon them. She made no bones about being disgusted with him. He had even kept her from being friends with Maria. "Twice I wrote her to come and see me," she railed. "But she's too fine for us Morgans. She's rich. She said it would be too hard on 'poor Carlos' seeing her. It would make him think of the days when you and she took out nuggets, and would only discourage you." Her lip curled in a sneer. "The feelings of 'poor dear Carlos' must be saved, I suppose, no matter what happens to us. But if you'd done as I wanted, we'd be friends now, good friends, and she'd have helped send Henry away—instead of him rotting on the hillside in a murderer's grave."

That cut hard, and angry words came up into the mouth of Charles, but before he had a chance to say them she was off on another tangent, as she shoved wood into the stove.

Were they always to be poor as crows? Why didn't he really work the claim at Experimental, now that his partner had left the whole mine to him? There was a vein close; everybody said so. He was just too lazy and liked hanging around town doing odd jobs for a living, so he could be near his everlasting schooners. Her eyes fired up with the glow of Satan and her face turned livid.

"Well, perhaps *you* can mine better than I can, you know so much," he snapped. "Those that gab so much about it better use some brawn."

"That I'll do, and show you, Charles Morgan!" she came back. "Maria did it, didn't she—and got rich? I've watched miners put in charges and set them off. I can use a pick and shovel— and I know gold when I see it in quartz."

"Then *take* the Experimental and be damned!" he roared and went out of the cabin.

After that Anne slogged day after day—and the lass had luck too. Some good stuff turned up and fair crazed her into work when she washed it.

She would dash in and put another charge of powder to work, so that it cleared while she cooked a meal or washed a few clothes. Before long she was in pants and shirt and heavy miner's boots. She didn't mind the muck at all.

"You be careful," Charles warned. "You've got to timber, to shore her up. You can't go too fast."

"When I want advice or timbering either, I'll ask for it," she snapped. "You and your 'be careful' is what's kept us as we are. Now let me mind my *own* business."

High Water Bill shook his head then. "Anne—Mrs. Anne, you got to watch them seams and timber, or sure as hell you'll have a cave-in."

"You'd better watch your schooners too, or you'll likely drown in them."

Bill wasn't offended, just laughed, but Charles saw worry come into the old miner's face. "Ain't she the high-tailin' mare though?" he told Charles later. "That woman's got more gimp in her than any woman I've ever seen—and more courage too."

Matt Brady had other ideas about what a woman should be. Margaret Banahan, the Irish beauty, had at last given in to his blandishments. They were to be married on the tenth of December. Matt was near crazed with joy. His head was so full of love-making and plans that he scarcely had time to wait on customers. He dashed in and out of the store like a cat at a fair.

"We're going to have the finest wedding ever celebrated in these diggings," he told Charles one morning, and paused with the scoop aloft over the bean sack.

"Don't it beat hell what a woman can do?" Bill asked. "There's old Brady holdin' off all these years until he's forty-five, and then love catches him and he's worse than any feller that ain't dry behind the ears. Matt ain't right in his head. He don't care that most of the diggings around here has gone to hell, and the flume busting down. He don't care that a lot of folks who used to buy has gone, and the stores closed. All he thinks about is that girl of his."

What a wedding it was! The bells of St. Anne's rang out merrily on the December air. Deep notes on the organ vibrated through the church. Matt, in his best suit, was like a creature transformed when he kissed little Maggie Banahan Brady after the ceremony.

"Must be great while it lasts," Bill whispered to Charles.

It was funny how weddings made women warm up. As they walked home to French Gulch that night, Anne told Charles that somehow seeing Matt and Maggie so happy and the Jim Johnstons too made her own heart lighter.

"A person feels that no matter what comes, if two people love each other and pull together there's hope for the world." She slipped her rough, work-worn hand into his and he squeezed it as they walked along.

"You've always been such a good man to me, Charles. So patient too," she said softly. "There'll be a good life yet—in spite of everything."

The day after Matt's wedding, Anne put on her miner's shirt and pants and fixed a bite of lunch for Charles to carry to his work, some for Aaron at school and a paperful for herself.

The lass was impatient to be off to Experimental. There was a good seam; and she was right where it widened enough to show.

"Maybe by night we'll be rich!" she cried, eyes bright. "That's how it comes when the seam is good."

Charles offered to knock off work and go to help her, but her head came up high. "No," she said. "You told me to take the Experimental and be damned. I've done the hard pick-and-shovel work myself and I'll find the gold and have the discovery myself!" She stamped out and up the trail.

When Charles reached home that night long after dark, High Water Bill was just spitting tobacco juice out of the cabin door. His face was white and strained.

"God!" he called out. "I thought you'd *never* come, Morgan." He stepped inside.

On the bunk lay Anne, white and limp—and lifeless. Little Aaron sat silent and frightened in a corner.

"I come up here before supper," High Water was saying. "She wasn't here, Morgan, and she's always home by half-past four——"

Bill took a great breath that was more a sob. "I waited awhile, then I went to Experimental. There was a cave-in, Morgan! I grabbed a shovel and dug like hell—but it was too late. I found her with her fingers around a chunk of rock with gold sticking out all over it. God, that gold was tremendous—she must have hit a seam!" The tears were streaming down Bill's cheeks.

Between sobs he told how he picked her up and carried her to the cabin. He had arrived just a few minutes before Charles. "She was *so* little and light," he finished, "and so full of courage."

Suddenly he turned close to Charles. "God, how I loved her, Morgan! It don't do no harm *now* to say it," he cried. "Only thing, I wish I'd had guts enough to tell her while she was living, but I was afraid she'd bash my head in—her being married and all."

Charles went over to the bunk, smoothed the tousled gray hair away from the brow and then turned away. "Yes," he repeated, "her being married and all! But I'm glad she got her hands on real gold at last—before it happened, Bill. That would make Anne happier than anything else in the world."

He went over to the door. His fingers, used to the action, caressed the nugget in his pocket. Soft words went through his brain: "I'll be here waiting, Carlos, if you ever need—your California wife."

THE END